ALSO BY REBECCA RASMUSSEN

The Bird Sisters

Evergreen

Evergreen

REBECCA RASMUSSEN

ALFRED A. KNOPF   NEW YORK 2014

THIS IS A BORZOI BOOK
PUBLISHED BY ALFRED A. KNOPF

Copyright © 2014 by Rebecca Rasmussen

Published in the United States by Alfred A. Knopf,
a division of Random House LLC, New York, and in Canada by
Random House of Canada Limited, Toronto,
Penguin Random House companies.

www.aaknopf.com

Knopf, Borzoi Books, and the colophon are
registered trademarks of Random House LLC.

Library of Congress Cataloging-in-Publication Data
Rasmussen, Rebecca.
Evergreen : a novel / Rebecca Rasmussen. —First edition.
pages   cm
ISBN 978-0-385-35099-0 (hardcover : alk. paper)
ISBN 978-0-385-35100-3 (eBook)
1. Brothers and sisters—Minnesota—Fiction.   2. Group problem solving—Fiction.
3. Families—Minnesota—Fiction.   4. Minnesota—Fiction.   I. Title.
PS3618.A78E94 2014
813'.6—dc23
2013016240

Jacket design by Kelly Blair

Manufactured in the United States of America
First Edition

For Ava, my little bee

Tell me the landscape in which you live,
and I will tell you who you are.

—ORTEGA Y GASSET

PART ONE

Evergreen, Minnesota

1938

1

╫╫╫╫ Eveline LeMay came after the water. She arrived on a
cool morning in early September, asleep in a rowboat without
paddles as if she knew the river currents would carry her past
the tamarack and black-spruce forest, around Bone Island, a
fen, and a bog, all the way to Evergreen and her new husband,
Emil, who was waiting for her on the rocky shore.

The flood had delayed Eveline's trip north two months
and forced her to travel by boat since the dirt roads had been
washed away and no plans were made to restore them. Emil
had sent word for her via the forest service to stay with her
parents in Yellow Falls, a lumber town twenty miles south of
Evergreen, until the water receded because he was living on the
roof of their cabin, subsisting on whatever happened to float
by. The newspapers blamed the flood on nature, but everyone
knew the government had been building a dam to harness the
power of the Snake and Owl Rivers in order to, in their words,
bring light to all that was dark, but in everyone else's: to build
a paper mill and clear-cut the forests.

"Mein Liebe," Emil said, and Eveline opened her gray eyes.

"I lost the paddles," she said, sitting up in the rowboat, stiff from floating all night.

On either side of the river, a forest of towering white pines shaded the shore. When the wind blew, long green needles fell onto the water like rain.

Emil lifted her out of the boat as if she were a child and waved away a mosquito from her face. "My poor baby," he said, kissing her. "But you're here now. You're home."

For the first time in two days, Eveline felt warm again despite her thin cotton dress, which she chose because Emil said the daisy pattern reminded him of the meadows in Germany where he played as a boy. She'd pinned up her long wheat-colored hair into a bun and let a few strands fall loosely around her face. Until she fell asleep, she'd pinched her cheeks every few hours to give them the rosy color Emil admired when they first met.

"Lob der Jugend," he'd said. In praise of youth.

Emil was ten years her senior, gray at the temples, which made him look both dignified and a little rueful. His shoulders were broad and strong from working outside, which belied the stiffness in his chest he called winter in the heart.

"They're boots," he said now, handing Eveline a pair of black rubber waders that rose to her thighs. "The country's all mud."

"And the cabin?" Eveline said, struggling with them.

"I stopped living on the roof three weeks ago," Emil said. "They're not like stockings. You won't break them if you pull harder."

Once she secured the waders, Eveline took Emil's hand, and the two of them walked up the rocky riverbank into the woods, which were alive with the hum of mosquitoes and groaning tree trunks. Emil set down pine boards for her to walk on in the places where the mud gurgled and spit sulfur. Where he didn't set down boards, the mud came up to her ankles and in one place her calves.

"At least the water came before the government did," Emil said. He pointed to a stand of old-growth pine trees the flood had uprooted and tossed like matchsticks onto their sides. "It'll make good firewood."

"Do we have a fireplace?" Eveline said.

"A woodstove," said Emil.

"Electricity?"

"A year or two yet. I'm working on running water."

Eveline had agreed to move to Evergreen because she wanted to be wherever Emil was, and Emil wanted to open a taxidermy shop on the edge of the wilderness like his father and his father's father back in the Black Forest. Eveline's mother had yielded similarly when she was nineteen and agreed to marry Eveline's father and live above the Laundromat despite her allergy to heavy detergents. Every afternoon for as long as Eveline could remember, her mother would sit in a spearmint oil bath to clear her sinuses, but she'd always be ready to greet her father with a kiss when he came home from the lumberyard, which made Eveline confident about her decision to marry Emil and move to Evergreen.

Before Emil proposed to her, Eveline worked at Harvey Small's, the only restaurant in Yellow Falls, serving plates of hamburgers to lumberjacks to relieve some of her family's financial burdens. After her shifts, she'd go across the street to Lenora's Fine Gowns, the place she'd met Emil, to brush against China silk and French chiffon, party dresses too fine for Northwoods parties. The dress shop was tucked between a live-bait stall and the Hunting Emporium, where camouflage jackets and buck knives hung from strands of twine in the front window. Eveline would circle the shop, reliving the moment when Emil had walked by, saw her twirling before a mirror, and was drawn to her side. After that, she'd go home to wash the scent of bacon fat out of her hair and freshen her skin with lemon juice.

Coming into the country meant Eveline no longer had to work in the restaurant, where children poured milk shakes onto the seats and stray dogs circled out back for bits of gristle, but it also meant she and Emil would have to eke out sustenance from the hard northern landscape and whatever supplies Emil had salvaged from the flood. Eveline was nervous about her instinct for survival, but she trusted Emil's completely. Emil had survived war as a boy and yet wasn't hardened. Eveline thought of his butterfly collection—the delicate purple emperor he gave her the day they met—and squeezed his hand. Around them great pines lay like injured soldiers, sap streaming from their bark like blood.

"I packed too many dresses," Eveline said, surprised at how the modest silver band on her ring finger had made her lose sight of the place she was packing for. She'd tucked a pair of dancing shoes into her suitcase at the last minute.

"You won't always have to wear waders," Emil said.

There's something else, Eveline thought, but couldn't say in the middle of all this death.

Before Emil decided to move them north, they shared her childhood bedroom in the apartment above the Laundromat and had only twice been daring enough to move together as man and wife, but it had been enough for life to begin inside of her.

Her mother didn't speak of her condition, but each morning she brought Eveline a cup of herbal tea with a spoonful of honey. She let out the seams of Eveline's clothes and found an oversize winter coat for her at the secondhand shop.

"Mom?" Eveline had said the morning before she left for Evergreen, when her mother passed by the threshold of her bedroom door. But the question Eveline wanted to ask her mother she couldn't find the tongue for, because even though her mother seemed cheerful enough and complained little, over the years her face had become weighed down by something Eveline recognized but didn't yet understand.

Are you happy? Eveline had thought.

Emil let go of Eveline's hand when they got to a clearing in the forest and the mud gave way to bright green moss, then switchgrass that rose to her thighs.

"It's not much farther," he said, tossing aside a dead weasel so Eveline wouldn't have to step over it. "Everything's been displaced."

Eveline wondered if Emil meant *perished.* Sometimes he used words that meant something different than they did to Eveline. When he asked her to marry him, he'd said "in case we're separated," which Eveline took to mean *so we won't ever be separate.*

The two walked through the thigh-high grass, over fallen branches that snapped beneath their feet and spongy earth that gave beneath them, Emil with a hand in his trouser pocket and the other wrapped around the handle of Eveline's tweed suitcase.

Overhead the clouds lumped together until Eveline couldn't discern their shapes individually anymore. The air smelled of wet earth. Oxeye daisies and milkweed thistle, which grew in the back lot outside her bedroom window in Yellow Falls, gradually took the place of the switchgrass and made Eveline feel more sure of herself. *What a good spot for a garden in the spring,* she thought. *My first real garden.* In place of the milk thistle, which scratched at her waders like fingernails, she imagined everything from pumpkins to malva flowers. Maybe even a row of walnut saplings, which would grow up with their child. When Eveline was a baby, her mother planted a forsythia shrub behind the Laundromat so Eveline would be the first one in town to glimpse spring in its bright yellow petals.

Eveline looked up at the clouds. "Do you think it's going to rain today?"

"Only if you wish it to, my wife," Emil said. "I've been practicing saying that."

"The wife part or the lying part?"

Emil smiled. "Both."

"Emil?" Eveline said, but before she could finish her thought the cabin rose out of the tangle of milk thistle in front of them like the prow of a ship on a wave.

For a brief stark moment, Eveline saw her future in the black water stains that licked the brown logs, in the boarded-up window Emil had yet to fix because he'd have to float a pane of glass twenty miles up the river. She saw it in the mud bubbling out from beneath the porch steps and the yellow liquid oozing like pus from the chinking between the logs.

And yet on the porch were two rocking chairs Emil had built and an evergreen wreath decorated with winterberries. A white-throated sparrow, what her father called a fortune bird, sat on the perch of a bright red birdhouse that hung from the eaves.

Emil set down her suitcase. "What is it?"

Eveline placed a hand on her stomach, a future that nudged her through the sunny material of her dress. "I'm pregnant."

2

Emil carried Eveline across the threshold singing, "A *Junge*! A *Mädchen*! Let us have one of each!" and everything turned sour. Though Emil had spent weeks cleaning the cabin, a few of the logs still dripped water like leaky faucets. He'd set pots and pans beneath the most eager of the streams and covered the stains on the floor with grass rugs, but the rugs couldn't contain what was beneath them, what was above them, what was all around: rot.

"It will get better," Emil said and set Eveline on her own two feet.

"Of course it will," Eveline said because she didn't want to hurt her husband's feelings or betray her own. She was certain she'd be sick if she didn't focus on what was pleasant about the inside of the cabin: the matching nightstands with delicate birdlike feet, the woodstove alight and crackling with blue and orange flames, and the narrow bed Emil had skirted with evergreen boughs and pinecones, which made it look like a nest.

"Would it be all right if I lie down?" Eveline said, hoping

sleep would transform her disappointment, her fears. She told herself she was tired—that was all. Just very tired.

Emil led her to the bed, turned down the dark blue patchwork quilt, and pulled the covers up to her chin. He touched the gentle curve of her stomach.

"Sleep, my dear," he said, as if he understood she was overwhelmed, as if he'd felt the very same way when he arrived in Evergreen.

Eveline fell asleep almost as soon as she closed her eyes. In her dreams, she heard the little bird on the front porch skittering across the wood planks, chirping her welcome song. She heard the tamaracks and black spruces bending in the wind beyond the cabin. She heard the *drip-drop* of water in the cast-iron pots and pans on the floor. All day, Eveline tried to open her eyes to her new life, and all day they remained closed.

Late in the evening, Eveline woke to the smell of rot, a still-sour stomach, and to Emil, who was snoring lightly beside her. His chest rose and fell with the sureness of a grandfather clock, and Eveline placed her hand on his ribs to steady all that was unsteady in her. She looked at the chipped basin Emil had set on the floor for her, but she couldn't bear the thought of an upheaval so close to him. On her nightstand, an oil lamp was burning. She lifted it with one hand and lifted herself out of bed with the other. Before he brought her into the cabin, Emil had steered her to the outhouse he'd built behind it.

Eveline put on her shoes, opened the heavy front door of the cabin, and stood on the porch a long moment in her daisy dress.

"It will get better," she said, clutching the oil lamp like an old friend.

After she found the outhouse, Eveline wiped her mouth with a handkerchief. She adjusted her underclothes and her dress, and in the process tilted the oil lamp too far south. When the flame went out, panic electrified the nerves in her spine and legs until she remembered a trick her father taught her when she was little. Eveline closed her eyes hard and opened them softly, and the dark wasn't so dark anymore.

On that night pulsing stars needlepointed the sky, and the moonlight, a pale harvest yellow, shone on the trunks of nearby birches, lighting their silver bark like streetlamps. The daytime industry of animals in the forest had slowed to an occasional *hoo* from an owl and the croak of a tree frog. Even the expanses of mud, which gurgled and spit during the day, eased back into themselves now. Eveline saw then that before the flood the country was beautiful and that it would be again.

During September, Emil worked on beauty's behalf outside of the cabin, clearing milk thistle and pricker bushes, while Eveline worked on its behalf inside. Emil had altered the frame of their one-room cabin to make it more structurally sound, but the people who lived here before them were the ones who'd built it and therefore decided its layout, which puzzled Eveline. The cupboards, for instance, were hung intermittently through the cabin instead of centrally in the kitchen, and Eveline was forced to put cans of beans in the cupboard above their bed and sacks of flour and rice in the one beside the closet door. The woodstove, where Eveline cooked their meals, sat on a pallet of bricks in the far corner of the room, and that, along with the placement of the cupboards, made Eveline wonder about the previous tenants, who'd left behind everything but their clothes and family photographs.

"Did they say where they were going?" Eveline asked one morning as she was cooking breakfast and noticed the path of worn wood between the stove and the table.

"Back to Canada, I think."

The woman had left behind a rosary and a silver hand mirror engraved with the words FOR MEG, LOVE, WILLIAM.

"I wonder why," Eveline said.

"They missed home," Emil said.

"They weren't able to make one out here?"

Emil touched the rosary. "It'll be different for us."

It was strange to be living among other people's things, and Eveline did what she could to make them feel more like hers. She pulled apart one of her dresses to make a floral curtain for the little window above the basin in the kitchen and filled the extra water glasses with stems of oxeye daisies and joe-pye weed from the meadow. There wasn't much to do about the boarded-up window, so that afternoon Eveline sat on the porch and on a page in her journal sketched what the view would have been. When she finished, she tacked her drawing to the rusty nail sticking out of the plywood board.

"I should make a wreath instead," she said when Emil came in from working.

"Don't you dare. I love it," Emil said. He handed her a blue porcelain teapot he found in the woods while he was clearing thistle. "I can fix the handle."

So far Emil had found a washboard, the teapot, and a worn-out teddy bear, which the flood had brought from someone else's home to the outskirts of theirs. The bear was missing its left eye, and though it was no longer fit for a child, Eveline sewed on a brown button in its place and set it on the bed. She would have been glad to return the items to their owners, but Emil only knew of one other family living in Evergreen on higher ground on the other side of the river. He'd left a note, but nobody had made the trip across.

"It's lovely," Eveline said about the teapot.

Emil touched the broken handle. "It reminds me of Germany."

Emil came to America because he thought it would be a less complicated place than Germany. He grew up during the lean years after World War I, when Germany was paying reparations to the rest of the world and starving as a result. Before the war, Emil's father was a naturalist and a taxidermist. After the war, instead of his father mounting the specimens he caught in the Black Forest and sending them on to the museums in Berlin, Frankfurt, and Munich, his family ate them. Once, when there were no specimens left, his father went into the forest with a wagon and came back with a wild horse from the pack Emil ran after with his boyhood friends. When Emil and his sister, Gitte, wept bitterly, their father told them to go to America. Perhaps there, he said, they only ride horses.

Even when prewar food appeared on the table again, Emil was intent on going to America because he read about the business opportunities for foreigners in the Dakotas. He only ended up in Minnesota because he ran out of money for train fare and because he walked past the dress shop and saw Eveline twirling in front of the mirror inside. After that he was intent on marrying her and opening a small taxidermy shop to support them.

After he finished the day's outdoor work, Emil would spread a cloth across the kitchen table and work late into the night, building a collection by which future customers could judge his craftsmanship. Emil preserved specimens the way his father and his father's father had. He didn't use the pernicious chemicals—arsenical soap and corrosive sublimate—

many taxidermists in America used. Emil used cotton and beeswax.

Watching him work was like watching an artist. Every few minutes, he'd stand up, rub his chin, and sit back down with the magnifying glass to fix whatever displeased him. He'd say, "I'm an elephant when I need to be a gazelle."

Eveline knew Emil was a fine taxidermist, but she wondered how he was going to find customers when only one other family lived in Evergreen.

"When hunters kill an animal here now, they have to take it all the way to Yellow Falls to get to a taxidermist," Emil said. "Instead of doing that, they can bring the animal to me. I'll preserve it and deliver it to them personally."

"By boat?" Eveline said.

"Next spring I'm going to get the money for a truck from Jeremiah Burr."

"What are you going to give him?" Eveline said.

"What everyone here seems to want," Emil said. "A wall full of bucks' heads."

"What do people want in Germany?"

"Sons who stay put."

When Emil had finally saved enough money for the trip across the ocean, his father wouldn't come out of his study to say goodbye. That morning, the women in his family were the ones who dropped him at the train station in Hornberg. Just before he boarded, his mother gave him his father's most cherished butterfly collection and suggested he use the butterflies to tip people along the way, which worked in Europe. But when Emil tried to give a porter a monarch butterfly in Grand Central Station, the porter crushed it in his hand.

Eveline fell in love with Emil precisely because of those butterflies. Other men left buckets of fish on her doorstep or dragged her out to the woods to watch them cut wood. Before they were married, Eveline would daydream about Emil's smooth fingers brushing hers in the dress shop the day they met and how, despite her parents' concern, she felt so certain his gentleness was meant for her and her alone.

Eveline looked at Emil's fingers now, which bullet burs and thorns had scraped raw. A blood blister had taken over the tip of his thumb; the nail was starting to turn black.

"I should get back out there," Emil said. "We're going to get snow today."

Eveline looked at the small pile of logs beside the stove. Even in warm weather, wood disappeared faster than Emil could cut it. "I can help you," she said.

Emil put his heavy wool coat on. He kissed her forehead. At the door, he smiled as if she'd said something funny. "I didn't marry you so you could wield an ax."

"Why did you?" Eveline said, but Emil was already gone.

Eveline set the lunch dishes in the basin and gathered Emil's wool socks, which needed mending. There was supper to think about and laundry to scrub against the washboard. Floors to wash, too. Eveline was amused now by all the nights she'd stayed up before she was married thinking about how freeing it would be when she and Emil finally had a place of their own. She didn't think about chores then or the silence she'd complete them in. Most days now, she went hours without speaking, when in Yellow Falls she'd scarcely caught a moment to herself, let alone a silent one.

Today was no different. The snow came home before Emil did, clinging to the silvery birch branches, the brown eaves of the cabin, and the red birdhouse. It softened Evergreen's sharp lines and the sparrow's hearty trill. Eveline wrapped herself in one of the left-behind quilts and sat on the porch talking to the sparrow, whom she'd named Fortuna.

Tuna.

"Why didn't you fly south like all of the other birds?"

Tuna hopped from the birdhouse perch to the porch rail-ing, stretching her white throat toward the falling snow so much like a child that Eveline half expected an eager tongue to spring forth from her beak to gather the flakes and savor them as they melted.

Eveline wondered what had happened to all the Yellow Falls girls who got married and moved south to Minneapolis and sometimes as far as Chicago, places that seemed like they were part of another world now. On a map, hundreds of rural miles separated her from them, but this distinction seemed more pressing than inches on a map: in Eveline's world girls talked to birds, and in the other one they talked to one another.

Were the girls lonesome for the Northwoods? Its forests? Its meadows? Its star-filled sky? Perhaps they all had closets full of pretty party dresses that kept them from missing the mud and the sand, the angles of the river and the anglers who fished it.

Tuna hopped from the porch railing back to the perch of her birdhouse.

"I feel the same way," Eveline said, unwilling to admit she was lonely.

3

⊁ Eveline spent the winter of her pregnancy reading Emil's taxidermy manuals, the only bound pages for mile after boundless mile. Of everything she packed that hurried September morning in Yellow Falls, books weren't something she'd considered stuffing into her suitcase, which meant she was stuck reading about dead animals now.

"Soon you'll be able to preserve me," Emil said when he came in from chopping wood on the first big snow day—two feet!—in November. He was growing a beard, which collected snow when he was chopping wood and, along with his foggy safety glasses, made him look a little like an owl until the snow melted.

"Just birds," Eveline said, even though she'd been secretly drawing pictures of babies when she was certain Emil was deep in the woods.

No woman in Yellow Falls, and probably anywhere, talked about what it felt like to be pregnant other than to say it was the Lord's miracle, so Eveline didn't know to expect the cramping and expanding, the tenderness of her breasts and hips. For the tenderness, she draped warm cloths over whatever parts were sore. She didn't know what to do about the expansion of her hips and breasts, except to take out the seams of her clothes and hope Emil didn't mind when they undressed beneath the sheets. The cramps were the worst; they caused her such indigestion Eveline didn't know how she'd survive their indignity. Often, while Emil slept soundly, she'd escape to the outhouse to spare them both.

And then December came, and Eveline and the baby reached sudden equilibrium. As the baby grew, the cramps and tenderness disappeared, and the expansion seemed more purposeful, since it confined itself to her stomach. The queasiness disappeared, too, which could have been because the cabin finally stopped smelling of rot and smelled instead of the applewood Emil cut for her. On the nights he preserved specimens, the cabin smelled of oil of cedar, too, which mixed with the smells of supper.

Cooking was difficult without a proper layout and running water. Eveline had to heat blocks of snow on the woodstove at the beginning of the meal and more at the end to clean the dishes. The pantry contained only a few items anymore—salt, flour, rice, dried beans, and bouillon—which made supper predictable: beef-flavored rice and beans. Occasionally, Emil would get a rabbit or a squirrel between chopping wood and bringing it to the cabin.

One day, he got a wild turkey, and how gloriously rich that meal was!

"Where did you find it?" she said when Emil brought the turkey inside. He'd already plucked all of the feathers, which made the turkey look like a newborn. Emil set a pot of water on the woodstove while Eveline coddled the turkey in her arms.

"The edge of the edge of the forest," Emil said.

"How smart you are!" Eveline said.

"How *lucky*," said Emil. "He let me take him."

"Let?" Eveline said.

"He leaped right into my arms," Emil said, taking the turkey out of Eveline's and placing it in the pot of boiling water.

While the turkey cooked, Eveline set the table. Normally, she didn't like the earthy smell of fat rendering out of animals, but just then the layer of yellow fat that bubbled at the top of the pot smelled like happiness.

The next day, Eveline turned the leftovers into soup. She couldn't wait to start a garden in the spring, to grow carrots, celery, potatoes, and a patch of herbs. Living in the woods had narrowed her longings; what happiness thyme (and the baby) would bring. Eveline took the most neutral of her cotton dresses and pulled them apart in order to make clothes for the baby, who nudged the project along when in the past she might have set down her needle and thread. In between sewing, she'd drink a cup of broth and read.

All but one of Emil's manuals were written in German, and though she was learning the language slowly from Emil (and from his German-to-English dictionary), the words on the page rarely came together in any sensible way. The sketches were what brought the words she did know to life. Eveline practiced tracing specimens in her journal and if she'd captured a likeness particularly well, Emil encouraged her to hang it on the wall, which was becoming crowded with grouse, foxes, deer, fish, and birds.

"You have a gift for drawing sparrows," Emil said.

"Only Tuna," Eveline said.

Each day the weather allowed her to, Eveline sat bundled in the rocking chair watching Tuna. At first, she drew Tuna in stationary positions, but as she got better, she drew her on updrafts. If she misplaced a shadow or shaded one too heavily, she began again.

Only one manual, the English one, showed sketches of the birds in their natural habitats, without accompanying sketches of horsehair nooses and thumbs on sternums—the means, their authors suggested, to put them to eternal sleep. Emil always asked of himself three questions when deciding whether or not to turn birds into specimens, since they would become part of his personal collection and wouldn't be for sale.

1. *Is it rare or endangered?*
2. *Is it likely to find a mate?*
3. *Will it stay put in its chosen habitat if left intact?*

If Emil could answer yes to any question, he'd walk away from whatever bird he was interested in preserving because he was a naturalist before he was a taxidermist.

That winter, however, Emil was mostly a woodcutter, and Eveline was mostly alone, which gave her too much time to worry about giving birth. Plenty of women had babies at home, but Eveline only knew of one woman who'd given birth in a cabin in the woods, and that woman, Lulu Runk, who'd been normal by Yellow Falls standards, now wore a coat made of coonskins and talked to people only she could see when she came to town for supplies. "Ain't no life in trees," she'd say, dragging her grubby child up and down Main Street by his sleeve. "No, sir, it ain't no life."

Emil was worried, too. "I think you should have the baby in Yellow Falls," he said on a blustery night in January as the wind rattled the windows. "It's too dangerous here. Besides, I think you'll need your mother. We can go back in March when the ice breaks up."

"Him," Eveline said, greatly relieved. "I see him in my dreams. He looks like you."

"Poor child," Emil said.

"*Handsome* child," Eveline said.

Emil was building a crib and a changing table made out of the maple tree he cut down when he first learned she was pregnant back in September. Emil said maple trees were lucky, according to a myth from the old country.

Though Eveline wasn't superstitious, she asked Emil to tell her the story. According to him, there once was a beautiful girl who lived with her family in the Black Forest. One late-fall night, while the girl's family slept in the cabin, the moon awakened the girl in the bed she shared with her little sister, drawing her to his bluish light. The girl went to the front door, dressed in only her nightclothes and slippers, her limbs long and graceful in the doorway, her hair trailing down her back like red silk.

Little girl, late night, the moon sang in a voice more lovely than any the girl had heard. *You belong with me.* The moon urged her outside, past the chickens and horses and outbuildings, farther and farther into the woods. Falling snow laid siege to her neck and face, but the girl didn't feel the cold flakes on her skin until she'd been walking a long while and the moon disappeared behind the clouds, and she realized she was alone in the dark.

Mama, she cried, for sense and fear took hold of her. She was too far away from the cabin now for the wind to carry her voice home. The girl huddled against the trunk of nearby tree for warmth and tried with all her heart to stay awake.

In the end, she couldn't stay awake or keep herself warm in the cold and fell first into troubled sleep and then sleep eternal. When the moon came down to make her his bride, just before morning banished him out of the sky, he found a small tree in the place the girl had been huddling. The tree had leaves as red as the dawn and sap as sweet as sugar.

"Why was she lucky?" Eveline asked Emil when he stopped talking.

"Because she became immortal," Emil said.

Eveline pointed to the frame of the crib. "But you cut her down."

That story was the only indication their lives wouldn't keep ticking along with the quiet sureness of a clock through the winter. On a windy afternoon in February, two months before Eveline was due, Emil was out cutting wood, and Eveline was reading the English taxidermy manual again. At first, she attributed the feeling in her stomach, like the tightening of a belt, to the manual's subject matter.

> Here, then, rests the shell of the poor hawk, ready to receive from your judgment the size, the shape, the features, and expression it had ere death and your dissecting brought it to its present still and formless state. The cold hand of death stamps deep its mark upon the prostrate victim.

After the belt loosened, Eveline gathered her mittens, hat, and coat for a trip to the outhouse. Maybe the beans she'd eaten for breakfast were causing the pains, she reasoned, since she'd never been in labor before. When she thought of giving birth, she imagined a quick, grueling pain that ended with her holding her little boy an hour or two later.

Huxley, they'd decided. After Emil's grandfather who died in the Black Forest during the war but not because of it. Hux.

In her most recent dreams, Hux had beautiful, saucer-shaped brown eyes and red cupid lips. He had Emil's gentleness, his even heart.

Eveline walked to the outhouse through the snow and wind, the thrust of both at her back, thinking about the pain in her stomach, which had dulled to nothing as quickly as it had surged, and about what kind of parents she and Emil would be. As an only child, she had all the attention she desired from her parents, but not so much as to turn her into a Murray—four sisters from Yellow Falls who shared the same first word: *mine.*

Eveline didn't worry about spoiling Hux in Evergreen because even the smallest comfort had to be earned here. If you were cold, you cut wood. If you were hungry, you made food. If you were lonely, you drew birds (and babies).

Eveline pried open the outhouse door, which had frozen shut since she was out there last. For light and ventilation, Emil had carved a half-moon and the North Star into the back wall of the outhouse, which he'd fashioned from a white pine killed by blister root. The growth rings were stained black and purple and patterned the wood slats like bruises.

The belt tightened around Eveline's stomach again. Her legs buckled, and she thrust her hand through the half-moon because it was the only thing that would keep her from falling over. The pain radiated from her stomach to her lower back. When a burst of warm liquid soaked her underclothes, Eveline knew for the first time that what she was feeling wasn't indigestion or taxidermy disgust.

If her mother had been with her, she would have rubbed peppermint oil on her lower back to numb the pain and lavender oil beneath her nose to calm her nerves. She would have told her about contractions and how to breathe through them and keep her body relaxed so that the contractions and the pain they produced could pass through her as if through an open door. In the end, when nothing else soothed her, she would have sent Emil and Eveline's father out to Harvey Small's and put Eveline in the bathtub and let her scream herself hoarse. But her mother wasn't with her and Eveline didn't know the liquid between her legs meant her water had broken; she thought it was blood or part of the baby or both.

"*Emil,*" she called, and the pain stopped as suddenly as it had begun.

Eveline ripped opened the outhouse door and stumbled out of it into the blowing wind and snow, latching on to the thick rope Emil had strung from the front porch of the cabin to the doorknob of the outhouse to make navigating easier during the winter. Eveline prayed she'd get back to the cabin before the next episode of pain—*Don't fall, don't fall,* she told herself—which was just when her ankle twisted and Tuna flew away from the red birdhouse and the white winter world went black.

Eveline woke to the sound of crying—a sound she assumed was coming from her, since her body hurt more than it ever had before. It took her a long moment to realize she was no longer outside, her cheek pressed against the snow, but that she was unclothed beneath the flannel sheet on the bed in the cabin, a metallic taste in her mouth. The sound was coming from Emil, who held a soiled blanket in his arms.

"He's dead," Eveline said, and Emil turned.

What Eveline felt now was worse than the burning between her legs and the unbridled zips of electricity radiating up and down her spine. If only she'd paid more attention to Hux during her pregnancy, recorded each of his stirrings in her journal instead of drawing one-dimensional babies while Emil was away in the woods. Maybe Hux had been trying to tell her everything wasn't all right, with his kicks and thrusts and flips.

In her dreams, Eveline had seen his sweet face again and again. When she woke, she'd patted her stomach when she should have said, *You are loved.*

Eveline covered her eyes with her hands, and then she uncovered them because she'd worried about only one of them dying in childbirth—her.

Of course Hux would live. He'd grow up strong and lean. He'd learn to climb trees and swim across rivers. He'd chase after wild horses with his friends like his father.

Except there weren't any wild horses in northern Minnesota. Any friends.

Emil walked over to Eveline, his thick black eyelashes wet.

"Hux is tiny but fine," he said, placing the soiled blanket, their boy, in her arms. "You're the one we were waiting for."

4

⊹∭∭⊹ Spring brought forth birch leaves on silver branches and tender green buds up from the softening ground. It brought bloodroot and wood anemones, southwest winds and melting ice, and on an afternoon in late April, the week Hux should have been born according to the medical world, it brought Lulu Runk.

Eveline was sitting with Hux in a rocking chair on the porch, trying to get him to latch on to her breast. If giving birth was the hardest thing she'd done, then getting Hux to eat was the second hardest. She couldn't tell if he was getting a flood of milk or none at all.

In the middle of one of her coaxing sessions, Lulu came marching through the forest and up to the cabin, her coonskin coat unbuttoned and flying behind her like a feral cape and her child flying in front of her to avoid getting swallowed by it.

"Straighten up!" she said, and Eveline pulled her shoulders back.

"It's not you I'm talking about," Lulu said, pulling back her boy's shoulders but looking at Eveline. Lulu spit into her palm and wiped it on her boy's cheeks, which smeared the circles of dirt but didn't get rid of them. Then she matted down his ragweed hair and made him swallow the blade of bluestem he was chewing on.

"One of us has got to be polite," she said, brushing a leaf off the front of her trousers, which were the color of mud and cut for a man. Her hair was short like her son's and stuck up in the same places, too. Lulu Runk was a tall, solid woman, made larger by her booming voice and the vigor of her coat.

"I'm sorry," Eveline said, dwarfish at five feet.

"It's not you I'm talking about," Lulu said. "Again."

More than six months had passed since Eveline had seen or talked to anyone other than Emil, who was down by the river fishing for bluegills in the cattails. Each morning after the ice had begun to heave and groan, he'd go down to the river with his rod, a feather jig, and a float he'd made from balsa wood and come back with that evening's supper. He and Eveline would eat as if they were trying to make up for winter's deprivation. They'd take turns scraping the blackened skin out of the cast-iron fry pan.

Eveline lifted the nursing blanket and looked at Hux pleadingly.

"I used to do that, too," Lulu said.

"He's hungry," Eveline said.

Lulu's mouth got crooked. "When aren't they?"

Without being asked and without asking, Lulu climbed the steps of the porch and sat in the empty rocking chair beside Eveline while her boy ran laps around the cabin, a toy gun in his hand. Tufts of matted brown fur from her coat fell to the porch floor during the maneuver, and though any other woman would have hastily stuffed the tufts into her pockets, Lulu put her feet on the porch railing, exposing a hairy ankle.

"Don't let him yank on your nipple," she said, offering a

cigarette to Eveline, who blushed. "He'll take until you have nothing left to give."

"I don't smoke," Eveline said.

"You should have seen mine with this one," Lulu said. "Raw as meat."

To her boy, who was zigzagging around the cabin, bushwhacking milk thistle with the barrel of his gun and yelling, *Yee-haw,* she said, "You're making me nervous. Why don't you go pick some mayflowers for our neighbor? I'm guessing she likes the pink ones."

"Yes, ma'am," the boy said, running off with his toy gun, yelling, *Pow, pow, pow!*

Lulu shook her head. "That's Gunther. Born with a gun in his hands."

"This is Hux," Eveline said, pulling aside the nursing blanket, embarrassed by the words *raw as meat* and *nipple* and yet relieved to hear them at the same time.

"Try giving him your finger to suck on," Lulu said.

Eveline offered Hux her pinkie finger, bracing herself for his fury.

"When you get tired of that, give him a bottle," Lulu said.

"I don't have a bottle," Eveline said as Hux lapped eagerly— *magically!*—at her finger. Why hadn't she thought of this? What kind of mother was so resourceless? So bottleless?

"I'll bring you one tomorrow," Lulu said.

Eveline wondered what she meant by *neighbor.* After a long winter, the very idea of Lulu made her hopeful. A friend!

"You just changed my life," Eveline said.

Lulu put out the cigarette with her boot and flicked it off the porch. "For the better, I hope." She held out her hand, which Eveline shook. "Lulu Runk."

"I know who you are," Eveline said. "I used to see you in Yellow Falls."

Because she realized how much she missed talking about things that husbands weren't interested in, she added, "Ain't something I'm likely to forget soon."

Lulu's mouth got crooked again. "I only do that so people will stay out of my way." She lit another cigarette and passed it to Eveline, who pulled the nursing blanket over Hux's face and held the cigarette between her thumb and index finger like Lulu.

"What's your name?" Lulu said.

"Eveline LeMay. I mean *Sturm.*"

"You're nervier than you look."

The two of them sat on the front porch most of the morning, enjoying the sun and cool spring wind, which made Eveline think of those lazy Saturdays and Sundays growing up in Yellow Falls, when her mother would make blueberry pancakes and her father would listen to his favorite radio program and Eveline would swipe spoonfuls of maple syrup when no one was looking. Tuna was flying herself dizzy, trying to keep up with all of spring's birds. While they rocked, Lulu smoked more and Hux fell asleep. For the first time in weeks the world slowed down, and Eveline could hear herself think again.

It turned out Lulu lived in what Eveline and Emil had thought was the abandoned cabin on the other side of the river.

"We were gone this winter," Lulu said. "Trapping up north. We're only back because Reddy was cleaning his rifle one day and shot one of his toes. You'd think he was dying for all the fuss he made. Reddy's my husband. Our trapping days are over."

"How long have you been married?" Eveline said.

"Long enough for him to drive me crazy. He's like a brother you want to punch."

"I don't want to punch Emil," Eveline said, waving to him

as he came up from the river through the forest, a rod in one hand and a string of bluegills in the other.

"Give it time," Lulu said. She stood up and called for Gunther to quit horsing around in the meadow and bring back those mayflowers straightaway. "You need a cowbell," she said to Eveline. "That's what I use to herd my menfolk in."

"Will you stay for lunch?" Eveline said, the taste of fish already on her tongue.

"No thanks," Lulu said. "I have a hard-boiled egg somewhere in here."

She reached into the pocket of her coonskin coat and, instead of an egg, which sounded wonderful—Eveline hadn't had one since September—Lulu pulled out a rumpled envelope. "I almost forgot why I crossed the river," she said. "When I was in Yellow Falls a couple days ago, Earl gave me this. He said you all moved out this way during the fall, but he says a lot of things that aren't square. If I'd known you were up here for sure, I'd have brought you supplies from the general store. Or a few chickens. Gunther got his hands on it if you were wondering about the dirt."

"You didn't get our note then?" Eveline said.

"What did it say?"

"My husband wrote it," Eveline said, motioning to Emil.

After Eveline introduced Lulu and Emil, Lulu tucked the cigarette she'd rolled but hadn't gotten around to smoking behind her ear and walked up to the meadow to retrieve Gunther, who was minding his toy gun instead of her. Even when they'd made it through the forest and to the swelling river, Eveline could hear Gunther yelling, *Pow!* and Lulu yelling, *It's not healthy to shoot your mama!* which made Eveline smile.

In the excitement of the morning and in the presence of the string of lovely bluegills, whose silver scales glinted in the sunlight and would blacken tastily in the fry pan, Eveline forgot to give Emil the letter, which she had slipped into the pocket of her dress.

"I'm glad you have someone to talk to now," Emil said. He leaned over and kissed Hux, who was still asleep. "Women need women."

"What do men need?" Eveline said, worried Emil might kiss her, too, and taste the tobacco on her lips and disapprove of her spending time with Lulu, even though now that the weather had turned away from winter he often took a rosewood pipe onto the porch after supper and smoked what was left in the canvas pouch he kept in his coat pocket.

But Emil only smiled. "Women."

Eveline went inside to put Hux down in the reed basket and get the fry pan and the woodstove ready for the bluegills, which Emil cleaned and gutted on the porch. If only they had butter, she thought, which brought her back to thinking about Lulu's egg and the good fortune of her and Reddy planting themselves on the other side of the river, one step closer to Yellow Falls and the roads, which had been mostly washed away in the flood but which Lulu said she and her red pickup truck could manage on in a pinch.

"What do you consider a pinch?" Eveline had asked Lulu.

"No whiskey, for one thing," Lulu had said.

When Emil finished cleaning the bluegills, he brought them to Eveline the way he used to bring her field flowers when he was courting her in Yellow Falls.

"What about Lulu's husband?" Emil said.

"She wants to punch him sometimes," Eveline said, marveling at the potency of Lulu's influence, since she would have simply said his name before her visit. Out in the bush it was easy to fall into the routine of saying only what was necessary.

After Eveline coated the bluegill fillets with flour and

placed them in the fry pan, Emil threaded his fingers through hers. "I'm glad for your little hands."

"I don't want to punch you if you're worried about that," Eveline said.

"Not now," Emil said. "But you probably will one day."

"That's what Lulu said."

Emil poked at the bluegills with a fork. "It's good to know Hux will grow up with a little friend. I had a wonderful playmate in Germany. Ava. She was better at everything than me. I'll cross the river tomorrow and introduce myself to the husband."

"Reddy," Eveline said.

"The fish?" said Emil.

Eveline gently swatted his hand away from the fry pan. "The husband."

Together, they ate lunch. After, Eveline cleaned the dishes with water from the rain barrel—another joy of spring! Hux woke with his usual hunger, and Eveline fed him while Emil worked on rigging up a shower in back of the cabin with the help of a second rain barrel, a brick oven, and a length of copper pipe he'd found in a pine tree after the flood.

When a half hour passed, Eveline offered Hux her pinkie finger like Lulu showed her. Lulu said a half hour was long enough for him to get what he needed and short enough to avoid chafing. Eveline put Hux in the cloth sling she'd made and walked around the cabin, arranging Gunther's mayflowers and wondering what Lulu's cabin looked like.

She thought of sketching her little son's face. Hux had thick black eyelashes like his father's and long thin fingers like Eveline's. Before Lulu's visit, Eveline had worried about Hux's endless supply of tears. After the visit, she stopped. Everyone was tired, that was all.

The three of them were up most nights now. Eveline would breastfeed Hux, and Emil would walk him around the cabin, bouncing him the same way he did when Hux was first born and Eveline was caught in that porous place between consciousness and unconsciousness, trying to figure out which way was home. They didn't speak of what Emil had done in the cabin that day, but Eveline was certain he'd saved her life.

Eveline's body was recovering slowly but steadily. Before she left Yellow Falls her mother packed her with small tins of arnica, *Hypericum,* and calendula—herbs meant to heal her from the inside out. Eveline and Emil were planning a visit next month, so her parents could meet their grandson and the local photographer could take a portrait of Hux for Emil to send back to his family in Germany. Maybe they could ask Lulu to take them in her truck. Eveline was already thinking about the bottle of whiskey they could buy her to show their gratitude. While they were in Yellow Falls, they'd stop at the general store so Eveline could covet licorice ropes while Emil purchased what he needed for the taxidermy business.

"Are you sure you don't want to preserve butterflies instead?" Eveline had said again this morning when Emil came back with a squirrel. "We could manage. I could plant a garden and sell the seeds at the general store. I've seen people do well with that."

"I'll skin deer for the rest of my life to keep licorice ropes in your belly," Emil said.

"Even if you have to do it for the worst kind of people?"

Eveline was thinking about the businessmen that came up in large hunting parties from the southern part of the state and shot at anything that moved until they got a buck. They never wanted the meat, only the heads. Even Jeremiah Burr, who'd lived in Yellow Falls his whole life, had offered Emil a dollar for every antler point.

"What you do isn't who you are," Emil said.

Eveline kissed Hux's warm cheeks and put him down in his crib. She watched him sleep for a while, wondering if the things you did didn't define you, then what did? What else could? Eveline wondered what Lulu would say. That's when she remembered the letter, which she brought out back to Emil, who was trying to figure out a way to make water move up in the copper pipe when it only wanted to move down.

"Für mich?" Emil said, wiping his hands on a handkerchief.

"Lulu brought it this morning," Eveline said.

"I thought it was from you," Emil said, pretending disappointment.

"My cursive's not nearly as nice."

Emil opened this letter and read its contents, at first with casual interest and then more and more seriously until whatever happiness his face had held in recent months gave way to panic. The way Eveline would remember it, there was a moment of absolute stillness when the future was still theirs before the wind blew up from the river and the first of spring's leaves shook as if they were afraid.

5

⁣ According to the letter, Emil's father had the kind of
aggressive cancer a person couldn't recover from. He'd lost control of his legs already and was confined to his bed, mired by
the indignity of a bedpan. The cancer had spread to his brain
and was making him confused and hysterical. Dr. Hayner was
waiting for Emil to arrive before he administered morphine.
Emil's sister, Gitte, had written the letter, which explained its
fine penmanship and its (perhaps) overly descriptive nature.
Gitte wrote for the local newspaper.

Emil folded the letter. When he tried to put it in his pocket,
the letter slipped from his hands to the floor. The news stiff
ened his body; his knee cracked when he bent to retrieve the
letter and again when he stood upright.

"I have to go to him," Emil said.

"Of course you do," Eveline said. "We'll go with you."

Emil looked at the crib, their son. "I don't think that's a
good idea. The boat could make Hux sick. That happened with
a boy on the way over. One day he was on the deck playing, the
next day he was dead."

"Are you certain?" Eveline said, though she knew Emil wouldn't lie to her.

"Would your parents mind looking after you and Hux until I come back?" Emil said. "I can bring you there this afternoon. Or we can ask Lulu. She has a truck, doesn't she?"

"I don't understand," Eveline said.

What she meant was: *Why is this happening? To you. To me. To us.* The three of them were just beginning to settle into life in Evergreen as a family. Summer was approaching, which was a cause for celebration in and of itself, and she had a new friend. How could a letter change all that? What right did it have? For a moment, Eveline despised Gitte. She despised the copper pipe outside, the sunshine glaring through the kitchen window.

Slow down, she thought, picturing herself walking up the back stairs to the apartment in Yellow Falls, to her mother and father, a life that didn't belong to her anymore.

Emil clutched his pocket. "The letter's a month old."

Only when Eveline thought of her own father did she give herself over to Emil's panic, which she'd never seen in him. He looked suddenly older, the lines on his neck and forehead more pronounced, his movements clumsy. In his eyes, Eveline could see what he would look like as an old man, how he would wear his hardships and even hers like a yoke.

"I don't have to go," Emil said, as if he'd heard her thoughts.

"Of course you do," Eveline said, as if she'd heard his.

Thus began the whirlwind of unstitching all they'd stitched together during the winter. It occurred to Eveline that Emil could go to Lulu's at once, and Eveline could stay back and pack up the cabin properly, so it would be able to defend itself against the weather and the animals, against Evergreen. She and Hux could go to Lulu's the next day.

"You can manage a trip across the river?" Emil said.

"If you left the rowboat, I could," Eveline said.

"What about the paddles?"

"I'll use a snowshoe."

Emil pulled her to him. *"Ich liebe dich."*

"I love you, too," Eveline said.

What were a few months away from each other? The boats were faster now, and the German borders were still open even if most people were leaving the country. And they were married, and Emil was a citizen of the United States; it said so on his passport. Eveline's parents would be happy to get to see their grandson and their daughter. Hux could use her old crib, which was up in the crawl space. Eveline could sleep in her canopy bed.

When Emil had filled a canvas duffel bag with clothes and a leather messenger bag with his identification papers and the German money left over from his first crossing, he handed Eveline a small stack of American money.

"It isn't as much as it should be," he said.

"We'll make do," Eveline said, though she wondered how they would, since food would have to be bought in Yellow Falls, and rent would have to be contributed to. Maybe she could get her old job back while her mother watched Hux.

Eveline walked Emil to the front door and onto the porch. The day was sunny but crisp. The air smelled of pines. Hux was sleeping in Eveline's arms.

"My son," Emil said, lifting Hux up. He kissed his cheeks and handed him back to Eveline. "Are you sure you can do this?"

"Yes," Eveline said.

"I'll be back by the end of the summer at the very latest," he said to Eveline, kissing her one last time before he laced his mud-caked boots, which he'd wear until he got to Yellow Falls and then switch them for the loafers he'd traveled across the ocean in the first time. He took the first step off the porch toward the woods and the river.

"I'll write whenever I can," he said, touching his pocket.

Eveline held Hux more closely. "Me, too."

Eveline spent the afternoon emptying the cupboards in the pantry of anything perishable and packing those items alongside hers and Hux's clothes. She put whatever could fit into the tweed suitcase, the earnestness of which made her smile now. To think she'd floated twenty miles with it in the bottom of the rowboat last September!

Eveline left her green scarf and her black dancing shoes on the shelf in the closet and scattered cedar chips over both to guard against the moths, which Emil said grew to be as big as hummingbirds by August, their wings patterned like old lace. The crib would have to stay. And the mattress made of pine needles and feathers.

Hux slept most of the afternoon in the reed basket on the kitchen table, aware, it seemed, that Emil was gone but not undone by it. He looked at her curiously, as if to say, *Now what? I don't know,* Eveline thought. Evergreen had always been a quiet place, but the absoluteness of it unnerved her now.

April. May. June. July. August, at the latest.

Eveline took down the English taxidermy manual from the bookshelf and a few of her sketches from the cabin wall. She wondered what would happen to Tuna, who'd become accustomed to the crumbs Eveline sprinkled on the porch railing for her and to Eveline's imitation of her song, which had improved over the months and was drawing Tuna closer to her outstretched hand each day. Had Eveline ruined her for the wild?

Had Evergreen ruined Eveline for Yellow Falls? What would it be like to sleep in her childhood bedroom with her child? To spend the evenings with her mother and father instead of with her husband? Only when Eveline was about to leave Evergreen did she realize how it had changed her. Since September, she'd grown out of being a daughter and was growing into being a mother and a wife. She thought of what Emil said: *Would your parents mind looking after you and Hux until I come back?* Did she really seem as helpless as a child?

I mind, Eveline thought now, because Emil had been taking care of her, and she didn't realize the completeness of his care until he was gone.

She could stay in Evergreen if she wanted to. Emil would be back by the end of the summer with enough time to cut and stack wood for the winter. She could help, too. She could learn to wield an ax. She could learn to catch fish instead of just frying them. She couldn't bear another winter of rice and beans, which was what would happen if she spent the summer in Yellow Falls. When Emil returned, they'd have to start from scratch, again.

Eveline could start the garden she'd planned up in the meadow and put up enough vegetables to last the entire winter. She could harvest the raspberries from the bush beyond the kitchen window and put up jam, too. She could even grow a row of tobacco plants with Lulu's guidance and surprise Emil with a pouchful for his rosewood pipe. How proud he'd be of her. How resourceful he'd say she was.

Yes! She'd stay.

Except that night came, and menacing shadows crept across the cabin walls, and suddenly Eveline wished there were a lock on the door. Though Hux was sleeping soundly in his crib, she brought him into the bed with her. *There's nothing to be afraid of.* But the moment the word *afraid* slipped into her vocabulary, so did the name *Annie Mae.*

The history books about Yellow Falls, if there were any, were marred by only one murder, which was still unsolved. A few years back, a mother was trimming flowers in her garden one morning while her nine-year-old daughter played in her bedroom. Neither of them noticed the man with the red beard watching them from across the way. When the mother went into the shed, the man walked through the front door, lifted Annie Mae up, and carried her away. Two days later, she was found in a drainage ditch beside a cornfield.

Eveline thought of Annie Mae now, in the cabin, while her own child slept peacefully beside her. If Emil were here, she would have curled up to him like a spoon, but because he wasn't, she turned away from her training. *This stops now.*

Eveline got up out of bed, opened the front door, and walked out onto the porch. She forced herself to look at the shadows and listen to the night sounds—the cries of owls, the creak of trees, the last of the ice breaking up on the river—until that was all they were.

The next day, when Eveline didn't go to Lulu, Lulu came to her.

"I thought a black bear got you," Lulu said, coming up through the woods the same way she had the day before, her coonskin coat flying behind her, Gunther flying in front of her. She'd tied a burlap sack to the end of a branch and was carrying it like a torch.

"They're more afraid of me than I am of them," Eveline said.

"That's a bunch of horseshit," Lulu said.

Eveline was pinning clothes to the line. She set down the yellow sheet she was holding and picked up the reed basket, Hux.

"I'm sort of kidding," Lulu said when she and Gunther got close.

"Then I'm only sort of mad," Eveline said.

Lulu untied the burlap sack from the branch and with the branch tapped Gunther on his backside. "Go on and play now."

"But I don't have anyone to play with," Gunther said. He brushed off the seat of his pants and messed up his ragged hair as if Lulu had touched that, too. He leaned over the reed basket. "*He* won't play with me, that's for sure. He can't even get out of that thing. I bet he doesn't know how to use the outhouse. He'd probably fall in. I'm *four.*"

"You were a baby once, too," Eveline started, but stopped when Lulu dragged her finger along her neck, and Gunther pretended to throw up.

"What about Buckley?" Lulu said.

Gunther poked at the ground with the torch stick. "He's mad 'cause I shot him."

His imaginary friend, Lulu mouthed to Eveline.

"You should apologize," she said to her son.

Gunther perked up a little. "And then he wouldn't be mad anymore?"

"Probably," Lulu said.

Gunther dragged Buckley to the porch steps. "I'm sorry I shot you, but I told you not to use my toothbrush. You were bad, and now I have gems."

"*Germs,*" Lulu said.

Eveline pinned one end of the bedsheet to the clothesline, but was struggling to keep the ends off the damp ground while she reached for another wooden pin in the bucket.

Lulu handed her one. "He's going to end up in jail, isn't he?"

"Maybe a straitjacket," Eveline said.

"Careful," Lulu said. "I'm not above shooting *my* friends."

Together, they finished hanging Eveline's wet laundry on the line.

"Are you going to tell me what happened?" Lulu said when their hands were empty. "I made Reddy take Emil to Yellow Falls so I could wait for you."

Eveline thought of Emil driving over washed-out roads in a beat-up old truck with a man who'd shot his own toe, on his way to a bus station, then a train station, then a boat, then his father. She wondered what they talked about, if they talked at all.

"Emil's father is dying," she said. "He went back to Germany to see him."

"You always think I'm talking about someone else," Lulu said.

Eveline looked down at Hux, who was staring up at the green trees, the blue sky, and the white clouds. "I was packing for home when I realized I'm already here."

"You know what you're doing?" Lulu said.

"No, but I'm sure of it all the same."

"I figured you might say something like that." Lulu reached into the burlap sack and handed her a baby bottle. "I was hoping anyway."

"Why?" Eveline said.

"We've got to start you a garden," Lulu said. "In that meadow where the sun's strong and the ground absorbs a little runoff from the hill. These are from my personal collection. The chafers and potato bugs don't like them as much as the kinds at the general store."

Lulu reached into her sack and pulled out a handful of tiny white envelopes with different words scrawled messily across the fronts: CARROT. TOMATO. DILL. BASIL. HORSERADISH. LETTUCE. CORN. SQUASH. PUMPKIN. TURNIP. ONION. BEANPOLE BEAN. SWEET PEA. BEET. CELERY. There were so many envelopes, and the name on each of them made Eveline's mouth water. The envelopes made her nervous, too, since she'd only ever grown a garden in the scraggly lot behind the apartment in Yellow Falls, and though it had seemed impressive, it was only the size of a sandbox, and Eveline had depended on it for beauty, not survival.

"Don't worry," Lulu said. "I'll help you. I already planted mine."

"Can I ask you something else?" Eveline said.

"Sure," Lulu said.

"Will you teach me how to fish?"

That night, Eveline sat at the table with a pencil and a piece of paper. *Dear Emil,* she wrote, but each letter she started, she stopped. She didn't know how to put into words what was in her heart. What if she couldn't take care of herself? Hux? What if she could?

A little after midnight, she ended up with this, the pale bones of truth:

Dear Emil,

I'm staying in Evergreen with Hux. I love you.

Eveline

6

⸺⫞⫞⫞⟨ Lulu came every morning for the next few weeks, until April turned into May and the buds turned into blooms, and thinking about Emil's departure turned into thinking about his return, since surely he was in Germany by now, saying good-bye to his father with Gitte and his mother before Dr. Hayner administered the syringe of morphine and Emil's father took his last breath. Though Emil hadn't translated the letter word for word, repeating the details he did translate made his absence easier for Eveline to bear, because they made it selfish for her to miss him too much or feel sorry for herself. Lulu said that was horseshit, too. Miss the man. Feel sorry for yourself. Downright wallow if you want.

"*He* wouldn't," Eveline said.

"Well, you're not *him*."

"It's complicated," Eveline said, thinking of her parents, who'd sent word through Reddy they were disappointed she wasn't coming home while Emil was in Germany—her mother had used the words *positively stupid.*

"No, it's not," Lulu said.

This morning, after Lulu and Eveline finished the thermos of coffee Lulu had brought and smoked a cigarette on the porch, and Gunther complained of Hux's helplessness and Hux spit up milk as if to annoy him further, they all went up to the meadow to work on the garden. Lulu lent Eveline her spade and hoe, but she turned the soil with her bare hands, which explained her black fingernails and her lack of flinch when she encountered a snake or an earthworm. When Eveline encountered either, she howled.

"They're not the biting kind," Lulu said.

"No, but they're the wriggling kind!"

In the afternoon, after Gunther and Hux napped in the cabin, the four of them—*And Buckley!* Gunther said—went down to the river so Eveline could practice fishing. She used the lures from Emil's tackle box because she wasn't nervy enough to use a worm.

"You have no problem piercing the flesh of chickens and turkeys and fish—other *alive* things," Lulu said. "You married a man who does that for a living, for God's sake."

"*Once* alive," Eveline said. "But you're right. I have to work up to it."

So far, with the lures she'd only caught river detritus.

"You might just be a wait-for-your-husband kind of girl," Lulu said.

Emil had never lorded his survival skills over her, but Eveline's lack of them irritated her now. Emil was the one who cut wood and dragged it through the snow. He was the one who carried Meg and William's belongings to the roof when the water came through, and he was the one who put them back when he found a way to get the water out.

I will bait this hook! Eveline thought.

And she did, though she squirmed the whole time while Lulu laughed and laughed.

"I'll shoot the worm if you want me to," Gunther said to Eveline, just before the hook pierced the worm's flesh, and Eveline felt both triumphant and a little sorry.

"Thank you," she said to Gunther. She was about to kiss the top of his head when she remembered what he did to his hair after Lulu had touched it. Instead, Eveline cast her line the way Lulu taught her and felt a tug on the end of it.

"I have something!" she said.

Eveline reeled in the line—*You have to think like a fish,* Lulu said—and just as she was about to declare triumph, she saw what she'd caught: an old leather shoe covered in algae.

Lulu unhooked the shoe from the line and cradled it like an infant. "So that's where you went. I've been looking all over for you. You poor baby."

Eveline thought of Emil and the day she'd arrived in Evergreen after falling asleep on the river and foolishly losing her paddles. And though neither Emil nor Lulu had meant anything by *poor baby,* Eveline was mad they'd both said it. Lulu could catch a fish with her bare hands. Probably Emil could, too.

"You have to think like a fish," Lulu said again.

"Fish don't think," Eveline said.

"Sure they do." Lulu thrust herself away from the rocky shore and jumped into the water wild eyed and fully clothed. While she spun around in the river like a crazed, cold fish, Gunther poked at Hux with his index finger, and Hux clamped down on it.

"Your coat!" Eveline said.

"He's got me and Buckley!" Gunther said.

Eveline freed his finger. "We don't bite, darling," she said to Hux.

"You might try meaning that," Lulu said, wringing out the ends of her coat, which smelled even more unpleasant and looked more alive than it had when it was dry. She came out of the water, red cheeked and dripping, and plunked down on a large gray rock that was warm from the sun. To Gunther and Buckley she said, "You're lucky he's all gums."

Eveline sat down next to Lulu. "He's *very* sorry."

Lulu poured the water from her boots onto Eveline's leg. "No, he isn't."

While Gunther and Buckley sat beside Hux with a healthy dose of fear in their eyes, and Lulu and Eveline sat beside each other on the rock sunning themselves, Eveline thought of Meg and wondered if she and Lulu had done the same thing together.

"I wasn't crossing the river then," Lulu said when Eveline asked her about it.

"Why not?" Eveline said.

Lulu tossed a pebble into the water. "I'm pretty sure we didn't come to Evergreen for the same reasons. Actually I know in my heart we didn't. Why did you come here?"

Eveline thought of Emil and his butterflies. "For love, I guess."

When Gunther and Buckley got up to chase after a low-flying bird downriver, Lulu said, "I came because Gunther needed a father and Reddy needed a wife. I used to work at the saloon, and Reddy was one of my regulars. He liked me because I knew just when to take away the whiskey and put down a cup of water and a plate of fried potatoes in its place. He said I was his angel. He's pretty uncreative when it comes to romance."

"Gunther isn't his?" Eveline said.

"Of course he is. Even if he isn't," Lulu said. She looked at the other side of the river. "Not everyone was sweet like Reddy. Some of them didn't ask for what they wanted."

As if she sensed Eveline was about to put an arm around her, Lulu sprang to her feet. She started downriver toward Gunther, who was standing in the water trying to catch minnows in the reeds. She threw a heavy stone into the water. Another.

"I wasn't always a wilderness master like I am now," she said, looking back. "I didn't know how to swim when I came here. Reddy had to teach me."

They spent the rest of the afternoon at the river's edge. Lulu ran up- and downriver with Gunther and Buckley, the three of them kicking and hollering, while Eveline fed Hux and thought about what Lulu had told her. As a true friend Eveline knew she couldn't say anything, but she wanted to for that reason.

Just before Lulu herded Gunther and Buckley into the row-boat and crossed the river for the night, Eveline said, *"Wait,"* to Lulu, who already had one foot in the rowboat.

Eveline picked up Emil's fishing rod and unwound the line from the reel.

"You take one end, and I'll take the other," she said to Lulu. "When you get to the other side, tie it to a tree branch and hang a bell from it. I'll do the same with mine."

"What for?" Lulu said.

Eveline placed the fishing line in Lulu's palm. "If you need me or I need you. It's like a doorbell. A way of knocking all the way out here."

"That's the dumbest idea I've ever heard," Lulu said, but before she pushed the rowboat away from the shore, she wrapped one end of the fishing line around her thumb and wrapped the other around Eveline's.

That night, Eveline wrote another letter to Emil.

Dear Emil,

I don't know if my first letter reached you or not, but if it did I'm sorry for its shortness. It's true that Hux and I are staying in Evergreen, but I didn't tell you how much we miss you and can't wait for you to return to us. I also hope you send a letter soon or that you've already sent one. I don't know how to picture you in the Black Forest. Is it really black?

Your son is beautiful and quiet these days. His demeanor has changed dramatically, which Lulu says happened with her boy Gunther at the same age (except he started off quiet and grew wild). Lulu seems so tough on the outside, but she's actually very tender. Kind, like you. She's been helping me with the garden. So far all we have is turned earth, but she tells me we'll have green soon. I can't wait for you to see it, to eat from it. I have been learning how to fish, too, although so far I've only caught an old boot!

Nighttime still makes me nervous, but I'm getting used to its noises more and more each time my ears encounter them. Sometimes, the noises surprise me. Sometimes, I surprise myself.

Have you ever been afraid?

Love, Eveline

7

⸺⧘⧘⧘⧘⧘⧘ According to Lulu, Reddy drove to Yellow Falls every week when the weather and the alfalfa and potato fields allowed a trip, ostensibly to pick up the mail but really to get drunk. At first, Eveline didn't understand why he had to drive the twenty miles each way to drink whiskey when Lulu kept a cupboard full of the brown bottles in their cabin.

"He saved my life," Lulu said. "That makes me obligated to save his."

She and Eveline were taking a break from the meadow garden and Eveline's side of the river, which long cold pine shadows took hold of in the afternoons. If you wanted direct sunlight, which Eveline and Lulu did on this day, you had to cross the river.

The two were sitting in a pair of tipsy diner chairs, which Eveline recognized from Harvey Small's. A sandy fire pit was in front of them and a sleeping child between them. Behind them stood Lulu and Reddy's cabin, which Lulu had painted red on one side and blue on the other because she couldn't decide which color she liked better.

June had taken over the land, the trees, and the river. Only at night, when the air turned crisp and the logs were lit, when the mosquitoes and blackflies retreated, could drifts of heavy snow be conjured. During the day, June bugs clung to the outside of both their cabins. At night, the moths, prehistoric in their oddness and Jurassic in their size, took the June bugs' place. Emil would have been able to tell Eveline their Latin names and might have preserved one for his personal collection. Eveline called them elephant moths and sketched a few of them in her journal for Emil to look at when he returned. *Eighty days, at the most.* She'd started brushing the moths off the cabin door and the porch railing, since cedar didn't deter them and she couldn't afford to lose any more clothing. *Seventy-nine.*

Gunther and Buckley were taking turns on the tire swing, which hung from a great old oak tree with branches nearly as thick as its trunk. Instead of them being annoyed with Hux, lately they were encouraged he could hold up his head for several minutes before it flopped to one side. Whenever they saw Eveline, they'd ask, "Can he walk yet?"

"A few more months," Eveline would say to keep up their hope.

Today the two seemed content to let Hux grow on his own terms, which allowed time for Eveline and Lulu to talk freely instead of spelling what they didn't want the boys to hear. "How is driving to Yellow Falls to drink saving Reddy's life?"

"He won't drink in front of Gunther. He thinks it would make him a bad father, since he doesn't do it for enjoyment," Lulu said.

"Why does he do it?" Eveline said.

"Reddy needs whiskey like the rest of us need water."

"What does he do in the winter?" Eveline said.

"I have to slip teaspoons of whiskey into his coffee to calm him down," Lulu said. "Once, I put a shot's worth in a bowl of beef stew."

"He didn't taste it?" Eveline said.

"He didn't say anything," Lulu said. "He went back for a second helping, though."

"Is that when he shot his toe?" Eveline said.

"He was sober for that, bless him."

"I've never had a drink," Eveline said. "Unless you count in church."

"I don't," Lulu said, getting up. "I won't!"

She went inside the cabin, crashed around the cupboards, and came back outside with a bottle of whiskey and two chipped glasses.

"I have to feed Hux," Eveline said, her breasts swelling at the thought.

"Give him some goat's milk," Lulu said to her. To Gunther and Buckley, she said, "Would you two go milk Willa Girl, please?"

"We're swinging, Mama!"

"It'll make Hux walk *a lot* sooner," Lulu said.

"What if he doesn't like goat's milk?" Eveline said, brushing Hux's silky dark hair with her fingers.

"Better hope he likes whiskey," Lulu said, pouring some into the glasses.

Eveline sipped the astringent liquid with as much grace as she could, even though the peppery taste on her tongue made her eyes water and her nose run. She wanted to spit it out, but Lulu would only make her drink more.

"It's not high tea," Lulu said. "What are you doing with your pinkie finger?"

"I'm being a lady," Eveline said.

"Stop. It's making me want to throw up."

When Gunther and Buckley finished milking Willa Girl in her chicken-wire pen beside the cabin, they took a shortcut through the garden and ended up trampling a row of young sweet corn and spilling most of the milk along the way.

"This will make him grow big muscles," Gunther announced, handing the glass to Eveline, which gave her an excuse to set down the one with whiskey in it.

"How should I feed it to him?" Eveline said.

Lulu laughed a little. "A spoon?"

"I see you've thought this out." Eveline set down the milk, lifted Hux out of the reed basket, and unbuttoned the top of her dress. "I think I'll feed him my way."

"My God!" Lulu said, staring, reaching. "They're *huge!*"

With one hand, Eveline covered her top half with Hux's receiving blanket. She swatted the top of Lulu's hand with the other.

"Your nipple's like a saucer!" Lulu said.

"Well, what do yours look like?"

"Not like *that,*" Lulu said.

The two of them stared at each other a long moment before they started laughing and belting out words like *Saucer!* and *Mushroom!* and *Bundt cake!* and Lulu took a swig of whiskey and spit it all over her shoe. After they calmed down, Lulu poured more whiskey, and Eveline asked the question she'd been thinking about asking for a while now.

"Do you ever take off that coat?"

Lulu patted the arms of the coat and a cloud of dust rose into the air. "Not in years," she said, waving away the dust as if it were nothing but finally succumbing to coughing.

"We're demented," she said when the coat reabsorbed the dust.

Eveline took the glass of whiskey from her. *"We?"*

Reddy came back from Yellow Falls with an armful of mail, a paper bag full of penny candy for Gunther, and a package of T-bone steaks from the butcher, one of which he'd bought for Eveline because he said women needed iron.

"Are you corrupting your friend?" he said to Lulu.

"She's corrupting me," Lulu said.

Lulu was right: Reddy may have looked like a rangy old mule, but he was soft as a lamb. Eveline had never seen him in anything other than a thick plaid work shirt, which concealed the boniness of his shoulders, and a pair of brown trousers, the same as Lulu wore.

He kissed Lulu's shoulder. "I don't think that's possible."

Lulu pushed the bottle of whiskey under her chair with her foot. "How was the trip?"

Reddy had been gone two days. One to drink and one to sober up. His hands were shaking a little. The whites of his eyes were yellow.

"Good," Reddy said.

Which brought Lulu to her feet, as if in the secret language of their marriage that word meant something different than it did to Eveline. "I'll fry up those steaks."

Reddy urged her back down in the chair and started for the cabin. "I'll heat some broth to tide me over."

Eveline was fond of Reddy and curious about him, too. Here was a man who'd given himself over to drinking and yet was completely honorable. Eveline didn't know any man—would Emil?—who would do what he'd done for Lulu, for Gunther.

Halfway to the screened door, Reddy returned to them.

"I almost forgot," he said, sifting through the letters under his arm. Last week he brought Eveline a note from her parents, but she hadn't received any postmarked letters yet.

"I mailed yours for you," he said, handing Eveline two

envelopes, one thick the other thin. "Earl said three weeks or thereabouts."

"Is that all?" Eveline said, cheered.

"One's from the government," Reddy said. "Probably trying to squeeze blood from a turnip. We got that one, too. I make Lulu open those. Bad news sounds better from her."

Eveline wasn't interested in the government letter; she focused on the thinner one. When she felt brave enough, she looked at the return address in the corner of the envelope.

Germany!

"It's from Emil," she said, hugging the letter. "I think I'll go home to read it."

"Should I take you?" Lulu said.

"I can manage," Eveline said. She tucked the letters into the pocket of her dress and picked up the reed basket. "Thank you. For the day. The letters. Everything."

Newly buoyant, Eveline started down the path to the river. The white lady's-slippers stood pretty and prim, like eager schoolgirls, on either side of the footpath. The light was lighter. How wonderful, too, the smell of the pines and birches and the electric-green moss.

And what lovely words: *my husband, my husband, my husband.*

Just as Eveline was about to step into the rowboat and push it away from the shore with the paddles Lulu and Reddy had lent her, Lulu came running down the path.

"Your steak," she said, getting tangled in the fishing-line-and-bell contraption.

Eveline placed the steak next to Hux and the reed basket in the bow of the rowboat. Then she got in herself, the toes of her canvas shoes wet from the water, her heart flapping like the fish she hadn't yet caught.

"That was a dumb idea, wasn't it?" she said.

Lulu untangled herself from the fishing line and gave the rowboat a push. "It's kind of like art. It's growing on me."

After Eveline got back to the cabin and had lit the oil lamps, which glowed warmly in the early evening light, she tucked Hux into his crib. When she was certain he was asleep, she went to the porch with a cigarette and packet of matches. She opened the letter from the government first because she wanted to savor the fact of Emil's a little longer.

Dear Resident,

On behalf of the Minnesota Water and Energy Commission, we are writing to inform you that thirty days after this third day of June, 1939, we will begin rebuilding the dam at the mouth of the Snake and Owl Rivers, eight miles north of Evergreen, in a government supported effort to bring you, those who live primitively in the wilderness, electricity by way of hydroelectric power. Light, my friends!

If you desire to stay in your home, which I'm certain you'll recall was built on land deeded to the government by the Chippewa Indians in exchange for tax clemency in the year 1889 and therefore which you have no legal claim to, you must sign and deliver this document within thirty days and thus will be able to remain where you are for a small monthly fee to be determined on an individual basis by our field agent who will assess all roofed structures (including but not limited to cabins, henhouses, outhouses, work sheds, and root cellars) as well as any and all cleared land in the months of July and August.

*In signing this document, I must remind you that
you retain no legal right to recover any damages,
fiduciary or otherwise, from the Minnesota Water and
Energy Commission or any branch of the government
for any future destruction to your homes or personal
effects or to the members of your family should an act
of man or nature bombard you during your tenancy on
government land.*

Remember, it is light we are offering you.

Sincerely,
    Albert Muldoon
    President
    Lead with Light Initiative
    Minneapolis, Minnesota

"Horseshit!" Lulu must have been shouting across the river, but the words and the official watermark beneath them on the heavy cream paper intimidated Eveline. Albert Muldoon from Minneapolis, president of the Lead with Light Initiative, had told her something she didn't know: the land beneath their cabin didn't belong to them and therefore neither did their cabin or the outhouse or the garden (including but not limited to). Did Emil know? Why wouldn't he have told her?

Which led her to opening his letter before she was ready.

Dearest Eveline,

I have no doubt disappointed (hurt?) you by not writing more often and sooner, but Father requires my continual attention. Everyone believed he was waiting for me to come home before he let go of his earthly concerns, but now that I am here, he continues to hold on for reasons unknown to all of us.

Yesterday when I was reading a passage from Goethe, To be loved for what one is, is the greatest exception, *he stopped me.*

"Are you happy?" he said to me.

"Very," I said.

"Then you are richer than I ever was."

Despite the war and its hardships, I always believed my father was generally happy. What a terrible shock to discover he wasn't. If he'd had his way, which I suppose means if my mother didn't get pregnant with me all those years ago, he would have become a naturalist in the tradition of Darwin.

Yesterday he said, "I don't believe in heaven. How can I be expected to die without that belief?"

I don't know how to answer that, so I sit next to his bed and read to him whether or not his eyes are closed. When we've both had enough, I tell him about you and Hux. He enjoys hearing about your rosy cheeks and your long, lovely hair. He's particularly interested in your efforts to learn German and your interest in taxidermy (which my mother thinks is a form of barbarism).

I wonder if I have made a mistake leaving you and Hux with your parents in Yellow Falls. Perhaps I should have stayed home, as I suspect it is not me my father really wanted.

Germany is not what I remember it to be. There is a movement here to involve all German boys in a program designed to promote nationalism, but one that excludes the Jewish population as well as other ethnic groups, among them the Gypsies. My father believes we will have another war on our hands very soon. He has heard Hitler speak on the shortwave radio. As have I now. Hitler is extremely persuasive; he makes hatred seem like a human right. The few Jews in our village have gone to stay with extended family in France and England, which my father thinks is wise since in Berlin and Munich a handful of synagogues have been burned to the ground and violence done to several of their worshippers. We're in trouble, I believe. We're already occupying Austria and part of Czechoslova-kia, according to the papers here. Have the American papers said anything? I wonder. You mustn't worry about me. I will be fine. I will come home to you soon.

Gitte and my mother have asked me to make sure you know you are welcomed into our family as is our little son. Gitte is making you a shawl. She and my mother are constantly bustling about as if household industry soothes their spirits. I wish it soothed mine, as it would be more convenient than running off to the forest to chop wood when my mood needs lightening.

On one of my wood-chopping adventures, my old friend Ava, whom I told you I used to play with as a boy, interrupted me. For as long as I can remember, she's been caring for her mother, who suffers from a mysterious illness that keeps her in bed. Ava has con-soled me greatly. She's taught me how to change my father's bed linens without rousing him from sleep. She was always more clever than me. Everyone, including Ava, thinks I should return to you and Hux at once, but I can't leave my father just yet.

Soon, my little dove, I promise.

I have enclosed whatever money I have been able to scrape together. It isn't as much as it should be, but will at least procure you the licorice ropes you love so much. I hope to hear from you soon and can't help but imagine our letters are crossing the ocean at the same time.

Kiss our boy for me. Kiss you for me.

Your loving husband, Emil

Eveline set the letter down on the porch floor. What had she expected? An easy death, her husband's swift return? Certainly not invasions, war.

Eveline forced herself to focus on the other parts of the letter. Gitte's shawl, their father's unhappiness. Emil didn't sound like himself, even though the gently leaning handwriting belonged to him. He'd never talked about German philosophy, which made Eveline feel very far away from him, since she'd been reading his blunt taxidermy manuals.

All she could think about was his friend Ava. Ava in the forest. Ava with a sheet in her hand, saying, *Like this, this.* Eveline was jealous of Ava's proximity to Emil, who hadn't even received her letters yet telling him she and Hux were in Evergreen. The only real thing she could do was put away the letter and the slim stack of green bills tucked into it.

Emil will be all right. Hux and I will be all right.

Tomorrow, she'd cross the river if Łulu and Gunther didn't cross it first. Together, they'd figure out what to do about the light man, Albert Muldoon.

Eveline went inside to fry the steak Reddy had bought her, which he'd wrapped in the front page of the *Yellow Falls Gazette.* The blood from the steak had made most of it illegible, but the headlines were still clear: "Little Bears Sweep the Play-offs," "Local Man Wins Regional Hot-Dog-Eating Contest," "Fifth Graders Sculpt Giant Loon out of Clay." The headlines made her miss news that wasn't news. "Woman Makes Steak for Sake of Iron, Distraction."

After Eveline ate, she went back to the porch to say good night to Tuna, who hopped onto the railing when Eveline approached her.

"That's a good girl," she said when Tuna pecked at the sunflower seeds in her palm. "You're spoiling me. One day you'll make a little bird friend and fly away."

Tuna gathered a beakful of sunflower seeds, hopped back onto the perch of the birdhouse, and gave a little chirp just before she disappeared inside it.

8

Crows were attacking the garden, tearing through the rows of deep green lettuce and orange heirloom tomatoes to get to the corn. Eveline woke to the jagged sound of cawing, followed by something that sounded a lot like chuckling, as if to say: *Got you!*

By the time she swaddled Hux in a blanket and ran up to the meadow, the garden had split its seams. The crows had uprooted Eveline's dill and broccoli and, just to be mean, a handful of yellow oxeye daises: her favorite flower. Eveline spent the morning restoring order to the garden, shooing the circling crows with Lulu's hoe, while Hux played with a rattle she'd made for him out of a dried gourd. She replanted what she could and harvested what she couldn't, thinking about how baby vegetables were prized more than their mature counterparts in the ladies' magazines now and wondering if the same held true for pumpkins and squash, tiny string beans. She didn't think of the word *scarecrow* until she got to the rows of violated sweet corn, the golden ears she wouldn't be dipping in pools of melted butter.

To build one, Eveline sacrificed a blue blouse and her black dancing shoes, but she couldn't spare any slacks, since she only owned two pairs and one of them was already in sorry shape. In the closet, she glanced at Hux's rompers. Unless she was going to make a baby scarecrow, she'd have to use a pair of Emil's slacks. She picked the least flattering of the heavy wool pairs—the ugly brown pair, if she was honest with herself—and laid the outfit out on the bed. *Sorry, dear,* she said, as if the slacks were Emil.

To make the scarecrow's skeleton, Eveline lashed together Lulu's hoe and a branch that had come down on the outhouse, along with rope leftover from the clothesline. He wasn't the world's handsomest scarecrow, but when she got him to his feet, Hux shook his rattle vigorously and Eveline felt a little surge of pride.

A few hours later, the crows came back.

"Scarecrows only scare people," Lulu said, after the second ransacking. She brought over one of Reddy's guns, a .38-caliber Smith and Wesson an old friend of his used to kill soldiers during the First World War. *German soldiers,* she meant but didn't say. "Even if they're not attacking your garden, sometimes you have to kill one just to make your point."

Lulu balanced an empty can of tomato paste on the scarecrow's arm, stepped back, and judging Gunther and Hux to be far enough away shot it off.

Eveline had never held a gun before and wasn't eager to hold this one, which was loaded with two-hundred-grain bullets. The worn walnut panels, along with the indentation of the previous owner's fingers, meant that someone had loved this gun well. The gun was heavier than Eveline thought it would be. The metal, cold and dull.

"This means you can't kill a crow," Lulu said, showing her how the safety mechanism, the hammerblock, worked. "This means you can."

Eveline held the gun as daintily as she could, wondering what Emil would think if he saw her with it. "I'm afraid it'll go off by itself."

"It doesn't have free will," Lulu said. "Apparently just like us."

Eveline, Reddy, and reluctantly Lulu had signed and returned the government papers, agreeing to let the field agent do his assessing because none of them wanted to vacate their land, which belonged to them in heart but not by deed. They were squatters. Lulu and Reddy knew this when they moved to Evergreen and took up residency in what was then an abandoned cabin. They said Emil must have known this, too, when he made the agreement with Meg and William, who were probably happy to get whatever they could. Money was what they'd most likely needed, not paperwork, which made her wish Emil was here so she could be mad at him in person instead of worried about him on paper.

Since she'd received Emil's letter, Eveline had been waiting less and less patiently for another one, hopeful whenever Reddy crossed the river and disappointed when he came with buckets of fish instead of an armful of mail. *He's not coming home,* she'd think then and would have to go to weed the garden or read the English taxidermy manual or take up some other project to distract herself from that possibility.

After some cleverness on her part, she and Hux now had a real outdoor shower when the rain barrel was full. Instead of fighting the flow of water, Eveline had raised the rain barrel onto the roof and lowered the copper piping, allowing gravity to do its work. She'd built a siphoning system out of cloth and gravel to slow the pressure of water. She and Hux had spent a whole day collecting smooth gray stones at the river and lined the shower floor with them. Eveline was still working on something that would approximate a showerhead, but she'd already placed a bar of castile soap in a dish and had hammered a nail into the cabin wall to hang her towel on. The temperature of the water depended on the sun, which meant the best time to shower was in the afternoon, when the sun was strong enough to heat the water to something between cold and comfortable.

Lulu and Reddy were impressed with her accomplishment, as was the Lead with Light field agent Cullen O'Shea, who showed up early one morning near the beginning of July to assess the property. He was wearing a crisp white shirt and freshly pressed trousers, which belied the lengthy trip up the river in his government-issued ten-horsepower motorboat. His eyes were an unearthly blue, his hair the color of cinnamon sticks. Despite the way he was dressed, he looked at ease in the wilderness.

Mr. O'Shea said he'd figure Eveline's ingenuity into his assessment, writing something on his wooden clipboard with a yellow school pencil. The air was humid, which made the pencil catch on the moist paper. Eveline was sweating, but he didn't appear to be.

"I believe that merits a five-dollar property rental discount, don't you?"

"I believe you may be right, Mr. O'Shea."

"Cullen," he said, a dimple appearing to the right of his mouth. "Friendly Irish surveyor at your service, Mrs. Sturm."

Eveline switched Hux to her other hip and held out her hand. "Eveline."

She went in the cabin to make a cup of tea for him. Lulu would have offered him a cup of dirt. He was going to Lulu and Reddy's cabin next.

"Lulu can be difficult," Eveline said.

"Are you friendly with her?"

"She's my *best* friend," Eveline said, smiling like a school-girl because it was true.

"Can I hold him?" Cullen said when she brought the cup of tea out to him.

"Your son," he added, when Eveline tried to hand him the tea. "I love children."

"Do you have any?" Eveline said, handing Hux over.

"Women worth marrying are usually already married," Cullen said, holding out his index finger, which Hux clung to like the rattle.

Eveline set the teacup on a stump. "He likes you."

"I like him, too," Cullen said, his dimple appearing again.

Cullen spent the morning walking around the cabin, the outhouse, and the surrounding woods, inspecting what the people at Lead with Light told him to inspect and writing the results on his clipboard. Though he was technically sup-posed to, he said he wouldn't come inside the cabin because whatever was in there wasn't his business and because Eve-line's husband wasn't there to agree to an invasion of privacy.

"What about the electricity?" Eveline said, though she wasn't particularly interested in having it, since she'd lived without for so long. The warm glow of the oil lamps made the cabin cozier at night and she'd finally mastered how to bake soda bread on the woodstove.

"An electrician will wire you when the dam gets closer to completion," he said. "It'll probably only be for a single bulb at first, which is pretty useless if you ask me."

Before he moved on to Lulu's, Eveline took him up to the garden, which was still growing despite the crows' efforts to destroy it. Lulu had brought Eveline a flat of geraniums to keep the grubs away from her leafy greens and suggested set-ting out dishes of soapy water for the potato bugs that weren't supposed to like this strain of seeds in the first place.

"Think of Gunther," she said. "He wilts in the presence of soap."

The corn was torn to bits, but the tomatoes were growing plump, some as large as grapefruits, and the squash vines were dropping their sunny petals onto the broccoli below them. Lulu kept urging her to harvest the garden, which Eveline kept delaying because the twist of vines and the spread of leaves, the vibrant rainbow of colors, gave her such pleasure to look at. The scent of her first real garden, too—soil and herbs and sun—was more intoxicating than any perfume she'd ever dabbed on her wrists.

"Maybe I'll marry her," Cullen said, shaking hands with the scarecrow. *"Him?"*

"The crows keep attacking the corn," Eveline said.

"See," Cullen said. "Even the scarecrow's taken."

"Only for the summer," Eveline said. "Then it could be yours."

"Nothing like marrying an *it*."

After Cullen gave her a copy of the report he was taking back to the office with him, in which he'd recommended charging her and Emil a very small monthly residence fee, Eveline gave him directions to Lulu's house and a last bit of advice.

"Don't ask her about her coat."

Cullen shook Hux's hand and then hers and started down the same path Emil had walked down months ago now.

Eveline spent the rest of the day doing her chores and playing with Hux, who'd begun to crawl. She set down a blanket on the porch and encouraged him with fingers full of honey from the jar Lulu gave her. When Hux grew tired, he rolled on his back and looked up at the cross of beams overhead and the slices of blue sky visible in the spaces between them.

"Your mama and papa love you more than anything else in the world," Eveline told him. She was worried Hux didn't know he had a father. She showed him the photograph of her and Emil taken outside the courthouse on their wedding day, her in the blue dress she was twirling in when they met and Emil in his traveling suit. "That's your papa."

After Hux woke from his afternoon nap and Eveline took in the laundry from the line, she started a supper of smoked trout. The last time Reddy went to Yellow Falls, he brought back a lemon for Eveline. Now, instead of rubbing the flesh of the fruit on her skin, she squeezed it over the smoked fish and on top of the dilled rice she made to go along with it. She cut a slice of soda bread for her and for Hux, although Hux mostly gummed whatever she gave him. Since it was just the two of them, she didn't set down a tablecloth or napkins. If she needed to wipe her mouth, she used a dish towel.

"Here we are then," she said to Hux when everything was ready.

Just then someone knocked on the front door. Eveline went to it, knowing that whoever it was wasn't Lulu because day or night Lulu marched right in. Maybe it was Reddy, come to invite them for supper.

"Hello?" she heard someone say. The voice was familiar, soft. She thought it belonged to Emil, which meant he was home again. Home. What a lovely word! She'd gladly put out a tablecloth again. She'd gladly dress for supper.

I've missed you so much!

Before Eveline opened the door, she picked an oxeye daisy out of the Mason jar on the bookshelf and tucked it behind her ear. She pinched her cheeks.

"You're home!" she said, skipping a little as she turned the knob.

Instead of Emil, Cullen O'Shea was standing at the foot of the porch with a bundle of wires in his hand. "I didn't know you were expecting me."

What a disappointment not to see her husband standing on the porch in his traveling suit, a duffel bag slung over his shoulder, a bouquet of white edelweiss—Emil's favorite flower—in his hand. "I thought you were my husband," Eveline said.

"No, ma'am," Cullen said. "I'm just a surveyor with a broken boat."

The sun was balancing low on the horizon, and Eveline shielded her eyes to see him.

"What's wrong with it?" she said.

He held up the bundle of wires. "One of these shorted out. I'm afraid I'm stuck on the river tonight. Tomorrow, I'll row myself back to town. I was wondering if I might trouble you for a blanket. I'll return it in the morning. The mosquitoes are getting to me."

"Of course," Eveline said, turning to retrieve one. Halfway up the porch steps, she stopped. "How rude of me. You must be starved."

"This is turning out to be pretty inconvenient, I admit. I thought I'd be up here half a day at the most, but your coat friend had me surveying in circles."

"She's a troublemaker," Eveline said, smiling.

"She's only protecting her own," Cullen said.

"I just put our little supper on the table," Eveline said, looking down at her apron, which was full of flour from the loaf of bread. *Nothing to be done now,* she thought, wondering what else in the cabin would embarrass her. "It's a simple one since it's just Hux and me, but we're happy to have you if you don't mind smoked trout."

"I love trout," Cullen said. "But I couldn't come inside, Mrs. Sturm."

"Eveline."

Cullen took off his hat. "It wouldn't be right."

"Those rules don't matter out here," Eveline said, taking his hand, which was softer than Emil's. She led him up the porch steps. "They probably don't matter anywhere."

Eveline sat Cullen down in her seat and made another plate for herself. Hux dropped his bread on the floor and though Eveline usually would have picked it up and given it back to him, with Cullen here she cut another slice for him and set aside the other one for Tuna. The kitchen was warm from cooking the rice, and before she sat down Eveline propped open the little window that overlooked the raspberry bush.

"You sure about this?" Cullen said.

Eveline sat in Emil's place. "Absolutely."

The three of them ate supper, Eveline and Cullen asking each other questions to fill the quiet and paying plenty of attention to Hux to ease the fact that they were two strangers sitting at a table together. *You're such a good little boy, aren't you? He's my angel. My love.*

"Have you always been a surveyor?" Eveline asked Cullen, thinking it was nice to have another person at her table again. Whenever she ate with Lulu and Reddy, she ate at their table. Afterward, one or the other of them would row her and Hux back.

"Not officially," Cullen said, studying her sketches on the far wall. "But I've always been somewhat of an observer. Looks like you are, too."

"Oh, those," Eveline said. "They're just something I do to pass the time."

"Where's your husband, if you don't mind me asking?"

"Germany," Eveline said. "His father's sick."

"I lost my father when I was a boy."

"I'm sorry," Eveline said.

"I only meant I know how hard it is."

After they finished eating supper, Eveline cleared the plates and made a pot of coffee with the grounds Lulu had brought over. Even though Lulu had showed her how to make a proper pot, loose grounds always floated to the top of Eveline's.

"You really don't want me to sleep tonight, do you?" Cullen said.

"Would you prefer tea?" Eveline said, lifting up the mug she'd set down for him and moving to replace the coffee with herbal tea. "Juice?"

That's when Cullen grabbed her wrist, which startled Eveline. She dropped the mug, which shattered when it hit the floor. Hux began to cry.

"I'd like some dessert," Cullen said, pressing so hard she thought she'd faint.

Eveline knew then that something terrible was about to happen and that she was helpless to stop it. "There isn't any," she said.

"You're the one who invited me in," Cullen kept saying, while the cabin spun and Eveline put her free hand on the wall, on her drawings, as if she could stop time from moving forward. She was standing on the edge of danger and knew she was about to fall in.

"Put that child somewhere else if you don't want him to see," Cullen said.

See what? Eveline thought, wondering if what was happening was real. How could it be? And yet it was. *Emil,* she thought or said or screamed.

There was nowhere to put Hux but outside on the front porch and Eveline did that when Cullen released her wrist, as if she was hovering above the ground, above herself, floating,

floating. Before Cullen forced her back into the hard lines of her body, she kissed Hux's pink cheeks and put a blanket over him. Still, he cried.

"Please help me," Eveline said to him, certain that going back into the cabin meant something terrible would happen and yet knowing she had to go there—a place that only moments before was pleasant, was home.

A plate of smoked trout still sat on the table. A lemon wedge.

"We were having dinner," Eveline said, thinking of Annie Mae in her bedroom.

"That's not what we're doing now," Cullen said.

"I could make a dessert. There's jam in the cupboard. Raspberry."

I can stop this, Eveline thought.

"I'm only going to hurt you if you make me," Cullen said, unbuckling his belt.

Before she could think of anything that would stop him, he pulled her inside.

"Why are you doing this?" Eveline said, crying because the cabin was spinning like a leaf on the river, crying because that's what her son was doing on the porch, because she couldn't go to him, because she couldn't tell him *Everything's going to be all right.*

"You can leave right now and I won't tell anyone," she said. "I won't say a word."

And then: "Lulu's coming over soon. The woman with the coat."

"Good," Cullen said, all dimples. "I wouldn't mind a visit with her, too."

"Please," Eveline said, and as if the very word enraged him, the courtesy of it, Cullen pushed her down to the floor

and the only thing Eveline could do was pray that unconsciousness would take hold of her the same as it did when she gave birth to Hux, when all she remembered was that someone had saved her. Someone would save her.

"You're the one who invited me in," Cullen said, and pushed her legs apart.

Ma-ma, she heard.

She heard the sound of wings beating at the front door.

"Look at me," Cullen said, forcing her eyes open with his fingers.

Annie Mae. Drainage ditch. You're the one who let him in.

Eveline was tethered to him, her hair loose and wild around her face, her pale elbows pressed hard against the wood. She was tethered to those dark pupils, those rings of blue—

"Why are you doing this?" she cried.

"Because you're good and dear and sweet," Cullen said.

When Cullen took from Eveline what he wanted, he guided his belt back through the loops of his trousers. Eveline lay on the hard wood floor, unsure of whether she was alive or dead. She should have listened to her mother and father and gone back to Yellow Falls. She should have listened to her husband. The mere thought of Emil shamed her.

"I'll give you a minute to collect yourself," Cullen said. "You should fix your hair."

"Are you going to leave?" Eveline said.

"Depends," said Cullen, smiling as if he'd done nothing more than eat supper with her. "Are you going to give me a proper send-off?"

"I need to freshen up first," Eveline said, shaking too much to stand up.

"I'll wait for you on the porch," Cullen said.

"My baby," she said.

"His eyes are closed," Cullen said at the door.

Eveline used a chair for support and pulled herself to her feet slowly because she couldn't trust her legs. She didn't know if Cullen was going to leave—if that was all he'd wanted—or if he'd decide he wanted something else from her. She picked up the brush and ran it through her hair, afraid to look at herself in the hand mirror. All her life, she'd never felt so deeply hated; it took hold of her sore limbs, it battered her heart.

For Meg, Love William.

Canada seemed so far way, so clean and pure, in contrast to what she saw—terror, daisies—when she looked in the mirror.

"Don't make me come in and get you," Cullen said. He cooed to Hux, who made no noise in response. *Was Hux dead?* Twice was too many times to think so.

Cullen moved on to the red birdhouse and to Tuna, holding his finger out for her to perch on. When she didn't come out, he held up a handful of sunflower seeds and clucked to her as if she were a chicken. "It's all right, little bird. I won't hurt you."

Eveline walked to the door with Lulu's gun in her hands. For a moment, the last moment of real thinking, she wondered if her heart was the thing in her hands. At the threshold, she raised the gun to the level of her shoulders.

"What do you think you're doing, darling?" Cullen said.

"I'm saying goodbye," Eveline said.

Cullen's dimples appeared at the corners of his mouth, but boyishly as they did when he arrived at her door the first time. "A woman like you shouldn't have a gun."

"It's not mine," Eveline said.

Cullen stepped backward carefully until he was standing on the sandy ground in front of the porch. "Of course it isn't. You're too good for it."

"I'll shoot you," Eveline said.

"No, you won't," Cullen said, stepping back even farther so that now he stood amid the milk thistle Emil didn't have time to clear before he went away. "You're going to let me go and raise that boy of yours and your husband's going to come home from Germany."

Eveline looked at Hux in the reed basket.

"You're going to tell your husband how much you missed him," Cullen said. "It'll be a true shame, but you'll forget all about me. You'll grow old. You'll get gray as a mule."

"I'll—" Eveline started.

"Jail's no place for someone like you," Cullen said. He was already at the edge of the forest, the place where shadows met shadows. "You don't want a rope around your neck."

A flash of steel bars. A broken neck. A headline in the *Gazette*.

"We were having dinner," Eveline said, the scent of trout and lemon on her hands.

Cullen tipped his hat like a gentleman.

"It was delicious," he said just before he disappeared.

9

꘏꘏꘏꘏꘏ Eveline didn't know how much time passed between firing Lulu's gun into the forest and Lulu running toward the cabin, calling, *Are you all right?* At some point, Eveline put the gun down and picked up Hux, who was crying like he used to when nothing would soothe him but her breast. Tuna came out of her red birdhouse, but she didn't make a noise.

"I know I gave you the gun, but I didn't expect you to use it," Lulu said when she reached the milk thistle. "I thought you shot your toe off. Are you all right?"

"We were having dinner," Eveline said, clinging to the porch railing, to Hux.

Tuna hopped onto the railing. She craned her neck strangely.

"I thought Hux only gummed things," Lulu said.

"The surveyor," Eveline said.

Lulu looked at her curiously. "Why would you invite him in? He's the worst kind of person. I'd have put him six feet under if Reddy had let me."

"His boat broke down," Eveline said. "Only it didn't."

Lulu looked back at the forest, the river, the last of the day's light.

Eveline dug her fingernails into the railing. "We were having dinner."

"What did he do to you?" Lulu said.

All at once, as if she could see into Eveline's heart, she came rushing through the milk thistle, up the porch steps.

"I knew something wasn't right with him," she said, unbuttoning her coat and wrapping it around Eveline's shoulders. She lifted Hux out of Eveline's arms. "Those dimples. I should have come sooner."

Eveline rubbed her cheek against the soft, worn fur of Lulu's coat. She didn't know if she was breathing or not. "I thought he was Emil when he knocked."

Lulu pressed her lips against Eveline's forehead. "Where is he? I'll kill him."

"Emil likes rosy cheeks. Sundresses. I let him go."

Hux kept touching his ears.

"Stop thinking," Lulu said, looking at the thin streaks of blood drying on Eveline's legs. "You can do that later."

Lulu took Hux inside, prepared a bottle, and laid him down in his crib. After a few minutes she came back out with Eveline's nightgown.

"Let's get you out of those clothes," she said to Eveline, loosening her grip on the porch railing and leading her to the back of the cabin to the shower.

She lifted Eveline's dress over her head and placed her beneath the splash of cool water. Eveline locked up her thoughts as Lulu rubbed soap up and down the length of her body like Eveline's mother did when she was a girl and Eveline used to catch soap bubbles on the ends of her fingers. Lulu washed her from head to toe, but Eveline didn't feel any cleaner at the shower's end. Her body hurt where Cullen had touched her; her neck was red.

Lulu wrapped a towel around her and slipped the nightgown over her head.

"They're so small," she said, fumbling with the buttons at the back.

"They're pearls," Eveline said, as if she were sleepwalking. "Only they aren't real."

How was it possible that she'd worn this nightgown on her wedding night? That life could change so quickly on an evening in July? She wanted her mother and father, Hux, Emil. She wanted to go back to the afternoon and the porch steps, the scattering of sunflower seeds. To say, *No, you can't have a blanket. No, you can't come in.* Her hair was wet against her back. When she closed her eyes, she saw herself reflected in Cullen's eyes.

Lulu went back inside to get Hux. When she came back out, she eyed her coonskin coat, which was draped over one of the rocking chairs.

"I'm going to bring the clothes you were wearing," she said, bundling the daisy dress and Eveline's underclothes in her free hand as if they were the offenders.

Eveline's parents were right: who did she think she was living all alone in the wilderness? All she'd wanted to do was continue the life she and Emil had started, to make him—her— proud. She thought of the words *I'm sorry,* the fishing-line-and-bell contraption, how inadequate they were then and now.

"You'll stay with us tonight," Lulu said. "Every night if you want."

When they reached the river's edge, there was no sign of the government boat or the man who'd steered it upriver that morning. The sun had set, and the stars, Orion's Belt and the Milky Way, pulsed like hearts in the sky. To the south, lightning flashed.

Lulu positioned Eveline and Hux in the canoe and pushed it away from the shore.

Dear Emil, Eveline wrote in her mind each time Lulu dipped the paddle into the water like a pen in a bottle of ink.

"We were having dinner," she said.

"Breathe," Lulu said from the stern of the canoe. "You're turning blue."

Eveline inhaled the cool night air, listening for something— what?—in the little waves that lapped against the side of the boat.

Eveline thought of that first trip down the river in her sundress. She thought of the lick of water on the cabin's wood, the story it told then, the story it told now.

Between the branches overhead, the moon appeared, yellow and glaring.

"You're underwater," Lulu said. "Now come up for air."

When they got across the river, they walked along the bank until they caught sight of the fishing line and the bell Lulu had rigged up. From there, they walked up the path to Lulu's cabin. There was a fire going in the pit. A chair tipped on its side.

"Today is almost yesterday," Lulu said, handing Eveline her bundled dress.

It was hard to believe the same thing that had happened to her had happened to Lulu, that a body could recover from that kind of disparaging, that kind of shame. Lulu walked around the fire, embraced Eveline, and backed away with Hux.

"Now put it in the fire," she said.

Eveline stood with the dress in her hand, thinking of the morning Emil had lifted her out of the rowboat. He loved this dress—the daisies marching up and down the length of the fabric—of all that it stood for. What would he think of her now?

Eveline tossed the dress and her underclothes into the fire and watched them turn to ash. Her neck throbbed.

"You have to let this go," Lulu said.

Together, they walked to the cabin, where Reddy had been waiting for them, pacing. He took both women in his arms, and though he probably wanted a drink, his breath smelled of buttery piecrust, which he'd pinched into a metal plate, filled with beaten eggs, and cooked over their woodstove.

"I thought something happened," he said.

Lulu looked at Eveline as if she were asking for her permission, which Eveline granted with a slight nod of her head. "It did."

Lulu handed Hux to Reddy. "Put him in with Gunther tonight."

"Of course," Reddy said, kissing Hux's forehead.

Lulu led Eveline to their bedroom. She tucked her into their bed, pulling the green cotton sheet to her chin. This was the first night Eveline would spend without Hux.

"Gunther will take care of him," Lulu said. "I'll be right outside if you need me."

"He said I'll forget all about him," Eveline said, the sheet over her mouth.

"That's goddamn rich," Lulu said, stomping her foot on the wood floor.

"Maybe if I hadn't been so friendly—"

Lulu swatted Eveline's cheek, but gently. "Don't ever say that again, you understand? This isn't your fault. Some people aren't good at the root."

"I feel so tired," Eveline said.

"It's all right to close your eyes," Lulu said, backing up.

"Will you leave the door open a little?"

"Of course."

Eveline looked around Lulu and Reddy's bedroom. On the nightstand was a photograph of Gunther when he was a baby, the last still days of his life. Beside the photograph were a half-drunk cup of tea and a scrap of paper, which said, *Reddy's snoring again. I can't sleep.* Being in that room made Eveline feel safe; the shadows beyond the window were comforting on this side of the river. Before she turned out the oil lamp, Eveline looked around once more. For a moment she forgot why she was here, until she heard the murmurs of her friends talking in the kitchen. After a while, Reddy sat down in the chair Lulu had positioned beside the bedroom door. Eveline watched him threading his fingers and unthreading them, picking up his rifle as if something could be done about the situation and then setting it down again when he realized it couldn't. She watched Lulu eat the entire egg pie as if long ago she'd learned how to stand what couldn't be changed.

Eveline woke to the sound of birds chirping beyond the window in Lulu and Reddy's bedroom and the sound of butter sizzling in a cast-iron skillet in the kitchen.

"Sit," Lulu said when Eveline came out of the bedroom in Reddy's trousers, which were nearly a foot too long for her.

Eveline lifted Hux out of the high chair he was sitting in; he was holding his body up as if overnight he'd grown stronger. She kissed him, wondering what kind of mother she could be after last night. Gunther was pushing eggs around his plate, complaining they were too runny. *There's a chicken in my eggs,* he said. And then, *Hux tried to kiss me with his mouth in the night.* Eveline looked around the cabin, knowing Lulu and Reddy would let her stay there forever. There were oxeye daisies in a mug on the table that weren't there the night before.

"If I don't go back now," Eveline said, "I'll never go back."

"I'll take you," Lulu and Reddy said at the same time.

"No," Eveline said gently. "Hux and I have to go alone."

Eveline kept waiting for the moment she would fall apart and wanted to be at home when it happened, to have the brown log walls around her, to see strength in their ugliness, that which even a flood couldn't take down.

Lulu and Reddy let her go.

Thank you, Eveline thought, but didn't say because it wasn't enough. What bothered her, what would always bother her, was that she hadn't done more, said more, that day by the river when Lulu had told her about the saloon men.

Before she left, Lulu took her into her arms one last time.

"I know what you're thinking," she whispered. "Don't."

"I'm not," Eveline said. "I won't."

She and Hux crossed the river in Reddy's canoe, rays of yellow morning light following her from the river's edge, disappearing in the forest, and appearing again when she reached the garden, which the crows had left intact, and finally the cabin.

Eveline saw the imprint of Cullen's shoes in the sandy soil beyond the front porch. She set Hux down in the reed basket between the rocking chairs, knowing she should go inside, get a broom, and sweep them away. The cabin needed to be fixed up, too, the plates cleaned and stacked, the floor washed of whatever was on it.

Eveline put on Lulu's coonskin coat and sat in one of the rocking chairs, drawing strength from the fur, the woman who'd worn it up until now.

Tuna came out of the birdhouse, chirping lightly, waiting for her morning sunflower seed fix. Hux, too, gurgled now and then, hungry for whatever Eveline's body could offer.

It seemed to Eveline that she had two choices: to keep living or to die, and like Lulu those years ago, she couldn't choose both.

Before the rain came that afternoon, falling in wide, windswept sheets, washing away what it could, Eveline lifted Hux out of his reed basket. As she guided his mouth to her breast, she thought of Emil coming home with a bouquet of edelweiss in his hands, of summer turning to fall: the life she'd said yes to at the courthouse in Yellow Falls.

10

August 23, 1939

Dear Eveline,

We've heard from Reddy twice now that you and our beloved grandchild will not be coming home this summer either and that you wish us not to visit you—a wish we will respect even if we don't understand it. Won't you at least write a letter, a few simple words of explanation? Even though we're only twenty or so miles apart, we feel so much further away than that. Try to remember that even though you know our routines by heart, we have no way of imagining yours. You're breaking our hearts, Evie. You really are. Did I raise you to be so unfeeling? Have we done something so gravely wrong? If we have, please forgive us. Please, my darling child, come home. It's never too late to come home.

Love,
     Your Mother

Eveline folded the letter and put it in the drawer of her nightstand with the others. She wanted nothing more than for her mother and father to take her in their arms and make everything all right as if she were a girl again, but Cullen had taken away their ability to tuck her into her bed, to believe what her father had always told her: *You can be anyone you want.* You couldn't. She couldn't. That kind of freedom belonged to the luckiest people. Everyone else's paths were decided for them, and nothing could be done about it.

Eveline was pregnant. Again.

She couldn't go back to Yellow Falls and let her parents see her body, the evidence of what had happened to her: what she'd done in its defense, what she didn't do, what she couldn't. They would still love her—of course, they would; she knew that much—but they'd feel just as helpless as she had when Cullen had asked for dessert. And even though they wouldn't want to, even though they'd go to sleep promising each other to picture cows jumping over the moon, they'd end up seeing her on the floor of the cabin.

This time around, sickness didn't overtake Eveline. This baby struck one note and one note only. *Please let me stay here,* to which Eveline said, *You can't.* It was as if the child was promising to be faultless, but that didn't ease the fact of it taking root like a walnut in Eveline's stomach. What good could come of her union with Cullen? What kind of child could be born from darkness and learn how to walk into the light?

Eveline had searched the woods for black cohosh root and boiled it for two days in a pot, extracting its life-ending potency. But even when she thought of Cullen on top of her and shivered violently, even when she thought of gnarled roots in the bog, how her body had felt black and twisted like them after he'd released her from the floor's hold, she couldn't drink it because she knew it wasn't the walnut's fault—hard-shelled as it was.

The same way Eveline knew Hux would be a boy, she knew the walnut would be a girl. She saw her in her dreams, always at the corner of her vision, a girl with hair as black as roots and eyes as gray as storm clouds, her skin cold to the touch. Sometimes, despite herself, Eveline would call to her, but the girl would never come; she'd only stand there from afar watching Eveline with love or hate or both rooting her to the ground.

Eveline woke from these dreams with a start. After what had happened to her, she was beginning to understand her limitations and that they were different than Lulu's, who'd kept Gunther under similar circumstances. Lulu said she never looked at Gunther and saw the men in the alley behind the saloon. She saw her little boy and his imaginary friend. She saw Reddy's fine heart. In her dreams, Eveline didn't see Emil. The only thing she recognized was the walnut's gray eyes and a question seizing them from the start.

If Emil came home and found Eveline round and full, she would let him decide what to do, since her body wouldn't be able to hide what had happened to it. He would have to determine if he could picture her on the floor of the cabin and still love her the same as he did before he left, when she belonged only to him. Though she hoped it was, she didn't know if his love for her was strong enough to withstand such a vision.

If Emil wasn't home by the time the walnut was born, which was what she was praying for, since then what had happened would belong to her alone—the shame of it, the press of the belt buckle on her skin—Eveline would go to the orphanage in Green River.

Eveline had heard of the term *shock* when it was applied to soldiers or to men who'd been trapped in coal mines, or to people who'd almost drowned. But she was fine. She was alive without water or coal in her lungs, fallen soldiers in her heart. Shock wasn't what plagued her. Or was it? *Tomorrow,* she'd sometimes catch herself thinking when the cabin began to whirl. *Tomorrow I'll fall apart.*

Lulu and Reddy were the only ones who knew about the walnut. Reddy didn't say as much, but Eveline knew he'd claim her as his second wife if it came to that. When he went to Yellow Falls the last time, Reddy saw an article in the *Gazette* about an ex-convict who'd stolen a government boat and had been posing as a government official. There was a reward out for both the man and the boat's return, he said, but it was an amount that wouldn't induce anyone to do any looking. As for the light project, during the second week of August, they all received a letter telling them it was on hold. Apparently someone at the top didn't think single lightbulbs in the wilderness were as useful as Albert Muldoon did. They still owed money though. An arbitrary property tax of thirteen dollars by November 21.

Since Cullen's visit, Reddy had been sleeping in a pup tent between the meadow and the forest, at the edge of Eveline's line of vision, each night eating cold cans of beans and each morning, before the sun came up, rolling up his pup tent, crossing the river, and going home. No one spoke of his routine or when it would stop.

"*Mama,*" Hux said again and again, but he didn't say anything else. He'd stopped tugging his ears, but if Eveline asked him if he wanted the rattle, he'd reach for his blanket.

Lulu said Reddy had lost hearing in one ear after shooting his toe, and it had yet to come back. Give it time, she said. You'll see. He'll hear.

What she seemed to be saying was that everything would

work out even if it seemed like it wouldn't. *You'll love that baby despite what's happened, despite yourself.*

September came, and a finally a letter from Emil—*I love you* was all she'd said in her last one—and though it made her fearful for him, his words carried with them relief for her.

Dear Eveline,

I don't know if you'll receive this letter or not. I haven't received any letters from you, though you've no doubt been writing often. The borders have closed and I am stuck within them until I can find a way out. Germany has invaded Poland, which you may or may not know by now. My father is still alive, although he is not what keeps me here. I have been commissioned into the German military despite my dual citizenship or maybe because of it. I am supposed to be in Berlin by the end of the week to report for duty. My poor mother and sister are fretting for the lives of two men now. If I desert my duties, according the new national laws, I can be shot if I am found. If I go, I will have to use force on another human being who has done nothing to me or to Germany. I keep wondering what you would do, gentle heart, if you were in my position.

You asked me once why I married you. I didn't know the answer that first day of snow in Evergreen. I simply knew I loved you and so I went to chop wood for you and our unborn son. But I'll tell you now in case you don't hear from me again. When I gave you that broken teapot I found in the forest, you displayed it at

once, despite its broken handle. You said, "It's lovely."
You have a certain grace in you, Eveline, which I've
always admired and which makes me the luckiest man
in the world. You deserve more than I've given you.
You've made do with so little.

I didn't leave Germany quickly enough, I'm afraid,
for which all of us will be punished. I will risk every-
thing to get home to you, my darling, but if I don't
make it there—and here, I don't mean to frighten
you—you must marry another and go on raising our
little son without me. How foolish I've been. I have no
money to enclose and little hope that this letter will
reach you—yesterday, a man was dragged away from
the post office and beaten in an alley, accused of trea-
son for writing a letter to a relative in England. And
this was in Hornberg. I can only imagine what's hap-
pening in the cities, in Poland. God help us all. Forgive
me if you can. If you get this letter. If you don't.

Love, Emil

Emil wouldn't have to know what happened to her—that
was her first thought. She could go to Green River in the spring.
She could let go of this ugliness inside of her she couldn't find
a way to want. As each thought rolled off the edge of the cliff
in her mind, she tried to gather it up, to hold on to it, before it
fell to the ground.

You selfish girl, she thought when she read the letter again.
You survived what happened to you. Your husband might not.

What was happening in Germany was worse than what
had happened to her. An army of Cullens had come together to
brutalize people—entire countries—overnight. And her hus-

band had been ordered to become one of them against his will, on behalf of which he would run and possibly be shot. What had happened to them: two quiet people who'd only wanted to live a quiet life in northern Minnesota?

Eveline imagined Emil in the Black Forest running between tree trunks and honey brush, looking for a way back to her and not finding one. He thought she was in Yellow Falls. He thought her cheeks were still rosy. He thought her heart was still light.

Meine Liebe, he was calling. *My darling. All you have to do is wish me home.*

Eveline placed a hand on her stomach. Even though she wanted her husband now more than she'd ever wanted him, she couldn't. Not yet.

She didn't know what reaction the news would have caused her to have if she'd read the letter in her mother's kitchen instead of her own. In Evergreen, Eveline picked up Hux, who was sleeping in the reed basket, tucked Emil's fishing rod under her free arm, and went down to the river. *If I can't catch a fish on my own we won't survive this. If I can, we will.* When she was a girl, she used to play a similar game with the daisies in back of the Laundromat. The yellow petals revealed whether or not she'd find love.

She knew how to win that game—she didn't know how to win this one.

On the way down to the river, Eveline dug into the soft soil on the forest floor with a trowel, turning the earth until fat brown worms wriggled up. She picked them up and put them into the pocket of her dress. How strange she could go on living after what Cullen had done to her and nearly faint at the thought of a handful of worms wriggling in her pocket.

At the river's edge, Eveline took the worms out one by one, pushed the hooks into their flesh, and cast out her line. Each time she felt a tug and reeled in her line, the worms were gone and the hooks bent backward.

You have to think like a fish, Lulu had said. Eveline imagined a school of them slicing through the dark water like silver knives. *How do you catch something that doesn't want to be caught? Whose life depends on not being caught? Maybe you don't. Maybe you give up.*

Eveline sat on the rocks. Hux had woken up and was looking at the blue sky and the birds crossing overhead, soaring on the updrafts. A cricket jumped into the basket and back out again. Eveline felt a tug on her line, but instead of reeling it in she let it out this time.

Another tug, and she stood up. Out in the middle of the river, a fish jumped.

Once she was sure she'd hooked the fish, Eveline began to reel in the line slowly until the fish was closer to her than it was far away. When she walked into the water, she could see it swimming circles in the shallows, panicked but alive. She kept reeling in the line. When all that was left between her and the fish was a few feet, Eveline held up Emil's rod and carried it and the fish out of the river onto dry land.

The fish, a lovely bluegill, opened and closed its mouth desperately. Eveline was on the verge of throwing it back, of eating beans and rice for the rest of her life. She thought of Emil and Cullen, two men forever part of her life, one she'd said yes to, the other no. She took that bluegill in her hands, slid the hook out of its gill, and with great sadness but a new resolve, *my God, my God,* she watched the life go out of it as it flapped against the rocks.

Eveline caught five fish before she walked back up to the cabin with Hux, tossed them in flour, and fried them in the skillet. Something inside of her was shifting even if she didn't know in what direction yet.

For the first time in weeks, she was hungry again.

She stood over the woodstove pulling the tiny bones out with her fingers and sucking the white flesh from them. When night came, Eveline placed Hux in his crib and brought a fillet out to Reddy's pup tent.

"I'm all right," she said, handing him the plate. "You can go home now."

Reddy picked up the fillet with his fingers. "I like to camp."

"Nobody likes to camp for this long."

"Emil would want me to," Reddy said. "I'd want him to if Lulu was out here alone."

"Emil's not coming home," Eveline said, thinking about the two of them in the truck all those months ago now. "At least not for a while."

"I figured as much," Reddy said. "The paper in Yellow Falls said Germany's invaded Poland. I didn't know how to tell you."

"Emil said that in his letter, too."

Reddy reached into the pup tent and pulled out a sleeping bag for Eveline to sit on. Stars were appearing overhead. Owls spoke to each other in the trees.

"Lulu thinks I should keep the baby," Eveline said.

"That's only because her parents didn't keep her," Reddy said.

"I didn't know that," Eveline said. "Maybe I did."

"When she came home from school one day, they were gone," Reddy said. "People said they went to Canada. Desperate people go north."

Eveline still had Lulu's coonskin coat, and though it gave her strength just thinking about it, she thought maybe it was time to give it back.

"This is your first fish, isn't it?" Reddy said, licking the ends of his fingers.

"How did you know?" Eveline said.

"They always taste the best." Reddy wiped the corners of his mouth with his sleeve. Scabs crisscrossed his face where he'd cut himself shaving in the garden the other morning.

"I'm not going back to Yellow Falls," Eveline said. "If you were wondering."

"I can help you cut wood for the winter," Reddy said. "Lulu thinks it'll be worse than last year, which was pretty bad where we were trapping. I'm sure she told you I shot my toe when I was cleaning my gun. She likes to tell that story for some reason."

Eveline thought of Lulu walking up to the cabin for the first time with a hard-boiled egg in her coat pocket.

"We're still figuring out how to raise the tax money, but I'm sure we can come up with enough for all of us," Reddy said. "We'll sell the truck if we have to. I don't have to go to Yellow Falls as much as I do either. Poor Gunther, having me for a father."

Reddy was eyeing the brown liquor bottle in the back of the tent.

"I'd have some," Eveline said, because he would do the same for her.

He already had.

Reddy got the bottle and a tin mug from inside the tent. He poured a little into the mug and handed it to Eveline, who squeezed his forearm lightly.

"You're a good husband and father," she said.

Reddy drew the bottle to his mouth. "You girls could break me in half."

The two of them drank together in the fading light— friends, family, whatever they were. When she woke in the morning, Eveline knew Reddy and the pup tent would be gone.

11

𝍩 By October men in orange hats, camouflage coats and pants, took over the woods the way Emil had said they would. They came to Evergreen to shoot what they couldn't kill in their hometowns, what didn't exist there anymore. They drank and smoked and crashed around like the land owed them something. During the day, Eveline cut wood and dragged it back to the cabin with Hux strapped to her back on a cradleboard she made out of plywood and the walnut weighing her down in front. Lulu and Reddy kept trying to get her to wear something orange so the men didn't shoot her. They wanted to give her some of their wood, too, so she didn't have to go out on her own as much. But that's what her friends didn't understand: Eveline wanted to be alone. She needed to be.

At night after she put Hux to bed, Eveline sat in front of the woodstove whittling arrows until their points were sharp enough to pierce the flesh of the buck she knew she had to get to pay the taxes she and Emil owed by the end of November. She knew it couldn't be just any buck either; he needed to have a rack that would satisfy Jeremiah Burr and his empty office wall. He needed to be a royal buck. Even though Lulu and Reddy kept offering to sell their truck to pay her taxes, Eveline kept saying no. If she couldn't pay the taxes now, she'd never be able to. Reddy lent her one of his bows because she refused to hold a gun again, and Eveline made a target out of a bundle of dried river grass and a tarp pulled taut across it. She decided she wouldn't go hunting until she hit the center of it.

Eveline's belly was growing rounder and softer, but the rest of her was growing stronger and harder. In September, the brush she cut for kindling would scrape her fingers raw, and even the gentlest application of salve would make her cringe. Now, her hands were full of calluses so thick the tip of a needle wouldn't penetrate them. Muscles she didn't even know belonged to her poked out of her arms and legs at strange angles. Ropy blue veins. Eveline looked like a different person than the one who'd arrived in Evergreen a year ago, one full of bruises and gashes and scars that looked exactly the way she felt.

Eveline usually kept her hair a few inches below her shoulder blades, but this year it got all the way down to her waist before she noticed it. One night after Hux fell asleep, she sat with the silver hand mirror and a brush, trying to untangle the leaves and bullet burs and hardened mud it had collected while she was in the woods. When she couldn't find her way through the knots, she cut it to her shoulders, then to her chin.

She'd worn out the last of her dresses, so she stripped the scarecrow of its trousers and wore those now along with one of Emil's heavy plaid work shirts. Hux was the only one who seemed to miss what she used to look like; when he was strapped to the cradleboard he'd suck on what was left of her hair.

"Mama," he said the first day it was gone.

He kicked and wailed until Eveline set him down on the ground.

"Do you want us to freeze to death?" she said sharply.

The walnut stayed quiet.

Cutting wood and dragging it back to the cabin was hard work, harder than Emil had let on last winter. But it was good, clean work, too, which kept her mind from wandering into visions of Cullen and herself forever entwined on the cabin floor. If she didn't pay attention she could cut off her hand with Emil's ax, which Lulu taught her to sharpen on the rocks down by the river one morning near the end of October.

"*I* could keep the baby," Lulu said that day.

Eveline touched the blade of the ax. The day was cool, the metal cold. The trees along the river shook their yellow leaves like fists. Snow was coming.

"How do you know when it's sharp enough?" Eveline said.

"I just know," Lulu said.

Of course Lulu couldn't keep the walnut—they both knew that. Eveline would have to stay on her side of the river for the rest of her life.

"I'm not going to leave her in the middle of nowhere," Eveline said. "Someone will adopt her. She deserves as much, don't you think?"

"You're the one with the coat," Lulu said, and went back to sharpening the ax.

"I'll give it back to you if that's what you want," Eveline said.

Gunther and Reddy had just come down from their cabin to the river, the opposite shore. Reddy waved to Lulu and Eveline. He began to lay putty down in the hull of the canoe, since the ice would be coming soon, and the canoe would have to be stored up in the rafters of their cabin. Either that or it would lay overturned in the chicken coop, and the chickens would have to come inside.

Gunther began to skip stones.

"Look at me, Hux!" he yelled. "I bet you can't throw as far!"

Lulu set the ax down. "I'm sorry. I don't know what's got into me lately. I have a lot more feelings than I want. A lot more memories."

Eveline touched Lulu's shoulder. "Why did they leave you?"

"I don't know," Lulu said, looking at the cat's paws on the river. "My mother dropped me at school and told me to mind my teacher and eat my lunch the same way she did every single morning my whole life. She didn't say a word different."

"This is different," Eveline said gently.

Lulu handed her the ax. "I know."

That afternoon, as the first snowflakes of the season fell, Eveline finally hit her target at its center. She strapped Hux to her back and went off into the forest, looking for the buck of all bucks, tracking disappearing footprints in the quickly falling snow. She heard the shots of other hunters in the forest, but she didn't see their orange hats between the low-hanging tamarack branches, the dark green boughs. She walked for hours in the forest, turning in circles until she didn't know quite where she was in relation to the cabin, until dusk came and she came upon a group of deer rubbing their antlers against tree trunks.

Hux was sucking on the end of her hair, gripping it with his fingers. Eveline kept him on her back. The walnut kept quiet.

The bucks looked at Eveline for a moment and went back to rubbing their antlers on the bark, as if she was different than the other hunters in the forest because she was a woman with a child in her belly and one on her back. The bucks weren't afraid of her like she thought they'd be, like she hoped they'd be, which reminded her of a day last spring, after Emil had left for Germany and before Cullen had arrived in his stolen boat, when Eveline was up in the garden and a doe and her two new-born fawns came out of the woods.

That day, Eveline had set a blanket out for Hux to rest on while she tilled the soil and pruned back whatever was grow-ing too leggy too fast. As she was slicing through a tomato vine, the doe and her fawns walked across the blanket. When Eveline noticed what was happening, her instinct was to run over and scoop Hux up in her arms, but something else told her to stand very still so she didn't startle the doe. At first, Eve-line was afraid the doe and her fawns would crush Hux with their hooves, but they didn't. Eveline looked at the doe and the doe looked at her, as if they weren't a deer and a woman stand-ing in a meadow on a cloudy day in May. As if they shared something essential that protected them in each other's com-pany. One of the fawns stopped to drink her mother's milk, nosing her way to the soft white fur covering her underbelly. The other one licked Hux's hand until the doe nudged them along, and they disappeared into the woods again.

Eveline raised the bow and positioned the arrow. All but one of the bucks leaped off in different directions when she pulled back the bowstring to her ear. The last buck, the most royal of them all, stood staring at her, his dark eyes open and unwavering, listening for what she was going to do in the beat of her heart. Eveline was listening, too.

She counted twenty-six antler points. Twenty-six dollars Jeremiah Burr would place in the palm of her hand. Twenty-six ways to survive.

She thought of the doe and her two little fawns. Their extraordinary understanding.

"I'm so sorry," she said, and let go of the bowstring.

The arrow pierced the buck through his neck, and he fell to the ground at once. When he tried to get up, his legs buckled. He didn't try to get up again. Eveline untied the cradleboard and set Hux down in the snow. She walked over to where the buck lay on his side. He was panting, groaning, quickly losing the light behind his eyes. Eveline knelt beside him. She stroked his fur, which a river of blood was turning red.

The snow was melting beneath him. Her.

The buck's breaths got further and further apart until foam came out of his mouth, and he stopped breathing altogether. The forest seemed to stop breathing as well.

The terrifying stillness of that moment, the way the wind and snow stopped blowing, the way even the leaves stopped falling from the trees, made Eveline realize what she'd always known. Her husband was wrong about preservation. You couldn't justify taking a life because it fit squarely into three paper rules. You couldn't justify taking a life even if it meant saving your own. All you could do was live with what you'd done.

What you were going to do.

Before the stillness passed and Eveline covered the buck with a tarp—she'd come back with the sled tomorrow and tow him to the cabin—she felt the walnut kick low and hard. First a foot. Then an elbow. Then a fist.

Eveline took her hand off the buck's underbelly and put it on her own.

"I know," she said.

For the first time in months, she started to cry.

When Eveline finally found her way home again, she put Hux to bed and lit a cedar fire more for the sound of the crackling logs and the comforting aroma than for warmth. After roasting a potato and eating it while she stood over the kitchen sink, she took down Emil's taxidermy manuals, praying she could do what they said she needed to in order to get her twenty-six dollars. She wondered if Jeremiah Burr would give her—a woman—the money for what he couldn't accomplish himself. He'd made the promise to Emil, a promise she was counting on. She'd strap herself to Jeremiah Burr's chair if she had to.

Of the tasks before her, first the buck's head had to be removed from its body, then the contents of its skull removed, its flesh torn then sewn, its body drained of blood and packed with snow. Then came the butchering if she didn't want to waste the meat—gruesome work Emil would never had let her bear witness to, let alone participate in.

Eveline dragged the buck back to the cabin on the sled the next afternoon. With a butcher knife, she separated the buck's head from his body in the snow beyond the cabin.

His blood had frozen overnight. His heart.

Dear Emil, Eveline thought, but now there was nowhere to send a letter.

When night came, Eveline wasn't afraid of it the way she was the first night Emil was wasn't there with her, when she stood on the porch listening to the forest's sounds. Since Cullen had come and gone, the only harm that lingered was the harm she could do to herself. Losing her ability to be afraid was a little like losing the vital red edges of her life. If there was no such thing as fear, there was no such thing as safety either.

Eveline took the buck's head inside the cabin but left his body outside. At the kitchen table, she studied the manuals, thinking of the people far away across the world sitting at their own tables—walnut, oak, maple—eating supper, perhaps, in their own small ways defending their lives. With a metal spoon, she scooped out the inside of the buck's head. The English manual urged caution. The German manual urged what, in their hard consonants grouping together like walls? Outside, Eveline heard Tuna chirping. She still wouldn't fly south. Eveline thought about bringing her inside, but couldn't bear to cage her.

Skinning the flesh from the buck's head required Eveline's complete concentration. While Hux slept in his crib, she put on a pot of coffee. She wound the radio Lulu had given her, and a Canadian program—the only thing besides static—came on. *A Day in the Life of . . .* , the announcer said from somewhere north of Evergreen. As she cut around the antler burs and tear ducts, she listened to a story about a woman from the northern reaches of Canada, who'd supposedly been raised by wolves. A group of scientists had found her in the wild and had taken her back to Ontario to study her.

Each time the announcer asked the woman a question, she'd howl, and the scientist who'd accompanied her on the show would have to answer for her.

Eveline had never seen a wolf in Evergreen; the trappers had gotten to most of them in the early part of the century, selling their pelts so women could have coats and men could have pride. The coyotes and caribou were mostly gone now, too.

Eveline skinned the buck's head, careful around the veins and tendons.

"We assume she was separated from her family when she was two or three," one of the scientists said about the wolf woman. "There's a small window of time where animals will care for other stray animals. When the window closes, the stray animal becomes prey, and only the very strongest will survive on its own."

"Does she speak English?" the announcer said.

"She knows a few French words. I can't say them on the radio."

"This is truly remarkable," the announcer said. "What will become of her?"

"Rehabilitation into civilization," the scientist said. "We're hoping she'll choose to live a normal life. One of our biggest challenges has been to get her to sleep in a bed."

The woman howled.

"Ouch!" the announcer said.

"We haven't been able to get her to stop biting people," the scientist said. "You should see my arms. Her canines are extremely sharp. A dentist is going to grind them down next week." There was a fumbling sound, a dropped microphone, a subduing. "You won't be so powerful then, will you?" the scientist said, out of breath.

Let her go, Eveline thought.

She wondered how the scientist had convinced the woman to come south with him, to part ways with the wolves who'd fed and protected her most of her life. She imagined a tranquilizer gun, a howl that would break any breakable heart.

"What happens if you can't rehabilitate her?" the announcer said.

The scientist cleared his throat, as if for a moment he was uncertain—regretful?—about what he'd done. "It's our belief you can rehabilitate anyone."

Eveline turned the radio off. Outside snow was falling; the sky was Chinook pink. Eveline thought about the wolf woman living in an apartment one day, one day going to work, one day cooking a meal on a stove, but at what cost? She hoped for the very least: that the wolf woman got another good bite in before her visit to the dentist.

When Eveline finished skinning the buck, she set the

brown fur on a towel to dry. From the cupboards, she pulled out Emil's container of beeswax, which she heated over the woodstove like the manual said. She found the bottle of sage oil and package of cotton she needed, along with what was left of the clay, to make a form for the buck. That was the peculiar thing about large animal preservation; a head on a wall wasn't really a head at all.

Emil had said the difference between a good taxidermist and a great one was his ability, through preservation, to bring an animal back to life. *Her* ability? Eveline had never heard of a female taxidermist; even the animals, the specimens, were male. Which led her to thinking about what kind of expression Jeremiah Burr would want to see in the buck's eyes. A man who wanted an animal head on his wall probably wanted nostrils flaring, exposed teeth, a fierceness that, to the customers who walked in his office, proved Jeremiah Burr's ability to conquer what didn't belong to him. To control it. Eveline knew she wouldn't be able to capture the buck as he was when she put an arrow in him in the forest—calm and majestic, demure almost—if she wanted her twenty-six dollars.

Eveline looked out the window again at the falling snow. Preserving the buck would take another week or maybe more. She hoped Lulu's truck would make it to Jeremiah Burr's office, over the potato and alfalfa fields, around the bog, and whatever else stood in her way, and she hoped that no one she knew saw her when she was there.

When she'd done everything she could, Eveline checked on Hux and went out on the porch to say good night to Tuna, who huddled in the corner of the birdhouse. Eveline lifted the birdhouse off its hook. She wouldn't cage Tuna, but they were bound together by sunflower seeds and time, and she wasn't going to pretend they weren't any longer. At the door's threshold, where cold met warm, Tuna came out of the birdhouse. She stood on the snowy perch for a moment, and with a great lurch forward into the cabin, spread her wings.

Eveline finished preserving the buck's head on a Monday morning. She cut and sanded a maple board to mount the head on. The fine, blond wood reminded her of the days Emil had worked on Hux's crib before he was born and of the story he'd told her about the lost little girl. Now, when she thought of Emil, she almost couldn't picture him.

Dear Emil, she thought, wishing for a campfire in the forest, a blanket around his shoulders. *Hold on a little longer. Just a little longer.*

Besides that one fist, that one foot, the walnut went back to being the walnut. She stayed so quiet Eveline sometimes wondered whether or not she was alive. If it had been Hux, Eveline would have gone to the midwife in Yellow Falls and made her listen for life with her wise ear. For the girl with black hair she saw in her dreams, Eveline did nothing because she couldn't. Everyone knew Emil was gone, and no matter how serious Reddy was about taking on a second child and wife, she didn't want that either.

In the afternoon, Eveline dropped Hux off at Lulu and Reddy's cabin. Reddy went back across the river to help her with the buck. When they'd loaded it into the back of the truck, Reddy showed her how to work the pedals, which she could barely reach, since she was so short. Though he'd offered several times to go with her, at first claiming he needed a few things at the general store, in the end he sent her off to Yellow Falls alone.

"Thank you for watching Hux," Eveline said, and put the truck in reverse.

"The chains are in the back," Reddy said, in case it started to snow.

But it didn't. Eveline and the truck made it to Yellow Falls without the snow chains. The tires caught on a patch of field ice only once.

Even though Jeremiah Burr's office was on the very edge of Yellow Falls, she felt strange being in the vicinity of Main Street, hamburgers and ice-cream cones, after so many months away. Jeremiah Burr wasn't expecting her, so she took a seat in the waiting room with Lulu's coonskin coat wrapped tightly around her to hide her belly. The men in the waiting room were called in first, even the ones who arrived after her, so that night was beginning to fall when Jeremiah Burr finally called her into his office.

"I don't like to deal with women in matters of landhold ing," he said before she had a chance to sit down. "Where's your husband?"

"Germany," Eveline said.

"There's a war over there," said Jeremiah Burr, a short man with ruddy cheeks and a sweaty forehead. His suit, though fine in material, strained at the seams.

"I've come about a buck," Eveline said.

"I don't hand out money to unfortunate wives, if that's what you've heard."

"My husband is Emil."

"The taxidermist," Jeremiah Burr said.

"You said you'd give him a dollar a point," Eveline said.

"I don't see him here."

"I'm here in his place," Eveline said. "I have a twenty-six-point buck."

Jeremiah Burr frowned. "A female taxidermist—I don't like the sound of it."

Eveline glanced at the photographs on his desk, at the woman in each of the frames smiling serenely. In her face was a look of uncomplicated happiness, one Eveline recognized from her wedding photographs, a year and forever ago.

Jeremiah Burr glanced at the photographs, too. His face softened at the sight of his bride, who was probably at home making supper for him on the stove, laying out linens for the table, freshening herself like a daisy.

"All right. You win. Show me the buck."

Eveline and Jeremiah Burr walked out of his office, through the waiting room, and out to the truck. "Now don't get it in your head I'm taking it. I'm just looking. Times are hard all around. I'm not made of money."

But he looked at the men in the waiting room when he said this, not at Eveline.

"You should sew or knit or something," he said when he lifted the tarp and saw the buck and the fierceness Eveline had managed. "This is no work for a lady."

"Will you take him?" Eveline said.

Jeremiah Burr looked over her work, which he said was good, better even than Emil's. "You have a gift for preservation. Fidelity to the animal."

Eveline didn't tell him that this buck was not at all like the buck she'd killed in the forest. Nor did she tell him she'd cried when the arrow pierced his flesh.

"When is your husband coming home?" he said.

"I don't know," said Eveline, looking up at the dark clouds tumbling by.

"I'll give you the money," Jeremiah Burr said, and she could tell then in his eyes that he wasn't the man he pretended to be in front of his customers, that a woman wouldn't have smiled like that if he were. "I want you to promise me you'll stop all this nonsense. You're in trouble, I can tell that. Or you're about to be. Where are your people? Wait a minute. Doesn't your father work at the lumberyard?"

"I'll be all right," Eveline said, huddling against the wind in the coonskin coat, thinking of her mother and father sitting in the kitchen, wondering what kind of daughter they raised, recalling all the things they'd done well as parents and all the things they didn't—*There was that time I yelled, that time she cried in the night and I didn't go to her*—wondering if any alteration would have made the difference.

Wait for me, Eveline thought. *I'll come home soon.*

Eveline thought of Lulu and Reddy, their fine hearts.

"I have good friends," she said.

Jeremiah Burr stood a long moment, deciding whether or not to push further into her life, trying, it seemed, with a wrinkle of his forehead, to foresee what would happen if he did, before he pulled out his wallet and handed her the money for the buck and a little extra.

"It's cold," he said, rubbing his hands together. "Buy yourself a new coat."

12

꧇ Winter came, and on its heels spring, another breakup of ice, another tightening of muscles and heart, another long-awaited birth. This one was different than the last; it hurt plenty, but Eveline wasn't afraid the way she was with Hux when she fell in the snow between the outhouse and the cabin. Nine months she'd been waiting for the moment her body released the walnut and she was free from Cullen and all that had happened on that warm day in July. Nine months until she could banish what remained of him—those dimples, the taste of smoked trout, what she saw when she looked into his blue eyes—from her memory. Nine months until she could come out of the fog and reclaim her life.

"Push," Lulu said, wiping sweat from Eveline's face and neck. Hux was over at Lulu's cabin, playing cowboys and Indians with Reddy and Gunther, touching his ears, no doubt. Eveline still had to raise her voice for him to understand her.

The labor had lasted all day, the tightening and loosening, the pain in her lower back. Lulu rubbed menthol oil on Eveline to cool her hot skin.

"You're almost there," she said, opening Eveline's legs.

Eveline was unclothed on the bed. Her toenails were dirty. Her feet swollen. For the last week, she hadn't been able to fit anything on them but Emil's slippers, which lay on the floor. Lulu was wearing one of Emil's undershirts, since she, too, had grown hot. There was a fire in the woodstove. The wood crackled and spit as if it were alive.

"I can see the head," Lulu said, rinsing her hands in the basin of water.

Eveline felt a burning in her lower body, that familiar zip of electricity. She thought she'd break apart or faint or both. But she didn't—not this time.

"You need to push now," Lulu said, her arms strong, waiting to catch a child, to keep her from falling to the ground, to her death.

"I'm not ready," Eveline said. She thought of Emil in the forest, the broken teapot on the kitchen table, the grace he saw in her but that she didn't see in herself.

"Push," Lulu said, and Eveline did.

She used every one of her muscles to do what Lulu asked. Her heart beat as if it would break away from the rest of her body. Even her eyes throbbed as they tried to follow the line of pain, which twisted all the way down to her toes like gnarled branches.

All of this was nothing compared with that last push toward freedom and the walnut's first cry, a howl, which Eveline would remember for the rest of her life.

"She's beautiful," Lulu said, cutting the umbilical cord and holding her up in the yellow lamplight. The walnut's hair was black as raven feathers, Lulu said, just like Eveline had dreamed. Her eyes were gray. Her fingers were long and thin, too—royal.

"Do you want to hold her?" Lulu said, wrapping her in a blanket and trying to hand her to Eveline.

"No," Eveline said inhaling for the first real time in months, thinking now only of the orphanage in Green River, the return to ordinary life. She didn't want to hold the child or even look at her. She loved Hux, babies; she just couldn't let herself love this one.

"She's your daughter, Eveline."

Eveline thought of Cullen's unbuckled belt.

Lulu bounced the walnut lightly, the same way Emil had when he and Hux were waiting for her to return to consciousness, to their life together in a cabin between a clearing and the forest. "Won't you at least give her a name? It's seven years' bad luck."

"That's when you break a mirror," Eveline said. She got out of bed, gripping the log walls for support. Tuna was in the rafters, watchful but quiet.

"You need to rest," Lulu said.

"Resting won't change my mind."

"You're still bleeding," Lulu said when Eveline slipped her nightgown over her head and picked up the reed basket. "Use the witch-hazel cloths I made for you."

Lulu looked for the cloths in the kitchen. When she didn't find them there, she looked on the porch.

Eveline looked for the little stack of pink paper she'd come upon earlier in the closet.

"Gravity is your enemy," Lulu said.

"Give her to me," Eveline said, after she found what she was looking for.

Lulu handed the walnut to her, and Eveline set her in the reed basket.

"How are you going to get across the river?" Lulu said.

"My best friend's going to help me."

Eveline put on Lulu's coonskin coat and draped one of

Hux's blankets over the walnut. With Lulu straggling behind her, she walked to the river's edge and Lulu's patched-up but still-leaky canoe. An owl *hooed* from the branches of a white pine. A fish splashed.

"Don't you even want to think about it?" Lulu said as she pushed the canoe away from the shore. She hopped in it at the last possible moment.

"I've thought about it every single day since last July," Eveline said.

Eveline dipped her paddle into the dark water, thinking about how many times she'd crossed this river—sometimes with joy, sometimes with sorrow. She looked at the reed basket and at the needlepoint of stars overhead.

You'll be all right, she thought.

A dry brown leaf blew into the reed basket, and the walnut reached for it with her tiny hand as if it were Eveline's breast.

When they'd crossed the river, they walked up to Lulu's cabin. Reddy had left the keys in the truck in case of an emergency, and Eveline set the reed basket on the passenger's side. The oil lamps were ablaze in the cabin; Reddy was feeding Hux in Gunther's old high chair, and Gunther was rooting him on with his toy gun.

"Eat your peas!" he said. "You're no sissy, are you?"

For the first time in their friendship, Lulu walked away from Eveline without saying goodbye. Without saying anything. She was halfway to her door and the slick of colors on either side of it when Eveline reluctantly started the truck, which groaned like an old man.

"Wait!" Lulu said, turning abruptly. "I'm coming with you."

She ran back to the truck with tears in her eyes, slid the reed basket over to the middle of the seat, and sat facing the passenger window, the darkness beyond.

They drove like that for miles and miles, over still-frosty alfalfa fields, until they reached the outskirts of Green River and the street the orphanage was located on, which was founded by a French Canadian nun in the early part of the century. The only French word Eveline knew was *au revoir*, which was what one of her teachers had said to their class when she finally got an offer of marriage: her ticket out of the elementary school. Eveline thought of Emil, of the letters they'd written to each other, of the letters they didn't. She thought, too, of the letter she found right before she went into labor and rang the bell on her side of the river and Lulu came running down the bank with a bag of supplies.

Eveline had been looking in the closet for clothes that could be spared for the birth, when she noticed a loose plank of cedar beneath her sweaters and the wolf spiders on the floor. She'd lifted the plank up, wondering if that was how the squirrels were getting in, thinking she'd go get the hammer and nail it back down. The little stack of pink paper beneath the plank she mistook for insulation. But when she pulled it out, she saw that the topmost piece was folded like a letter and words were scrawled across its front.

For you.

Eveline had thought it was from Emil—some last pink thought before he left Evergreen for Germany—so she opened it and read it.

To you, whoever you are,

We're leaving in the morning. Going back to our town in Canada after trying to make a life here and failing.

*Last winter, my husband fell from a tree he was trying
to cut down and broke his legs and we almost starved
to death. We ate old newspapers when there was
nothing left. This is a hard place. But you must know
that by now. What I want to tell you is this, what the
woman who lived here before us, whose foundation we
built our lives on, told me: when the time comes to let
go, let go.*

Good luck to you.

Love, Meg

Eveline parked the truck behind the tall iron gates in front
of the orphanage. It was late now, and the street was emptied
of everything but stray leaves tumbling by; the metal swing
set beside the orphanage creaked. The building was made of
red bricks, warm and solid. Inside, through one of the lighted
windows, Eveline saw a few nuns sitting around a table eating supper. They were wearing black habits. One of them was
reading from a Bible.

Eveline got out of the truck with the reed basket, the walnut. Lulu stayed inside, her hand pressed against the window
as if she were trying to reach something.

Eveline walked through the gates to the front door of the
orphanage, knowing she wouldn't go inside, she couldn't fill
out paperwork, she couldn't say the reasons she was leaving
the walnut on their doorstep either to them or to herself.

The air was cool, the sky lighter above Green River than it
was in Evergreen.

They would take this child and raise her to be mindful of
the Lord. They'd watch her take root like a tree in the world. Or
maybe a family would adopt her, since she was just born and

people wanted babies more than they wanted older children. She'd survive this hour, the walnut. She'd survive being left behind, just as Eveline had. Lulu, too.

Eveline looked back at the truck, at her best friend, who was still pressing her hand against the glass, which her warmth was fogging.

"You'll be all right," Eveline said to the walnut, who started to cry.

Eveline's instincts took over, and she picked up the child to comfort her. It was then that Eveline saw her daughter's lovely gray eyes, the specks of spring green in them, the earth in all its forms.

Eveline could take her back to Evergreen. She could keep her. Summer would come. Another garden. Another season of rain and growth. She could sit on the porch with her like she did with Hux. She could give her what she'd given him.

Eveline buried her face in her child's neck, inhaling her sugary smell.

All at once her child latched on to Eveline's cheek and pulled at it hard the way Cullen had pulled on her wrist. *I'd like some dessert.*

Eveline unlatched her tiny hand from her face. She was afraid again.

There isn't any.

One of the nuns walked by the window, and Eveline got down on her knees. She could see the moles on the nun's face—black hairs growing out of the brown lumps—and the heavy silver cross she wore around her neck swinging back and forth.

When the nun sat down, Eveline stood up. She wrapped Hux's blanket—the one with little ducks on it and his name embroidered at the corner—around her child and set her in the reed basket. "I have to let you go," she said, drops of blood falling from between her legs onto the front walkway like tears. Her child stopped crying.

Eveline leaned over her daughter one last time.

"I love you," she said.

Eveline rang the orphanage's doorbell and ran, because unlike with Cullen, this time her legs would carry her wherever she wanted to go. She thought of broken legs and dreams, of a woman named Meg who'd left behind her silver hand mirror, perhaps because the vision of her life in Evergreen would only haunt her. When Eveline reached the truck, she saw that Lulu had moved over to the driver's seat, and Eveline sat where Lulu had been sitting; the passenger window was still foggy from the warmth of her hand, her heart.

"Drive," she told Lulu, who said, "Are you sure?"

"Yes," Eveline said, although as they drove away from the orphanage, from her sugary daughter, she wondered if this was the biggest mistake of her life, leaving a child on a doorstep at half past ten o'clock. She thought of the day last spring when she saw the doe and her two fawns in the garden. Her two fawns. She felt herself letting go of the bowstring.

Go back, she thought as they turned the corner, which would lead them to the county road and eventually to the alfalfa fields and home, but she couldn't say it out loud no matter how much she wanted to. Back there was stillness. In front of her was life. Eveline kept thinking of Emil in the Black Forest, shivering around a dying fire for months and months, waiting for her to do what must have seemed so simple to him: to wish him home.

And that's what she did finally on this cold spring night halfway between Green River and Evergreen, on a dark country road illuminated by the truck's yellow headlights. She could see a light go on in the Black Forest, and her husband running toward a clearing, a road much like this one that would steer him home. She could see him crossing the ocean, boarding a train in Grand Central Station without his butterflies but with no need for them after all he'd survived. She could see him paddling upriver in a leaky old boat.

Lulu reached for Eveline's hand, and there they were, the dwarf and the giant.

In the dark, Eveline kept hearing a voice, a howl, which would pull her back to this moment the rest of her life. She thought of the wolf woman in a cage somewhere in Canada, and a powerful longing sprung up in her. She dug her fingernails into the door handle, hoping it would give beneath the pressure, praying she'd fall out of the truck onto the cold hard road.

The moon appeared between the clouds, and though Eveline was miles from the orphanage, she was bound to it now, to the woman with the moles and the cross, to the moment she laid her child down in the reed basket beneath a blanket full of cheery ducks, to the moment she turned her back on the past, believing she could for an instant—you couldn't, she knew now—and steered toward the future.

As they turned onto the first of many alfalfa fields, Eveline saw a girl with black hair and long thin limbs in the headlights. She saw the crackling fall leaves in her hands, the sticks in her hair, the question, always the same question, in her startling gray eyes.

Why did you leave me?

PART TWO

Hopewell Orphanage
Green River, Minnesota
1954

13

That girl with the black hair and the long thin limbs was Naamah, and Sister Cordelia took up her cause from the start. She said the devil had hold of Naamah's soul, and for the last fourteen years she'd been trying to drive him out. That was why Naamah had spent the first week of her life in a crib positioned beneath the holy-water font and this last one banished to her cot, which Sister Cordelia had moved out of the dormitory Naamah shared with the other girls and into the broom closet. This time Naamah's crime was being hungry and plucking a beautifully purple grape from the vine in the garden without asking for permission.

Each morning Sister Cordelia made the girls walk past the broom closet before they went down to breakfast to deter them from falling into temptation's arms like Naamah had.

"Don't be fooled into feeling sorry for her," Sister Cordelia said as she hurried into the closet this morning. The hem of her habit stirred up the fine layer of dust on the floor and sent it whirling in the air. Her moles and the wiry hairs that grew out of them started to quiver, and her upper lip curled back, exposing a rotting tooth among a row of twisted yellow ones. "This is about more than a grape," she said to the girls. "This is about giving in to your desires the moment you have them. It's about lust. Think about what would have happened if I didn't knock the grape out of her hand in time. If she'd actually eaten it."

"Yes, Mother," the girls said, and each of them made the sign of the cross.

If the other nuns had still been at Hopewell, they might have tried to convince Sister Cordelia to let Naamah go back to the dormitory, or at least let her move an inch or two on her cot, but they might not have. Most were as fearful of Sister Cordelia and her very particular interpretation of the Bible as the girls were. The other nuns usually stayed only as long as it took to be transferred to other, more pleasant orphanages down south. After the last nun left and no one came to take her place, Sister Cordelia walked the halls with her cane held high once again. That she'd had a mother and father once, a history outside of Hopewell, seemed impossible to Naamah. Sister Cordelia belonged to Hopewell, and Hopewell belonged to her.

The only nun who'd ever tried to stop Sister Cordelia was Sister Lydie, who'd grown up milking cows and making cheese on a dairy farm in a place called Racine, Wisconsin. During her first week at Hopewell, Sister Lydie intervened when she saw Sister Cordelia striking Naamah's hand with a ruler in the hallway because her locker wasn't up to scratch.

"Stop striking her this instant," she'd said, putting herself between them. Her voice and her body were tiny but bold. She was only twenty years old then. "Children need love in order to follow the rules we impose on them. God would be ashamed, Sister. Naamah's an innocent in his eyes, as she should be in ours."

"Don't you dare talk about him that way," Sister Cordelia said. Without warning, she stopped striking Naamah's hand with the ruler and struck the top of Sister Lydie's.

Sister Lydie only lasted sixty-four days before she left Hopewell, but the impression she left behind was everlasting. Sister Lydie was the only person who'd ever rubbed Vaseline on Naamah's hands to take the sting out of them or offered her a cold glass of milk when she was thirsty or a hug when she was lonesome. She was the only person who ever sang a song to Naamah, for her. Naamah liked to imagine Sister Lydie walking through fields of sweet grass on her parents' farm, a pair of marmalade barn cats purring in her arms. She thought Wisconsin must have been full of gentle people like her.

After Sister Cordelia and the girls finally went down to breakfast, Naamah moved a few inches this way and that to disperse the pain radiating from the lower part of her spine from lying down too long. She was careful not to creak the metal springs too much because other than going to the bathroom she wasn't supposed to get up. She was supposed to lie on her cot and think about what she'd done. Today, Naamah mostly thought about how much she wished Sister Lydie would come back to Hopewell, though no one who left ever did.

Well, almost no one.

Once, when Naamah was nine years old, she was cleaning the windows upstairs in the dormitory, and a car pulled up to the iron gates at the entrance of the orphanage. Naamah had never seen a car as fancy as that. She thought it belonged to a king or a queen. The wheels looked like they were made of gold. Naamah didn't recognize the young woman who stepped out of the car until she took off her feathery green hat. Ethelina,

who'd slept in the cot next to Naamah's until she was six-
teen and was sent out into the world without any warning.
Ethie. Her hair was still red as a strawberry. Her eyes still like
blue ice.

That day, Ethelina stood on the gravel driveway with a
hand on her cheek and the other stretched across her heart,
staring up at the orphanage. She stood that way for a very long
time before she got back into the car and drove away. Even
though she'd dropped her pretty green hat on the gravel, she
never came back for it.

Naamah didn't know what Ethelina saw when she looked
up at the orphanage, but it made her wonder what the world
was like outside Hopewell and what had made Ethelina come
back. All her life Naamah had dreamed of turning eighteen
and walking through the front gates for the first and last time,
of Sister Cordelia finally having to let her because the law said
so. Most of what Naamah knew about the world, which the
high stone wall surrounding Hopewell obscured the view of,
she'd heard from the two girls who went to town weekly to
help Sister Cordelia carry whatever she bought at the market.
Sister Cordelia said the world was full of liars and thieves and
murderers, but Mary Elizabeth and Mary Ellen told everyone
it was full of shops and restaurants and cars that came in all
colors of the rainbow. They said there was a large stone fountain next to the market, and people who walked past it would
toss pennies into the water to make their dreams come true.

The rest of what Naamah knew, she learned from books
or from Sister Cordelia. The broom closet was situated on the
second floor of the orphanage, above the classroom, and in
the afternoons Naamah heard the girls doing their sums
on the blackboard and reciting the meanings of the words
Sister Cordelia made them memorize the night before. *Defer-*

ence. Authority. Dominion. Again. Again! Sister Cordelia said a stupid girl was a useless girl, and neither she nor God would abide that inadequacy. She expected their letters and numbers to be formed perfectly, and if they weren't she'd make them kneel on a ruler for the rest of the lesson. Naamah was the only girl unfortunate enough to have been born left-handed, with a proclivity for smudging and cursive that leaned toward hell instead of heaven.

All the other girls shared the name Mary there. Their middle names were what distinguished them. Mary Margaret. Mary Catherine. Mary Elizabeth. But even those could be confusing. Mary Alice. Mary Alise. Purposely so, it seemed, as if Sister Cordelia didn't want them to be told apart. Naamah and Ethelina were the only girls who'd ever been given different first names. Ethelina's meant "noble" in the dictionary. Naamah's meant either "pleasing to God" or "pleasing to the devil," depending on religious interpretation.

The devil, a few of the Marys had decided.

"At least my name doesn't rhyme with *comma*," Mary Helen liked to say. "KOM-ah. NOM-ah. You have the ugliest name in the world."

Even before Naamah plucked the grape from the vine in the garden, most of the girls avoided her because they were afraid if they got too close Sister Cordelia would start believing the devil had hold of them, too. Some would tell if Naamah wet her bed, which she still did when she had nightmares, or if she forgot to bring her rosary beads to morning mass or if a thread were loose at the hem of her uniform, and they'd be rewarded with wedges of cheese or one of Sister Cordelia's beloved figs, which she had shipped in little oval tins all the way from Turkey. Naamah didn't blame them even when she did. Even though in a room full of girls she always felt very alone. She might have done the same thing if a fig or wedge of cheese had ever been within her reach, which was why she didn't scowl at the girls who scowled at her or tell on them when they broke a rule. She didn't even tell when a girl got her monthly blood, though there was always a girl who told when Naamah had hers, and then Naamah would have to stand in the bathtub while Sister Cordelia washed her down with a bleach solution because of how dirty the blood made her in God's eyes.

Sister Cordelia said God was the only one in the world who deserved unconditional love and that you had to give yourself to him completely, like she had, before he'd ever consider loving you. She said he knew the difference between empty gestures and real heart. Each morning after the girls were sent outside to rake the yard of its birch and bigtooth leaves, Sister Cordelia came into the broom closet with a bowl of cornmeal and spoon-fed Naamah her breakfast, even though Naamah knew how to feed herself perfectly well.

"If only you'd let God into your heart," she said today as she guided a spoonful of cornmeal toward Naamah's mouth. Her heavy silver cross swung across her habit like a pendulum. "I can see it, Naamah. It's still flecked with black."

Sister Cordelia had a way of sounding sincere sometimes, like she really did want to help Naamah but Naamah was the one making that impossible. When Naamah was a little girl, she believed what Sister Cordelia told her: that the cross gave her the power to see into Naamah's soul as if through a window. Naamah would put all of her effort into trying to change the view. She'd pray until her knees went numb. She'd scrub the floors until she saw her reflection in them. She'd memorize Sister Cordelia's favorite passages in the Bible. Still, her devotion was flawed. She'd confuse the order of someone begetting someone else or the floor would shine in a less-than-holy light. Naamah didn't think Sister Cordelia could see into her soul anymore, but part of her still clung to the belief that if she could just scrub a little longer or pray a little harder she'd become lovable.

Naamah lay all day watching the sunlight move across the walls. When night came she watched the moonlight move across them. She soothed herself by thinking of her favorite of the songs Sister Lydie used to sing to her. *Go to sleep my darling, close your weary eyes. The lady moon is watching from out the starry skies. The little stars are peeping, to see if you are sleeping. Go to sleep, my darling, go to sleep, good night.* Naamah thought about her mother and why she left her at the orphanage with only a blanket to know her by. That small white square of cotton with rows of yellow ducks on it was the only thing Naamah owned that her mother had once touched. When no one was looking, Naamah would press her lips to each of the ducks, as if her mother were in there somewhere and only needed to be coaxed out.

It's all right that you left me. It's all right if you come back.

Sister Cordelia allowed her to keep the blanket as a reminder of the low place she came from. She told Naamah her mother was a prostitute at a logging camp up north, which Naamah thought meant her mother was a cook or a nurse or a special kind of woodcutter who climbed high up into the branches of trees until Sister Cordelia described the crimes of the flesh her mother committed daily, *nightly,* for money. Every night since then, Naamah would trace the letters stitched into the corner of the blanket—HUX—wondering what they meant, pretending it was a secret message. Maybe it was Morse code like they'd used in the war. Maybe it meant *I'm sorry, my little duck. I love you.*

Of everything she was deprived of in the broom closet,

Naamah missed her blanket, which she kept hidden behind a towel in her locker during the day, the most. She missed the thinning fabric, the fading ducks, her only true friends at Hopewell. She didn't care what Sister Cordelia said about her mother and the men who paid her money to take off her clothes. She didn't care how many sins of the flesh her mother had committed. She didn't even care that one of those men was probably her father. One day she was going to find her mother and push all those men down into the sawdust where they belonged, and she was going to hold her mother tight until her mother held her and everything was all right for the first time in their lives. That's what kept her going.

That night, Naamah dreamed of her mother's face, her skin, the shape of her heart. In her dream, she and her mother were meandering through a garden like the one at Hopewell. Her mother was humming a tune about everything blue in the world. *Blue skies, bluebirds, blueberries.* When they passed a vine full of jam grapes so ripe some had already burst and fallen to the ground, her mother reached for a small cluster of them.

You can't, Naamah warned her. *You'll get in trouble.*

But her mother picked the grapes anyway and put several of them in her pretty pink mouth. As she chewed, she let the sugary juice run down her chin. She picked another grape from the vine; this one she handed to Naamah.

Try one, she said. *They taste like love.*

Just as Naamah was lifting the grape to her mouth, anticipating its sweetness, she woke with a start and found herself on the floor of the broom closet. She didn't know how she'd arrived there or what kind of noise she'd made on her journey down from her cot, but she braced herself for a late-night visit from Sister Cordelia. Sister Cordelia knew everything that happened at Hopewell. Her moles were detectives. The hairs that grew out of them were antennae. She knew things about Naamah that Naamah didn't even know.

Naamah listened for Sister Cordelia's footsteps on the stairs. She listened for the swishing sound of her heavy black habit against the tile floor. She listened for how quickly Sister Cordelia was breathing, how much trouble she was going to be in. She listened until the pool of silvery moonlight flooding over the windowsill slipped from one wall to another.

Still, Sister Cordelia didn't come. Maybe she didn't know everything.

Naamah waited until the moonlight gave way to daylight before she climbed back into her cot as noiselessly as she could. She drew her knees to her chest and closed her eyes, trying to call forth an image of her mother. *Blue skies,* she whispered. *Bluebirds. Blueberries.* Only when Naamah finally stopped listening for Sister Cordelia and the hem of her habit brushing against the floor in the hallway could she hear her mother singing in the garden once more. Only then could she see the grape juice dripping from her mother's chin.

14

Although Sister Cordelia had bent herself to the task of saving Naamah's soul, she had to delay her plans because the town of Green River had invited all twenty-six of the orphans at Hopewell to its harvest festival on the following Saturday. In the letter, which was hand delivered by an assistant clerk from the town hall and which Mary Elizabeth had brought up to the broom closet straightaway, the board of trustees wanted the Hopewell girls to sing one of the Lord's songs on a stage in front of the whole town. They wanted the girls to feel like they had a real place in the community instead of simply sharing an address with them. Afterward, cups of warm apple cider and plates of sausages would be served, and the girls could mingle with the townspeople.

"Whores mingle," Sister Cordelia hissed as she read.

Surely Sister Cordelia wouldn't be opposed to the request, the letter said, since she could select any of the Lord's songs she saw fit. The town's board of trustees said they were looking forward to hearing the girls sing because they were certain their voices would sound more poignant than the voices of girls who were blessed with (yet spoiled by) mothers and fathers. They were looking forward to enjoying a bright future with Hopewell.

"Fools," Sister Cordelia said.

Sister Cordelia was feeding Naamah spoonfuls of cornmeal, reading the letter, and reacting to it all at once. She wasn't aware she'd been reading out loud until Naamah started choking because Sister Cordelia had pushed the spoon too far into her mouth.

"Singing is for heathens," Sister Cordelia said, retracting the spoon.

While Naamah lay on the cot with bits of cornmeal strewn across her face, Sister Cordelia looked over the letter very carefully, as if she might have missed something in the blocky print (*print!*) and Naamah was waiting for it to be her fault.

Warm apple cider and sausages? The sounds of the words, the fragrant steam rising off of each letter, made Naamah's mouth water. She licked the stale cornmeal from the outer edges of her lips, pretending it was anything other than what it was, even the slender piece of chalk Sister Cordelia had made her suck on so she never forgot Pythagoras' theorem again, the geometry of fear. Naamah hated cornmeal.

"There's no community out there," Sister Cordelia said. She held the letter away from her cross. "People lie to each other. People cheat. Out there people have babies and leave them on my doorstep like dogs."

"Maybe they don't mean to," Naamah said because she thought Sister Cordelia was talking to her and therefore awaiting a response.

Sister Cordelia tucked the letter into her habit. She told Naamah she could get up from her cot now and return to the dormitory with the other girls, but she kept hovering over Naamah as if she had something else to say. A fat blackfly was darting around the broom closet, buzzing across the length of the floor, the ceiling, the cot. When it landed on one of Naamah's toes, Sister Cordelia's hand came crashing down on her foot.

"There's good and there's evil," Sister Cordelia said. "There's in here and out there. You're foolish if you believe anything worthwhile exists on the other side of our wall."

Sister Cordelia always said there were two worlds—the one at Hopewell and the other one—and that the other one had different rules. Out there, plenty of good Christians got punished for following God's laws, and plenty of bad ones lived like kings for breaking them.

"Think about that when you see people stuffing themselves with sausages."

"I get to go, too?" Naamah said, trying to picture the fountain, the colorful cars, the market with an entire aisle devoted to salty canned foods.

"I can't very well leave you alone, can I?" Sister Cordelia said. "But you certainly haven't earned a trip to town. A trip anywhere other than the broom closet." Sister Cordelia put her hand on Naamah's cheek. "What happened here? You have dust on your face."

Naamah thought about the time she spent on the floor of the broom closet last night. She thought about her mother's pink lips, the sweetness of her voice. Naamah didn't want to lose her garden dream by giving it to Sister Cordelia.

"I do?" she said, waiting for Sister Cordelia to see the truth in her soul and punish her for lying. For dreaming of her mother. For dreaming at all.

But Sister Cordelia didn't say anything. She simply went to

the bathroom and returned with a washrag and a basin of tepid water. She wiped down Naamah's face the same meticulous way she would a corner of the floor to prove her loyalty to God and whatever humble work he required of her. Though Sister Cordelia had seen every one of Naamah's angles from her head to her toes, Naamah had never even seen Sister Cordelia without her habit on. She didn't even know what color her hair was or if she had hair at all.

"Sometimes I wonder if you're ever going to follow the path to God," Sister Cordelia said, wringing out the washrag. "Don't you see it, Naamah? It's right in front of you. All you have to do is open your eyes. I can't keep prying them open for you."

From the window in the broom closet, Naamah saw a group of girls huddling together in the garden to try to keep warm in their threadbare uniforms, pleated gray skirts and white blouses pintucked at the sleeves, while they harvested the last of the season's tomatoes and corn and the first of the squashes and root vegetables, which they carried to the screened door at the back of the kitchen, where the oldest girls worked very hard to make whatever meals Sister Cordelia requested.

From where she stood now, Naamah could also see above the high stone wall. She could see beyond the iron gates. To the south was Green River. To the north, the woods. Tall evergreens. Green as far as she could see.

"Do you have any idea what God thinks of you?" Sister Cordelia said. "What he tells me while you're sleeping? He thinks you don't have a chance at redemption. Maybe I should stop fighting for you like he tells me. Maybe I should move on to another girl."

"I'll be good," Naamah said, thinking, *Maybe you should.*

For the first time in her life, fear wasn't the only thing steering her into good behavior. Fear wasn't the only thing flooding her heart. Naamah imagined herself standing on the stage at the harvest festival with the other girls. She imagined a whole town of people clapping for them after they finished singing, a whole town of people rushing onto the stage to shake their hands and hand them plates of sausages and glasses of cider, to welcome them to the community. She imagined slipping away from the stage in all that commotion and running toward her mother, the forest ever green.

This was Naamah's chance to change her life. Maybe her only one until she turned eighteen and could walk out of Hopewell immediately thereafter. By then where would her mother be? How many more grapes would she offer Naamah before she gave up on her altogether? Wasn't that what her mother was trying to say in her dream?

Be brave, Naamah. Fight for me. Fight for you.

Sister Cordelia put the washrag in the basin. "I'm all you have," she said, as if she'd heard Naamah's thoughts. "I'm all any of you have. Don't forget that."

"I won't," Naamah said, but there was no heart in it.

That was on Sunday.

On Monday, after a night of sleeping in the dormitory again, Naamah awoke to three girls standing over her, sneering as if she'd done something terrible to them while she was in the broom closet. They followed her to her locker with the same angry expressions until she took off her nightgown to change into her uniform, and they saw the sores on her back from lying on it too long. One of them asked her if they hurt. Another said of course they did. The last one, Mary Margaret, said Naamah still looked pretty; she always looked pretty.

"That's why she picked you," Mary Margaret said.

The other two tugged hard on Mary Margaret's arm. "*Shh.* You'll get in trouble."

Just before they pulled her away from Naamah and the lockers, Mary Margaret looked at her as if she were sorry. She said, "Don't let her make you ugly."

Naamah had never thought about the way she looked unless it was to straighten her skirt or smooth a wrinkle from her blouse or unless it was to pull her dark hair back from her face like all the girls were made to do each morning before they went down to breakfast. There were no mirrors in the dormitory or in the bathrooms—anywhere Naamah knew of. The only time she ever saw her reflection was when she was washing the windows and sunlight came through the glass in just the right way, and even then she didn't recognize the girl she saw. She didn't even know what color her eyes were.

Sister Cordelia had once said beautiful girls were born with ugly souls, and Naamah had felt sorry for orphans like Ethelina because even then, though she was just a little girl, Naamah sensed what Ethelina's beauty would cost her. During her nightly prayers, Naamah used to wish for vast brown moles to appear on her own skin overnight to protect her. She'd wish for wiry black hairs. The more revolting the better. And though her wish never came true, and her skin remained pure as milk, no one, not even Sister Cordelia, had ever accused her of being beautiful. Stupid, but not beautiful. Naamah touched her cheek, wondering if what Mary Margaret had said was true and what it meant if it was.

Sister Cordelia spent the first part of the week spreading lard onto pieces of bread and watching Naamah eat them in an effort to fatten her up, so the townspeople wouldn't know she'd been starved. Naamah was tall and thin by nature; the week of lying in her cot and eating mostly cornmeal had made her gaunt.

"People are fat as hams out there," Sister Cordelia said. "They stuff themselves to bursting. They don't care what God says about excess. They eat whatever they please. Whenever they want. They don't understand the virtue of skin and bones."

To Sister Cordelia's dismay, each of the lard sandwiches Naamah ate wouldn't stay put in her stomach. The same thing happened when Sister Cordelia dipped pieces of bread in oil and when she forewent the bread altogether and placed a pat of butter on Naamah's tongue while she read from the Bible, hoping the Word of God would make it welcome.

What Sister Cordelia didn't know was that Naamah was making those sandwiches, those pieces of bread dipped in oil, those pats of butter, come up. *Fight for me, Naamah. Fight for you.* Every time she swallowed, Naamah thought of her mother and that stage, freedom, and she'd go running to the bathroom with a hand over her mouth. She thought that if people were really as fat as hams on the other side of the Hopewell wall, when they saw how thin she was they'd rescue her from Sister Cordelia and help her find her mother. Naamah had to keep reminding herself to curb her smile, her first little victory, on the way back.

As well as the long mealtime hours spent trying to get Naamah's stomach to cooperate, Sister Cordelia had spent two afternoons in a row trying to organize the girls into a choir and get them to sing, which they wouldn't do because they thought it was a trick—normally at Hopewell, singing was forbidden—and because other than Sister Lydie no one had ever sung to them, and they didn't know how. Each of the girls kneeled, awaiting her punishment. Sister Cordelia raised her voice, but she didn't raise her ruler this time.

"After the festival you'll all get what's coming to you," Sister Cordelia said.

Naamah wondered if people out there didn't like to see lash marks on girls' hands.

On the third afternoon, Sister Cordelia came marching into her office, her habit flying behind her like a black tongue. Naamah was still sitting in front of a stack of sandwiches, willing herself to look green when she felt as bright and yellow as the sun.

"You're going to make yourself useful," she said, herding Naamah from the table into the dining room, where the girls were lined up against the wall according to age. They were standing at attention like Naamah imagined soldiers did, except that two of the girls were only five years old, with such small voices and hands and feet.

When the girls saw Naamah, they looked relieved as if now that she was there they wouldn't be scrutinized as closely. Some let their shoulders inch forward. Some let their knees bend slightly. One of them scratched the back of her neck and a brown spider fell to the floor, and though regular girls might have screamed or jumped or let out their ponytails to check for spiders in their own hair, the Hopewell girls stood still.

Sister Cordelia placed a dusty book of hymns in Naamah's hand. On the front cover was a photograph of a man and a woman standing together before a microphone. Their mouths were half open as if they were in the middle of singing a song. Each of them was holding one side of a Bible. The woman wore a dress with flowers all over it. The man wore a wedding ring. They looked like they loved each other as much as they loved God.

"Your job is to pick a song and teach it to them," Sister Cordelia said. "They won't sing for me, but I have a feeling they'll sing for you."

Sister Cordelia opened the songbook for her. The pages were stiff and yellow and smelled like mold. One of the corners disintegrated in her hand.

"Careful," Sister Cordelia said.

Naamah read through the first song. While she understood the words, she didn't understand the melody, only that there was one hidden somewhere in there. The little round notes in the top corner looked like a pair of eyeglasses. She wished Sister Lydie were here, even if she could only stay the afternoon. Sister Lydie's voice was like the cottony clouds rolling past the windows in the dining room; always her voice had left behind blue.

"That's middle C," Sister Cordelia said, pointing to a dark note. "These are accidentals. This means sharp. This means flat."

"Accidents?" Naamah said.

"Just teach them the words," Sister Cordelia said to Naamah. "I'll be back soon." To the rest of the girls, she said, "I suggest you listen to Naamah. You've seen what it's like to lie in the broom closet. You may ask her if you've forgotten."

After Sister Cordelia was gone and they were alone in the dining room, Naamah stood as still as the row of girls in front of her. *Listen to you?* they seemed to be thinking, looking Naamah up and down. Why would any of them do that? And why would Sister Cordelia want them to? Naamah didn't know anything about music other than the happiness she remembered feeling when Sister Lydie sang to her all those years ago and when her mother sang to her in her dream. She didn't know about notes or accidentals, sharps or flats, and she didn't know why a person who thought music and singing were for heathens would know about them either. *Listen to me?* Naamah thought. But the girls did listen. Out of curiosity. Hope. Fear. She didn't know why. Even the girls who'd told on her when she had her monthly blood listened, even the girls whose hands were still sticky from figs.

The littlest girls came to her first.

"Can we help pick a song?" they said, and in their eager expressions, their still-trusting brown eyes, Naamah saw who the girls could have been if they were brought up somewhere else. In the older ones she saw what they would become if they stayed at Hopewell.

Naamah put the book on the floor, and the girls gathered around it with her. They took turns reading the titles of the songs out loud as Naamah flipped the pages.

"Do you really think she'd put us in the broom closet?" Mary Helen said.

"I don't want my back to bleed," said Mary Rose.

Naamah stopped turning the pages when she got to a song called "Angel Band." Instead of the northern Minnesota sky, which was the only entity that could ever match Sister Cordelia's moods exactly, Naamah imagined a sky full of yellow-haired angels. She imagined a pretty golden harp and even prettier golden notes floating up to them on a breeze.

"I like the name of that one," Mary Margaret said, from the outer edge of the circle. She was kneeling with her hands pressed together as if she were at a real mass led by a priest in a church, instead of the one led daily by Sister Cordelia in the classroom during which they stood. They'd heard of churches with stained-glass windows and even of men who preached right out in the open, but Sister Cordelia said only Holy Rollers needed props. She said the cross was enough for a true Christian. Only a sinner went down to the river to pray.

"Will you read it to us?" Mary Margaret said.

"Are these even Catholic songs?" another girl asked. "They sound sacrilegious."

"Why would Sister Cordelia give them to us if they weren't?" said another.

"You mean if they were?"

"Maybe it's a test."

"Let her read," Mary Margaret said.

And so Naamah did, and the words, which conveyed a kind of religious love none of them had ever known, stilled the girls' fidgeting with the hems of their skirts and the buttons on their blouses, as well as the ones staring off into space because for a moment they could.

My latest sun is sinking fast, my race is nearly run
My strongest trials now are past, my triumph has begun
Oh, come Angel Band come and around me stand
Oh bear me away on your snow white wings to my immortal
*   home*
Oh bear me away on your snow white wings to my immortal
*   home*

"That one, that one!" the littlest girls said. "Because it has a bear in it."

"It's not that kind of bear," another girl said.

"Grrr," said another.

"It means *Please take me away from here,"* Naamah said, and the girls looked at her and at one another with a kind of knowing no one outside of Hopewell would ever be able to offer them, and that was all it took for them to agree. "Angel Band" was their song.

Naamah read the first line again.

The next, and the next.

All the girls, including Naamah, were very good at memorizing what Sister Cordelia told them to memorize, at recalling exactly the definitions of words and reciting them days, weeks, months, even years later. They were good at remembering what got them in trouble and what didn't. But memorization wasn't the same as thinking, as feeling; it was the difference between reciting the meaning of the word *orphan* according to the dictionary and having to live as one. In Sister Cordelia's world, there was never any room for interpretation, and there certainly wasn't room for angels or their snow-white wings.

The littlest girls leaned against Naamah, and the other girls leaned against them, and there they sat huddled together on the floor in the dining room in silence as if what they had found was so delicate a shift of a foot or a cough or a sneeze could make it disappear again. If this was happiness, Naamah thought, if this sudden warmth she felt was love, then it really was worth fighting for.

Sister Cordelia came back to the dining room with a gramophone, which was one of the most beautiful things Naamah and the girls had ever seen, even though they didn't yet know quite what it was or how it worked. The base of it was square and made of sleek dark wood, out of which sprouted a shiny brass piece shaped like a great trumpet flower.

"It makes music," Sister Cordelia said, and showed Naamah how it would work if a record was placed on the turntable. "I don't want you to play it until I leave."

"Yes, Sister," Naamah said.

She and the girls might have been more curious about why Sister Cordelia didn't want to be in the same room with the gramophone or about where it came from, but the answers, whatever they were, couldn't have been as compelling as the gramophone itself and the idea that it could somehow, *would* somehow, make music out of the thin Hopewell air.

"You have an hour to teach them a song," Sister Corde-lia said. "All of you will perform Saturday afternoon at three o'clock. You won't have the gramophone. It'll be just your voices in a crowd of people. Once it's over we're coming directly home." She fingered her cross. "If it were up to me, we wouldn't go at all."

"Yes, Sister," Mary Margaret said quickly, as if to rush her out.

Sister Cordelia looked at Mary Margaret and the rest of the girls circled around Naamah and the songbook. "Don't be fooled, Naamah. They don't care about you. You're worth only as much as a fig to them. Or a piece of cheese."

How much am I worth to you? Naamah thought.

When Sister Cordelia was gone and they were alone again, Naamah turned the metal crank and placed the record on the turntable as she'd been shown. Maybe Sister Cordelia was right about the girls' attention, but having them circle around her made her feel special even if they did it only because Sis-ter Cordelia had told them to. Being chosen was what each of them had dreamed of after being unchosen by their par-ents and after being passed over by new parents because they weren't darling enough or they were freckled or they were too old. Once when Naamah was six years old, a woman came very close to adopting her. During her visits, she told Naamah about the room she would have and the toys she would play with. But then one day the woman's husband came with her to Hopewell, looked hard at Naamah, and told his wife they couldn't adopt her. She never knew why.

Naamah set the needle on the record, and after a startling crackle and spit, a song came on, and each of their faces lit up. Naamah sat with the songbook on her lap, wondering how a page filled with heavy black notes could sound so light and alive. The girls listened to song after song until they got to theirs, which was even more beautiful than the others, more delicate, and their practice time was nearly up.

"We're going to be in big trouble," one of the little girls said.

"Huge," said the other.

"No, we aren't," Mary Margaret said, still on her knees. "One of us can sing, and the rest of us can hum like they do on the record. It'll be pretty that way."

"Who should sing?" Naamah said.

Mary Margaret tapped the songbook with her finger. "You should."

"That's a good idea," said one of the girls who'd pulled Mary Margaret away in the locker room. "If Sister Cordelia doesn't like it, which she won't, she'll be the one to blame."

"It'll be Cotsville in the broom closet," said the one who'd taken her other arm.

"That's not why," Mary Margaret said, looking at Naamah as if she knew something about her even Naamah didn't know.

"Why then?" Naamah said, but it was too late.

Sister Cordelia came sweeping into the room, fury on her face. Or maybe it was panic. The girls scattered to the outer edges of the dining room, but Naamah stayed where she was on the floor with the songbook in her hands. All at once, Sister Cordelia lifted the black record from the gramophone and broke it into as many pieces as she could.

"I've suffered enough today," she said with what was left of her breath.

The girls disbanded to finish their chores, leaving Naamah alone with Sister Cordelia, the songbook, and the gramophone.

Sister Cordelia got down on her hands and knees to collect the broken pieces of the record, which she tucked away in some hidden place in her habit instead of putting them in the garbage bin across the room. She looked diminished somehow.

If she was anybody else but her, her eyes might have welled up just then and overflowed with salty tears.

"Leave," she said to Naamah, but in a way someone else might have said, *Stay.*

Naamah got on her hands and knees, too, as she did whenever there was a mess to clean up. She picked up a jagged piece of the broken record and handed it to Sister Cordelia, who took it from her and tucked it into her habit without a word.

Sister Cordelia reached for the songbook. She sat on the floor, staring at the worn cover, the photograph of the man and woman at the center of it.

"This is my mother," she said, touching the paper. "She used to be the soprano in our church's choir in Minneapolis. People said her voice was like an angel's, but I don't remember it that way. She used to tell me to be silent."

Naamah handed Sister Cordelia another piece of the record.

"She fell in with a Holy Roller and went south with him to bring his false god to the backwaters of Mississippi when I was eight," Sister Cordelia said, covering the man's face with her finger. "They wouldn't see it that way, but that's the way it was. Magic and light shows and speaking in tongues, even though God gave us the Word."

Naamah tried to give her another piece of the record, but she didn't take it.

"She was pretty," Sister Cordelia said, rubbing her thumb along the woman's cheek and through her hair. "She was disappointed I didn't take after her. She's dead now."

"I'm sorry," Naamah said, because she didn't know what else was safe to say or why Sister Cordelia was telling her the story. Maybe it was meant as a cautionary tale. *This is what happens when you worship false idols.* Maybe it was a warning. *I know what you're planning, Naamah.*

Sister Cordelia smiled strangely at the gramophone. "Now I have this unwieldy old thing to remember her by." Even though she'd carried it downstairs perfectly well by herself, Sister Cordelia asked if Naamah would help her carry the gramophone back upstairs.

"Yes, Sister," Naamah said.

Sister Cordelia carried the songbook and Naamah carried the gramophone up to a room on the second floor that was always locked. Naamah and the other girls were forbidden to even pause in front of it. If the other girls thought about the room or wondered what was inside, they didn't say so in Naamah's company. Naamah didn't wonder about it either. She'd accepted that a great many things at Hopewell, and probably in the world, didn't belong to her and never would. With a tarnished brass key, Sister Cordelia opened the heavy wood door. She nudged Naamah forward when Naamah wouldn't move.

"You may pick one thing for yourself," Sister Cordelia said, turning on the light. "But you mustn't tell the other girls about what's in this room."

In all directions Naamah saw variations of pink: light pink on the walls, dark pink on the border that the circled the top of the room, *pink* pink on the dolls that were adorned with sparkly shoes and hairpins and sat primly on row after row of shelves. There were pink puzzles, a pink rocking horse, a pink spinning top, and a bookshelf full of pink books—stories that seemed like they would take a lifetime to read. There were even pink curtains gently gathered over a pink crib in the corner of the room, as if they were only waiting for a pink girl now. As if they'd only ever been waiting for one.

"What do you want?" Sister Cordelia said, her habit even blacker against all this light.

Naamah knew better, but she allowed herself to walk around the room inhaling the scent of pink. She allowed herself to come under the spell of all the pleasure it promised. Naamah looked over the dolls and toys, this foreign land, with pure bedazzlement, instead of asking silent questions. *Where did all this come from? Why haven't I seen it until now?* No one had ever given her a gift. There was no Santa Claus. No Easter Bunny. No birthdays. Nothing but longing to mark the passing of time.

"This," she said, and lifted a ceramic bird off a shelf full of tiny figurines—men and women, animals and flowers, a whole miniature world of them. Naamah cradled the little bird in her hand as if it were injured and needed her to become well again.

"That?" Sister Cordelia said, turning the key over in her hand. "It isn't even pink."

"It has wings," Naamah said. Snow-white wings.

Naamah used her baby blanket to make a nest for her bird on the shelf in her locker. The rest of the girls had either gone outside to harvest that day's store of vegetables from the garden or down to the kitchen to chop and boil them for supper. Now and then Naamah heard girls humming between the rows of vines, and then, inside, Sister Cordelia's office door would slam, and the girls would harvest in silence again for a while.

Naamah stood in front of her locker, cradling her pretty white bird in her hand.

"You need a good name to have a good life," she said, stroking its shiny ceramic wings, the ridge of feathers soft beneath her fingers. "You can't have one like mine."

Sister Cordelia once said Naamah was lucky to have a name at all; at other orphanages girls had numbers.

Step forward to be struck, number 134682.

"You can't have a number," Naamah said to her bird, stroking her orange beak. "I'm going to call you Gracie."

Naamah kissed the top of Gracie's head, at first with only a tinge of suspicion about what she'd seen in the pink room, which she tried to block out with adoration. When that didn't work, she held Gracie tightly, as if someone were already trying to take her away. *You belong to me now,* she said. But the longer Naamah stood in front of her locker, the more she wondered where everything in the pink room had come from and why Sister Cordelia had shown the room to her. To reward her for teaching the girls the song? That hardly seemed likely. To keep her quiet at the festival? Maybe so. Did the other girls have dolls and toys and pretty pink books hidden away in their lockers, too? Naamah held Gracie with one hand and opened every single locker with the other, but all she found were clothes, shoes, towels, and the occasional wet sheet a girl was trying to dry out before Sister Cordelia noticed.

No other girl had a baby blanket or a little book about wilderness survival like the one she'd swiped from the library in Sister Cordelia's office when she was supposed to be eating lard sandwiches. No one else had a white ceramic bird.

Naamah kissed Gracie again. She was so sweet, so tiny.

I've earned you, Naamah thought.

The more she thought about it, the more she believed everything in that pink room had been donated, and even though Sister Cordelia didn't want what was offered she'd been forced to take it. Some of the dolls Naamah had seen still had price tags attached to their dresses and to the bottoms of their sparkly shoes. Were people outside of Hopewell that generous? That kind? Maybe there really were cars in all colors of the rainbow and a fountain that made dreams come true. Maybe Sister Cordelia really did have a mother once.

Naamah kissed Gracie a third time. She didn't know what

she'd bargained for by taking her, or if she'd bargained anything at all, but she was glad for Gracie's springy feet and her
triangle beak. She was glad for her snow-white wings. Before
Naamah placed Gracie in the blanket nest in her locker and
told the ducks to protect her, she heard a rustling of feathers,
the call of somewhere other than here.

15

❦ On the morning of the harvest festival snow began to fall in wide, wet flakes. While the other girls took turns bathing, Naamah stood in front of a tall window in the dormitory. She'd been ready to go to the festival since the first brush of light in the sky. She'd been ready to go all her life. Outside, the rows of plants in the garden were beginning to turn white. White the earth. White the sky. White the last ripe grapes clinging to the vines. What if this was the last time Naamah looked out a Hopewell window? Wasn't it? She didn't know why, but she wanted to remember the wavery old window glass and the tiny drops of water that clung to it. She wanted to remember the sound of the radiators gurgling steam into the air. The few pleasant things about Hopewell.

"What do you think it feels like?" Mary Margaret said, sidling up to her at the window. She pressed her hand against the glass.

"Out there?" Naamah said. "I don't know."

None of them was allowed outside when it became too

cold to wear the thin blouses and skirts, which was most of the year in northern Minnesota. Only the girls who helped Sister Cordelia in town each week had ever felt snow on their skin or had stuck their tongues out to catch it when Sister Cordelia was tending to business.

"Maybe it's like the icebox, except a giant one," Mary Margaret said.

Naamah was thinking about the song she was supposed to sing and the crowd she was supposed to get lost in afterward. She'd memorized the words, but wasn't certain about the melody, since she'd only heard it once before Sister Cordelia destroyed the record. Sister Lydie used to say you could only remember a melody if it found its way into your heart.

When Mary Margaret lifted her hand from the window, narrow rivers of water pooled at the sill. "Maybe it's like heaven, and all this time we've been so close to it."

Little fingers of fear started to pinch at Naamah's heart. She was going to have to leave Gracie and her baby blanket behind. The book about how to survive in the wilderness—how to avoid hypothermia and frostbite, black fingers, missing toes. She was going to have to keep running and running and running, even though she'd never run more than a few yards her whole life. She was going to have to believe the world beyond the Hopewell wall wasn't what Sister Cordelia said it was. She was going to have to believe in the logging camps up north and not believe in them at the same time.

"You're going to be all right," Mary Margaret said, as if she knew what Naamah had been planning. "You were always going to be all right."

When all of the girls had bathed and dressed, they went downstairs together. Twenty-six coats, twenty-six scarves, and twenty-six pairs of mittens had magically appeared on the table where they usually ate their meals. No one knew where the winter garments came from, but they made for a lovely sight, all those reds and wools and blues.

"Make sure each of you has a coat, a scarf, and a pair of mittens," Sister Cordelia said, coming into the dining room. "Naamah, come with me."

Naamah followed Sister Cordelia to her office, wondering if like the pink room there was one full of all things winter: ice skates and coats and snowmen that came to life when nobody was looking. Maybe there was a room for each of the seasons, a room for each of the girls filled with their hearts' desires.

"I have something for you," Sister Cordelia said. "Close your eyes."

Naamah did as she was told, even when she felt Sister Cordelia's hands at the front of her neck and then at the back of it. Even when they formed a collar for a moment.

When Sister Cordelia allowed her to open her eyes, Naamah saw the small silver cross and chain dangling from her neck.

"This is so you remember whom you belong to," Sister Cordelia said.

Sister Cordelia carefully looked Naamah over, adjusting the fit of the clothes she'd chosen for her earlier that morning. Naamah was wearing a gray sweater, thick gray tights, her gray uniform skirt, and a pair of dull-black shoes that had appeared at the foot of her cot before she woke. Her coat was gray, her scarf. Naamah didn't know what she looked like—a storm cloud? She didn't care. *Goodbye,* she thought.

Sister Cordelia stared at Naamah as one might stare at a window, waiting for the glass to yield to the view. She placed her hand over her cross, as if she didn't want God to hear her. "Everything I've done has been to protect you, Naamah. You're still too young to understand what I mean. Too willful."

Naamah touched the cross around her neck.

Sister Cordelia touched the window. "Your soul is like this glass."

A moment later Mary Elizabeth knocked on the office door, announcing the arrival of the bus. She said she'd brushed all the girls' hair and put the ribbons in and that Mary Catherine had done the same for her. They'd all pinched their cheeks until they were pink.

"We get to ride on a bus?" the littlest girls were saying in the hallway.

"A bus! A bus!" said the others.

"Remember what I said," Sister Cordelia said to Naamah before she came out of the office and reminded the other girls about the rules. Sister Cordelia's hands, which had just been so definite in their movements, were shaking slightly.

"Don't be worried about the snow, Sister," the bus driver said when Sister Cordelia let him in. "It's just showing off for us today, since it's the first of the season. I'll get you there in one piece." He turned to the girls. "I'm Mr. Philips. How do all of you do?" When none of them answered, he scratched the back of his head. "I don't blame you. Nothing's worse than a bald bus driver who's got snow for hair." Water dripped down his face faster than he could wipe it off. "All right, then. Let's get you to town."

The whole way to town Naamah sat beside a rattling window, staring out at the earth and sky beyond the bus. Each girl, except the five-year-olds who were told to sit together, sat alone on the brown cloth seats. Mr. Philips kept looking back at them as if what he saw was strange, but he didn't say anything. He only smiled, hoping, it seemed, someone would smile back at him. He turned the heater up because he said they looked cold.

Shortly after they drove through the Hopewell gates, the

bus made a turn and then another, and out her window Naamah started to see smoke pouring out of brick chimneys between the cover of trees. She started to see houses. Front yards. Backyards. Fences whitewashed with fresh snow. She even saw a snow family perched beside a rusty swing set; the family had carrots for noses, buttons for buttons. The bus continued past them. Past bright red berries. Wet black branches. An old schoolhouse that had boarded-up windows and a heavy leftward lean. Past more than Naamah could see at one time.

She looked down at the white line on the road, wondering what it meant and why the bus kept crisscrossing it. She looked up at the wires strung between the high wooden poles, knowing they made telephones work even though Hopewell didn't have one. She saw a bushel of apples overturned on the side of the road. She saw a blue plate.

The bus continued into town, which was full of buildings and cars and signs painted red, white, orange, green, blue. SODA FIVE CENTS. GORDON'S BAIT AND TACKLE. A bank, a park, an empty bench. MARYANN'S QUILTING SUPPLIES. THE CORNER STORE.

How could all of this new color and these words and this life be here, so close to the stern white walls of Hopewell? How could that white be so different than this white racing past the bus windows to the ground? Sister Cordelia looked back at Naamah, momentarily distracting her, but Naamah saw the sign anyway. LOVE'S CAFÉ, WHERE THE BAKED CHICKEN IS AS GOOD AS YOUR MOTHER'S. *Your mother's. Your mother's. Your mother's.*

The bus made another turn before it slowed and stopped altogether, and Naamah saw the sea of hats and coats and mittens. She saw the stage and the shiny instruments covered with snow. She saw husbands helping wives out of front seats and wives helping children out of backseats and children tumbling forth with red cheeks and noses.

"Snow!" one of them yelled, and then they all did.

One by one, the Hopewell girls stepped off the bus into the snow with them. Unlike the other children, the Hopewell girls flinched when the first flakes touched their skin.

Mr. Philips looked back at Naamah. "Aren't you coming, little girl?"

"I'm fourteen, sir," Naamah said, getting up from her seat at the very back of the bus where Sister Cordelia had positioned her.

"That isn't so little, but it isn't big either," Mr. Philips said when Naamah reached the front of the bus. He pulled out his wallet and within it a photograph. "I have a granddaughter your age. You look like her. See?"

"What's her name," Naamah said.

"Elena," Mr. Philips said. "She wants to be a doctor when she grows up. The kind that delivers babies. What do you want to be?"

"I don't know," Naamah said.

No one had ever asked Naamah that before. She and the other girls at Hopewell had spent all of their time thinking about what it was going to feel like to pass through the Hopewell gates once and for all. They didn't think about what would happen after that because it didn't really matter; the *after* had to be better than the *before*.

Mr. Philips put the photograph away when Sister Cordelia stepped onto the bus.

"Don't wait too long to think about it," he said, winking.

Sister Cordelia took Naamah's hand and led her down the steps of the bus out into the snow, which the wind whirled around and around. *Snow,* Naamah thought. She couldn't help but smile.

The first flakes landed on her eyelashes, and there they glinted like tiny stars until the heat of her skin melted them into droplets of water, which she blinked away and which rolled all the way down her cheeks and disappeared into her scarf. The next snowflakes fell onto her shoulders and then her gray mittens and then the snowflakes fell everywhere. The accumulation was so startling Naamah stopped moving forward.

Cold, snow, ice: these were old words, but their meanings were entirely new. They were filled with magic, overflowing with it. Anything seemed possible. Everything. At the exact moment Naamah stuck her tongue out to catch a snowflake like the children around her, Sister Cordelia jerked her forward, but not before she caught one.

"There's the stage," Sister Cordelia said. "Everyone keep your order."

All the Hopewell girls were together now, walking in a straight line, past folding tables full of empty cups waiting to be filled with cider and empty plates waiting to have sausages placed on them. The women behind the tables were trying to wave away the snow as one would wave away flies in the summer, some with their hands, some with spatulas. They were wearing white aprons over their coats, turning sausages in pans.

They were laughing.

"The sausages," they said. "The snow."

Sister Cordelia led the girls past the tables, past a crowd of people tossing balls of snow into the air and then trying to figure out whose ball went the highest. Some of the people were jumping up and down to keep warm. Some were blowing on their mittens and gloves. All of them were smiling. *Were regular people always so happy?* Naamah wondered.

A little girl, of four or maybe five, dropped her doll on the ground, and her mother was helping her wipe the snow off with a handkerchief she'd pulled from her coat pocket.

"There," she said gently, as Naamah passed. "Miss Lilly's all better now."

"But she had snow on her, Mommy," the little girl said. She and her doll had bright blue eyes and blond hair that curled under at the ends. Both were wearing shiny black shoes with little bows at the heels. Both looked like they'd only ever been loved.

The mother kissed the girl's forehead in a way Naamah had always dreamed of being kissed. First by her mother, then by any mother, then anyone. Mary Elizabeth and Mary Ellen had told stories about seeing families holding hands on the walkways in town or families throwing pennies into the fountain together, and all of them had wondered what it would be like to have their own coins, their own hands to hold. Once, a passerby had given Mary Ellen a penny and was disappointed when she wouldn't toss it into the water, but the Hopewell girls understood perfectly well: she was waiting for a family to throw it with.

Sister Cordelia urged Naamah and the other girls forward toward the stage. A snowflake landed on Sister Cordelia's cross, and she brushed it away as if it were unholy.

"Keep moving, girls," she said. "Don't get distracted by all of this sin."

As Naamah and the other girls climbed the steps of the stage, Naamah memorized how many there were—one, two, three, four—so her feet could navigate them on the way down. She looked back at the bus and then at the stand of trees on the opposite side of the park. She thought of what the wilderness book said: *If you want to survive, you need to figure out where you are in relation to where you want to go. If you don't have a compass, you'll have to make your own.*

When they were all on the wooden stage, which was covered in a layer of snow marred by trails of footprints that went everywhere and nowhere, a member of the town's board of trustees introduced the girls as a whole and then

155

asked each of them to come up to the tall silver microphone and say her name individually. Mary Catherine. Mary Elizabeth. Mary Margaret. Mary Alice. Mary Jo. Mary Constance. Mary May. Mary Alise . . . Naamah.

"That's an unusual name, isn't it?" the trustee said, stopping Naamah from returning to the other girls with his hand. "What does it mean?"

Naamah looked at Sister Cordelia, who told her to go on and answer the question. By this time, the crowd of people had mostly stopped talking and had directed its attention to the stage. A few babies were crying, and their mothers were bouncing them on their hips. Children were swiping sausages from untended pans and hiding them in their coats. The snow was falling faster now than it was melting, and the people of Green River were starting to look like the snow people Naamah had seen from the bus window.

"It either means 'displeasing to God' or 'pleasing to God,'" Naamah said.

"Depending on what?" the trustee said.

"My behavior, sir," Naamah said, and the crowd erupted in laughter. Naamah didn't understand it.

"The Hopewell girls, everyone," the trustee said, waving his hand dramatically before he hustled Sister Cordelia away from the stage, and Naamah and the girls were alone.

Naamah stayed in front of the microphone just as they'd planned, and the other girls formed a half circle around her. She looked out onto the sea of people loving and laughing and living their lives. Instead of families she wasn't a part of, in their place Naamah saw trees. She saw her mother. She saw green after green after green.

"'My latest sun is sinking fast, my race is nearly run,'" she sang.

Naamah thought of all the nights she'd spent in the broom

closet unable to sleep because she was so afraid. All the days she'd spent on her hands and knees trying to scrub her way into Sister Cordelia's heart, the Lord's heart, anyone's heart. She thought of all the years she'd spent watching the other girls eat wedges of cheese and fat purple figs.

"'My strongest trials now are past, my triumph has begun.'"

Naamah was never going to get down on her knees for anyone ever again. She was never going to let anyone stuff cornmeal into her mouth. She was never going to let anyone cleanse her with bleach.

"'Oh, come Angel Band, come and around me stand.'"

She was going to tear up every Bible she ever saw.

She was going to spit on every cross.

"'Oh, bear me away on your snow white wings . . .'"

She was going to be free.

When Naamah stopped singing, the crowd started clapping and cheering and whistling. People were moving toward the stage quickly, just as Naamah had hoped they would. The trustee who had introduced them told the girls to take a bow.

"Especially you," he said to Naamah. "You have a beautiful voice."

As Naamah stepped forward and curtseyed, she looked to the left side of the stage and saw Sister Cordelia surrounded by a group of people trying to congratulate her. On the right side of the stage, Naamah saw the stairs and started running.

Naamah was down the stairs—one, two, three, four—and on her way across the field, to the woods on the other side of the park, to the logging camps and her mother's tender arms, when a woman wearing a worn-out fur coat blocked her way.

"Is it you?" she said, as if her heart were breaking.

The woman's face was a strange yellow color; her skin had sunken in on itself like a piece of old fruit. Mucus gathered at the corner of her eyes. The woman was too young to look old. To look that weathered. Her hair was the color of wheat.

"I can't cry anymore," the woman said, wiping the mucus away with a handkerchief. "This is what comes out of me now."

The coat she was wearing was missing big patches of fur.

"You haven't had a good life, have you?" the woman said.

Naamah looked toward the woods at the other end of the park. She thought of the wilderness book. *Hypothermia. Frostbite. Black fingers. Missing toes.* If she went now, she could still make it there. But she had to go now. Her legs would have to move as fast as her heart was beating. As fast as she was breathing. "No," Naamah said.

The woman reached for Naamah's hand, and though Naamah hesitated—the woods, the woods—she gave it to her because the woman looked so sad and sick and alone.

The woman pressed her lips to the top of Naamah's hand; it was the first time anyone had ever kissed her. The first time since Sister Lydie that Naamah had felt the warmth of another person's heart on her skin. Just before the woman let go of Naamah's hand, and Sister Cordelia came running down the last of the stairs, her habit white with snow, chanting *Our Father, Who art in heaven, Hallowed be Thy Name,* and seized Naamah with her claws, the woman leaned to one side as if she might tip over.

"Please forgive me," she said. "If you're you. If you aren't."

16

❧ Naamah didn't make it to the trees. She didn't make it to the logging camps. She didn't run and run and run until she was holding her mother and her mother was holding her and everything was all right for the first time in their lives. She didn't even get to say goodbye to the woman who'd kissed her hand. Sister Cordelia steered her back to the bus by the collar of her coat saying nothing but the Our Father prayer over and over again. When Mr. Philips greeted them with a wide smile—You should be a singer, that's what! How lovely your voice was, like those angels you were singing about—Sister Cordelia quieted him with a sharp wave of her hand. *And lead us not into temptation,* she said.

On the way back to Hopewell, Naamah sobbed in her seat while the glass rattled, while they passed the blue plate, the overturned apples, the people made of snow. Sister Cordelia was sitting next to her and would make her pay dearly for her tears and for what she'd done at the festival, but Naamah couldn't stop crying.

She wasn't free. She wasn't free.

When they arrived at the orphanage, Sister Cordelia didn't say a word to Naamah. She didn't drag her to the broom closet or strike her in front of the others or set a bucket in front of her and tell her to scrub until God forgave her for trying to run away—one day for each step, one week for each glance at the evergreen trees. She didn't say or do anything.

That night while the other girls slept, Naamah turned and turned in her cot, the metal creaking beneath her, wondering why Sister Cordelia didn't pull her away from the other girls to punish her the moment they walked through the front door, wondering why she'd been allowed to pick at her supper with the other girls, to brush her teeth, and to recite her nightly prayers on her knees. What new punishment awaited her? How much would it hurt? How long would it take? Naamah had never been more afraid.

"You're going to be all right," Mary Margaret had said that morning, but before they went to bed she'd said, "You're letting her make you ugly."

When Naamah couldn't sleep and couldn't wait any longer for her punishment to come, she got up from her cot. She stood in the middle of the dormitory, shivering in her thin cotton nightgown. She watched the girls nearest to her sleep, their faces awash in blue light. The littlest girls had climbed into bed with one another and lay together like spoons. The others slept alone. How was it no one had wanted any of them? How was it that at the exact same time one woman could be turning sausages and another woman could be dying?

Naamah made her bed as neatly as she could in the darkness. She kissed her pillow the way the woman at the festival had kissed her hand. She touched the cross Sister Cordelia had placed around her neck. She knew whom she belonged to. She always had.

Naamah left the dormitory and walked into the broom

closet. *You can't punish me if I punish myself first,* she thought, and lay down on the cold floor. When freezing wasn't punishment enough, Naamah dug her fingernails into her back until she reopened the sores from the last time she was in here, and the blood rose. With that blood—pain she understood, pain that was safe, pain that felt like home—she was finally able to rest.

Hours later Naamah woke to Sister Cordelia standing over her, shaking her head lightly in the moonlight. Sister Cordelia was wearing a white nightgown just like Naamah's, just like all the girls at Hopewell. Her silvery hair trailed down her back, ending in waves at her waist. In this light, Naamah couldn't see Sister Cordelia's moles. She couldn't see her crooked yellow teeth. Naamah thought she was dreaming.

"What are you doing in here, child?" Sister Cordelia said, sighing deeply.

When Sister Cordelia kneeled before her, her bones creaked. She helped Naamah up from the floor and led her out of the broom closet down the dimly lit hallway. Back to her cot, Naamah thought. She didn't understand why she wasn't being punished.

Sister Cordelia's feet were bare. Were they also bare in the broom closet? Naamah had never seen her toes or heels or arches; up until this very moment she'd believed Sister Cordelia had hooves instead of feet. Naamah had never seen the patchwork of red and blue veins around her ankles— evidence Sister Cordelia had a heart.

Instead of the dormitory Sister Cordelia took her down to her office, where Naamah found her baby blanket and her pretty white bird on Sister Cordelia's desk.

"Are you taking them away?" Naamah said. Of course she was. She was probably going to make Naamah smash her bird and burn her blanket.

"No, you are," Sister Cordelia said. "As well as the rest of this." She handed Naamah a white laundry bag stuffed full. "Open it."

Naamah untied the strings and reached inside the bag, expecting to feel something sharp snap at her skin. At the very least, she thought she'd see soiled linens she'd have to scrub clean. But on top of the bag, she found the gray winter coat she'd worn to the festival, the pair of mittens, and the scarf. Beneath that layer was a pair of winter boots. Beneath that a loaf of bread, a wedge of cheese, and a tin of figs.

"I don't understand," Naamah said.

Sister Cordelia leaned against her desk. "Keep going."

The last item Naamah pulled out of the bag was a hat, which was covered almost entirely, intricately, with green feathers. Naamah recognized it at once.

"Ethelina dropped this in front of the gates," Naamah said. "I saw her when I was cleaning the window."

"You were a little girl then," Sister Cordelia said, fingering the material at the collar of her nightgown. She looked very old without her habit on. Her skin hung from her neck as if it were about to peel away from her and fall to the floor.

Naamah touched the green feathers. "I waved to her, but she didn't wave back."

Sister Cordelia looked out the darkened window as if Ethelina were still standing there with her hand stretched across her heart. "Ethelina was special," she said. "Most of the girls who come through here aren't."

"Where did she go?" Naamah said.

"I opened a door for her, and she walked through it," Sister Cordelia said.

She turned from the window and faced Naamah.

"Do you know you were only a few hours old when I found

you? The umbilical cord was still warm. You were special, too, Naamah. Your eyes were so gray."

Sister Cordelia walked behind her desk, opened the top drawer, and closed it again.

"We were so close to having everything, Naamah. You and me and God. Your mother didn't want you, but I did."

Naamah let go of the laundry bag.

Your mother didn't want you. Naamah had always told herself that one of the logging-camp men had forced her mother to leave her on the doorstep on the night she was born. Every girl at Hopewell told that kind of story because if their mothers had left them by choice, then no one had loved them even for a minute.

Sister Cordelia came out from behind her desk.

"Put the coat on, the boots, the mittens," she said. "It's cold out there."

"Where are we going?" Naamah said.

"You're going," Sister Cordelia said. She tucked the bird and the blanket into the laundry bag. She put a hand on Naamah's back and urged her out of the office and toward the front door of the orphanage. When Sister Cordelia opened it, the icy wind came tumbling through, unhinging the wooden cross from the wall in the entryway.

"You wanted to go, so go," she said.

Naamah looked past the snowy yard and the front gates toward the dark woods on the other side of the road. *Hypothermia,* she thought. *Frostbite. Black fingers. Missing toes.* From the steps of the orphanage, she heard tangles of branches scraping against one another in the wind. Trunks creaking. She heard the cry of the wind itself.

All her life, she'd waited for the day she'd finally get to leave Hopewell, and yet now that the moment had arrived she was afraid to go. And it wasn't just because the snow was falling and the wind was howling and the woods were dark. The idea of running through all that toward someone who might not love her, who might not have ever loved her, felt like running off the edge of a cliff. Blue skies. Bluebirds. She couldn't hear her mother's voice.

The wind lifted Naamah's nightgown; it blew open her coat.

"Keep moving or you'll freeze to death," Sister Cordelia said.

Your mother didn't want you.

If that was true, then Sister Cordelia was right about what was on the other side of the wall. Naamah already felt the ice crystals following her veins to her heart.

"I'll be good," she said and let herself fall to Sister Cordelia's feet the way people in the Bible did when there was nothing left to do but beg for God's mercy.

Sister Cordelia tried to shake her loose. "You already made your choice."

Naamah looked up at Sister Cordelia through the snow. She thought of the pink room. The pink dolls. The pink curtains gathered over the empty pink crib. People may have donated all of that stuff, but it didn't explain the careful way Sister Cordelia had displayed it.

"I'll be your pink baby," she said. "That's what you want, isn't it?"

At that moment, everything, even the wind, stopped.

Sister Cordelia unwrapped the strings of the laundry bag from Naamah's wrist and set the bag beside the door. She was smiling a little, the way she did when she was finished scrubbing Naamah down with bleach, the way she did when she knew she'd won.

"Do you understand this is the only time I'm opening this

door for you?" she said. "If you come inside, you'll live your life here with me and God. That's the promise you'll be making when you cross the threshold."

Naamah looked at the woods and then at the open front door.

Hopewell was the only place she'd ever lived. The only place she knew by heart.

Naamah looked up at the tall dormitory windows, at the place on the roof where a paper airplane she'd made carrying the message SAVE ME HUX had landed and the place on her arm she was struck for it. She tasted the cornmeal at the corners of her mouth, the smears of lard on dry white bread. She saw the Word in the bricks.

Naamah looked toward the frozen kitchen garden, hoping to see her mother walking among the vines once more. Hoping to see the grape juice dripping from her mother's chin. Hoping to hear her say, *Fight for me, Naamah.*

Instead of her mother, when Naamah closed her eyes, she saw the woman at the festival with the worn-out fur coat, the worn-out heart. She felt the woman's cracked lips on her skin. The woman was the one saying, *Fight for you.*

Sister Cordelia took Naamah's hand when Naamah crossed the threshold.

"I did a better job with you than I did with Ethelina," she said.

Naamah thought of Ethelina's strawberry hair. Her blue-ice eyes. The way she had looked standing on the other side of the gate in her feathery green hat, as if, for the slightest moment, she'd wanted to come back inside, too.

"I knew you wouldn't be able to leave, but I had to know for sure," Sister Cordelia said. She reached into the front pocket of her nightgown and pulled out a small gilded Bible with Naamah's name printed on the cover. "I've been waiting a long time to be able to give this to you. To be able to tell you of my love."

Naamah took the Bible from Sister Cordelia and leafed through the pages in the dim light of the entryway. She paused when she came to the long passages about people begetting other people she'd worked so hard to recite perfectly when she was small. She saw the floor she'd been scrubbing since she could hold a rag. She saw the rulers she'd been kneeling on since she could kneel. Naamah felt every pinch and poke and prod in the name of God. She smelled every drop of bleach.

But it wasn't until she saw the words from 1 John 4:18 and looked up at Sister Cordelia and realized her moles and her loose skin and her twisted yellow teeth weren't really what made her ugly that she knew what she had to do even though the snow was falling and the wind was howling and the woods were dark.

There is no fear in love.

All at once a cold black wave came rising up from somewhere very deep in Naamah.

"I hate pink," she said.

Naamah pushed the Bible hard against Sister Cordelia's chest, against her heart, which made Sister Cordelia lose her balance. Sister Cordelia cried out on her way down the front steps. She cried out when she landed on the walkway with a thud.

Her toes were covered with snow. Her hands were covered with snow. Snow was collecting in her old-woman hair.

Sister Cordelia looked up at Naamah with utter surprise.

With fear, which made Naamah strong.

"It was my mother's favorite color," Sister Cordelia said.

Before Naamah picked up the laundry bag, before she ran

through the Hopewell gates for the very first and last time, toward the woods and the logging camps, she bent over Sister Cordelia, lifted her hair away from her face, and pressed her lips to her wrinkled ear.

"You'll never be my mother," she said. "You'll never have my love."

PART THREE

Evergreen, Minnesota

1961

17

Hux should have told Leah he loved her—he knew that. When she announced she was leaving last month, he'd only said okay from his place in front of the woodstove. Leah had come to Evergreen because she had gotten separated from her canoeing group on the river. She'd stayed with Hux in a cabin without indoor plumbing an entire year. He was lucky for that, wasn't he? Most of the time he was fine about being alone again. He could leave out as many mugs of half-drunk coffee as he liked. He could listen to his favorite old-time program on the radio without Leah calling him Grandpa. Sometimes, though, especially when he came in from preserving animals in the work shed at night, and she wasn't there to reach for her nose plug anymore, he'd miss her below and above the belt enough that last week he threw out her comb, her flowery perfume, and her wool bunting.

Gunther said he was a damn fool, if you asked him.

"Good thing I wasn't asking," Hux said.

The two of them were standing in the oxeye meadow on

Hux's side of the river, getting ready to cut logs from the birch tree Hux took down in the forest that morning and dragged here with his truck. It was the beginning of October, but the afternoon sun was still warm enough they couldn't see their breath. The ground still gave a little beneath their feet. Hux pulled a carrot up from the soil, brushed it off, and bit into it. When he was a baby his mother started a garden up here, which she stopped tending by the time he could walk. Twenty-odd years later, and stray vegetables still cropped up among the milk thistle.

"I'm going to chop you into the ground," Gunther said.

Hux was wearing an orange hat because it was hunting season and he didn't want to get shot. Gunther's was camouflage.

Hux put on his safety glasses.

"You're seriously wearing those?" Gunther said. "No wonder Leah got fed up. Or maybe it was because you wouldn't get rid of those bunk beds. Or maybe it's the beard."

"Can we please just cut some wood," Hux said.

They'd have to cut at least another cord before the first hard frost. Everything about fall in the Northwoods seemed like a race. If you didn't chop enough wood, you'd freeze come winter. If you didn't put up enough food, you'd starve. There were stories about fur trappers who went into the woods in the fall and didn't come out again. When Hux's father was alive, he never let Hux leave the cabin without promising to pay attention to what was around him. He wanted Hux to understand who he was by where he was.

Hux chopped and stacked birch logs thinking of his father, who'd had the strength of two men but could pin butterflies and insects to velvet with the delicacy of a woman. His father had learned Latin growing up in Germany and garnered a great sense of well-being from knowing more than what was commonly known. The monarch butterfly was *Danaus plexippus*. The stick bug was *Phasmatodea*. When he was little, Hux resisted learning these complex names because he didn't like that they always applied to dead things. *Phasmatodea* were pinned to velvet and encased in glass, while his beloved stick bugs clung to trees in the forest and could be cajoled with a light brush into his hand.

"You should come to the tavern with me," Gunther said, splitting the last log. He cradled his ax like it was a woman. He was smiling his crooked smile just like his mother used to when she was up to no-good good. "I'll find you a real sweet girl."

"I have to be at Phee's first thing in the morning," Hux said.

"I could have built ten porches in the time it's taken you to build one."

"I'm still not going to Yellow Falls with you."

When all the wood was stacked, they tarped it up and secured it with bungees in case the wind picked up or it rained. They'd come back tomorrow or the next day to load it into the truck. They'd split it evenly, maybe even take some over to Phee's place, since she was living out in the bush all by herself. She'd protest, but she'd take the wood.

A yellow butterfly landed on the blue tarp as if the tarp were a stretch of water.

"You remember the year all those caterpillars came?" Gunther said.

When Hux was a boy, he and Gunther used to play in the meadow while their fathers discussed animals. One year there was an explosion of caterpillars on account of the heavy summer rains. Hux and Gunther spent hours transferring monarch caterpillars from overcrowded milkweeds to less crowded ones so they didn't starve.

"I kept thinking you were going to crush them," Hux said.

That year, Hux's father let him and Gunther bring a chrysalis into the cabin and they watched it turn into a butterfly. Though he and Gunther rarely agreed about anything at that age, or at any age, for that matter, they agreed not to pin it to velvet.

"I can be gentle," Gunther said, chewing on a bluestem and then spitting it out again. "You sure you don't want to come with me to town?"

"Have fun," Hux said.

Gunther slung his ax over his shoulder and walked toward the river, which he swam across unless it was frozen. It was the only kind of bathing he liked to do.

Hux put his ax in the truck. The afternoon was too nice for driving, even the quarter mile back to his cabin, so he left the truck and walked. Along the way, he stopped to pick up a red oak leaf the size of a plate. Every fall since he was little he collected leaves and pressed them in his father's heavy taxidermy manuals. His collection was like a farmer's almanac. You could tell by looking at each season's worth, some bright and others dull, whether or not the year had been warmer or colder than usual, or more or less snow had fallen. Hux put the oak leaf into his bag, wondering what its unusual brilliance would mean.

Hux followed the footpath into the woods, a path created by the weight of his boots and a steady stream of whitetails that ate blueberries off the bushes. After cutting wood, all he could ever think about was eating something hearty. Leah used to make venison stew that melted in his mouth. She did something special to the meat but would never say what.

"You won't need me if you can make it yourself," she said.

When he got home, Hux went to the back of the cabin to check the level of the rain barrel, which wasn't full enough to justify taking a shower, albeit a freezing one. He'd been thinking about getting a propane heater so he could rig up a four-season shower, but he'd either have to preserve more animals or charge Phee more than he wanted to. And there was the problem of the water supply; it seemed like there was always too much or too little of it. Maybe he'd just keep going over to Gunther's when he wanted a warm shower.

"Get a well already!" Gunther would say, but he'd always let him in.

Hux loved Gunther's cabin—the red and blue swipes of paint on the front of it, the fact that it had actual bedrooms and a bathroom instead of an open space and an outhouse like at Hux's. When Hux was a kid, he'd spent as many nights over there as he'd spent here.

Hux walked to the front of his cabin, figuring where the squirrels were burrowing into the spaces between the logs so he could chink them before the weather turned. No matter how many precautions he took, the squirrels always found a way in. The last squirrel chewed through the loaves of bread in the kitchen. The container of honey, too.

Hux stepped onto his front porch, took his boots off, and clapped them together before he saw the limp buck sprawled out between the rocking chairs on the porch floor and the note attached to its fur.

Cheer up, Buddy. This one's all yours. Go get that propane heater.

Gunther.

Sometimes Hux couldn't believe how alike Lulu Gunther turned out to be. He was feisty and loud and downright obnoxious sometimes, most of the time, but he was also more generous than anyone in the Northwoods. He had more heart.

Before he got to the buck, Hux stepped around it and went inside to heat a can of chicken soup and drink a glass of milk while the refrigerator still worked. During the winter, when the storms cut off the electricity, he'd have to put whatever was perishable in the snow, and unless he tied a rope to it he wouldn't find it until the spring. Probably he should have stocked up on powdered milk, but it seemed unnatural to him when for years all he'd drunk was milk from Gunther's goat Willa Girl and then Willa Girl II. It was bad enough drinking gallons of the store-bought stuff while they waited on a Willa Girl III.

After Hux ate, he boiled a pot of water on the woodstove for coffee and sterilized his tools. Before he began to separate the buck's head from his body on the porch floor, he gave thanks like his father taught him. In his father's view, respect was the most important part of preserving an animal. When Hux was first learning how to mount, his father would take away his tools for a week if he forgot to say a few kind words. Hux didn't love the work the way his father did, or the hunters he mostly did it for, but he was good at it, and more often than not that made the difference between failing and prospering in Evergreen.

Once Hux freed the buck's head from its body, he decided to spread plastic garbage bags over the kitchen table instead of going out to the work shed. The light was better for skinning here, and Leah wasn't around to protest anymore. He went out to the shed for the shortwave and set it up on the counter.

While he worked, Hux liked to listen to the Canadian program *A Day in the Life Of*. Recently, they'd done a story on polar bears in Churchill. Hux liked the part about the bears knocking over a tundra buggy and scaring tourists into going home. His father said there were two kinds of men in the world: the kind that respected animals and the kind that got killed by them. Hux had witnessed the rise of a third category: the kind that sprayed themselves with Rusty's Doe-in-Heat, waited with whiskey in a tree stand, and took a kind of grace that didn't belong to them.

Hux knew he ought to bring the buck inside, but what he really wanted to do was drink a cup of coffee and reread his favorite childhood book, which his father used to read to him first as a boy and then again as a young man. After Hux's mother got sick and couldn't easily join them in conversation anymore, and Hux and his father ran out of conversation themselves, his father would read out loud from the top bunk while Hux listened on the bunk below him like he was a little boy, even though that year he turned fifteen. The book was about an explorer in the Arctic Circle. When his father read to him, the cabin filled up with the midnight sun. When Hux was growing up, there were no schools to go to and only Gunther to play with, so Hux became friends with the stars in the sky, the trees in the forest, and the people in books. Gunther made fun of him for talking about igloos and sled dogs, but he had an imaginary friend he dragged around everywhere, too.

When the kettle whistled, Hux filled a mug and added a spoonful of instant coffee grounds from the tin on the counter. He took his coffee out onto the porch and went back inside for the wool camp blanket on the bottom bunk and the book on the shelf beside it. He sat in the rocking chair closest to the door. The afternoon was beginning its slow slide into evening. The air smelled of Phee's cedar fire.

Just a few minutes, Hux told himself, and he'd go back inside and work.

He looked out at the garden he'd started between the tangle of raspberry bushes and the south side of the cabin. He was proud of his little plot of earth. The beets and spinach were making way for pumpkins and squash. The last lonely tomato dangled from the vine.

Hux opened the book and closed it again.

An owl hooted in a distant tree. The echo of it took awhile to reach him; the delay reminded him of how alone he was just then.

Maybe he should have gone to town with Gunther after all and made merry with shots of cheap whiskey and flushed girls until he forgot how much he missed Leah. How much he missed his father. His mother. Lulu. Reddy.

Until he forgot that everyone who ever mattered was gone.

Sometimes Hux felt like a child living out here this way. Sometimes he felt like an old man. Sometimes he heard his mother calling to him from the grave, her chest rattling like wet bones. *Do the right thing, Hux. Go get your sister. Bring her home.*

18

❧ Until the day of her death, Hux's mother kept a grim secret. Whenever she felt the truth bubbling up, she swallowed it down until her insides turned black from its poison.

All the years of her girlhood, Hux's mother had worn a green ribbon in her long wheat-colored hair. Her cheeks were pink. Her heart light. Her eyes were the only part of her that pointed to something heavier; they were the color of river stones.

According to Hux's father, his mother looked like the girls who worked in the *Bier* gardens in Berlin, girls who charmed customers with plates of sausages and flashes of milky skin. On the day Hux's father arrived in Yellow Falls from Germany and saw Hux's mother spinning in front of a mirror in the dress shop, he wanted to marry her. At the time, he only knew how to say two things in English. *How do I get to the Dakotas?* and *Would you like a butterfly?* He said both of these things to Hux's mother, who laughed, but not unkindly.

Hux didn't know the girl who wore a ribbon in her hair;

he'd only known a woman who wore her disappointments like a saddle on her face. A woman who wanted to be happy but couldn't. Hux still didn't know what provoked her to tell the truth the last day of her life.

"I can smell my own death," she'd said when the sun came up and Hux passed by the foot of her bed on his way to his shoes and the door. "It doesn't smell good."

"You're not going to die, Mom," he'd said. He was afraid of her. Her skin had yellowed and hung from her body like drapes, and in his heart he knew that meant she was right about dying, and he didn't want her to go. He still needed her. He was only fifteen.

"Everything's been spoiled," his mother said.

Hux didn't know his mother had a blockage in her heart, which was why purple rosettes made veiny bouquets of her legs and brown mucus gathered in the corners of her eyes. He didn't know her liver had stopped working.

"Can you keep a secret?" she said.

"Yes," Hux said, although no one had asked him to keep one before.

"Because I don't feel like dying without telling someone," his mother said. "I suppose I don't feel like dying at all, and yet here I am."

That day Hux sat on the edge of the bed next to his mother's feet, which were blue and scaly and swollen to nearly twice their normal size. His father had gone to Yellow Falls to get the doctor, since his mother couldn't travel over the rough roads to see him anymore. Hux was supposed to spoon-feed her warm broth while he was gone, but when he'd brought out a mug of it, his mother said, "It's no use feeding me now," and Hux took it back to the kitchen. She wouldn't let him put a cool washcloth on her forehead either, which he was glad for; he didn't want to touch the skin that wasn't hers anymore.

"Do you remember the year your father was in Germany?" his mother said.

Hux shook his head.

"I suppose you don't," his mother said. "You were just a baby. A lovely baby."

Both his mother and father had referred to the year they were separated by an ocean before, but Hux didn't remember living alone with his mother in the cabin. He didn't remember how his mother had waited each time Reddy went to Yellow Falls, hoping for a letter from Hux's father and being disappointed when Reddy didn't return with one.

"I wanted to prove I could take care of us," his mother said. "You and me."

Hux's mother hoisted herself up in the bed, groaning like an animal. If his father had been at home, Hux would have run out to the work shed to hide. Ever since his mother had gotten sick, he'd put a blanket over the window and pretended he was in the Arctic.

"Lulu came with seeds to start a garden that first day," his mother said. "She was good to me from the start. The coonskin coat—where is it?—belonged first to her."

Hux went to the closet to get the coat, which he draped over his mother's legs. Over the years, most of the fur had fallen away, and the coat had lost its warmth. Still, his mother wouldn't get rid of it. She said whoever wore it wore strength on her shoulders.

"Lulu saved my life," his mother said. "Where is she?"

"She died last year, Mom," Hux said.

"Oh," his mother said. "I remember now."

Lulu had been walking in the forest a few miles north, surveying whether it was a good year for trapping or not, when she stepped on an old iron bear trap and it closed around her ankle, its teeth all but severing her foot from her leg. She bled to death before Reddy found her and the scrap of paper in her hand.

Goddamn poachers! the paper said. *They got me.*

Gunther took a gun out to the forest after they buried her and came back with a buck even though it wasn't hunting season. Reddy took to drinking in the open. Once a week until she got sick, Hux's mother would go over there to straighten up. She'd make a pot of chicken broth and wouldn't leave until Reddy had eaten a bowl.

Once Hux saw her put a splash of whiskey into the broth.

"He's a great man," she said when Hux asked her why she did that.

Sometimes his mother would make an egg pie the way Reddy did for her when Tuna, his mother's beloved little bird, died. Hux remembered that bird, her throat white as snow. He remembered her flying around the cabin in the mornings after his mother had given her a handful of sunflower seeds. He remembered how one afternoon she fell from the rafters like a stone. How his mother took Tuna in her arms like a child. How she wept and wept.

"I hope you don't hate me for what I'm about to tell you," Hux's mother said to him from her bed. "You were always such a good boy. Do you know that? We were doing so well. The garden was growing. Your grandparents were going to come for the first time."

Hux didn't remember their first visit to Evergreen, but he remembered the other ones. They'd bring him candy from the general store, and his grandfather would take him fishing for trout down by the river. Hux only visited their apartment once, and he'd stayed in his mother's old bedroom, playing with all of her treasures instead of sleeping. On the night table was a book about a woman who went west to pioneer with her family. Hux didn't like the story much, but he liked how one of the characters shared his father's name.

"I should have listened to your grandmother," Hux's mother said. "We got a letter from the government that summer. They were going to rebuild that dam they've been talking about forever. They were going to bring us light."

His mother slumped back down in the bed, a movement that shifted the metal pan beneath the lower half of her body. Urine spilled onto the sheets, which were stained yellow from previous accidents. When Hux moved to get a dry cloth, his mother grabbed his hand.

"He could tell I didn't have a survival instinct."

"Who?" Hux said.

"Cullen O'Shea," his mother said. "He came one morning to survey the property. I've never forgotten those dimples. Some people are evil to the core."

When Hux didn't say anything, his mother said, "His hands were scissors for me."

"You need to rest if you want to get better, Mom."

His mother looked at him sadly. "I didn't shoot until he was gone. That was the second-biggest mistake of my life."

Hux didn't want to know what the first one was. "You need to stay quiet."

"I'm glad I didn't live long enough to see the light come in," his mother said, looking up at the ceiling. "I wouldn't have been able to bear it."

"You're still alive, Mom," Hux said, thinking, *Don't go, don't go, don't go.*

"I had his child," his mother said, her chest starting to rattle the way the doctor said it would near the end. "Then I gave her away to some nuns in Green River."

Before she rolled over, she said, "You have a sister, Hux."

Then, after a few strained minutes, "I think I'll join Lulu now."

19

At first light, Hux headed over to Phee's place to finish building her porch. He didn't sleep well again and was hoping pounding nails and sawing boards would wear him out enough to set him straight for the next night. Gunther was right: he'd been lingering on the project longer than was necessary, reinforcing the porch floor and then reinforcing it again. If Phee had noticed, she didn't say anything. Sometimes she'd bring out mugs of coffee so bitter Hux could barely choke it down. Other times, though, she'd bring out a perfectly sweet apple pie. Maybe she had her own reasons for not wanting him to finish.

Phee lived on the western edge of the bog, which meant they probably wouldn't have crossed paths except they were in the general store at the same time, and Earl, the owner, introduced them. That day, Phee's basket was stacked with tins of sardines. Hux's was full of sweets. He figured he could grow the healthy stuff, and Gunther could supply the meat, but neither of them knew their way around a pie tin. The one time

Hux had tried to make cookies, they got so black even the birds wouldn't touch them.

"We make some pair, don't we?" Phee had said in the checkout line.

Phee was an older woman, with silver hair twirled up on her head like a nest, but with a brightness of eyes that made her seem younger than she was. That first day, she was wearing a long yellow dress with a pair of muddy waders. Hux liked that about her from the start—how she could be practical and impractical at the same time, tough and dainty.

"For Liddy. My cat," she'd said, motioning to the sardines in her basket. "She likes the ones packed in oil. She's a brat."

Hux had looked down at the bags of rainbow-colored candy in his basket with more than a twinge of embarrassment. "I guess I'm doing my part to keep the dentist in business."

"I'd rather pull my own tooth out than see him again."

Hux had thought of Gunther standing in front of a mirror with pliers and a cotton ball soaked with whiskey, his homespun version of dentistry. "That's what my friend does."

"He sounds smart," Phee had said.

Hux had laughed. "Not really."

Ever since then, he'd been building a porch for her.

The fall sun shone brightly as Hux drove around the southern tip of bog to the western side where Phee lived. Woodland caribou used to thrive here until their migration routes were cut off by the northern timber industry. The small bands that were stranded in Evergreen eventually died off or were poached by hunters. You could still see their old bleached bones reflecting in the sun sometimes. You could still hear the clicking of their feet. Hux rarely saw an animal or a bird at work in the bog, but if he paid attention he'd see evidence of their industry. The great gray owl bred here during the summer along with the warblers and thrushes. To Hux the most interesting part of the bog wasn't the birds or the animals; it was the plant life. The pitcher plants were the most cunning of them all.

"Sometimes I forget how fortunate we are to be on top of the food chain," Phee said when Hux showed her how they trapped and dissolved insects.

Hux worked on her porch all morning with the same pre-emptive regret he'd felt before Leah left, when he knew he could still stop her but couldn't make himself block her way. When he was around Phee, he felt like that sunny-yellow dress of hers, and in Evergreen that was a hard thing to give up, especially with winter coming, all those blue hours.

All night Hux had sat up in his bunk bed thinking about his mother and father, about Lulu and Reddy—everyone that was gone. Gunther's last bar girl said Evergreen was probably cursed and gave Gunther a small bundle of sage tied with twine, which he was supposed to light on fire and wave around the cabin to clear out old spirits and bad luck. Gunther had laughed at her, but Hux wouldn't have minded waving the sage around.

A few weeks before Leah came to Evergreen and a few weeks after his father finally succumbed to pneumonia, Hux found a cedar box with a flower etched on the front beneath a stack of his father's wool sweaters in the closet. Sometimes Hux doubted his mother had said anything about the light coming in and the man named Cullen O'Shea who was going to bring it to her. Sometimes he thought he'd made the story up, like his stories about the Arctic. But what she told him was the truth, and his father must have known it for years. Inside the box were two pieces of pink paper. Another woman's letter took up the first piece. A woman named Meg. On the second piece, there was a small red footprint, a thin curve of an arch on paper, and words his mother had written next to it.

My daughter. Born April 16, 1940.

"Where's your mind this morning?" Phee said, handing Hux a mug of coffee.

"About a million places," Hux said. "I'm sorry, Phee. I'm taking too long."

Hux set down his hammer. The mosquitoes and blackflies had already died off, which made the going easier than when he'd started the project. The last of the season's frogs were calling to one another in the bog.

"Do you want to hear the truth?" Phee said, sitting on the step beside him. "I think we both don't want you to finish this porch. I'm sure you've noticed I don't have a whole lot of neighbors out here."

"I bet Earl would like to move in with you," Hux said.

"He doesn't discount sardines for you, too?" Phee said. She rubbed her hands together as if she were cold. "If I'm old enough to be your grandmother, how old does that make Earl? Wait. Don't say it. I don't want to know."

"Ancient," Hux said.

Phee tapped Hux on the knee with her index finger. "I've still got a few years' worth of vanity left in me. Maybe less if we count my arthritis."

"Does it hurt?" Hux said.

"On the good days I can open a jar. On the bad days I can't."

"What kind of day is it today?"

Phee looked at her almost-finished porch, which would probably outlast both of them. She leaned against the railing. "A good one."

The two of them sat next to each other on the top step with

their coffee, looking out at the bog and up at the sky, listening to the birds chirping in the branches of trees, as if they'd been friends for a long time.

"Can I ask you something?" Hux said after a while.

"Sure," Phee said.

Hux didn't know why then or why her, but he wanted to tell Phee about that cedar box and his sister's footprint inside. He wanted to tell her about the light and Cullen O'Shea. About how he didn't know why his father had kept the box hidden in the closet all those years. Hux hadn't even told Gunther he had a sister somewhere out there in the world. He'd just sat alone with the truth, figuring if he sat long enough he'd know what to do with it.

"You want to know why I came out this way, don't you?" Phee said, granting him a little grace, a little more time, with the touch of her hand. "My husband and I couldn't have children," she said. "I'm all twisted up in the places I need to be straight and straight in the places I need to be twisted up." Phee touched the silver ring on her finger. "Milty wanted children more than anything else."

Hux wanted to tell Phee he was sorry, but he didn't want to embarrass her the way Gunther got embarrassed when they talked too close to their hearts.

"I came here because I was always looking out a window at the kids playing in our neighborhood," she said. "What a waste those years were. I should have closed the blinds."

"What happened to your husband?" Hux said.

"He's still sitting in the chair I left him in," Phee said.

What if his sister had been waiting for him like that? Hux thought. He thought of his mother, too—of all she'd endured and how that endurance had disfigured her from the inside out. He wanted her to finally be happy, wherever she was.

Phee finished her coffee and called to Liddy, who was sunning herself on the woodpile, her throne, and then said to Hux, "Can I ask you something now?"

"Sure," Hux said, bracing himself.

But Phee only smiled. "You think my coffee's too bitter, don't you?"

20

✦ Hux didn't like the idea of going to an orphanage, especially a religious one. He'd never set foot in a church before,
and his only knowledge of them came from what Gunther
told him about the Catholic church in Yellow Falls, where the
priest could supposedly take one look at you and tell you all
the ways in which you were eternally damned. Gunther loved
the idea of that. He loved the fervor of it all, the gore. Heaven
versus hell! God versus the devil! Sometimes he'd sit in the
pew with a flask or a girl or both, daring the priest to come
over and assess him. Sometimes he'd try to get Hux to go with
him for entertainment's sake (*the sake of your soul!*), but Hux
didn't like the idea of someone being able to look through him.
He liked the words *winter* and *woods* and *snow*. He liked a good
covering. A thick coat.

Halfway to the orphanage in Green River, Hux pulled over
to the side of the road. He didn't feel like himself when he
wasn't in the woods. The road to Green River was flat and
the view open. Brittle alfalfa fields stretched to the horizon

in every direction. Hux was thinking about turning back altogether. He looked at the piece of pink paper on the passenger seat, the imprint of his sister's slight foot. Even though she was only a year younger than him, Hux kept thinking he'd find a bright-eyed little girl waiting for him at the orphanage. He kept thinking he owed this girl something.

Unless his sister had become a nun, like a few orphans probably did, deep down Hux knew she wouldn't be there anymore and that she wasn't little anymore either, and there was some comfort in that. He figured he'd sit with one of the nuns, and she'd hand him an address or some other vital piece of information to move him closer to her.

When he wasn't thinking about that little girl, Hux liked to imagine his sister was married by now with a child of her own, like the prettiest girls in Yellow Falls who married their high school sweethearts and gave birth to the next generation of them all in the same year. He liked to imagine a group of nuns having reared her as if she were their own, taking turns singing little hymns and bouncing her on their knees. Hux wondered what she'd look like, if seeing her would be like seeing his mother again in her true unburdened form. *My sister,* he thought. He made up names for her when he couldn't sleep. Maybe she was a Catherine or a May. Or something fancier than that. Lorraine. Victoria. Maybe she'd turn out to be like the priest, and she'd be able to see through him and understand why he was sitting on the side of a road in the middle of nowhere.

Hux wished Gunther were in the passenger seat, pointing a gun at him to make him keep going. *Buck up,* Gunther would have said. *At least your ma didn't get poached.* But that was the other thing, the dark thing, the thing named Cullen O'Shea. What if he saw her for the first time and, like his mother, wanted to let her go again?

Hux sat while the wind rocked the truck and his breath fogged the windows. He thought of the cabin and the oxeye meadow, the river and the porch. Even though he didn't want to, he thought of his mother helpless on the cabin floor, the same floor Hux used to crawl across before he could walk, the same floor he used to eat crumbs from like his mother's bird, Tuna. Hux thought of his father stuffing that cedar box, this pink paper, beneath his wool sweaters in the closet—the only unbrave thing he ever did.

Hux steered the truck back onto the road.

You should have done something, Dad.

Hopewell was the name of the orphanage, which seemed pleasant enough until Hux drove through the iron gates and sat with the head nun, the only nun as far as he could tell.

Sister Cordelia, she called herself.

Hux had never met a nun before and was intimidated by her black robe, along with the straight way she sat in her chair as if God himself were pulling her shoulders back. Sister Cordelia had a large brown mole on her cheek and one above her lip. When she spoke, the moles and the thick black hairs that grew out of them spoke, too. She wore a heavy silver cross around her neck and seemed strangely powerful for being so old.

The office contained a metal desk, two chairs, and a cross on the wall with a ceramic Jesus affixed to it. The two of them sat on either side of the desk, schoolmarm and schoolboy, the way Hux imagined he would have sat at the school in Yellow Falls if it had been closer and he'd been allowed to go. Sister Cordelia looked at Hux as if she could tell he'd never been to church or read the Bible. Hux could barely meet her dark eyes, and yet there was nothing else to look at in their place unless he looked at the bloody arms and legs of Jesus on the cross or the moles between the deep wrinkles on her face.

The yellowed window shade was drawn.

Sister Cordelia didn't speak for a long time. She only stared at Hux, which prompted him to open his mouth. Even though he spent most of his days in silence, this kind made him nervous. He wondered out loud where all the children were. Why didn't he hear them in the hallways? Since being invited in, Hux hadn't seen any signs of childhood. No toys. No little shoes by the door. No drawings. Whatever else little girls adored.

His questions went unanswered.

So Hux went on. He told Sister Cordelia he was looking for his sister, his name was Hux, and he lived in Evergreen.

"So you're Hux," Sister Cordelia said, quieting him with the rise of her hand. "I've been waiting a very long time to know what those three letters meant."

"You know who I am?" Hux said.

"Now I do," Sister Cordelia said. "Your name was stitched on her baby blanket."

Hux leaned forward. "My sister's?"

Sister Cordelia rested her chin in the palm of her hand. She looked at Hux from different angles, as if she were deciding something important about him.

A full minute passed this way, and then another.

"I let her go when she was fourteen," she finally said, with what Hux recognized as pity. It was the way Earl talked to him whenever he went to the general store for supplies. *Poor boy,* he would say though Hux was a grown man now. *It's a great hardship to be all alone in the world.* The man would always put an extra can of soup into his bag.

"Don't you have to keep kids until they're eighteen?" Hux said.

"You should stop troubling yourself and go home," Sister Cordelia said. "You're a decent young man, I can tell. No religious training, but that can be overlooked in some cases. I suggest you get yourself to a church and find a nice woman to marry. Have the Lord's children and *keep* them. Then you'll have lived a more Christian life than your mother."

"You knew her?" Hux said.

Sister Cordelia opened one of the desk drawers and took out a worn manila folder stuffed full of yellowed paper, debating, it seemed, whether she was going to give it to Hux or not. "I watched your mother leave your sister on our doorstep. For a brief time, I thought she'd change her mind, but she didn't. She bled onto the walkway, which I scrubbed clean."

Hux had assumed his father was the only one with a war story; he'd escaped the Nazis and Germany with nothing but the clothes on his back and had worked his way home by stoking the fires in a steamship first and then cleaning the floors in Grand Central Station until he'd earned enough for a ticket to Minnesota. Until Hux's mother was in his arms once again. His father had said that was the best day of his life, seeing his family again.

His mother said she was disappointed he didn't bring her a bouquet of edelweiss.

"She was a prostitute, wasn't she?" Sister Cordelia said. "They all are, coming to us in the middle of the night like they do. They think I can't see them or their tarnished souls. I wonder why she kept you. Maybe a boy seemed more useful to her."

"She wasn't what you say," Hux said, raising his voice more than was right in front of a woman. "She was my mother. She was wonderful. She died when I was fifteen."

"If you say so," Sister Cordelia said, getting up from the desk. She lifted the window shade and stood staring at a group of girls huddled together outside. The girls were wearing white blouses and gray skirts when they should have been wearing coats and hats.

"Aren't they cold?" Hux said, wanting to give them his work shirt, his warmth.

"Nobody grows strong by being coddled, young man," Sister Cordelia said. "That's my work here: to take the sins these girls are born with and restore them through the Word."

"But they're only children," Hux said when one of the little girls met his eyes. She was just like the sister he'd been picturing all this time. Her hair was swept back into a ponytail. Her cheeks were pink. "Why weren't any of them adopted? Why wasn't my sister?"

"Naamah was meant to serve God. I suppose the others weren't cute enough."

"That's her name?" Hux said. He didn't know what it meant or even how to spell it, but he was happy to finally know it. Naamah. In it, he saw the future. He saw home.

"It was when she belonged to me," Sister Cordelia said, turning away from the window. She walked over to Hux. "Do you believe in the devil?"

"I don't know," Hux said.

Sister Cordelia handed Hux the folder. She rolled up her black sleeve, exposing her forearm, which was purple and scarred, as if, like Jesus, she'd been nailed to the cross. "You should. He's everywhere. For a long time he had hold of your sister. Maybe he still does."

Hux opened the folder and read the topmost piece of paper in it.

April 16, 1940. Another infant has been brought to us by her mother, who abandoned her to our care like all the other mothers. Why do they keep opening themselves up in such unholy ways? We've decided not to pursue the mother and instead, in accordance with the laws of Minnesota and the greater laws of God, raise the child as a Christian to be adopted by a family who practices our values or raised by us if no one sees fit to take her home. I shall call her Naamah, for she is a fallen angel and I intend to restore her through the Word.

May 5, 1940. Naamah has been crying for daylong spells. I have taken over her care completely, since the doctor is useless in this matter and thinks she's simply adjusting to life at Hopewell. I've positioned her crib next to the holy-water font and hung a cross directly over it, so that she may know the Lord's sacrifice and behave accordingly. I don't care what the other nuns think. We must take swift and grave action now, so the Devil doesn't steal Naamah's soul out from underneath us. She's wooing him with her tears. He's going to get her. I know it. I'll do what I can with the help of the Lord.

October 9, 1940. No matter how hard I have tried to keep her from him, Naamah has let the Devil take hold of her. I see him in her gray eyes now, the way she hoards whatever milk I give her, the way she stuffs her fingers greedily into her mouth. I must strike now with my arsenal. I'll starve her if I have to. I must drive the Devil out.

Hux turned over the papers as if he'd find something that made sense of the first ones the farther in he got. What he was reading didn't seem like it could be real. His mother and father had never laid a cross finger on him, let alone a cross religious one. They never talked about the devil. Or even God. They were gentle woods people—sad, maybe—who taught him to be kind and treat others the way he wanted to be treated.

September 21, 1945. One war may have ended, but another one goes on here. Naamah has lost a tooth in the holy bread. I know she did it on purpose. God is stronger than the Devil, she will see. Until she repents stale bread is all she'll get to eat. She has so much potential, but sometimes I have to hurt her just to see it, to get down to the truth of it all. She doesn't understand what a kindness this is. She's still selfish enough to sit before me looking heartbroken. She doesn't understand His sacrifice.

"But everyone loses teeth," Hux said, letting a handful of the papers fall to the floor.

"They don't all do it while taking Communion," Sister Cordelia said.

June 4, 1950. Naamah's monthly blood has come. I've told her how unclean that makes her in God's eyes and she submitted to me cleansing her private parts with bleach. She's finally freeing herself from the Devil's hold. She's finally becoming mine.

"Why did you give this to me?" Hux said. He couldn't bear to read a single word more. "What would make you give this to me?"

Sister Cordelia closed the shade again. Gone was the girl with the ponytail, the pink cheeks, and the flicker of light in her eyes. Sister Cordelia kneeled before Hux and gathered the papers he'd dropped on the floor. She took great care to put them back in the folder in their original order. While she was sorting them, the covering she was wearing on her head shifted, exposing her bald and pale scalp, which only a few stray silver hairs crisscrossed anymore. "God punishes me, too," she said when she realized what he was looking at.

"Where is she?" Hux said.

"I've heard stories about her in the logging camps up north."

When Sister Cordelia stood, the bones in her knees cracked, and she reached for the corner of the desk to steady herself. She was weaker than Hux had originally thought, but he didn't offer her his hand. Her silver cross swung back and forth. She was breathing heavily.

"Holy Father," she said. "Give me strength."

And then Hux saw it. In front of him was a woman who'd lived her life on a leash of her own making and would die on one, and he felt sorry for her the way he felt sorry for wounded animals when there was no one to put them out of their misery. He wondered what had happened to make her this way. Had she ever been a little girl with a tender heart?

Sister Cordelia got herself back in her chair. When her cross stopped swinging and her breath belonged to her again, she touched the manila folder as if she were touching the trees it was made from, the forest, the ancient history.

"I loved her," she said. "I love her still."

21

🍂 Hux drove away from the orphanage with only one thought: if his mother had spoken up earlier, that manila folder would have been half as thick. Together, his mother and his father could have mustered their courage and brought Naamah back to Evergreen. They could have shown her what it was like to be loved without also being hated.

Hux thought of the girl he'd seen outside the window at Hopewell. He imagined teaching her how to split logs in the forest. How to preserve what was beautiful about an animal. What was everlasting. But with each new mile he drove, his vision of her faded until all he saw was the blurry outline of her face.

Hux drove to the first of the two logging camps he knew were still in operation. The rest of them were positioned closer to towns and had been shut down when the roads were paved and the loggers could travel back and forth easily. Hux went empty-handed, hoping he would find his sister and hoping he wouldn't all at once. He parked the truck and searched the scattering of cabins, the camp store, and the tavern, repeating her name—*Naamah, Naamah, Naamah*—to strangers who looked at him with yellow whiskey stares.

"I might've had a good time with her," one of the men said, nuzzling his face into his arm as if it were a woman when Hux walked past him.

"We all might have," another one said, laughing the way men did sometimes.

"Got any booze?" said a third.

These men were more grizzled than any Hux had seen in Yellow Falls. He walked past them without saying anything because his father had taught him never to fight a man who wasn't worthy of his fist.

"You up for some fun, mister?" a girl not much older than the one at Hopewell asked Hux. She was wearing red lipstick, which was badly smeared. One of her plaid knee socks was pulled up, and one was pushed down to her ankle.

"No," Hux said. She belonged in front of a blackboard at school. Or in her mother's care. What kind of man would press his lips to hers?

Cullen O'Shea, Hux kept thinking when he looked at those knee socks. Hux wondered if he would have taken that shot. Gunther would have made sure the man was lying under an outhouse for all eternity. Nothing would have made him happier than nature's call.

"No," Hux said again to the girl.

He slipped back into the camp store with a tightness in his chest that had been expanding upward and outward ever since he'd left Evergreen. He walked up and down the aisles and bought the first cheerful thing he found: a bag of striped peppermint sticks.

The girl was still standing outside when he came out.

Hux wasn't fool enough to think he could save all the lost girls. All he could do for this one was give her some candy.

Hux drove farther north, alternating between running the heater when he was able to trick himself into thinking about the weather or the woodpile or the canning he still had to do before winter set in and opening the window when he thought about Sister Cordelia and Hopewell and that knee-sock girl instead. From inside the truck, Hux could smell the crisp pine needles on the forest floor, which was why he kept the window open the rest of the way: the scent of the needles reminded him of home. One year when Hux was little, he boiled a pot of the green ones in water and poured the liquid into a glass bottle, which he gave to his mother for her birthday because she said the scent of pine made her feel clean and feeling clean made her happy. He didn't understand what she meant, but he remembered how she smiled when she took the top off that bottle. He remembered smiling, too.

The second logging camp was more remote than the first. There were still forests that hadn't been touched by the blade of a saw up here, a sight almost harder to bear than the forests that had. Hux was part of the destruction, but he didn't ever use more of anything than he needed. Except for maybe whiskey once in a while. Or salt.

Leah used to make fun of him for that. *You're so moderate,* she'd say. *Sometimes I want you to eat a whole turkey or throw one or yell.*

She probably would have done better with someone like Gunther, only his idea of faithfulness was different than hers. Fat, thin, tall, short, blond, brunette, redhead—Gunther loved every kind of woman. And they loved him, too. He could be with a different girl every night, and none of them would ever throw a drink in his face.

Hux parked the truck next to a few others more beat up than his. Instead of cabins, this camp was scattered with canvas tents. Nothing was paved. Everything was dirt. When the wind blew, so did the dust. Here, as in the first camp, men made their wages by destroying the forest. The few Hux passed wore coarse expressions as if life had chopped them down and they were glad to return the favor.

Men went to logging camps because there were no jobs in the places they came from, at least not for them. Usually they were people who couldn't live the normal way without getting in trouble. Some of them had lost their families. Some of them never had families. Hux guessed the women came for the same reasons. In this camp, they sat on the ground outside the scattering of tents, waiting for the men's workday to be done so theirs could begin. None of them was as young as the girl with the knee socks. They didn't look like they could be saved. They didn't look like they wanted to be.

When Hux was growing up, his father took him to this logging camp to buy planks for the woodshed because they were cheaper than at the lumberyard in Yellow Falls, where they'd gotten a discount until Hux's grandfather died. His mother had wanted to come along for the ride and the fresh air, but his father had told her it was better for her to stay in Evergreen. She was just beginning to get sick then. He said he didn't want her to catch a cold. Hux remembered waiting outside the lumberyard office while his father did business. He remembered thinking the women were pretty, which shocked him now.

When his father came out with a purchase slip and they were on their way back to Evergreen, Hux had asked him why all those women were sitting in the dirt.

"Where else are they going to sit?" his father had said.

Hux stopped to talk to each of the women now, hoping his sister wouldn't turn out to be one of them. He declined their offers of whiskey and good times and gave them each a peppermint stick, which made him feel bad because it made him feel better.

He walked until there was nowhere left to walk but into the bar, the only building in the camp with walls. He slipped in through the saloon-style doors and sat down at the bar, which was made of plywood no one had bothered to sand smooth. He ordered a glass of beer and a shot of whiskey, a hamburger, and fries. The bartender wrote his order on a slip and went back to the kitchen where a man was peeling a giant pile of potatoes and smoking a cigarette at the same time. When he read the order, he looked over at Hux.

"You mind if it's venison?" he said. "That's all we've got this time of year."

Hux said he didn't mind and went back to his beer and the bowl of peanuts the bartender set in front of him. Though Hux wanted to find his sister, not finding her here would bring some comfort, too. The longer he was away from the orphanage, the more he knew he should have gone to the police about Sister Cordelia. *I'll starve her if I have to.* She believed in what she'd done—he could tell that because she'd looked him in the eye while he read the pages in that folder. But he could also tell there was more to the story than she'd been willing to say. *I let her go when she was fourteen.*

"You up here looking for work?" the bartender said.

"Thinking about it," Hux said.

The bartender offered him a cigarette, and he took one even though he didn't normally smoke anything other than his father's old pipe and the tobacco Earl set aside for him once in a while at the general store.

"They lost one on the blasting crew last week," the bartender said. "You've got to have steel balls for that. It pays double though."

"I think I have regular ones," Hux said, exhaling a cloud of smoke.

"Too bad," said the bartender.

When Hux finished the cigarette the bartender offered him another. "Rough day, huh? They all are, aren't they?"

Hux thought of all the days he and Gunther had spent by the river fishing and swimming and drying off in the sun during the last year. Sometimes Leah would come down, too. Or one of Gunther's girls, who'd say silly things that made all of them laugh.

"Some are better than others," Hux said.

The bartender looked at the door and at the woman who was on her way into the bar. He gathered up the condiments on the shelf behind him, stuffing what he could back into jars and putting them in the kitchen.

"Brace yourself," he said. "Here comes a tornado."

Even though he'd never seen a picture of her, Hux knew the woman who came through the door was his sister the way he knew in his heart what she was doing in the logging camp. She walked in wearing a white undershirt and tight jeans that were stuffed into a pair of scuffed cowboy boots. She had long black hair down to her waist, which was full of leaves and sticks and pine needles. Out of all the women he'd seen today, she was the only one who still had a mouth full of teeth. Her body was long and lean and leggy, coltish, but there was steel in her stone-colored eyes. Something old and hard and sad.

They were just like his mother's.

"I'll take a shot of rye," she said to the bartender, plucking an olive from one of the jars he didn't have time to hide. The bartender glanced at her skeptically until she looked around the room, set her sights on Hux, and said, "You know I'm good for it."

"Just this one," the bartender said. "After that I need to see some money."

"You don't think I'm charming anymore?" she said, swinging her hips as if there were music playing. Unlike the women outside, she wasn't wearing makeup or cheap perfume. Hux didn't know what that meant. "You used to like when I came in here. You used to call me darling. Don't you remember that? We'd go out back in the sweetgrass."

"You used to pay for what you took," the bartender said.

"You used to, too." She looked at him seriously for a minute before deciding the whole thing was funny. She laughed but in an awful way.

Hux put out a few bills on her behalf, which only made her laugh more.

"You're all the same," she said. "Every one of you."

A single dimple appeared at the left corner of her mouth, and it broke Hux's heart to see. All he could think of was getting her out of here. The smell of grease from the kitchen was making him sick. His thoughts were making him sick. The words *out back* and *sweetgrass*.

A bell rang outside, which meant the men would be getting off work soon and would come in here looking for relief. Hux couldn't let her go with one of them or more than one of them or all of them. He couldn't watch her sell herself for an olive or a shot of rye or whatever it was she wanted this far north.

The cook brought out his food, but Hux couldn't touch it.

"You want some?" he said sliding his plate over to her. She

was hungry, he could tell. Her expression was the same as the strays that lived in the dirt alleys back in Yellow Falls.

"What do you want for it?" she said. She eyed the hamburger but made no movement toward the plate of food or the empty stool next to Hux.

"Nothing," Hux said.

Naamah, he thought. *Naamah.*

"Did you hear that, Bill?" she said to the bartender. "He's my fairy godfather. He doesn't want anything."

"I heard," the bartender said.

"Yeah, I've heard that one before, too," she said.

"I have something that belongs to you out in my truck," Hux said, visualizing the piece of pink paper in the glove compartment. He wanted to take off her boot and see if that curve was still there.

"It'll take more than a hamburger to get me in your truck, Bud," she said.

Hux handed her his wallet, which contained just under a hundred dollars, what was left of the money his father had put in the sugar tin before he died. Leah had tried to get him to spend it on a kayak. She said a leaky old rowboat was no way to cross the river. When she was mad about her shoes getting wet, she used to hide the oars in the forest.

Naamah looked through the wallet, took out the crisp bills, and counted them one by one before she stuffed them into the pocket of her jeans.

"I'll call you the Lord Almighty, if that's what you want," she said. "You're one of the sick ones. Drive up here even though you have a wife and kid, right? You're either going to be rough, which'll cost you extra, or you'll want me to hold you. I know your type."

"I just want to talk," Hux said.

"At least you're not bad looking," she said, plucking a fry off his plate. "Your beard's going to scrape me up, but I can live with that. Some of them you have to wait till dark to be with. You'd think they'd smell pure like the trees with what they do all day, but they don't. It's disappointing, if you want to know the truth."

She narrowed her eyes. "You sure you know what you're doing, Bud?"

No, Hux thought, because he didn't. He offered her a peppermint stick, which she tucked into her shirt pocket. The next one he offered her she ate right in front of him. When she licked the peppermint stick, she closed her eyes for a minute as if the sugar were transporting her somewhere bright and sweet and cheerful. She swung her legs a little on her stool, but stopped when she noticed Hux looking at them.

When she'd chewed up the last of the red-and-white swirls, Hux got up from the stool, hoping he wouldn't have to ask her to follow him, which he didn't. She took his arm, and the two of them walked to his truck.

"So you're a gentleman then," she said.

"Do you mind if we drive a bit?" Hux said, opening the passenger door for her and closing it when she got in.

"That'll cost you more," she said.

"All right," Hux said, putting the key in the ignition and trying not to think about what she thought he was enlisting her for.

The two of them drove up the twisting dirt road, past a group of men who were working on taking down an old-growth pine tree in what was left of the light. A few of them were standing on stakes and harnessed to the trunk high up in the tree, and the others were looking on, waiting with chain saws and the chipping machine that would make mulch out of the branches. When they first moved to Evergreen, Hux's father had cleared the land around their cabin. He said he'd never worked harder on anything than all those stumps, all that pesky milk thistle. Hux's mother said he used to leave when the sun came up and come home when the sun went down. She saw him as much she saw the moon.

"Can I smoke?" Naamah said, putting her feet up on the dashboard. She pulled out a pack of cigarettes and lit one of them. "Want one?"

"No," Hux said, breathing easier once they'd turned out of the camp and were headed down the county road in the direction of Evergreen. When the pines that towered over the road turned into grass and weeds, Hux steered the truck to the side of the road.

"The county police might drive by," Naamah said. "They come out here sometimes."

Though he didn't want to frighten her, Hux locked the doors.

"So that's how you want it to be," Naamah said. "I knew you were too nice to be normal. Can I at least finish my cigarette before you unbuckle your belt?"

"*Sister Cordelia*," Hux said because he didn't know how else to tell her why he was there. He hated that he was wearing a belt. He hated Sister Cordelia, his father, even his mother, for a few beats of his heart. This wasn't how it was supposed to be. They were supposed to have grown up together like he and Gunther had. They were supposed to be brother and sister, not what she thought they were right now.

Hux expected her to try to unlock the door and run away from him. He'd been so occupied with trying not to hurt her he hadn't thought about the possibility of her hurting him. As if she were an animal, she started clawing at his face and neck.

She growled at him. She bit. She snapped.

"Christ! Christ! Christ!" she said, swiping at Hux's eyes with her fingernails before he could raise a hand to protect himself.

She was yelling and crying all at once.

"You don't get to do this to me," she said. "You let me go."

Hux wasn't sure whom she was talking to. When she'd scratched his skin raw, and the blood turned his collar red, she started scratching her own face, and Hux used his force to pin her to the seat so she couldn't hurt herself.

"I know what happened to you, Naamah," Hux said. "My mother is your mother. I'm your brother. *Hux.*"

As if his name was made of magic, Naamah stopped fighting and looked up at him with her big river-stone eyes. Unlike Hux's mother's, hers had tiny streaks of green running through them. The streaks were tenuous, like the first of spring's leaves.

"Your name was stitched on the corner of my blanket," she said.

Hux was still holding her wrists against the seat. He was tangled up in her long hair.

"It wasn't even really my blanket, was it?" she said as if that possibility hurt her more than the scratches on her face.

"I don't know," Hux said, easing his grip on her.

Naamah closed her eyes the way she had when she was eating that peppermint stick and only opened them when the heater came on, blowing summery air onto them.

Outside the light turned from yellow to orange to pink.

"What do you want?" she said, softening, which made Hux wonder which girl—this one or the one who'd traded herself for so little in the bar—was his sister.

Hux didn't know what he was doing in the logging camp any more than he knew what he was doing living alone in a rustic cabin deep in the Northwoods.

Hux looked down at his sister. He thought of all the lost years, and even though he knew he couldn't get them back—they couldn't get them back—he wanted to try anyway. He wanted to make what was wrong right.

Naamah was wearing a small silver cross on a chain around her neck, which pinched her skin a little at the clasp. She smelled like tobacco and peppermints.

"I want to take you home," Hux said.

22

✦ Hux didn't know what was more depressing: that all his sister's earthly belongings fit into a cloth laundry bag or the bag itself, which she'd reinforced with electrical tape, or the fact that she wouldn't let go of it. The whole way back to Evergreen, Naamah sat with the bag on her lap and a hand on the door as if at any moment she might change her mind, lift the handle, and tumble out of the truck onto the side of the road. The few moments she wasn't holding the door, she was smoking or eating the beef jerky Hux bought at one of the gas stations near Yellow Falls because he was hungry (and nervous) and figured she was, too. He avoided Green River altogether because he didn't want to think what Naamah would do if she saw Hopewell or Sister Cordelia again. Hux couldn't get her moles out of his mind, her creaking bones. *I love her still.* He wondered if what he was doing was right.

"You warm enough?" he said to Naamah when they were crossing the river, which had always felt like it belonged to

Gunther and him alone. Hux saw her looking at the water, which the moonlight was making diamonds out of.

"Is it cold?" she said.

"I'm comfortable," Hux said.

"I mean the water," Naamah said.

"Another month, and it'll be ice."

Naamah pressed her hand against the window. "Will you stop for a minute?"

"All right," Hux said, thinking she had to go to the bathroom or tend to some other womanly matter and didn't want to say so. He pulled over when they got to the boat landing canoers used when they got tired and wanted to be taken back to Yellow Falls. Sometimes Hux found beer cans down here or bags of half eaten potato chips or waterlogged hot-dog buns. He didn't understand that kind of disrespect for the land but knew it was only a matter of time before those things started showing up around the cabin, too; people weren't afraid of the woods the way they used to be. The pull of the river's current.

As soon as Hux parked the truck and put on the brake, Naamah was out the door, and though she left the laundry bag in the cab, she fled so quickly he thought she was running away from him. Her hair flew behind her like a black veil.

"Wait," he said, but she was already in the water, breaking its gemstone reflection.

Hux got out of the truck and walked down to the river's edge. After a few minutes, the water settled and the waves stopped lapping at his feet and he couldn't see where she was anymore. He called for her, even though he didn't feel like he had that right.

She didn't answer.

Hux stood a whole hour at the river's edge, listening for signs of his sister as the water floated by. Sometimes a branch would get caught on a rock out near the middle where the current was the strongest, and he'd think it was her for a minute. Or a frog would croak. Or a fish would splash. But Naamah never materialized. Maybe you couldn't wake up without a sister and have one by nightfall and expect everything to be on its way to fine. Maybe all she'd ever agreed to was a ride out of the logging camp.

A little after midnight, Hux went back to the truck to wait some more. He had a sleeping bag in the back and a jacket he could bunch up into a pillow.

When he opened his door, he saw Naamah sitting there, and though he had no idea how she'd gotten herself out of the river and into the truck without him noticing, he was glad to see her. She was combing her long, wet hair with her fingers. River water pooled in the seat beneath her. The cab smelled like moss and fish.

"I was watching you from a rock on the other side of the river," she said. "You looked sad the way you were standing."

"I didn't see you," Hux said.

"I didn't want you to," she said.

The laundry bag was on the floor by the stick shift now. Her cowboy boots, too. The windows were fogging from all the moisture in the cab.

"How long were you going to wait for me?" she said.

"Until morning," Hux said. "See if you changed your mind."

Naamah smiled, but not the brash way she did back in the logging camp. Sweetly. Her hands were shaking a little. Hux could see she was cold and rooted around until he found the sleeping bag, which he wrapped around her shoulders.

"This is a mistake," she said, fumbling for her cigarettes.

In this light, her lips looked blue.

"How do you figure?" Hux said.

Naamah offered him a cigarette, and he took one out of the package. Her matches were wet, so he pushed the lighter in and waited for it to glow red.

"I wouldn't have waited that long for you," she said when it finally did.

Hux turned on the defroster, which cleared away the fog. After that he turned on the heater until she stopped shaking. He thought of his mother, *their* mother, how much she must have missed Naamah over the years. When Hux was little, she used to linger in the craft section of the general store. Hux would go off looking for candy or toys or both, and when he found what he wanted, he'd walk up and down the aisles searching for her. Almost always, he'd find her exactly where he'd left her: in front of the girls' dress patterns or the boxes of hair ribbons. Sometimes he'd find her in front of the skeins of pink yarn, touching them as if they were made of more than just scratchy wool.

"It doesn't matter," Hux said. "I already know my way home."

The first night in the cabin was strange and not strange and strange all over again; Hux would remember it for the rest of his life. At half past two, he and Naamah walked through the cabin door together for the first time. Hux had left the kitchen light on, which made the navigation up the uneven porch steps easier.

Usually he didn't think much about the way the cabin looked, but tonight he was distinctly aware of all its little flaws and eccentricities. To start, the window above the sink was covered with curtains made of two different kinds of fabric—one with strawberries all over it and the other with ears of corn—because years ago the general store ran out of one or the other. In the main part of the room, a plywood board was still nailed to the wall where a window should have been. After his father died, Hux brought back the tradition of putting up a sketch like his mother did when she was still alive. A larkspur was up there now. The cupboards were too high. The shelves were too low. And even though Hux liked sleeping in the bunk beds his father built, despite Leah's protesting for a year straight about their lack of intimacy, they made him feel like a child now.

Hux walked into the kitchen and set his keys on the counter. He'd done his best to clean up the mess from Gunther's buck, but he saw now he'd missed a few thin streaks of blood on the tabletop. He should have made the cabin nice for her. Picked whatever wildflowers were left and stuck them in a vase. Bought her something at the dress shop in Yellow Falls. Perfume. Jewelry. A scarf. Something just for her.

"What do we do now?" Naamah said. She reached out to touch the sugar bowl on the table but pulled her hand away suddenly as if she were afraid she was going to break it.

"We sleep," Hux said, because he didn't know what else to do or to say and because his father used to say a good night of sleep gave a man's nerve back to him. Hux knew Naamah would want to know more about their mother, about the reasons she was dropped off at the orphanage and he wasn't, but he was hoping she wouldn't ask tonight. He didn't know how he was going to tell her what had happened.

"All right," she said.

Before they settled in for the night, Hux cleared out a shelf in the closet for her, but she wouldn't let go of the laundry bag.

"Whatever's in there is yours," Hux said. "I won't touch it. I promise."

He got out a hammer and a few nails and tacked a yellow

sheet up over the opening to the closet. "I'll change in the mud-room when I need to. You can change in here."

After Naamah put on a pair of old gray sweatpants and an equally old sweatshirt, Hux showed her to the top bunk bed, but she refused it. He even offered to switch with her and sleep up there instead, but Naamah wanted to sleep on the floor. She said the last time she slept in a bed was on a cot at the orphanage.

"At least take a pillow," Hux said.

She patted the laundry bag. "I already have one."

"What about a blanket?"

"I have one of those, too."

"Okay then," Hux said and turned off the light. A moment later he turned it back on. "I forgot to show you the outhouse."

"I'll find it if I need it," she said.

"It's out back."

"They usually are."

"Okay then," Hux said again, realizing how stupid he sounded after he turned out the light. He was relieved he couldn't see her and she couldn't see him, and wondered if she was, too. He didn't regret bringing her back here; he just hadn't thought far enough ahead about what they were sup-posed to do after they walked through the door. Maybe she hadn't either. Tomorrow Hux needed to cut wood and haul it back to the cabin. He needed to catch some fish—bluegills, bass, pike, trout, walleyes—and smoke it, so he wouldn't be stuck with potatoes all winter. He needed to work on Gunther's buck so he could sell it to someone and get more supplies at the general store. Maybe he'd smoke some of that meat, too. Thinking about work calmed Hux a little, except he didn't know what his sister normally did during the day up at the logging camp, what she'd do here. He didn't take her for a woman who liked to bake pies, but she didn't seem exactly like a lumberjack either.

Normally Hux fell asleep easily. Leah used to say he was like a bear hibernating on the bunk bed. Tonight, though, he didn't fall asleep until Naamah finally stopped thrashing around on the floor, clawing the air in her sleep.

In the logging camp, she said she'd slept outside on the forest floor, and that's where Hux found her when he woke after the first rays of golden light came through the kitchen window and swept across his face.

"I'm sorry. I tried. I just couldn't breathe in there," she said when he asked her why she was curled up on a bed of brown pine needles just beyond the cabin. Her long black hair was twisted around her. She looked like a bird in a nest.

"Okay," Hux said, which wasn't ever sentiment enough for Leah.

"Okay," Naamah said.

Hux asked her if she wanted to chop some wood. He didn't want to subject her to Gunther yet or share her with Phee. In a few days he'd take her across the river. "You don't have to chop it, I mean. You could just come."

"I know how to use an ax," she said, rising.

So Hux took her, the axes, a few thick slices of bread, and a thermos of coffee into the woods. As they walked along the footpath, he pointed out different types of plants and mosses, showing her which were edible and which weren't—*This one I rubbed on my face as a boy, and I looked like a tomato for three days*—but she already knew about them. He didn't want to ask her how because he thought the story might involve the logging camp and the men there. He wanted to erase that part of her life by filling it with his.

"This is a stinging nettle," he said. "This is milk thistle."

Where else are they going to sit? he could hear his father saying.

Hux didn't know what his father would think about Naamah. Or what his mother would think. He didn't even know what he thought yet. More than anything, he wanted to know why Naamah left that orphanage when she was so young, but she didn't owe him that.

When they reached the cedar tree Hux had felled a few days before, he opened the thermos and handed it to Naamah.

"I love the smell of coffee," she said. "The taste not so much."

"I put a lot of sugar in mine," Hux said.

Naamah took a sip, made a face, and handed the thermos back.

"You want some bread?" Hux said.

Naamah picked up an ax. "I want to chop wood."

While he drank coffee, Hux watched the way her black hair slid across her back each time she swung the ax. There were twigs and leaves stuck in it from sleeping on the ground in the logging camp and last night in Evergreen, and now little splinters of wood from the cedar tree were stuck to it, too. Naamah was used to working hard; he could tell that. When she got warm, she took off her sweatshirt, leaving her with only the white undershirt from the day before. He couldn't tell if it was still wet from the river or wet from her sweat.

Hux joined in after he finished the coffee. He could barely feel the moment of impact between the ax and the wood anymore, his calluses were so thick. Leah used to wear gloves when she went with him, but Naamah worked until she had blood blisters at the base of her fingers, and those blisters broke, and then she worked more.

It was like the two of them had chopped and stacked wood

together all their lives. They weren't competing the way Hux and Gunther did. They weren't betting anything. The sun was shining through the narrow spaces between the branches overhead. The air smelled of pine and cedar and tamarack sap— their hands and clothes were sticky from it.

Occasionally Hux thought he saw in Naamah the beginnings of a smile. A bird would land on a nearby branch or the wind would blow and the trees would rain needles on them and they'd stop swinging for a minute. Once, Naamah held her finger out and a grosbeak grazed it. Like Hux, she seemed to love being outside all the way to her bones.

She looked sorry when they cut the last of the wood.

"We'll come back soon," Hux said. "Wood's one thing I never have enough of."

Naamah sat on a log. She wiped her hands on her sweatpants, which stained the gray material with blood. "I know what you're thinking," she said.

"I've got stuff for that at home," Hux said, visualizing the package of bandages and the tin of salve he kept in the mudroom. Naamah was beat up pretty good. Her hands were swollen; parts of them looked like raw meat.

"You could have stopped without any hard feelings on my part," he said. "Out here you've got to know when to say mercy."

Naamah looked down at her hands. Her hair fell around her face like a curtain; a pinecone toppled out of it onto the forest floor.

"I didn't like it—all those men," she said.

"It isn't any of my business," Hux said, but his mind got caught up in the words *all those men* anyway. He thought of the girl with the knee sock pushed down around her ankle.

Naamah fumbled at the front of her neck until her fingers found her silver chain and cross. "I went there for her."

23

Naamah left the orphanage in the middle of an October snowstorm with only the clothes on her back, the boots on her feet, and the same laundry bag she'd brought with her to Evergreen. She didn't say why she left, and Hux didn't ask her. Until that day, she said she'd never felt snow on her skin. She didn't know it could be soft and biting all at once. She didn't know anything until she was alone in the woods for the first time.

Naamah rocked as she talked. She and Hux were sitting on the porch trying to hold on to the last of the day's sun. The waxwings were flying through the garden, plucking up what was left of the berries and dropping them on the ground.

A few weeks had passed since he and Naamah had first chopped wood together. Hux was still sleeping in his bunk bed and Naamah in her pine-needle nest beyond the front porch. In the mornings Hux would come out with a mug of coffee for her, which she'd sip from the frosty forest floor. She said all that sugar was growing on her.

Hux kept telling Naamah she didn't have to sleep outside, but she kept saying she did. He didn't know what she was going to do when the snow came, but he hoped she'd want to stay the winter and by then he'd find a way to lure her inside.

"I thought leaving Hopewell would make me free," Naamah said, rocking more and more slowly until she stopped altogether. She looked out into the woods.

"Did it?" Hux said, slowing down, too.

"Not exactly," Naamah said.

Hux thought she was going to tell him about the logging camp—why she stayed when she found out their mother wasn't there, that she'd never been there. But she didn't.

"I stood all night in a stand of evergreen trees a few hundred yards from Hopewell," she said. "I thought I was going to freeze to death like Sister Cordelia said."

Hux was listening to Naamah as if what she said were pieces of a puzzle that was going to take time to put together. He was listening for the corner pieces, the foundation.

"When I was bitten up by frost but still alive in the morning, I started walking through the woods," Naamah said. "There was a fountain in Green River that was supposed to make people's dreams come true, but when I got there it was empty."

Naamah lifted herself out of the rocking chair. She put her cigarettes in the pocket of the work shirt Hux had lent her. "I think I'll go inside now."

Hux handed her the matches, picturing her standing all by herself in the snow, thinking about how afraid she must have been even though she didn't say so.

"Are you hungry?" he said. He didn't want to push her into telling him more, but he didn't want to let her go either. About all he could think to do right then was feed her. "I could make pancakes. With that syrup you like so much."

Naamah smiled a little but not enough for her dimple to show, which seemed a kindness even though she didn't know the story of her face the way Hux did.

"Okay," she said.

That night, after they finished supper and Naamah was washing the dishes, Gunther came by for the first time since Hux had brought Naamah to Evergreen. Gunther had been out hunting royal bucks the last few weeks, and when he didn't find any of those he trapped a few foxes. He said he'd told Hux he'd be gone.

"I guess I forgot," Hux said.

"It's the Leah fog," Gunther said. He leaned against the doorframe. He was chewing on a twig, which was his version of a toothbrush. His cheeks were flushed. His hair ragged the way women liked it. He was wet from swimming across the river. He was also drunk.

"Aren't you going to invite me in?" he said, handing Hux a bottle of whiskey. "I sold a few nice pelts today. I brought the good stuff. Didn't you even miss me?"

"Not tonight," Hux said. From where he stood, he saw Naamah rinsing the dishes from supper. He could hear her humming, but he didn't recognize the tune.

Gunther leaned across the threshold. "You got someone in there?"

"No," Hux said, trying to close the door. "Good night."

Gunther hopped over a rocking chair and hurled himself off the porch, somehow managing to land on his feet. He ran to the kitchen window before Hux could pull the curtains shut. Naamah watched as Hux ran back to the door. Her hands were full of soap.

"You old dog," Gunther said. "Here I was feeling sorry for you. I was about to go out and find you another buck. Who is she? Where did you find her? What are you hiding?"

"She's my sister," Hux said because he'd never be able to get Gunther to leave without telling him the truth, and even then he didn't know if he'd be able to get him to go.

"And I'm your uncle," Gunther said. "I didn't take you for a paying customer."

Hux made a fist, but Gunther caught it before it did any damage to his face.

"You don't know how to fight," he said. "You're going to break your hand." He forced Hux's thumb out from beneath his fingers. "Now you can hit me."

Naamah sidled up to Hux at the door. "What's going on?"

"I was just telling your friend to hit me right here," Gunther said, pointing to his jaw.

Naamah put a hand on her hip, which she tilted ever so slightly in his direction.

"Why should he?" she said.

"I said something he didn't like," Gunther said.

"Maybe I should hit you, too, then," Naamah said. "I'm his sister after all."

After Hux was finished feeling proud Naamah would call herself his sister so soon, he recognized what was going on. She and Gunther were flirting with each other.

Naamah wiped her wet hands on her jeans and held one out to him. "I'm Naamah."

Gunther took it and kissed the top of it. When he finally let go of it, his lips had soap on them. "I'm in love," he said, licking them.

"All right. Enough's enough. You have to go," Hux said, pushing Gunther away from the door and down the steps.

Gunther's boots were wet and untied, and he kept falling over himself. "I'll come over tomorrow. I'll explain everything."

"She's the prettiest girl I've ever seen," Gunther said, looking up at the porch. "It's not just because I've been drinking either. That hair. Those eyes! She's like a wood angel."

"Go drink some more," Hux said. "It'll do you good to pass out. Just don't do it in the river. I don't want to pick crayfish out of your mouth."

"A fairy?" Gunther said, finally turning toward the river. "No, that's not it."

Gunther was halfway to the river when he found the word he was looking for.

"Nymph!" he called back, and Hux waved him off and closed the cabin door.

"I'm sorry about that," he said to Naamah. "Gunther's a handful."

"I don't mind," Naamah said, returning to the sink.

When the last of the dishes was clean, she dried them and put them away in the cupboard Hux normally used for his skinning tools, but she seemed proud of herself and Hux didn't want to discourage her. Hux got out the old book about the Arctic Circle. He should have been thinking about preservation—what was going to get them through the winter besides wood—but he kept thinking he had time to settle in. They had time.

Before they went to sleep that night, Naamah did something surprising. She brought the laundry bag inside, along with a blanket made out of old potato sacks she'd stuffed with goose feathers and stitched together with heavy twine. She said she thought she'd give the top bunk bed a try. When she spread her blanket over the existing wool one, a few of the white feathers floated down to the floor.

"Okay," Hux said, trying not to make a big deal about it, even though he didn't know why Naamah had changed her mind. Tonight wasn't any colder than the others. The sky was clear. The ground was dry. He tried to stop thinking; he didn't want his thoughts to scare her off. Sometimes he had the feeling she could hear them without his saying anything.

Hux changed in the mudroom, and Naamah changed in the closet. Both of them took turns with the flashlight in the outhouse. Before they got into the bunk beds, Naamah kneeled on the floor. At first, Hux thought she'd dropped something and was looking for it, but then he heard her say, "Amen," and she was on her feet again. He didn't ask her about it or the cross around her neck. He kept thinking of what he'd read in the file at the orphanage. *I intend to restore her through the Word.* He wondered if she believed in God or if it was some kind of reflex. Hux believed in the trees and the river and the sky.

When Naamah climbed up into the bunk bed, Hux turned out the light. They lay in silence for a while before Naamah spoke up in the darkness.

"Why did she leave me and not you?" she said.

Hux was grateful Naamah had waited as long as she had, but he still didn't know the best way to tell her what had happened, since he couldn't think of it, of *him,* without feeling sick to his stomach. Sick in his heart.

"Our fathers weren't the same person," he said.

"Who was mine?" Naamah said.

Hux shifted in the bunk bed. He didn't feel himself clenching his teeth until he released them. He heard his sigh, though. His deep exhale.

"He wasn't a good man, was he?" Naamah said.

"No," Hux said, trying to spare her his name if she would

let him. "He came the year my father was in Germany. Our mother couldn't keep him out."

"Do I look like him?" Naamah said.

Hux turned on the light and got out of bed to get the photograph of his mother and father on their wedding day. Even though the photograph was black and white, he knew his mother's dress was blue with tiny crystals sewn into the fabric and that she'd worked at Harvey Small's in order to buy it. His father wore a traveling suit made in Germany. Both of them had a certain glint in their expressions, a happiness to have found each other in a lumber town in northern Minnesota.

"You look like her," Hux said, handing her the picture frame.

Hux got back in the lower bunk to give Naamah some privacy. She didn't say anything for a long time, and Hux resisted the urge to fill the silence. He wondered if she was studying the photograph for traces of herself, if she was following the lines of their mother's face with her fingers like he did sometimes. He wondered, but he didn't ask.

Another feather floated down.

"Sister Cordelia used to say she was tainted by the devil," Naamah said finally. "She said that's why he wanted me so much. She said she could have kept me if she'd wanted to."

"I don't think it was that simple for her," Hux said.

Hux thought of Naamah's footprint on the piece of pink paper—the words *my daughter*—which he put in the glove compartment of his truck the night he took Naamah away from the logging camp when his name was the only proof she needed in order to believe he was who he said he was, who he said *she* was. He thought about getting up to get it. He thought about how, when he was little, sometimes his mother would look at him as if she expected to see someone else or at least hoped she would.

"I used to have dreams about her when I was still at Hopewell," Naamah said, the bunk bed creaking beneath her. "One time she and I were walking through the garden at the end of summer. She was singing a song about all these beautiful blue things. Even though I told her she'd get in trouble with Sister Cordelia, when we passed a grapevine she picked the biggest grape she saw. I watched her eat that grape like it was made of happiness."

"What happened after that?" Hux said.

"I woke up."

"Do you still dream about her?" Hux said.

"Yes, but the dreams aren't as nice. The last one I had I was standing in an alfalfa field and she ran over me with a truck."

Hux twisted his blanket in his hands. He couldn't change what his mother had done. In order to understand it, Hux had to let Cullen O'Shea in all over again. He had to picture him at the door. At the table. On the floor. A man with scissors for hands. Stones for a heart. He had to picture his mother with a gun in her hand.

Hux leaned out over the bunk bed and looked up at Naamah, who was hugging the picture frame as if it could hug her back. She asked Hux to turn out the light, which he did.

"Not a single person in this world has loved me," she said.

Hux reached up for her hand but couldn't find it in the dark. "I do," he said, and even though he did, albeit in a way he didn't understand, it didn't sound true.

"Guilt and love aren't the same thing," Naamah said, but kindly.

The next morning she was gone, and Hux wished he'd told her about how their mother used to linger in front of the pink yarn at the general store. He wished he'd told her about how she used to look at him and want her. He was sorry for the piece of paper in the glove compartment. He was sorry about it all.

Hux searched for her on the bed of pine needles at the forest's edge but didn't find her there. He walked through the meadow, where they'd sometimes drink their coffee, thinking maybe she'd gone for a walk. She liked to wander through the woods when there were no more chores left for her to do. He walked across the creek, over the springs, in and out of the little ravines. He sat on a stump for a while and then went back to the cabin, hoping she'd be waiting for him on the porch like the night she was waiting for him in the truck. Maybe she was watching to see what he'd do.

When she wasn't at the cabin, Hux took the rowboat across the river. Gunther could track people as well as he could track animals. According to him, Hux had the footfall of an old sap. Gunther was lighter on his feet, like how pond skaters balanced on the surface of the water but never broke through.

Hux knocked on Gunther's front door, but Gunther didn't open it.

Naamah did. She was wearing one of Gunther's plaid work shirts and looking back over her shoulder in the direction of the kitchen, laughing her logging-camp laugh.

It'll take more than a hamburger to get me in your truck, Bud.

Her dark hair trailed down the length of her back and was full of twigs and dirt and feathers. A strand of algae was stuck to her neck. Her feet were caked with dried mud. She squinted in the bright morning light.

"I was thirsty," she said, before Hux could say anything.

Gunther walked out of the bathroom with a towel wrapped around his waist. Before he saw Hux, he said, "I've got the worst goddamn headache in the world. Between your hands and the whiskey, I don't know which way is up. I think you drank more than me."

Gunther turned, and Hux saw the claw marks on his back.

"I don't see how you could have grown up in some orphanage. You belong out here in the trees." Gunther stopped talking when he saw Hux standing at the screened door.

"I'm going for a walk," Naamah announced when Hux made a fist.

"You don't have shoes on," Hux said.

"I like the way the forest feels on my feet," she said.

Hux looked at her bare legs. "What about pants? It's cold."

"They're down by the river," she said and set off in the opposite direction.

Hux opened the screened door, which was still caked with dead blackflies and mosquitoes from the summer. He was happy to have found Naamah, but not like this.

"What do you think you're doing?" he said to Gunther.

Gunther secured the towel around his waist and put a kettle on for coffee. The cabin smelled of sweat and dirt. On the floor, Hux saw Naamah's footprints.

"Living my life," Gunther said. He took down two mugs and heaped sugar into them. "You want milk or something? Whiskey?"

"She's my sister," Hux said.

"*Half* sister. She told me all about it. Funny you never did."

"How was I supposed to tell you that?" Hux said.

"You know about how I came into the world," Gunther said. "You think that's an easy truth for me to tell?" He put on a pair of pants while the water heated up. "You've got to figure out how to stand what you can't help."

"I didn't bring her here for you," Hux said.

"No, you brought her here for you," Gunther said.

"You can't treat her like some bar girl from Yellow Falls."

"Careful," Gunther said, making the coffee. "My mother was some bar girl."

Hux sat at the table. He thought of Lulu and her old coonskin coat. "Your mother wasn't just some bar girl."

"Neither is Naamah," Gunther said.

"I know that," Hux said.

"Then what's the problem? Unless you think I'm not good enough for her."

"I didn't say that."

"But you're thinking it," Gunther said. "I can't be celibate like you."

"Women don't leap at me like they leap at you," Hux said, thinking of the woman he was with—the only other one—before Leah. Milly McKay, who ended up choosing someone else because Hux couldn't get his feelings for her together fast enough.

"That's because you don't leap at them," Gunther said. "How long did it take you to ask Milly out? A year? She got married and had a baby faster than that. A girl, I think."

"I'm not you," Hux said.

Gunther had always been able to do everything—catch a bucket of fish, chop down a tree, milk a goat—twice as fast as Hux. He'd made a life out of tracking wild things, taming them with the barrel of his shotgun, and mounting them on his walls. Hux had made a life out of preserving what was dead. Of course Naamah would go to someone like him.

Gunther added some whiskey to his coffee. "I'm going to marry her."

"That's the most ridiculous thing I've ever heard. You've known her for eight hours," Hux said. "You have no idea who she is."

Hux pictured the country road outside the logging camp—Naamah clawing at his face in the truck and then at hers. She'd already clawed at Gunther. He thought of her taped-up laundry bag, how long she'd been carrying it, how damaged it was.

"Besides, I don't think she's the marrying kind," he said.

Gunther smiled the same crooked way his mother did when she was still alive. It was a smile that could turn a black sky blue. "Then why did she say yes?"

24

❦ Gunther and Naamah were married on a Tuesday at the courthouse in Yellow Falls, with Hux and Phee looking on as witnesses. There were no promises to cherish each other, no declarations of everlasting love, no *for better or worse*. One minute they weren't married, and the next they were, and the civil servant was asking the four of them to exit through door B and sign the papers that would make the whole thing official.

Everyone but Hux had signed and was now waiting on him.

Hux stood in the lobby of the courthouse with the pen in his hand. He looked at Naamah, who was wearing the dress Phee had sewn for her; Naamah didn't care what the dress looked like as long as it wasn't white or black, like a habit, so Phee chose a pretty silver material from a bolt at the general store that matched Naamah's eyes almost exactly. Phee had made a hair wreath, too, out of evergreen branches and berries and tiny fall orchids from the bog. Gunther was wearing the corduroy suit Reddy had married Lulu in and a camouflage tie he bought at the Hunting Emporium. He had dirt under his fingernails. He was smiling his crooked smile. Maybe this really was the way love worked.

"Are you sure you want to get married?" Hux had asked Naamah that morning when he was helping her get ready at the cabin, when there was still time to back out.

"That's what people do when they love each other, isn't it?" she'd said.

Hux looked down at the piece of paper. Gunther had scribbled his name so quickly Hux could barely make it out. Gunther wanted to kiss his bride, damn it. Twirl her around a little. Take her back to the woods. Naamah's signature was looping and intricate and measured, surprisingly so for a woman who slept outside and walked barefoot through the forest most of the time; the look of it gave Hux some assurance she knew what she was doing. Phee's signature was the one that gave him pause. It was bold as newspaper headlines, but Hux couldn't tell which direction it was leaning.

"Grave Mistake Made by Young Couple Today in Yellow Falls"? "Young Couple with Fine Future Marries Today in Yellow Falls"?

"We'll all be dead before you sign your name," Gunther said.

What if I don't sign it? Hux thought, even though he knew Gunther would grab a stranger off the street if it came to that. Hux thought of his mother and father in the picture back at the cabin, his father's traveling suit, his mother's blue dress. They'd started with so much happiness, and in so little time it was whittled down to nothing.

Naamah sidled up to Hux. Her dress rustled like wind in the trees. She put a hand on his forearm. *It's all right,* she seemed to be saying with the light press of her fingers.

So Hux signed the piece of paper, and Gunther picked Naamah up and whooped like a cowboy all the way down the steps of the courthouse. At Phee's urging, Hux took several pictures of them. His thumb was in the way of the lens in every photograph except one. Only the one would turn out and only after the camera was lost and found again, and all it would take then was a glance for Hux to know which headline their coupling implied.

After Gunther finished showing Naamah off to strangers on Main Street, the four of them drove back to Phee's cabin to eat a pot roast with carrots and potatoes and a loaf of bread, which Gunther and Naamah barely touched. The whole time their legs were tangled up beneath the table like vines. Their hands were anchored on each other's laps, as though if they let go they might get pulled down into their private underworld altogether.

Hux felt bad Phee had gone to so much trouble and ate twice as much as he normally would have to show his appreciation. After the roast, Phee served pieces of chocolate cake and tiny glasses of red liqueur that was sweet and bitter at the same time. After that, she excused Gunther and Naamah from the table as if they were children, for which they looked grateful and guilty and relieved.

In no time they were outside, chasing each other around the woodpile and the garden, taking turns tackling each other to the ground. Gunther had finally found someone who didn't mind wrestling with him. Someone who liked it, even. Once, Naamah pretended she was hurt, and when Gunther skidded to her rescue beside a pile of kindling, she bit his arm, and he howled and they laughed and did it all over again.

Phee opened the window above the sink in her kitchen.

"Your dress!" she started, but then she closed the window

suddenly as if she were sorry she'd said anything. Phee's fingers were covered in bandages where she'd pricked them with the needle when she was sewing Naamah's dress. She said it had been a long time since she'd worked without a pattern, but Hux wondered if her arthritis had flared up while she was sewing, if that's what made her hands clumsy.

"You want me to go get Naamah and tell her to take it off?" he said.

Phee wiped her hands on a dish towel. She opened a can of sardines for Liddy and whistled lightly for her to come. "My wedding dress is sitting in a pile of mothballs somewhere. This one will tell a more interesting story."

They stood side by side looking out the window like parents. They watched Naamah and Gunther run around and around the fire pit and eventually disappear into the bog. Every so often Hux would hear the echo of their laughter.

After the last dish was washed and put back in the cupboard, he and Phee went out to the porch with bigger glasses of the red stuff, which reminded Hux of cough syrup and chokecherries. "What is this anyway?" he asked her.

Phee put a pair of gloves on and draped a wool blanket over her lap. The snow had held off through October and the beginning of November, but the sky finally looked ready for it even if Hux's woodpile and his pantry weren't. The air was heavy with moisture. The clouds were low and pink.

"I thought it would suit you," Phee said, lifting her glass.

"Because it's bitter?" Hux said. He missed Naamah. He missed his best friend. He was happy for them, but he couldn't help feeling like he was being left behind, which was exactly how he felt when his mother died.

Phee smiled. "No, you fool. Because it's sweet."

The two of them sat out on the porch talking and rocking and waiting for Gunther and Naamah to return until it became clear they weren't coming back, at least not tonight. Hux offered to light a fire for Phee, but she said sometimes she liked being a little cold.

After a while, Phee fell asleep in her chair, and Hux went inside for another blanket and placed it around her shoulders as well as he could without waking her. He listened for Naamah and Gunther in the bog but didn't hear them. He wondered if they'd decided to walk home, and if that was so, he tried not to feel hurt they didn't come back to say good night.

Late in the evening, the first snowflakes started to fall, and Phee woke with a start. She dabbed at the corners of her mouth with a handkerchief, as if she'd been drooling.

"You never know what's going to happen when you close your eyes at my age."

"You're not that old," Hux said.

Phee used the railing to pull herself up. "You're not that young." She leaned her head out over the porch. "Is that snow?"

"It started a few minutes ago," Hux said.

Phee walked down the steps and held out her hands to catch the flakes. "This is worth being cold for," she said, slipping off her gloves.

Hux followed her. There was something special about the first snow of the season. Even though it brought with it months of low hanging gray skies, below-zero temperatures and wind chills, the first snow temporarily covered everything fall had exposed.

"You think it will stick?" Phee said.

Hux thought of Naamah, of Gunther. "It's too early to tell."

25

✤ Almost overnight, late fall turned into early winter, and the first featherlight snowfall turned into daily snowfall heavy as stones. The transition was hard to appreciate, especially when Hux had to strap on snowshoes to go anywhere but the outhouse or the woodpile.

It was Phee's first winter in Evergreen, which Hux figured would be overwhelming for her. He made a weekly trip over to her place with wood, which he stacked by the door so she didn't have to walk through the snow. Sometimes they'd play one of her word games.

When the roads were clear enough, Hux would make trips to Yellow Falls to pick up a few luxuries at the general store with the money he got from Gunther's buck. He'd get butter and cream for Phee. Eggs and cheese for himself. He'd even pick up a few things for Gunther and Naamah, too, but he'd always end up eating them himself because they stayed out trapping longer than he expected. Still, he'd buy little bags of peppermint sticks with the same sense of anticipation every time.

Naamah had moved her few belongings over to Gunther's cabin, and even though he'd never seen what was inside of the laundry bag, he missed seeing it around. He missed the routine of going outside with a cup of coffee in the morning, and he missed the relief he felt when he saw her snuggled up under her tree. He missed wondering how that flimsy burlap-and-feather blanket kept her from freezing.

Sometimes Hux would sit in the truck with her footprint in his hand, wondering if the reason he didn't want to sign that piece of paper at the courthouse was selfish all the way to its root. Maybe he wasn't looking out for her at all. Naamah and Gunther had gone out trapping after the first snow, and by the time they finally came home in December, for the first time in his life Hux understood wanting to tackle someone to the ground.

The three of them were down at the river, drilling holes into the ice with augers so they could fish. Naamah was wearing her cowboy boots and a pair of jeans with holes all over them, clearing snow away with a shovel. Her hair was so badly tangled, so full of the woods, it looked like it belonged to one of the animals in their traps.

"I've never met anyone who loves being outside as much as me," Gunther said about Naamah. "Except my ma, maybe."

Gunther said he and Naamah would walk for ten or twelve hours at a time, setting lines and checking others, and his fingers would have about fallen off, and she'd want to keep going to the next stand of trees, the next river, the next vague horizon line. He said she was better at figuring out where to set the traps than him. She'd blind-set them without bait even, which he never did, and the animals would still come. The only lure they needed was her.

"At least that's how it is with me," he said.

Gunther looked good. His hair was long. His beard thick. He looked happy.

"You still trucking to the tavern every night?" he joked.

"Oh, yeah. I've had some real sweet times," Hux said.

"You still going over to Phee's place?"

Hux knew what Gunther was doing, but there was no stopping him.

"She's married still, you know."

"It isn't like that," Hux said, pretending to be irritated but not doing a very good job of it. Without Gunther here, he'd had no reason to cross the river, which he loved to do in the winter. When he was a boy, he used to think that when the river froze it froze all the way through to its rocky bottom, until his father told him there was a whole winter world down there, alive and well and rushing by.

"You're still hung up on Leah," Gunther said. "You should go after her."

"Why don't you go back into the woods and leave me alone," Hux said.

Gunther reached for Hux's arm and at the same time hooked his leg around Hux's and before Hux knew it he was on his back on the ice, the wind knocked out of him. His head hurt. His tongue was bleeding. His ear was full of snow.

"I missed you, too," Gunther said and helped Hux to his feet.

Naamah had stopped shoveling the snow. She was leaning over one of the holes they'd drilled, holding a pocketknife and staring intensely at the dark water below. The sky above was clear and deep and blue, and the sun reflected off the snow and the ice with such strength Hux had to close his eyes every few seconds to stop them from burning.

"What is it?" Gunther said.

All at once Naamah plunged her hand into the hole, and

when she brought it back out again she was holding a good-sized bluegill, which she'd speared with one of the short blades on her pocketknife. Even though Hux counted himself an accomplished fisherman and had known quite a few of them, too, he'd never seen anything like this. Naamah quieted the bluegill with the pocketknife and filleted it right there on the ice as if she'd been doing it all her life. The scales she scraped off shone like little jewels in the sunlight. Lulu was the only other person Hux could think of who might have been capable of this same feat. He'd always wondered how she'd gotten tangled up in that bear trap with a sixth sense like that.

"I told you," Gunther said. "They jump onto blades for her."

"How did you know when to put your hand in?" Hux said.

When Naamah was done cleaning her bluegill, she wiped her hands, the entrails and blood, on her jeans. She put the fillet in the little leather satchel she was carrying.

"Sister Cordelia taught me," she said, standing up.

"They taught you how to fish at that orphanage?" Gunther said.

Even though Hux didn't know why Naamah had lied like that, the fact that Gunther was still smiling concerned him more. It meant Gunther didn't know about Sister Cordelia or what she'd done to Naamah. He didn't know anything.

Naamah tugged on Gunther's beard. "Don't be jealous, you old goat. I just have more patience than you do."

"You could wait out a goddamn glacier," Gunther said. He grabbed her hand roughly and kissed it tenderly and just like that dissolved Sister Cordelia's ghost.

Maybe it didn't matter Naamah hadn't told him about her. They were together on the ice in Evergreen, and Sister Cordelia was miles away in Green River, sitting behind a yellow window shade with an unworthy heart. Maybe the past didn't have an equal hold on everyone. Maybe it was gracious sometimes and let people go without following their tracks.

"I guess we know what we're having for dinner," Gunther said, licking his lips. He lifted the satchel off Naamah's shoulder. "We'll dip it in cornmeal and fry it up in butter."

Hux thought he saw something change in Naamah's expression—a little dark twinge—but before he could figure it out it disappeared.

"That sounds good," she said, leaning into him. "I love cornmeal."

26

❦ December slowly turned itself over to January, and January blew around snow and branches and little signs that everything wasn't all right no matter how much Hux wanted it to be. Instead of the trees and the river and the next horizon, Naamah was living behind doors and walls and closed windows now. Steady heat from the woodstove.

She was trying hard to be a perfect wife for Gunther, who saw the freshly baked bread on the table but not the burn marks on Naamah's fingers. He didn't see that no matter what apron she wore it choked her at the neck. Phee tried to teach Naamah how to bake bread without hurting herself. Hux was no cook or seamstress or handyman, but he tried to help her as much as he could, too, when Gunther was off in the woods.

At this time of year, Gunther favored his gun over trapping. While he was out, Hux would bring over dinner fixings for them and whatever else he could think of. Near the end of January he brought over the curtains he ordered for Naamah in a catalog at the general store. Unlike his strawberry and

corn ones, hers had squirrels all over them. He figured maybe
if some were already inside, the others would stay out.

"Why don't you go with him?" Hux said when the curtains
failed to stir her one way or another. "I'm sure he'd like you to.
You'd probably bring back more than he does."

"He doesn't like when that happens," Naamah said.

Her hair was brushed smooth for the first time; the strands
were shiny as lacquer. On anyone else but her it would have
been beautiful. Naamah was wearing an apron with flowers
all over it. Beneath that a housedress with a prim little collar, something like his mother used to wear and Lulu used to
make fun of her for. *Why do you insist on dressing like a house-
wife? You're more than that dress. At least you're more than
that to me.*

"Besides, I like being here," Naamah said. She held her
head high, but the gesture didn't belong to her. "I sleep on a
bed now. With pillows and everything."

"I figured as much," Hux said, thinking, *Who are you trying to be?*

"I take bubble baths sometimes, too. Gunther got me some
at the general store. He likes how wrinkled up I get. He said it's
nice knowing what I'll look like when I'm old."

Hux sat at her table. He offered Naamah a cigarette, which
she said no to at first. Eventually she gave in and smoked one
over the sink. Even with bread baking in the oven and meat
and onions simmering on the woodstove and cigarette smoke
hanging in the air, Hux could smell something else beneath it
all, but he couldn't figure out what it was.

"You don't have to come over so much," Naamah said. "I'm
fine here."

"I like seeing you," Hux said, putting out his cigarette,
which he'd been smoking more for her sake than for himself.

"Gunther's right," Naamah said, turning away from him and toward the window above the sink, which looked out onto the green and white of the woods. Her voice turned dark like the long shadows the spruces cast over the snow. "You should get yourself a woman. That way you won't have to cross the river so much."

Hux put the box of matches in his pocket and stood up. He was suddenly embarrassed. "I'm sorry," he said to Naamah, and he meant it.

They were newlyweds. They probably needed their space. Maybe that's why she looked uneasy every time he was there. Maybe she was trying to figure out ways to get him to go home without hurting him.

"I just missed having you on my side of the river," he said.

Hux put his hat and coat on and laced up his boots, which had been drying beside the woodstove. He balled up his wool socks and put them in his coat pocket. He was halfway through the front door when Naamah rushed over and blocked his way.

"Come back inside," she said, with the kind of wild-animal panic he saw in her the day he brought her back from the logging camp. "I didn't mean it."

Hux was busy thinking about his own hurt feelings until he saw she was crying.

"Please forgive me," she said, pulling on his arm, his hands, his neck.

"It's all right," Hux said, trying to calm her down.

"You have to forgive me. You're the only one who understands."

"There's nothing to forgive," Hux said. He took her hands in his and drew her to him like she was a child. Her tears wet his heavy wool shirt and soaked all the way through to his skin. She was shaking. "It's all right," he said again.

He didn't know how to help her, only that she needed it. He untied her apron so the only thing around her neck was her cross and she could breathe again. Naamah tucked her head beneath his chin. That's when Hux realized bleach was what he'd been smelling.

Maybe he should have said something to Gunther about it, but Hux didn't that day or any day because he wanted to protect Naamah from what he considered an indignity— one that wasn't his to share. He only went into the bathroom, found the bottle of bleach beneath the sink, and poured it down the drain.

He only held her face in his hands and said, "You're already good and clean and pure, Naamah. You don't need this. You don't need *her*."

He didn't know he was failing her so badly at that moment.

He didn't know it wasn't enough until Gunther showed up at his door one morning a few weeks later without Naamah or his crooked smile.

"Is she here?" Gunther said when Hux opened the cabin door. The skin beneath Gunther's left eye was black. His neck was scraped up.

"No," Hux said, trying to figure out what had happened to him.

"I woke up, and she was gone," Gunther said. He brushed past Hux and sat down at the table inside, which was full of Hux's preservation tools. Gunther picked one of them up.

"Maybe she went for one of her walks," Hux said.

"In the middle of the night?" Gunther said.

"She doesn't like to sleep inside. At least she didn't when she lived with me."

Gunther helped himself to a cup of coffee but didn't add sugar or whiskey like he usually did. He looked genuinely miserable. "I can't figure her out. She's like a handful of people even though she's only her."

Hux knew exactly what Gunther meant.

"Do you know she prays?" Gunther said. "One minute we'll be drinking whiskey and making snow forts and the next minute she'll be on her knees."

Hux knew the things he wasn't telling Gunther and why he wasn't telling him, and for the first time he wondered if Gunther was doing the same thing.

"Sometimes I get the feeling I love her more than she loves me," Gunther said. He touched his eye. "I can live with that, I guess."

"What do you want me to do?" Hux said.

"Go look for her. She'll think I'm checking up on her if I do it myself."

So Hux laced up his boots and layered up for what he knew would be a long cold day out in the woods. "I'm sure she just wanted some air."

"I should be the one who needs air, don't you think?" Gunther said.

"I don't know the rules," Hux said.

Gunther slumped forward in his chair. "Yeah, me neither."

Hux put his snowshoes on and headed north through the pines with a backpack full of supplies. Aside from food and water, no matter what time of year it was he brought with him a few yards of nylon cord, a pocketknife, fishing line, fish hooks, a compass, a lighter, an extra-large garbage bag, a water tablet, a small handsaw, a first-aid kit, and a plastic whistle. Gunther said if Hux went down in the woods, he might as well just accept it.

Hux didn't know where Naamah went in the middle of the night, but she didn't take Gunther's truck or his, which

Hux figured she would have done if she wanted to go south to Yellow Falls. If she wanted to run away. So Hux kept walking north, calling her name, uncertain if he should be genuinely worried or if she was fine and had only wanted a little space. If he should be glad she'd found her way back outside.

The day was cold and windy; icy black branches clacked against one another overhead. Frozen blueberries clung to the bushes at his knees. The snow was mostly crusted over, which made the going slippery. Ice crystals clung to Hux's beard.

After an hour or so of walking in wider and wider circles under a heavy winter sky, listening to the sounds of the forest, the crunching of snow beneath his feet, Hux started to hear music like the kind they played at the tavern in Yellow Falls—the kind meant to get people dancing and sweating in order to keep them thirsty.

Hux had heard of the Mosquito Net: a plywood shack set far back in the woods, taken down each summer and pieced back together by fur trappers each winter. Inside, men supposedly did what they did in Yellow Falls: smoked and drank and hung up pictures of naked women they'd found in magazines you couldn't get at the general store. Pictures that Hux felt bad for enjoying.

Gunther had been to the Mosquito Net once, but he said the men were too rough there even for him. Plus, he said there weren't any three-dimensional women there, which defeated the purpose of going out in his mind.

Hux knew Naamah was inside even before he pushed open the door. Even before he saw her spinning around with a trapper that had Paul Bunyan blood. He just knew.

The trapper was twice as wide as Hux. Twice as tall. Black hair sprouted from his thick hands, his thick neck, his thick head. His incisors were long and sharp. He looked like a bear only without any of a bear's magnificence. Just big and mean and furry.

"What are you doing here?" Hux said to Naamah.

Naamah had a half-crumpled paper cup in one hand; the other was wrapped around the trapper's waist. "That's my brother," she said to the trapper.

"Gunther's worried sick," Hux said. "Why are you here? You should be at home."

"My brother thinks he's the pope," Naamah said to the trapper.

"I'll be the pope if you want me to be," the trapper said, scratching his beard against Naamah's neck. Even though it was freezing outside, lines of sweat trickled down his face and landed on Naamah's green blouse. "See how salty I am for you?"

Naamah licked the trapper's neck, and Hux lunged forward.

"She's married," Hux said.

A group of men turned from their stools. They looked like the kind of trappers who would snare an animal, skin it for its pelt, and leave the rest behind to rot.

The music was saying something about horses and dirt roads and broken hearts.

Naamah turned to the trapper, whose hands moved down her body and caught on the button of her jeans. She showed him her silver ring, which Hux had given her.

"Isn't it pretty?" she said. "It was my mother's. Our fingers were the same size."

"I wouldn't do that if I were you," Hux said to the trapper.

The trapper twisted the button on Naamah's jeans. "What are you going to do?"

"I'm taking her home," Hux said.

"Not before she pays up for what she's drunk."

"How much?" Hux said.

The trapper put his hand down Naamah's blouse before Hux could stop him. He ripped off the top buttons, exposing her breasts. "This should do it."

Hux took a swing at him but was on the floor before his fist had a chance to connect to the trapper's face. He'd bitten his tongue on the way down. His blood tasted like metal. The men at the bar were laughing at him.

The trapper buried his face in Naamah's chest, pressing his lapping-dog tongue against her skin. "Run along home with your daddy now," he said when he came up for air.

Naamah frowned. "You're just going to let me go?"

Hux got up from the floor. "I'm her brother, not her father."

"You two are something else," the trapper said. He looked at Hux. "You're not even going to thank me? I got her primed up for you. All of us did."

Hux cocked his arm back, and with all his force he took another swing, and this time his fist connected with the trapper's hard jaw. In the moment of connection Hux felt his thumb snap, but no pain had ever felt as gratifying.

"Go to hell," he said.

Hux lifted Naamah up as if she weighed no more than a feather and carried her out of the shack the way Gunther had carried her into Phee's cabin after they were married.

When they were outside, Naamah bit his forearm, and Hux let go of her.

"Why did you do that?" she said, whacking at a pile of iced-over bullet brush. The thorns scraped her hand, and little drops of blood came together like beads on a necklace. The torn pieces of her blouse flapped in the wind. She looked sober suddenly, clear eyed, so much so that Hux wondered if she'd been drinking at all in there.

"I was having a little fun," she said. "You don't like to have fun, do you?"

"This isn't my idea of fun," Hux said, looking down at his thumb, which was already swollen. "Where's your coat? Your gloves? Your hat?"

Naamah pointed to the bar.

Hux took off his coat and put it on her. He zipped it up to her chin. Then he put his hat on her, his gloves. He was starting to feel less and less heroic.

The two of them walked through the forest, back the way Hux had come. Even though he offered her his snowshoes, Naamah didn't take them, and yet her boots hardly sank through the top layer of crusted snow. Many times along the way she offered to give Hux's coat back, and even though he was freezing he kept saying no.

Just before they got to the cabin, where Gunther was scratching his bride's name into Hux's kitchen table with one of Hux's preservation tools, Naamah stopped him.

"I'm sorry about your thumb," she said. "I don't know what's wrong with me."

"Let's just forget about it," Hux said. "Gunther's waiting for you. He loves you, and you agreed to love him."

Naamah tilted her head like a little girl. "His breath smells like raw meat."

"Then tell him to brush his teeth," Hux said and pulled her forward.

27

✤ Hux couldn't get that little head tilt out of his mind and what it meant, at least what it meant to him: Naamah had been robbed of her childhood. It was probably foolish, but he thought if he could give it back to her in some small way she could be happy here in Evergreen. Maybe she wouldn't go back to the Mosquito Net. The logging camp. The orphanage. Wherever else she'd been. Maybe she'd leave all of that behind.

On a sunny morning in late February, Hux drove to the general store. He walked up and down the aisles looking for something he remembered being fond of as a child. He settled on a box of sparklers until he was at the cash register and saw a pair of white ice skates sitting on the shelf above Earl's head. The silver blades gleamed under the store's yellow lights. The white leather beckoned. Hux couldn't afford the skates, but Earl let him have them on consignment. Hux bought the sparklers outright. A packet of bubble gum, too.

When he got back to Evergreen, Hux cleared a patch of ice on the river. After that, he built four chairs out of snow like he and Gunther used to do when they were kids and put a few sleeping bags on them for extra cushioning. Hux found his and Gunther's old hockey skates in the mudroom and brought them down to the river with Naamah's. He even brought a thermos of cocoa and a basket of homemade chocolate-chip cookies, which he was pretty proud of. He only burned them a little and only because he didn't immediately figure out he needed to turn the baking sheet every few minutes on the woodstove.

That afternoon Hux herded everyone down to the river, including Phee and her cat, Liddy, who liked to go for rides and would even stick her head out a window if one was rolled down for her.

"What's all this?" Gunther said.

"I thought we could teach Naamah how to skate," Hux said, placing the skates in her hands. He couldn't contain his excitement. He was up on his toes.

Naamah stared at the skates. "These are for me? They're mine?"

"Careful," Hux said when she touched one of the blades. "The metal part is sharp."

"I don't have any way of paying for these," Naamah said.

"They're a gift," Hux said.

When Naamah realized Hux wasn't going to take them back and he didn't want anything for them either, she jumped a little. "There's not even a tiny scuff on them. They smell so good, too. So clean."

"That's the leather and the polish," Hux said.

Naamah kissed Hux's cheek. "I love them. Thank you."

"Let's get them on her already!" Gunther said, nearly tackling her to the ground. He yanked Naamah's boots off. "You're going to love this."

When Gunther got Naamah's feet into the skates and double tied the laces so she wouldn't trip over them, Naamah held one of her feet up to the sunlight, twisting and turning it admiringly. Before Gunther pulled her up from the snow and told her to hold on to his shoulders and he'd lead her around the ice until she got the hang of it, he mouthed *Thank you* to Hux as if Naamah's happiness was so fragile two little words would shatter it.

Naamah wrapped her arms around Gunther so tightly his face got red. He didn't tell her to ease up, though. He kissed each of her arms and kept walking her forward.

"That's my girl," he said whenever she screamed or laughed or cried out. Once Hux was sure Gunther jostled her a little to get her to hold on to him tighter.

While they walked and slid and wobbled on the ice, Hux helped Phee and Liddy into one of his snow chairs. "Do you know how to skate?"

"I used to," she said. "Thirty or forty years ago."

For Hux it had been at least six or seven years. Maybe more. When he and Gunther were young, they'd come out with their hockey skates when the hard work of clearing the snow became more enticing than watching wood in the stove burn down to ashes.

"I don't know if it's like a bike or not," Phee said. "If you remember."

She was petting Liddy, who hissed when Phee got too close to her face. Liddy hissed whenever Hux tried to touch her, which was why he'd given up trying to be friendly anymore. Once, she nuzzled against his pants, and he thought she'd turned nice, but then she clamped down on his ankle hard, and he had to shake her loose.

"You're afraid of her, aren't you?" Phee said.

"Actually I was thinking of how nice she'd look on my wall," Hux said.

"Naamah, I mean," Phee said, watching her on the ice.

"It's like flying!" Naamah said when she found her footing. She eased her grip on Gunther and then let go of him altogether.

Naamah skated to the edge of Hux's little rink and looked frustrated she had nowhere else to go until she figured out she could turn around and go back the way she came. She went back and forth like that, her hair soaring behind her.

"I keep holding my breath," Phee said. "But she keeps not falling."

"I've been holding mine, too," Hux said.

After a while, Naamah skated over to them.

"Can we come back tomorrow?" she said, plunking down in one of Hux's ice chairs. Her cheeks were flushed. Her hair wild. She was glowing from the inside out instead of the other way around. "And the day after that? And the day after that, too?"

"Sure," Hux said.

Naamah looked at the cookies. "Can I have one?"

"You can have all of them if you want," Hux said, pleased by her pleasure. Maybe his idea wasn't so foolish after all.

"You better save one for me," Gunther said. He was lacing up his old hockey skates, which were still sharp after all these years.

Liddy jumped from Phee's lap to Naamah's.

"Oh, Liddy, leave her alone," Phee said.

"Your cat's name is Liddy?" Naamah said, eating a cookie with one hand and petting her with the other. "I used to know someone with that name." She was stroking Phee's cat in all the places you weren't supposed to, but instead of biting or fleeing Liddy purred. "She would sing to me when I was little. Before she went back to Wisconsin."

"What would she sing?" Phee said.

"Lullabies," Naamah said. "She was a sister. A nun, I mean."

Liddy climbed up the front of Naamah and licked her face.

"That means she likes you," Phee said, which made Naamah smile.

"Why didn't you ever have children?" Naamah said. "You would have been good at it. You're so nice to everyone."

"*Naamah,*" Hux said. "Some things are private."

"I did want children," Phee said. "My body just wasn't put together that way."

"Why didn't you adopt one?" Naamah said.

"*Naamah,*" Hux said again.

Gunther was clearing snow off the ice, moving farther and farther down the river. At first, he'd look back, but after a while he just kept going. Hux wasn't sure if he was clearing a longer and wider path for Naamah or for himself.

"My husband was a stubborn man," Phee said, looking downriver after him.

"At Hopewell only babies ever got adopted," Naamah said. "And only the ones that didn't cry. Sister Cordelia said a lot of people pretended to be Christian, but when it came down to it they weren't really interested in charity."

Hux was lacing up his skates and getting ready to go downriver, too.

"I miss her sometimes," Naamah said. "I know I'm not supposed to, but I do."

"At least Naamah's talking about it," Hux said to Phee that night when he was driving her back to her cabin. "That has to be a good sign, right?"

The sky was still clear, and because of that the night air was even colder, but it was worth its chill because of how many stars were out. Hux's father used to point out the constellations and teach Hux the stories behind their names. His mother was the one who said the names didn't matter or even the shapes they made: crows and serpents and bears. Each little star mattered. Each little glimmer of light.

Hux pulled up to Phee's cabin. His hand was already on the door handle so he could help her and Liddy up the steps of the porch and through the front door.

"I don't know how to tell you this, so I'm just going to tell you," Phee said. "She's pregnant, Hux. She's already starting to show."

"Naamah?" Hux said, letting his hand fall. His heart. "Did she tell you that?"

"I don't think she knows," Phee said.

28

❧ Naamah did know. She'd known since before she went to the Mosquito Net, before she cleaned herself with bleach. Hux knew those events were connected, even more so now that a pregnancy underlay them, only he still didn't know how. Whenever he thought he was starting to understand his sister, she'd surprise him like she did when she told him she'd already gone to a doctor in Yellow Falls, who took some of her blood away and gave her a booklet about pregnancy she kept under the mattress so Gunther wouldn't see.

"You and Gunther haven't talked about having kids?" Hux said.

They were sitting at Naamah's table with cups of coffee, except Naamah wasn't drinking hers because she couldn't stomach the taste.

"We talk about being in the woods," Naamah said. "Hunting. Trapping. Gunther wouldn't ever love anything that got in the way of that."

It was true: Gunther only liked people who could be left in the forest and find their way out again, and even some of those people he didn't like.

"How do you feel about it?" Hux said.

"I don't know," Naamah said. She put her hands over her ears as if the conversation were suddenly too loud for her. What was she going to do with a screaming baby? Hux thought. A hungry baby? Sometimes Naamah went all day without remembering to eat.

"There are different kinds of doctors than the one you went to," Hux said.

Naamah touched her cross. "I couldn't do that."

"Because of her?" Hux said, thinking of Sister Cordelia. Sometimes he wanted to rip that cross off Naamah's neck. He wanted to see if it would set her free.

"Because of me," Naamah said.

Naamah got up from the table and walked over to the couch where she made a nest out of old blankets, which she burrowed into as deeply as she could.

"I wonder what she'd say. I'm married at least. Not in a church, though."

"She's probably dead by now," Hux said. He didn't understand how Naamah could miss a person like that, even a little. "At least I hope she is."

"I feel like I did something wrong," Naamah said.

"You didn't," Hux said, but he couldn't help thinking about the trapper at the Mosquito Net, the scent of bleach on her skin. How was she going to do this?

The light in the kitchen kept flickering.

"A girl at the logging camp went to one of those doctors you were talking about," Naamah said. "She never came back from that appointment."

"Maybe she decided to have the baby," Hux said. "To change her life."

"I like to think that, too," Naamah said. She put a hand on her stomach and the other on her heart, as if she were trying to connect them.

Hux got up from the chair he was sitting in and burrowed into her couch nest with her. He didn't know anything about babies or what they needed besides diapers and milk, but he knew about mothers. He knew about their deep well of love.

"I'll help you," he said.

Hux did what he could the next few weeks. He brought over warm cups of chicken broth, which Naamah gulped down and which came back up just as quickly until she learned how to sip. He sat with her. Phee made tea from ground ginger and raspberry leaves to ease her queasiness. Both she and Hux agreed not to say anything to Gunther until Naamah did.

Gunther may have been a sharpshooter in the forest, but at home his farsightedness didn't do him any favors. Gunther figured it was a good sign to see Naamah sitting in her blanket nest when he came in from hunting. He thought she was finally relaxing into their life together, finally letting Evergreen nourish her like it nourished him.

He started calling her his little bird.

As predictable as he was, his reaction when he found out Naamah was pregnant surprised Hux. Hux was sitting with Naamah when Gunther came in from hunting that day.

"I think it's about time for the breakup," Gunther said, and out of nowhere Naamah threw up. Gunther looked to Hux. "What did I say wrong? It happens every year. The ice melts. The green comes out. The flies start biting."

"She ate something bad," Hux said.

"No, I didn't," Naamah said when she stopped heaving. "I'm pregnant."

Gunther stepped forward. "You're what?"

He seemed like he was doing the same thing Hux had done when he first found out: deciding whether or not this would drown Naamah or bring her up to the surface.

Naamah was standing now, yellow vomit stuck to her shirt. She was looking out the window at the forest as if she might try to walk through the glass to get there.

Before she could move, Gunther blocked her way.

"Do you think it's a boy? Because I could teach him to hunt and trap and fish. He could run the business with me. Little hands are good for making lures."

"He won't come out walking," Naamah said. "He won't understand about the forest."

"I knew it—he's a *he*."

A smile spread across Gunther's face. A wide, amazingly crooked one.

Gunther set down his rifle. With a great swoop downward he picked Naamah up and spun her around and around the cabin. When he finally set her down, her face was drained of its color, but she looked relieved, which seemed as good as happy.

Each week that spring after the ice on the river broke up, Naamah would sit on either hers or Hux's porch studying that little booklet about pregnancy, which seemed to help her connect what she couldn't connect with her hands. She memorized the chronology of what was happening inside her and started to measure everything according to weeks.

When she was at Hux's, she would read parts of the booklet out loud. Hux knew that at week eight the baby was starting to grow fingers and at week ten tiny fingernails. He knew about the fine dark hair that covered the baby by fourteen weeks and the gooey protective coating that came after that, which the book compared to a layer of cream cheese. He didn't want to know what the book said about birth.

"It'll fall out, won't it?" Hux said to Naamah that day about the hair.

"I don't know—the book doesn't say," Naamah said.

"I guess if it doesn't fall out you could shave it," Hux said.

"You can't shave a baby, can you?" Naamah said, and they both laughed.

By May, the weather had turned so nice Naamah stopped putting a blanket over her belly when she rocked on Hux's porch. Open windows suited her. Blooming flowers. Toothy weeds. She seemed to be lengthening right along with the days, the greenery.

Naamah helped Hux start his garden again, and she started one for her and Gunther again, too. Even though the crows always attacked whatever corn was planted in Evergreen, Naamah planted a few rows of it anyway. She said corn was an excuse to eat butter. She liked how the kernels left imprints, like little teeth, in the softened sticks. She started tomatoes and onions and carrots, too—anything and everything, so long as she could put her hands in the warm black earth. Always, she had dirt under her fingernails and garden detritus in her hair. Like their mother used to, Naamah would pick bouquets of wildflowers up in the oxeye meadow and put them in Mason jars on both sides of the river.

Whatever had sent Naamah to places like the logging camp and the Mosquito Net seemed like it was finally gone. Gunther thought so, too. He knew about the cream cheese stuff and the hair. In the evenings, he'd sit with her on their porch even though he hated to sit still. He used to say sitting made his legs so bored he wanted to shoot them just to feel something. Now he said he liked how the book compared the baby to a minnow.

At week twenty, Naamah felt the baby move for the first time.

The next day she paddled across the river and walked up to Hux's cabin. She was wearing Phee's long yellow dress and a fancy green hat with feathers all over it. Hux was working at preserving a muskrat for a customer in Yellow Falls, who kept changing his mind about what kind of mount he wanted. He was glad to see her, glad for the break.

"I need you to take me to Hopewell," she said from the other side of the screened door, which a few moths clung to. Her long hair was twirled up under the hat somehow, and for the first time Hux saw how delicate her neck was.

"I don't think that's a good idea," Hux said.

"Then I'll walk," Naamah said. "It's not that far."

"Does Gunther know about this?"

"He wouldn't understand," Naamah said. "I wouldn't want him to have to."

Hux stepped out onto the porch. He wanted to do what was right, but he didn't know what that was. Naamah was pregnant, and he couldn't see any good coming from her and Sister Cordelia sitting down together in a room. He could see Sister Cordelia hurting her all over again without even laying a finger on her. On the other hand, maybe it was what she needed to get on with things and have this baby. This life.

"I feel like I shouldn't take you," he said. He motioned to her hat. "You don't have a gun or anything under there?"

"It isn't that kind of trip," Naamah said.

"You know what you're doing?"

Naamah put a hand on his forearm. "No, but I'm sure of it."

So Hux drove his sister to Green River.

On the way they listened to the radio, which came in more and more clearly the farther away from Evergreen they got. The river and hills gave way to alfalfa and potato fields, blanketing the land beneath them with purple and white flowers. Hux and Naamah rolled down their windows at the same time— he liked when that happened, these little synchronicities. It made him feel close to her. The air smelled sweet and rich and young. Yellow buttercups were growing up alongside the road.

"You think my corn is going to make it to harvest?" Naamah said.

She was leaning toward her open window, looking at herself in the side mirror, but not in the way Leah used to when she was putting on makeup on their way to Yellow Falls or doing something else to doll herself up. Naamah was looking at herself with real wonder.

"The crows are pretty persistent," Hux said.

"Gunther doesn't think it will make it either," Naamah said. "He said he remembers our mother making a scarecrow one year. It's still strange to say that—our mother. To think of her living somewhere besides in my dreams. He said the crows got the corn anyway."

"I don't remember that. Gunther's a little older than me, though."

Naamah smiled. "A little wiser, he says."

"He's full of it. He's always been full of it."

"He says that, too."

The two of them stopped talking when old farmhouses started to crop up alongside the road instead of just the buttercups, the crops. They were getting close to Green River, to

Hopewell. Naamah started to fidget a little in her seat, which made Hux doubt his decision to bring her here. If she didn't think it was bad for the baby, he would have offered Naamah some whiskey to calm her down, to calm both of them down. All he had was one of the pieces of bubble gum he'd bought at the general store during the winter.

"You sure you don't want half?" Naamah said, unwrapping it.

"I got it for you," Hux said. "I just forgot about it."

Naamah put the piece of bubble gum in her mouth and chewed it vigorously while Hux drove the rest of the way to Hopewell. He figured she'd want to go inside, and he was preparing himself to insist on going in with her. He was preparing the steel toe of his boot in case Sister Cordelia did anything to hurt Naamah. If she talked about the baby as a sin in the eyes of the Lord. Or the Lord at all, though that seemed inevitable. Even though it was summer now, Hux didn't want to see those girls huddled together outside. He didn't want to see Sister Cordelia's bald head. Her oversize cross. Her moles. And yet he wanted to see her get what she deserved, even if he didn't know what that was.

Naamah swallowed the gum the moment Hux pulled up to the iron gates, as if chewing it in the presence of the Hopewell sign would have made her guilty somehow. The gates were closed but not locked. Hux asked her if she wanted him to park there or open them and drive up to the front door, which was his way of asking her if she was sure being here was what she really wanted, what she really needed.

"I don't know what I'm going to do yet," she said, so Hux parked the truck in front of the gates. "I always imagined coming here and burning this place down. Hurting her for hurting me. For making me ugly."

"You're not ugly," Hux said.

"Sometimes I am," Naamah said.

When Hux turned off the engine, Naamah slid out of the truck as quickly as she had the night he brought her home and she disappeared into the river. This time, she didn't disappear. She walked right up to the iron gates and pressed her face against them. The hem of Phee's yellow sundress blew in the wind. A green feather came free from Naamah's hat, floated into the cab of the truck, and landed on the passenger seat.

Naamah was standing in front of those gates as though her feet were rooted all the way to the center of the earth. He wondered if that hat was like Lulu's coonskin coat.

Lulu would have loved Naamah. She'd have made a pair of trousers for her that would have lasted a lifetime. She'd have admired Naamah's persevering spirit, even though she wouldn't have said it that way. Her courage. Which Hux never really possessed.

When she was still alive and Hux broke his arm following Gunther up a tree, Lulu carried Hux to her couch as if his legs were injured. "I want to tell you something about yourself," she'd said. "You got hurt because you're too careful. I saw you hesitate on that branch. That's when you fell down. What were you thinking?"

"How I didn't want to fall down," Hux had said.

Lulu laughed a little. Hux loved Lulu like a second mother. He loved her man pants and her thick plaid lumberjack shirts. He loved that mysterious bond between her and his mother, how his mother would come in from an afternoon with her saying she suddenly felt like baking a pie or eating ice cream. Something decadent. Sometimes, when she didn't have the ingredients for a pie and the trip to Yellow Falls was too daunting, she'd dip her fingers into the sugar container. Sometimes she'd let Hux dip his fingers in, too.

"Gunther's going to fall off a cliff one day," Lulu said. "I think we all know that. He'll holler the whole way down because he won't have seen it coming."

"I don't want to fall off a cliff," Hux said.

"You're like your mother," Lulu said. "She fell down hard once, and she never climbed high enough to do it again."

"But she loves you more than anything," Hux said.

Lulu smiled her crooked smile. "I love her that way, too."

Hux watched Naamah at the gate, thinking of Lulu. Naamah was looking up at the orphanage with an expression Hux could only guess at because her back was to him. She stood that way for a long time. Hux thought he saw someone pass by the front windows on the second floor of the orphanage. He thought he saw Sister Cordelia's black robe.

He thought of what Sister Cordelia had told him—*I love her still.*

After a while, Naamah let go of the gates. When she came back to the truck, there was rust on her face.

"I'm ready to go now," she said.

Hux tucked the green feather into his pocket. Maybe a little strength would rub off on him, too. Maybe like the feather, they were supposed to float for a while. Land softly. Hux decided to drive the other way out of Green River, through the center of town. He and Naamah could make wishes on a handful of old change that was rolling around on the mats.

Before he started the truck and steered it away from the orphanage for what he hoped would be the last time, he pointed to the gravel.

"You dropped your hat. Should I get it for you?"

Naamah looked at herself in the side mirror. She touched the front of her sunny-yellow dress. "It isn't mine anymore."

29

❦ Everyone made it through the summer admirably, even the corn. The thick green stalks were as tall as Naamah by August. The ears golden as the sun. Before they harvested it, Hux took a picture of Naamah with her crop. The doctor in Yellow Falls had said the last few months of her pregnancy would be uncomfortable with all that extra weight bearing down on her. Right then, though, between the rows of sweet corn, Naamah looked round but light. She looked proud of herself.

"Take another one," Gunther said that day. "I want to remember this forever."

Naamah's feet were bare. Her toes were curled into the damp soil. She was wearing one of Gunther's white undershirts and a pair of overalls with the seams let out by Phee.

"You get in there with her," Hux said to Gunther.

"Brother and sister first," Gunther said.

Hux gave up his camera and walked into the corn, pushing some aside to make a space for himself. He put his arm around Naamah's waist, and she put hers around his.

"You guys look like lovebirds," Gunther said. "My turn now."

In one of the pictures, Gunther got on his knees and pressed his lips against Naamah's stomach. In another, he kissed an ear of corn.

The whole time the corn rustled, the flies darted, and the heat radiated from all directions. It was the height of summer, the height of everything.

Even though it tasted wonderful when it was grilled over Gunther and Naamah's fire pit and dipped in butter, Hux thought it was a little sad to eat that corn. To see the corn silk blow around in the dirt. Gunther said he was too sentimental—corn's corn—and he was probably right. It was just that Naamah had worked so hard to grow it.

Naamah was still reading her book about pregnancy, but she wouldn't look at the chapter about birth no matter how much everyone encouraged her to. She said the doctor had scared her enough when he told her what would happen if the baby wouldn't come out on his own. She didn't like the idea of being put to sleep or having an IV stuck in her hand. The idea of a room you had to be wheeled into and out of. Hux didn't like the sound of it either. When you lived in a place with nature all around you, you were bound to get nervous being stuck between four white walls, weren't you? Naamah wanted to know how you could give someone a C-section when they were landlocked in Minnesota.

"It's not that kind of 'sea,'" Hux explained. Sometimes he couldn't tell if she was joking or if she really didn't understand what most people did. "It stands for *Cesarean*."

"I don't care what it stands for," Naamah said. "I still don't like it."

Naamah started to have nightmares about it.

One day in early September, she was taking a nap on the bottom bunk at Hux's cabin and woke up having wet the bed.

She'd grown heavier like the doctor said she would. She hunched more. Slept more. Wanted to be alone more, too, so Hux let her use his cabin and would walk around Evergreen until he couldn't walk anymore. He pulled bad weeds and picked good flowers and pruned the garden. Eventually, he'd sneak onto the porch and rock in one of the chairs until Naamah woke up. Sometimes he'd read. Mostly he'd just sit.

"Please don't be mad," Naamah said when she realized what had happened to the bed. Her uncertainty in that moment reminded Hux of the first days she was with him in Evergreen. It made him think of her taped-up laundry bag. It made him nervous.

"The book says something about a loose bladder, doesn't it?" Hux said. He didn't want her to be embarrassed and he didn't want to read too much into her expression either.

Naamah balled up the sheets and carried them toward the screened door. When she opened it, a few lacy moths flew in. "I'm going to take these down to the river. Don't tell Gunther, okay? He'll just worry. He already wants to camp in front of the doctor's office."

"Only if you let me come with you," Hux said. "If you stop fretting over old sheets."

"Okay," Naamah said, finally returning to the girl he'd stood with in the corn.

The two of them went to the river, scrubbed the sheets against the warm rocks, and pinned them between birch trees to dry. A little yellow butterfly landed on the white cloth, which made Hux think of his father. His father wouldn't have pinned one so common to velvet. He was always looking for the most unique butterflies for his collection, which was why all his life Hux had preferred the most common ones. They were the safest to love.

"You want to come in? It's already getting colder," Naamah said, wading into the water fully clothed. She reached down to her feet and pulled a piece of dark green algae out from between her toes. "You can be upriver of me if you want."

"You go ahead," Hux said. "This rock is suiting me just fine."

When she was deep enough, Naamah rolled over onto her back and floated. Her stomach rose above the surface of the water like a half-moon. Her hair fanned out around her like seaweed. "I love to swim," she said. "It feels good to be weightless. Free. It was the best thing I ever bartered for at the logging camp. The lessons, I mean."

"Who taught you?" Hux said, even though he didn't think he wanted to know.

"Just someone I used to know," Naamah said. "She was one of the good ones."

"She?" Hux said, relieved.

"You're one of the good ones, too."

"Thank you," Hux said, feeling the heat come into his cheeks. Gunther would have taken a bow. He'd have stripped down and run into the water after her.

"Too good maybe," Naamah said, squinting at him even though the sun was behind her. "You always let everyone go ahead of you."

"I'm not in a rush," Hux said.

"I'll say." Naamah took in a mouthful of sparkling blue water and spit it, like a fountain, in his direction. She went beneath the surface for a minute, but just as Hux started to worry about her she came back up again, sending little waves in all directions.

30

Even though there wasn't a storm in Evergreen or even a cloud visible on the late-October horizon, a few hours before Naamah gave birth the electricity went out. At first Hux thought he didn't pull the cord hanging from the rafters hard enough, so he pulled it again. Then he tried the switch next to the sink. No luck there either. *Remember, it is light we are offering you. Light, my friends!* Gunther still had that old government letter. He still got riled up about it, too. He said it was taxation without representation. Clear-as-day bullshit. Most of the time Hux let him rant without joining in. But something bothered him about the bulbs not working today. He didn't feel like sitting in the dark with Naamah.

"Tell me about our mother again," Naamah asked him.

It seemed like it was always dark when Naamah asked about her.

"She was glad she didn't have to see light come in here," Hux said. He'd just come in from rocking on the porch. The cabin was full of shadows.

"Because of my father?" Naamah said.

Hux was thinking about how much and how little Naamah looked like their mother. How much and how little he remembered what made her *her* anymore. Sometimes he couldn't even remember his mother's voice.

Naamah was resting on the lower bunk bed. Her belly rose toward the top bunk like an unexpected lift of earth. She was staring at the slats of wood above her, counting the black knots in the wood.

"What was his name?" Naamah said.

"I wish our mother never told it to me," Hux said. He sat on the floor beside the bunk bed. "Trust me. You don't want to know. You should let this go."

Naamah stopped counting the knots in the wood. "Please tell me, Hux. I need to know before the baby comes."

"Why?" Hux said.

Naamah touched her belly. "So I don't pass on everything that's bad about me."

"You're nothing like him," Hux said.

"Then tell me his name."

"Cullen O'Shea," Hux said.

They were going to bring us light.

"He was Irish, then?" Naamah said.

His hands were scissors for me.

Naamah touched her face the way Hux had seen a blind person touch a stranger's face in Yellow Falls. "Did he have dimples?"

I've never forgotten those dimples.

"Yes," Hux said.

Naamah let her hand fall. "That's why you hate seeing mine so much."

"I don't hate it," Hux said.

"I knew a few men like him," Naamah said. "Girls got hurt sometimes up north when they weren't careful. Sometimes even when they were."

"Why did you stay there for so long?" Hux asked because he was close to asking, *Did you get hurt?* and he couldn't know the answer to that. He just couldn't.

"Where else was I supposed to go?" Naamah said. "I was fourteen."

"But she wasn't even there," Hux said, thinking of their mother, the men.

Naamah looked at him as if she were still a little girl. "She's everywhere."

The two of them stayed silent for a while staring at the knots of black wood, the wood's history. Hux wondered if he should have lied to her. At least about the dimples. Maybe about everything. He didn't know what Naamah was thinking about.

"Thank you for telling me," she said eventually. "I know that was hard for you."

Naamah rolled over onto her side and closed her eyes. It didn't take long for her to fall asleep or at least to pretend she was. Hux continued to sit on the floor beside her. He counted the rafters, the logs beside the woodstove, anything he could count. After a while he lay back, too.

Late in the afternoon, Hux woke to the sound of Naamah's breathing, which had turned from slow and steady to jagged at some point while he slept. Sweat was pooling in the space between her neck and shoulders. Her cheeks were red, her veins swollen. Hux jumped up to find the keys to the truck so he could take Naamah to the hospital.

"Please don't take me there," Naamah said. "They'll stick me with things."

Hux thought about the bag Gunther had packed for her to take to the hospital, the tiny diapers folded up inside of it and God only knew what else. Gunther had tried to put a pocket-knife in there. "I don't know anything about giving birth other than women do it. I don't want to know anything more about it than that either."

"You were born here," Naamah said.

Hux put his hand on his sister's hot forehead. "So were you. That doesn't mean we know what we're doing. Gunther either. Where's that book?"

All at once, Naamah arched her back. She latched on to Hux's hand with the strength of a lumberjack. She clutched her stomach with the other.

"She's coming," Naamah said, fighting for her breath.

"*She?*" Hux said.

"I couldn't tell Gunther—he made a camouflage bib out of a tarp."

"We've got to get you to the hospital," Hux said.

"I see her," Naamah said, gripping him harder. "She rocks me to sleep at night."

"You mean you rock her?" Hux said.

When the contraction was over, Naamah let go of his hand. "I mean it how I said."

Hux and Naamah spent the next hour or so that way—with her holding on to him one minute and letting him go the next. Naamah still wouldn't agree to go to the hospital in Yellow Falls. She still wouldn't budge from that bunk bed.

"This isn't the right time to be stubborn," Hux said. He was the only one who seemed to be panicking. Naamah was strangely focused.

Between contractions, Hux did everything he could think of to get ready for what was coming. He heated the water to sterilize the scissors and the tools he used to sew up animals. He brought a stack of clean towels over to the bunk bed. A clean sheet. He lit the candles he had and kept matches nearby. He wished his father were here. Hux's mother told him he saved both their lives the day Hux was born.

Naamah started exhaling knives. She spread her legs apart.

"I'm going to push now," she said.

"No," Hux said. "No. No."

But she started pushing anyway.

"How could she leave me, Hux? I didn't do anything wrong."

"I don't know," Hux said, wiping down her forehead with a cool cloth.

Naamah started breathing so fast and hard Hux thought she was going to pass out. Her face tensed up. The muscles on either side of her jaw bulged.

"She hated me, Hux."

Naamah's eyes were as fierce and gray as they'd ever been; the green in them was overcome. "She left me on the doorstep like a dog."

A few minutes later, the baby was born.

A girl, just like Naamah said she would be.

Hux didn't have to twist and pull his niece's shoulders to get her out. He didn't have to make sure the umbilical cord wasn't wrapped around his niece's neck, squeezing her life before it could begin. He wasn't the one who'd had to reach into dark places no one belonged. All he did was pick his niece up and lay her on her mother's chest.

Even though her eyes were still closed, Hux's niece did something incredible. She charted her way beneath Naamah's shirt until her mouth found Naamah's breast. She reached for Naamah's tangled hair with her tiny fingers.

With her heart.

"She's beautiful," Naamah said, looking at her daughter, who was making little sucking sounds. Her legs were tucked up underneath her.

"She looks like you," Hux said. She and her mother shared the same curving arch, the same dark hair, the same lips. Hux thought all babies were born with blue eyes, but when his niece opened hers he saw that they were a gentle shade of brown.

"I'll turn on the light," he said to Naamah. "You'll see."

Hux pulled the cord he'd been pulling all day. This time the lightbulb snapped yellow, a sudden ugly exposure that all of them shrank from. Naamah pulled her hair free from her daughter's hands and tried to sit up. Though his niece didn't cry when she was born, she cried now. She wailed. Hux didn't know a baby could make that much noise.

"How do I get her to stop crying?" Naamah said with real alarm.

"I have no idea," he said, draping a clean towel over Naamah and his niece, so the blood wouldn't spook them. "Feed her? Rock her a little? Let me go get Gunther."

"I'm afraid I'm going to hurt her," Naamah said.

"You just need your husband," Hux said, not thinking much about it then. Hux's hand was at least twice the size of his niece's foot. Anyone would be afraid of holding her the wrong way, of straining her neck—whatever Naamah was afraid of.

After Hux cut the umbilical cord, he went to get Gunther, who'd been shooting at bucks all day and finally got one in honor of his son. His future trapper.

"It's a girl," Hux said when he found him and the buck in the forest.

Gunther looked up from field dressing. Hux could tell he was deciding whether or not to be happy, because, in Gunther's view, you could decide things like that. Despite the buck and the fishing rod and the camouflage bib, he decided to be happy.

"I'll buy her a pink tackle box, then," he said, more tenderly than he'd ever said anything. "A goddamn pink tackle box."

He dropped the knife he was holding and a flap of the buck's soft white underbelly fur and started running through the woods toward Hux's cabin, whooping and hollering.

When Hux reached the cabin, the door wide was open, and Gunther was inside holding his daughter up like a prize trout. He was kissing her cheeks and cooing to her.

"You're the greatest little girl who ever lived," he said. "I'm going to spoil you and then spoil you some more. Who says girls can't fish? Look at those perfect hands."

Naamah was still on the bottom bunk.

"Can I get you anything?" Hux said to her while Gunther held his daughter up to the light, which in his hands she didn't shrink from.

"I'm so thirsty," Naamah said, so Hux brought her a glass of water, which she drank down without stopping. He brought her another one.

"She stopped crying the moment he picked her up," Naamah said.

"That's just luck," Hux said. To Gunther, he said, "Come see your wife."

"My wood goddess!" Gunther said and brought the baby over to them. He'd wiped his daughter off with a damp towel and wrapped her up in a dry one. "I had a feeling today was the day. How are you doing? Why didn't anyone come get me?"

"I'm all right," Naamah said, cheering a little.

"That's all that matters, then," Gunther said. He tucked his daughter into the crook of his arm, where she fit perfectly. He gave her his pinkie finger to suck on.

Hux saw tears in his eyes, but unlike when they were kids Gunther didn't wipe them away. A few drops landed on his daughter's cheeks. He didn't wipe those away either. "What do we call a girl as precious as you?" he said. "What name could ever do you justice?"

Naamah looked up at Gunther and their daughter as if she didn't see how she fit with them. Hux wondered if her hesitance had something to do with their conversation earlier. Even though she'd asked him, he couldn't help but feel like he'd poisoned her.

Naamah reached for the silver cross at the front of her neck, but instead of stroking it like she usually did, or cupping it for comfort, she pulled it until the chain broke.

"Racina," she said.

31

🌿 When they'd recovered enough to make the trip, Gunther took Naamah and Racina to Yellow Falls to have them checked out by the doctor, who said they were banged up a little more than was usual but were fine. Naamah didn't act like she was fine, though. If Gunther tried to go hunting, Naamah would beg him to stay. If he went to get another log from the wood-pile, she'd run outside barefoot in the cold after him. If he had to go to the bathroom, she'd follow him in before he could shut the door.

"You've got to help me," Gunther said to Hux when Racina was three weeks old. He'd slipped out of the cabin and crossed the river in a canoe while Phee sat with Naamah and Racina. The canoe told Hux something was wrong before Gunther did.

They were sitting at Hux's kitchen table, waiting for the water to boil for coffee. Gunther looked as bad as he used to after a hard night at the tavern.

"I can't rock both of them," he said. "I've slept a total of two hours in the last two days. Three if you count when I fell asleep standing up."

"Give it a little time," Hux said, even though he'd been worried about Naamah ever since she broke that chain. "She's still finding her footing."

Gunther traced the letters he carved into the wood the last time Naamah wasn't fine. He said something about getting formula in Yellow Falls, even though they'd planned on breastfeeding. Naamah had planned on it anyway.

"I hold that baby more than she does," he said, which Hux could tell hurt him to say out loud. "You'd think it'd be the opposite. Her clamoring for Racina and me shrugging her off. Men aren't even supposed to like babies. But women . . . all the women I've met know how to hold them right. Naamah holds Racina like she's holding a porcupine."

"I'll go see her," Hux said.

He went over to Gunther's place that afternoon while Gunther drove Phee home and continued on to the general store. Hux had been so preoccupied with the birth of his niece he didn't notice that fall was starting to let go of Evergreen. All along the river, the trees were turning red and brown and gold. Frost was settling on the rocks. On the river grass. On the outermost boughs of the evergreens. The air smelled like fire again, winter in the Northwoods. It seemed like such a long time ago now that Naamah was harvesting her corn and swimming in the river beneath a warm sun, her belly poking up like a half-moon.

Hux let himself into Gunther's cabin. Phee had knit a tiny pair of red mittens for Racina and a hat the same color, which she'd left on the table.

"How's my little niece?" Hux said. "My sister?"

Naamah was sitting on the couch with her feet tucked under her. She was staring at the window. The room smelled like spoiled milk. Spit up.

"Gunther sent you over here, didn't he?" Naamah said.

Her eyes didn't look right; even though she was sitting on the couch right in front of him, they were very far away. "Will you open the window? I can't breathe."

"Maybe just a crack," Hux said, looking around for his niece. "It's cold out."

"She's in the bedroom," Naamah said. "Phee got her to sleep for me."

"Can I see her?"

"Yes," Naamah said. "Don't wake her, though."

Racina was asleep in the middle of the bed, swaddled in a worn yellow blanket with ducks all over it. It was his blanket, Naamah's. He saw his name stitched into the corner of it, and though the blanket alone might have drawn him backward to Hopewell or Sister Cordelia or his mother making a hard choice on an April night, seeing that blanket wrapped around Racina made him feel like everything was going to be all right despite what Gunther had said. The blanket was Naamah's dearest possession, and she'd given it to her daughter.

Hux bent over Racina, who was breathing quickly but easily. He kissed her warm cheek. He didn't see how skin could be that soft, that perfect. His skin was somewhere between sandpaper and pine bark. Hux watched Racina sleep awhile. He loved that he got to see her take her first breath. Come into her life with so much grace. In a way, it made up for having to watch his mother and father go out of theirs without it.

Before Hux went back to the living room, Racina opened her eyes. The baby book said it was too early for her to smile, but she did it anyway.

"You were awake this whole time, weren't you?" Hux said to her. "Already tricking your poor old uncle. Winning me over with those big brown eyes."

Racina kicked her foot a little. She made a gurgling noise.

Hux put his finger to his lips. "Don't worry. I won't tell anyone."

Hux waited until Racina closed her eyes before he went back out to sit with Naamah on the couch. He offered to get her something to eat, but Naamah said she wasn't hungry.

She put her head in her hands. "Something's wrong with me, Hux."

Naamah was shaking, so Hux put a wool blanket around her shoulders. "You and Gunther are new parents. That's a lot to take in."

"I'm afraid I'm going to do something terrible," Naamah said. "When babies cried at the orphanage, Sister Cordelia would pinch them until they learned how to be silent."

"You're not going to hurt her," Hux said.

"How do you know that?"

"Because you love her," Hux said.

Naamah picked up a pillow and hugged it close. "Sister Cordelia loved me."

Even though Hux wanted to tell Naamah that wasn't real love, his instinct was to stay quiet. Maybe she counted on Sister Cordelia for that. At least that.

"You want to know the last thing I said to her?" Naamah said. *"You'll never have my love."*

Hux stayed very still, as if Naamah were an animal in the forest and a sudden movement might scare her away. "It was true, wasn't it?" he said gently.

"I knew it would hurt her," Naamah said. "That's why I did it."

Naamah tucked her feet deeper into the couch.

"I thought when I ran into the woods, she was going to follow me. That's why I stayed there all night. That's why I did a lot of things, I guess."

Hux thought about the logging camp, the men.

"There was only one other girl at Hopewell who had a name as different as mine," Naamah said. "Ethelina. She left like I did, a few years before me. I wonder if she stood all night in the trees, too. I wonder which direction she went in the morning."

"Maybe you could find her," Hux said.

Naamah looked toward the window, the trees. "Sometimes I wish I didn't know how to fish and trap. Those other things in my blood now. Sometimes I wish I went south."

Hux thought about the girl with the sock pushed down around her ankle.

"You're here now," he said. "That's what's important."

"Gunther's sick of me, that's for sure," Naamah said.

"You just need to ease up on him a little. Let him go to the bathroom by himself."

"I'm sick of me, too."

"Racina's not going to be a baby forever," Hux said. "Before you know it, she'll be running around the woods. You, too."

"Gunther wants to get her a pair of snowshoes," Naamah said.

"You have to do that, too," Hux said. "Think about the future."

"Sometimes I think about what her first word will be. *Dad,* probably. *Daddy.* I was hoping it would be something like *forest* or *cedar* or *green.*"

"Why *cedar*?" Hux said.

"When I was at the logging camp, there was this old-growth cedar tree I used to sleep up in," Naamah said. "It had great big branches in all the right places. When the wind blew at night, it felt like the tree was rocking me. It felt like the safest place in the world."

Hux heard Gunther's truck coming up the drive.

Naamah heard it, too. She got up to close the window.

"One day when I was up there, I woke up to a group of men yelling for me to come down so they could cut up my tree," she said. "They said I couldn't do anything about it. The sun had come up. The work orders were in."

Naamah put a log in the woodstove.

Gunther was rattling his keys.

"They didn't even look sorry," Naamah said. She sat back down on the couch and hugged the pillow again. "They just started up their chain saws and cut down all that beauty."

32

🌼 Naamah not only started to let Gunther out of her sight, she encouraged him to go. She said she was being foolish before and was done with it now. On the days Gunther went out hunting, she'd pack a lunch for him and kiss him like she did before Racina was born. She'd stand at the door with Racina in her arms, waving until he disappeared into the trees.

Neither Hux nor Gunther knew what she was doing to get her courage back until the first snow of the season came. That night, Gunther said he'd better go out and pull up the new traps he'd been trying out downriver and asked Hux to go with him.

"It'll take half as much time that way," he said. "Unless you have a date with Phee."

"Would you shut up already?" Hux said, getting up from the couch where he was sitting with Naamah. "I'll go."

Naamah was reading the *Yellow Falls Gazette,* which Gunther had brought back from town a few hours before. News about the annual sale at the Hunting Emporium took up the front page. Camouflage was half off.

Gunther walked over to Naamah. "Aren't you going to send me off with a kiss?"

"Kiss," Naamah said, but she didn't look up from the newspaper.

"I want a real one when I get back," Gunther said, pretending to be offended. He was in a good mood. He finally thought things were getting back to normal.

"You should get some sleep," Hux said to Naamah, and he and Gunther left.

The whole time they were out pulling up the traps, Hux felt like something was wrong, but he kept telling himself Racina was asleep in the bedroom and Naamah was awake on the couch; his worries were old ones. But Hux worked hard and fast in the snow anyway, which made Gunther work that way too, and they were back at the cabin in a few hours.

"Where is she?" Gunther said when he went into the bedroom to check on Racina and found an empty bed. He walked all over the cabin, opening and closing doors, overturning things along the way.

"Naamah!" he yelled, as if, despite Naamah's sugary send-offs, he knew there was something to be worried about deep down.

"Your truck's still here," Hux said.

"Where would she have gone? It's night and it's snowing," Gunther said.

Gunther started tossing pots and pans around in the kitchen as if his wife and his daughter were beneath them. After the pots and pans, he moved on to the container of oatmeal on the counter, then the cornmeal, which he emptied on the floor.

"Racina's too little to be outside on a night like tonight."

He stopped when he got to the flour. "She's seven goddamn pounds. She'll freeze."

Gunther dumped the flour on the floor and an empty whiskey bottle tumbled out.

"What in hell is wrong with her?" he said, looking at the bottle.

Hux was looking at the *Gazette,* which lay open on the couch.

Ethelina Thompson, former Hopewell orphan, age 28, of Green River, Minnesota, passed away early yesterday morning surrounded by her family. Ethelina, *Ethie* to those who loved her most, is survived by her husband, Gerard Thompson of Green River, and her three children, Mary Sue, Mary Grace, and Mary Beth.

On the opposite page was a news story, a headline:

MOTHER OF THREE HANGS HERSELF FROM BALCONY
OF RIVERFRONT HOME

Hux read about the wash bucket Ethelina had stood barefoot on. The rope she'd cinched around her neck. He thought about how Naamah must have felt that rope around her neck, too, when she read the article with no one around. She must have felt the cold metal on her feet. She must have panicked when she read about how, before Ethelina turned over the wash bucket to stand on it, she'd been scrubbing herself with steel wool and bleach.

Hux didn't think any direction could have been worse than the one Naamah chose when she left Sister Cordelia at fourteen, but he was wrong. Ethelina didn't even choose a direction; she'd stayed in Green River, a few miles from Hopewell, all this time.

"I think I know where she is," Hux said.

"Where?" Gunther said.

"The Mosquito Net."

"How would she know about that place?"

"She's been there before," Hux said with so much reluctance, so much sadness, he wasn't sure he said it at all. "That time you came over to my cabin looking for her."

Hux thought of the Paul Bunyan trapper, the way he'd ripped open Naamah's green blouse as if he owned her. He thought of the trapper's lapping-dog tongue, all the lapping-dog tongues—why Naamah needed them when she was unsure of herself.

Why she could never let herself be all right.

Gunther picked up the whiskey bottle. "Did you know about this, too?"

"No," Hux said.

"I'm going to find my daughter first and kill you second anyway."

Gunther put his coat back on. He grabbed the keys to his truck.

"I'm coming with you," Hux said.

Gunther looked at him the way they did when they were boys. "Of course you are."

Gunther drove fast but carefully through the snow until they got to the bridge that would take them across the river, and he lost his measure and just plain accelerated. When they passed the boat launch, Hux thought of the night he brought Naamah to Evergreen. He thought of her diving into the water, of the water pooling on the seat beneath her.

He and Gunther never made it inside the Mosquito Net.

When they pulled up, the truck's headlights landed on a cedar tree and the little yellow bundle tucked into its crook. Both of them jumped out when they saw that the bundle was Racina. She was breathing very slowly when they got her down. Her cheek was frostbitten from being pressed against the snowy bark.

Gunther held her in his arms. "Keep swimming, my little fish."

Hux drove them to Yellow Falls as fast as he could, but Gunther kept telling him to go faster. "She's so cold," he said, weeping just like he did when he found out Lulu had gotten caught up in that bear trap. "I should have kept her safe."

When Hux pulled up to the hospital, he left the keys in the ignition, and he and Gunther ran with Racina through the snow, yelling for help. A doctor in a white lab coat met them at the sliding doors. His stethoscope swung like a pendulum. After Gunther explained what had happened as best as he could, the doctor took Racina from him.

"Get a security guard," he said to a nurse.

A moment later, two guards dropped the cups of coffee they were holding and came running out. The doctor pointed to Gunther, who put his hands up in the air.

"Take care of her," Gunther begged. "Make sure they take care of her, Hux."

The guards pushed Gunther down to the ground and handcuffed him, while the doctor put a plastic mask over Racina's face and strapped her little body to a stretcher. He cut the yellow blanket off her, slicing through years of history, and stuck a needle in her tiny arm. Racina cried and cried, and all Gunther could do was watch from the ground.

Hux followed Racina as far as they would let him. He waited by that green door two hours before someone told him

Racina was going to be all right. Before someone said she was a good little fighter. She had a lot of heart.

On his way to tell Gunther, who'd somehow convinced the guards to uncuff him and was already gone, Hux found a scrap of the yellow blanket on the floor. He picked it up and held the ducks against his face. He thought of Naamah's story about her cedar tree, how, even though he didn't hear her, she'd tried to tell him she was falling.

Gunther, Hux would soon learn, was already pulling up to the Mosquito Net. He was parking his truck, running toward the bar door, picturing Racina strapped to a stretcher, a needle in her arm, hearing her cry and cry, all the while yelling for Naamah to come out.

He was kicking his way through the plywood, through the heap of melting snow on the floor. He was looking hard at the roughneck men and the woman passed out in a pool of her own vomit they were laughing at.

Before Gunther could think, he was lifting Naamah up by her tangle of black hair, slinging her over his shoulder, and walking out the door. He was thinking about losing Racina as he was throwing her mother down in the snow.

As he was telling her not to come home.

33

🌸 Even when Hux offered Naamah his bunk bed, his porch, his side of the river entirely, she wouldn't go back to Evergreen. She wouldn't go back inside. She was living deep in the woods, if you could call what she was doing living, waiting for Racina to come home from the hospital, to be all right like Hux said she was.

During the day Hux would leave the hospital while Gunther was in with Racina, drive home on the back roads, and walk out to the woods. The first day he brought Naamah a pair of Phee's boots, since she'd lost one of hers somewhere between the bar and Gunther throwing her down in the snow. He brought her a pair of his warmest gloves, a sleeping bag, and a plate piled high with chicken and vegetables he roasted on the woodstove for her, but Naamah wouldn't touch any of it. The second day, Hux brought a thermos of coffee and a little container of cream, but Naamah wouldn't touch that either. She just stood there in the forest, looking at the canopy of green. A week of this, and her foot didn't even look like a foot anymore—it was purple and swollen and alien.

"At least put the boot on," he said, thinking of their mother's feet right before she died. "Losing your foot isn't going to make any of this better."

"I'm not going to put it on," Naamah said.

Hux set down the trash bag he was holding. He and Naamah were standing close to each other. So close Hux saw the trees reflected in her eyes. He'd been so careful of her for so long, patching her together the best he knew how, and it had gotten them nowhere. Hux wasn't the one who'd left Racina in the crook of a tree, but he knew the blame belonged to him, too. He didn't realize how much he'd been using her to patch himself together.

"You're going to put that boot on," he said, and with a great thrust forward that surprised him as much as it surprised her, he tackled her to the ground.

Hux grabbed her swollen foot and jammed the boot on it. When it wouldn't fit all the way, he twisted the boot like a screw. When it still wouldn't go on right, he took out his pocketknife, cut the leather tongue out, and forced her black-and-blue toes into the heel.

Naamah cried out, and Hux finally let go of the boot. He was breathing hard. Her foot was in his hand. "You made a mistake. People make them, Naamah."

"Not like this they don't," Naamah said.

Hux let go of her foot and lay back in the snow.

Racina was in the hospital with frostbite, pneumonia, and a list of other things he didn't understand written on her chart. Gunther was worrying over her with everything he had, bullying doctors one minute and begging them to take extra-special care of Racina the next. Naamah was going to lose her foot if she kept this up. Everything was such a mess, and, even though he wanted to more than anything, Hux didn't know how to clean it up.

"I'm so sorry," he said.

"I'm sorry, too," Naamah said.

After a while, she put the boot on and lay back with him. The two of them lay shoulder to shoulder in the snow, looking up at the trees above them, the branches swaying in the wind. The canopy was so thick they couldn't see the sky; it made the light look green.

"I'm so far away from who I want to be," Naamah said.

"Me, too," Hux said.

He leaned into her gently, as if the wind were blowing him there. He thought of the girl with the knee sock around her ankle. All that had happened to her. All that would.

"Come home with me," he said, reaching for her hand.

"I can't," she said, but she let him have it.

"Why?"

"Do you remember the first day we chopped wood together?" Naamah said. "I had blood blisters all over my hands and you told me I could have stopped?"

"I used all the bandages I had to patch you up," Hux said.

"That's the thing," Naamah said. "They're all gone now, and I've still got sores."

"What are you saying?" Hux said, even though he knew in his heart what was coming, what had been coming a long time now.

Naamah's eyes were gray and green and clear.

"I'm saying mercy," she said, and let go of his hand.

Hux wondered what their mother would have done if she were here. Would she stop Naamah? Would she let her go? Hux got up and walked over to the trash bag he'd brought with him. He riffled through it until he found what he was looking for.

"This was Lulu's before it belonged to our mother," he said, laying the coonskin coat across Naamah's lap. All these years later, and dust still rose up from it. "The story is whoever wears it wears strength on her shoulders. Whoever wears it will be all right. Both of them would want you to have it."

Naamah ran her fingers along the back of it where the most fur was missing. "I know this coat."

"How?" Hux said.

"The day I left Hopewell Sister Cordelia took us to a festival in Green River," Naamah said. "We sang a song in front of everyone, and when we were done, a woman wearing this coat blocked my way. She was really sick. She knew my life at Hopewell wasn't a good one, and she asked me to forgive her for that. I figured she gave up a child once and was sorry about it and just wanted someone to hear her say so. It was her, wasn't it?"

"I don't know," Hux said, trying to work through his memory so he could see what she was seeing, feel what she was feeling. How many old coonskin coats could there be?

"All this time I've been picturing her walking through grapevines."

"There was this one day she took the truck in the morning without telling anyone and didn't return until late that night," Hux said. "My dad and I borrowed Reddy's truck and drove everywhere we could think of, but we couldn't find her. When she finally came home she wouldn't tell us where she went, but her trip made her more peaceful. She stopped crying out in her sleep. She stopped trying not to die."

"She was the first person who ever kissed me," Naamah said. "I remember the way her lips felt on my skin."

Naamah nuzzled into the coat as if their mother were still in there somewhere.

Maybe she was. Maybe she always had been.

Naamah touched every part of the coat she could get to, letting her hands linger over the missing patches of fur, the white buttons made of bone, the hide Lulu had pieced together from animals she'd trapped so long ago now.

"Thank you for this," she said when her hands had nowhere else to explore.

"I should have given it to you sooner," Hux said, thinking of his mother and Lulu rocking on the front porch of the cabin season after season, year after year, talking and laughing and smoking the way only they knew how.

If you want to catch a fish, you've got to think like one.

I've caught plenty of fish, thank you very much.

Naamah put the coat on, as if she knew Hux needed her to in order for him to leave her alone in the forest like she wanted. "You gave it to me at exactly the right time."

That day, Hux walked back to the cabin the longest way he could think of. He circled trees and dipped down into ravines and dragged his feet in the snow, which would melt tomorrow or the day after, like it always did at this time of year. It would take a few more snows yet before it started to stick for good. When there was nothing left to circle, Hux started following the path the whitetails took, which would take him home.

He could see himself opening some beans and eating them out of the can, hearing the fork scrape against the tin: the sound of being alone. He could see himself turning on the radio and sterilizing his tools and preserving something he didn't really want to preserve.

In the middle of the oxeye meadow, Hux stopped walking. He watched the birds flying low over the snow. He thought of how much his mother would have loved to draw them, how she used to tack her sketches up on the plywood board, which was supposed to have been a window for so long now. The sun dropped low in the sky. Hux's heart dropped low, too. Naamah was alone in the forest, which was full of shadows now. He didn't see how that could be merciful, but he let her go because she asked him to. Because with that old coonskin coat on her shoulders now, he believed she would be all right.

When the sun was completely gone, he walked the rest of the way back to the cabin in the dark. All the lights were on inside, casting a warm glow against the old log walls, which he'd patched about a million times now. Hux walked up onto the porch. Before he could get in the door, Gunther came out of it holding Racina in the crook of his arm.

"We've been waiting for you," he said, as though they hadn't been fighting the last week straight, blaming each other for everything. "They set her free today. I was so happy I bought a whole goddamn turkey from Harvey Small's. Gravy. Potatoes. Cranberry sauce. Phee's going to come over in a while, too."

A large piece of gauze was taped to Racina's cheek. Hux wondered what kind of scar was forming under there. What kind of scars they'd all end up with.

"We started some coffee," Gunther said.

Hux knew he had to find a way to tell Gunther about Naamah, and he knew it would break Gunther's heart, but he wasn't going to tell him tonight. Tonight Hux was going to do the opposite of what he felt like doing: He was going to celebrate his niece's homecoming with his oldest friend in the world. He was going to eat turkey and cranberry sauce and whatever else made it onto his table. He was going to give thanks. Tomorrow he'd order that pane of glass for the window. Before he went to town, he'd walk back to the woods, and even though Naamah wouldn't be there, he'd see the imprint they'd made together in the snow, and it would look to him like two angels, the grace both of them had been looking for.

Hux leaned over Racina, who was making little gurgling noises with her tongue while Gunther bounced her lightly in his arms. When she noticed Hux watching her, she stopped making noises. She looked up at him curiously with her pretty brown eyes.

"What's she doing?" Hux said.

"Still deciding if she likes you," Gunther said, nudging him.

"How do you know she likes you?" Hux said. When he nudged Gunther back, Racina smiled like she did that day in the bedroom. As far as Hux could tell, hers wasn't going to be a crooked smile or one that set off dimples either.

It was going to be a smile all her own.

"Uncle Hux is funny, isn't he?" Gunther said to her, but he was smiling, too.

Hux didn't know how a little girl was supposed to prosper with two craggy men and an old woman looking after her in a place like Evergreen, but he had a feeling she would.

"Don't listen to him," he whispered in his niece's ear just before they went inside.

PART FOUR

Evergreen, Minnesota

1972

34

🐇 For her eleventh birthday, Racina wanted a pair of purple cowboy boots more than anything else in the Northwoods. Ever since she saw them in the general store in Yellow Falls, she couldn't stop thinking about how perfectly they matched the color of the butterfly Uncle Hux showed her last week after one of their walks. A purple emperor, he called it. He said it came all the way from Germany before the war and was the reason, or at least one of them, Racina's grandmother decided to marry her grandfather. Racina liked to think of the cowboy boots that way. She liked to make up stories for them. *There in the leather patch the purple boots were born. Here in the forest they met their first friend.*

The day her dad saw her sketching them in her notebook, he offered to take her to the general store and buy them right then, since her birthday was still months away. As long as it didn't jeopardize her health, her dad couldn't stand for her not to have what she wanted.

"I want to earn them," Racina said, and her dad stopped

jingling the keys to the truck in front of her, trying to lure her out of the cabin with them. She didn't want to hurt his feelings, but she thought the boots would be more special if she worked for them. Like how finding a four-leaf clover yourself was luckier than someone giving one to you.

"You're too young to get a job," her dad said. "You can't even drive yet."

"I was thinking I could do the things you and Uncle Hux don't like to do. You guys are pretty messy. I could help Phee, too. She's been wanting to alphabetize her books, but her hands are hurting her. It could be like an allowance."

"How do you know about allowances?" her dad said, fake squinting like he always did when he was about to say yes but didn't want her to know it yet.

"Evergreen's not as far away from the rest of the world as you think, Dad."

"As I'd *like*," he said and kissed her cheek in the same place he always kissed it.

Her dad hated that more people had moved out to the woods in the last few years. He said it was only a matter of time before Evergreen turned into something it was never meant to be. He used to make fun of Uncle Hux about not having running water, but now he told him to hold out because wells attracted the wrong kind of people. People at all. He said if it weren't for Racina's sickness, he'd have filled theirs in a long time ago and turned back to the river, the rain. Thank God, he said, no one had ever built that paper mill or dam.

If it weren't for her sickness.

Racina had heard those words all her life. They were the six most powerful words in the English language. Strung together like that they meant no matter how warm the river was, her dad wouldn't let her swim in it. They meant overdressing all year long to keep the chill off and the infections away. They meant not running even when the crickets in the meadow clung to her socks and made her want to lift up her legs more than anything. They meant never standing in the rain. Never playing in the snow. Once, Racina made a list of everything she wasn't allowed to do because of her sickness, and it filled most of a notebook. When she showed it to her dad, all he said was that it took a lot to keep her safe.

The doctors agreed Racina had a rare immune disorder, but over the years they'd disagreed about how to treat it. Some wanted to stick her and her bones with needles. Some wanted to send her to faraway places to be studied. Some wanted to take her away from her dad because sometimes he'd get so mad he'd grab her file out of their hands and tear it in two. Dr. Beller, their new doctor, was the only one whom her dad didn't do that to. She was the only one who said Evergreen was exactly where Racina was supposed to be.

Racina wondered what Dr. Beller would think about the purple cowboy boots. The last time she saw her in Green River, Dr. Beller was wearing a bright orange dress underneath her white doctor's coat. She said she guessed she was ready for hunting season, all those poor deer. Racina said she didn't like to hunt either—not that she was *allowed* to.

"Stop making me look bad," her dad had said.

Now he put his keys back on the hook by the door. He said he didn't want her sweeping anything and stirring up her cough, but she could get wild with the sponge as long as she wore rubber gloves. He said that ought to be worth a pair of purple cowboy boots.

"*Dad,*" Racina said. "I want to really earn them. Not fake earn them."

"Fine," her dad said. "I'll give you five dollars."

"One dollar," Racina said, wishing everyone would stop being so careful of her lungs and her cough and *everything* and treat her like a normal girl for once.

"Not a penny less," her dad said and held out his hand for her to shake.

Theirs was the first cabin she cleaned from top to bottom (as high as she could reach on her tiptoes, anyway). She wiped down the cabinets, then the counters, and then the floor. After that, she hoisted herself up on the counter to open the curtains above the sink. When she was little and didn't want to eat whatever weird food her dad put in front of her because someone told him it worked miracles, she'd sit at the table and count the squirrels on the curtain fabric. She remembered once getting as high as two hundred and four before her dad made her move to a different chair and count what was left on her plate instead. They both knew a lot about things like wheat germ and brewer's yeast and tea that tasted like dirt.

When Racina was done with the main part of the cabin, she cleaned her room. She made her bed more carefully than she would have if she weren't getting paid for it. She picked her clothes up off the floor and put them back into her dresser. She tried peeling the pink stickers off her mirror again, but they still wouldn't budge. She didn't like how everything for girls was pink and everything for boys was blue anymore. She wanted to be like her history book said Switzerland was during the First World War.

Racina loved studying history. Studying in general. Since she wasn't allowed to go to the school in Yellow Falls and make real ones, sometimes she'd pretend people like Watson and Crick and Einstein and Eleanor Roosevelt were her friends. She liked learning about the world. Unlike her dad, she didn't mind seeing a few more cabins on the drive to Yellow Falls.

Uncle Hux didn't mind either, as long as the people in those cabins were good to the land. He said as much when her dad dropped her at Uncle Hux's cabin a few days later when the rain cleared and the river calmed down and the sky turned blue again.

"Did you see that barn the new people put up by Phee's place?" her dad said. "Someone should burn that down. They cut an acre of trees."

"*Dad,*" Racina said.

"What else am I supposed to say?"

"Not that you're going to burn a barn down," Racina said.

Her dad tapped the top of her head. "I only said someone should."

Uncle Hux held the screened door open for Racina to come inside. "You're dad's right this time. It would take a hundred years to get those trees back to what they were."

Racina's dad put his hand on her shoulder. "Hold up a minute. You're not going to get rid of me that quickly."

He handed Uncle Hux the usual list of instructions he'd put strips of clear tape all over to strengthen, the first-aid kit, and the bag of remedies in case she got sick.

"If she starts coughing, give her a spearmint leaf to chew on. If she sounds gravelly, make her a cup of this tea. If she does anything else, go to the hospital. You know the rules. Don't give her caffeine. Don't ply her with candy either. I know you give her those licorice ropes. You might as well give her a spoon and a goddamn bowl of sugar."

"I'm not a baby," Racina said. "I know what to do when I cough."

"All right," her dad said. "I'll be back in a few hours."

On her way inside the cabin, Racina saw the nail polish still stuck to Uncle Hux's pinkie finger, which he had let her paint when he came over last week. They drew a picture together then, too, which Uncle Hux had put up in the same place he always did.

"Why do you hang pictures right on the window like that?" she asked.

"It's something your grandmother used to do when this was a piece of plywood."

"For decoration?" Racina said.

"Yes," Uncle Hux said.

"Is that why Aunt Leah collects all those tiny teacups?" Racina said, looking at the shelf above her uncle's bed, which was full of them. The only miniature thing she owned was the white ceramic bird that had appeared on her windowsill one morning when she was six years old and she returned from a two-week stay at the hospital in Green River.

"I have no idea," Uncle Hux said. "I just try not to break them."

"When will she be back?" Racina said.

"A few more weeks still. Her sister's having the kind of wedding that lasts a lot longer than one day. Your aunt's ready to send her on her honeymoon."

"I don't think I want to get married," Racina said.

"It's nice being married," Uncle Hux said. "Especially to your aunt."

Racina loved the story of how Aunt Leah came to be her aunt. Whenever she stayed over on one of the bunk beds, she asked them to tell it. Her favorite part was about how Uncle Hux realized he'd made a terrible mistake letting her leave Evergreen and in the middle of the night got in his truck and drove hundreds of miles. Racina loved hearing about how he promised to build her a bridge across the river if she didn't want to get her feet wet.

"Dad probably wouldn't let me get married anyway," Racina said, wondering if a boy would ever want to build a bridge for her.

"Your dad loves you so much it makes him crazy sometimes," Uncle Hux said.

"Sometimes?" Racina said.

Uncle Hux smiled. "That may have been generous."

"He won't even let me sweep."

"I won't either. I have a much more important job for you. A museum in Wisconsin asked me to bring a badger back to life for an exhibit. I thought you could help."

"Do you really need my help?" Racina said. Sometimes she had the feeling that people weren't always telling her the full truth, maybe because she knew she wasn't always telling them the full truth. "Because I want to earn those boots."

"I need your little hands," Uncle Hux said. "Your artistic sense. Right now his fur is so bleached he's the color of an old bone. He's missing an eye, too."

Racina sat at the kitchen table while Uncle Hux put a kettle on the woodstove. He said he needed to sterilize his tools and drink some coffee before he got started. He had to mix some paint, too, which she could help with. The only time he ever worked inside was when Aunt Leah was gone, because the only animals she wanted on the table were the ones that ended up on her plate, and she wasn't even sure about that anymore.

"You want some of that tea your dad packed you with?" Uncle Hux said when the kettle whistled. He opened the tin of sugar and got out a spoon.

"I'll have coffee actually," Racina said.

"Your dad wouldn't like that."

"He wouldn't have to know," Racina said.

When it was done brewing, Uncle Hux poured a little in

a cup for her and added some cream and a teaspoon of sugar. "One of these days you're going to get me in trouble."

"You and Phee are the only ones who let me do things," Racina said. She puckered her lips when she tasted her coffee. "It's so sweet."

"People always say that, but they get used to it," Uncle Hux said.

He looked out the window above the sink for a minute, as if something more than a raspberry bush stood in front of it. Her dad and Phee did that sometimes, too. Racina wondered if all adults did that or just the ones in Evergreen.

"I'm used to it now," Racina said, unpuckering.

Uncle Hux went into his closet and came back with a cardboard box of fake glass eyes for Racina to look through. Then he went and got the badger from the shed and set the small museum crate on the table. Racina's dad said that before she was born, Uncle Hux used to preserve animals for hunters who wanted heads on their walls. When she asked him why he stopped, her dad said Uncle Hux got soft. They all did. Her dad used to be a trapper. Now he mostly made fishing rods and sold them to people who didn't know how to fish.

"They look like marbles," Racina said about the eyes.

"Marbles would be a lot cheaper," Uncle Hux said. "These are custom eyes. A man in Canada makes each one of them by hand. No two are exactly alike, just like in life."

Racina held up a blue eye that looked just like river ice. "This one's pretty."

"The museum will probably want brown ones," Uncle Hux said.

"Why?" Racina said.

"Because they want the badger to look real."

"By using fake eyes?" Racina said.

Before he uncrated the badger, Uncle Hux put on a pair of

plastic gloves. He told her not to touch the badger's fur because a lot of old taxidermists used to preserve with arsenic, which was a poison. A lot of them didn't know what they were doing either, he said, which was why this guy had seams all over the place. Each person who'd worked on him had tried to cover up the previous person's mistakes but had ended up making his own.

"How will you fix him?" Racina said.

"I don't know yet," Uncle Hux said. "That's what the coffee's for."

The two of them sat together at the table with the box of eyes and the badger between them, drinking their coffee. Hux asked her how her studying was going, which she said was better for her than it was for her dad. Her dad didn't understand the kind of math that was in her book, and even though he said he'd never once had to divide fractions in his life he stayed up all night until he figured out how to do it.

"He's one of the most stubborn people I've ever met," Uncle Hux said.

"You should see him around my French book."

"We never had to learn another language when we were your age. We didn't have to go in and take those tests you take either. Your dad learned what to do by trying it, and I learned what not to do by watching him. I bet he went up every tree within a mile of here."

Racina liked to imagine Uncle Hux and her dad playing in Evergreen as kids, climbing trees and jumping in the river and running until they couldn't run anymore.

She set her coffee cup down. "Uncle Hux?"

"You don't have to drink it if you don't like it," he said.

"If I ask you something, will you tell me the truth?" Racina said.

"I'll try," Uncle Hux said.

Racina swept her dark hair away from her face and touched her cheek, her scar, which looked almost exactly like the leaf of a pitcher plant. The edges of the scar formed the shape of a trumpet. Inside, the skin was marbled with tiny veins. More than her sickness, which made the skin underneath her eyes red most of the time and kept her smaller and thinner than other girls her age, her scar was what made people stare at her.

"How did I get this?" she said.

Uncle Hux let go of his coffee. His face didn't look soft like it usually did. His beard either. He looked worried or sad or both maybe. "What does your dad say?"

"He says it's a birthmark," Racina said.

"That seems right," Uncle Hux said.

"I'm almost eleven," she said, glaring at him. "I know the difference between a birthmark and a scar."

Uncle Hux looked at the badger as if the answer were somewhere in that crate. If he didn't tell her about the scar, she didn't know who would. Uncle Hux wasn't built for lying. At least that's what her dad had said when the three of them were on their way to Yellow Falls and her dad stopped to put up NO TRESPASSING signs on public land.

"I know it has something to do with my mother," Racina said. "I saw it in my medical file once before dad took it out. I know I was in the snow."

Racina knew other things, too. She knew she was three weeks old the first time she went to the hospital, and she knew her mother never came to visit her.

Uncle Hux looked at her as if he were deciding something important and needed her face to do it. He'd never looked at her scar with anything other than love, and because of that she didn't know what his expression meant; right then, his eyes looked like they were holding on to all the feelings in the world. After a while, he took off his gloves and went into the closet, where he stayed so long Racina wondered if he was ever going to come back.

When he finally did, he said, "I don't think I can tell you what you want to know."

"Why?" Racina said.

"Because your dad wouldn't want me to." Uncle Hux pushed a little cedar box in her direction. "This is the best I can do until you talk to him."

Racina reached for the box, which had a flower on the front of it.

"It's yours now," Uncle Hux said.

Racina lifted the top off the box and looked inside, expecting to find one of Uncle Hux's wood carvings or a present Aunt Leah had picked out for her in one of the stores in Yellow Falls. What Racina found instead were photographs.

"That's a picture of your mother with her corn," Uncle Hux said, moving his chair so he was next to her. "She's the only one of us who could grow it without the crows getting it."

Racina looked at her mother, who was wearing overalls and a white T-shirt in the picture. Her feet were bare. Her toes were buried in the dirt. The corn was all around her. Racina had only ever seen one other picture of her mother—the day she and her dad were married—and her mother looked scared in that one.

"That's you in her belly," Uncle Hux said.

"It is?" Racina said. She touched the picture before she remembered it was bad for them. Her mother was holding her stomach with one hand and holding the corn back with the other. She looked so pretty. Her dark hair went all the way down to her waist like Racina wanted hers to do. She was smiling the way her dad did when he was in a really good mood.

"She was very happy that day," Uncle Hux said. "We all were."

In another picture, Uncle Hux had his arm around her mother—his sister—and in another one her dad was kissing an ear of corn. The last picture was the one she loved the most. In that one, her dad was kneeling in front of her mother with his hands on her waist and his lips on her stomach. Her dad had told Racina he thought she was going to be a boy before she was born. He even said he thought that was what he wanted. But when he saw her for the first time, he said he wouldn't have traded her for all the boys in the world.　•

Racina knew her mother left Evergreen when she was a baby, and she knew it wasn't because of anything she did—at least that's what her dad used to say when she was little and asked about her mother. Her dad said her mother grew up in the orphanage in Green River. He said she had a very hard life, which made her sick, and she had to go away to get better.

"Why didn't he ever marry anyone else?" Racina said.

"It takes your dad a long time to figure out how to let go of things," Uncle Hux said. "It takes me a long time, too."

Racina looked at the picture again. "I can't tell what color her eyes were."

"They're gray with just a little green in them," Uncle Hux said. He sifted through the box of glass eyes and put one of them in her hand. "This one's pretty close."

Racina held the eye up to the light. The gray in it made her think of the stones by the river, which she liked to sit on when the sun was shining because they made her warm. The streaks of green running through the gray made her think of the river grass and how, when she was little and the wind blew, the grass seemed like it was waving to her.

"Do you think you can love someone you never really knew?" she said.

"Yes," Uncle Hux said. He put his arm around her the way he put it around her mother all those years ago in the corn. "I think they can love you, too."

After her dad picked her up and they crossed the river and walked up the bank to their cabin, Racina decided to take a nap. Her dad asked if she wanted him to tuck her in, but she said she was fine. All she wanted to do was sleep a little. Cleaning was hard work.

"How about I make you some of those noodles you like for dinner?" her dad said.

Usually, Racina liked to help with the noodles because her dad let her make a little hill of flour and a well and crack an egg into it. Usually, she savored each noodle she twirled onto her fork. "I don't like them that much."

"Since when?" he said.

"Today," Racina said, thinking of the pictures of her mother in the corn and wishing her dad had been the one to give them to her.

"You sure you're all right? You don't sound like you."

"Who else would I be?" Racina said, but she meant if her mother had stayed in Evergreen. If her eyes were gray with a little green in them, too.

When her dad finally stopped staring at her and began measuring out flour for the noodles, Racina went into her room and closed her door. When she heard the radio go on and the familiar clang of pots and pans start up, she lifted the corner of her mattress and moved her hand around until she felt the folder she was looking for. Even though it was just she and her dad in the cabin and he didn't go through her belongings, or at least she didn't think he did, when she first started putting things in the folder she wrote *Property of Racina* on the front and beneath that *Please Keep Out*.

Racina took the cedar box Uncle Hux had given her out

of the bag that held her medicine. Out of that she took the photographs of her mother in the corn and put them into the folder along with the little book about having a baby Phee had given her, the scrap of her baby blanket, which was supposed to have belonged to her mother first, and the tarnished cross she found on the floor at Uncle Hux's when she was four or five and would make forts under the bottom bunk bed. She pretended the cross belonged to her mother, since the orphanage in Green River used to be a religious one when she lived there. Uncle Hux said that had all changed a few years ago when the head nun died.

Sometimes Racina would rub the cross like a crystal ball and see her mother walking through a meadow like the one on the other side of the river. Other times she'd see her catching a fish with her bare hand like Uncle Hux said she did once.

Today, Racina looked at the picture of her dad and her mother in the corn together. She didn't want to say so in front of Uncle Hux, but she was worried about her dad, and even though it didn't make sense to her, she was mad at him at the same time. She'd heard him and Uncle Hux talking outside by the fire pit last week. Uncle Hux had told her dad he'd watch Racina if he wanted to go to town like he used to before she was born. If her dad wanted to spin a woman around a dance floor for a few hours. Eat some dinner.

"I'm beyond all of that now," her dad had said.

"You can't be beyond love. It isn't healthy."

"Then I'm on death's door," her dad had said.

As far as Racina could tell, her dad wasn't beyond love; he was still stuck in it, which was why she'd stopped asking about her mother. Every time she did, he'd look like the buck's head on the wall above the woodstove. That was why she didn't tell him about the baby book or the cross, and that was why she wouldn't tell him about the picture of him and her mother in the corn either. But she wanted to, and she wanted him to tell her things, too.

After they ate dinner that night and listened to the radio awhile, Racina got ready for bed, and her dad came to tuck her in. She knew she was getting too old to be tucked in, but she didn't want to be the one to say so. Her dad pulled the covers back and sat on the bed next to her. He always started with stories and ended with a song. Tonight Racina asked for a shadow story because she knew how much her dad liked to tell them. He'd cup his hands and release them and suddenly there would be an alligator on the wall. Or a bear. Or a wolverine, because of how rare they were.

Tonight her dad told about a woman, walking through a forest, who had a special sense about the outdoors, so much so that animals and birds would come up to her instead of the other way around. Even the trees would lean toward her as she walked by.

As he spoke, Racina watched her dad as much as she watched the shadows on the wall. Her night-light was on in case she got sick in the middle of the night, and it illuminated his face enough that she could see this story, or at least this part of it, made him sad. He said the lady was a wood angel and that nobody knew it until they took her out of the woods, and she wilted like a plucked flower. He said by the time people realized what was happening to her, she had only one little petal left.

"She didn't die, did she?" Racina said.

"No," her dad said. "She found her way outside again."

"Did the people leave her alone?"

Racina's dad moved his hand in a sweeping motion in front of the wall as if he were erasing the wood angel lady.

"She left them," he said.

After the story was over, he pulled the covers up to her chin like he always did. The moment he left, she'd free herself from the covers, pull off her socks, and sprawl across the bed with just the sheet over her. If he didn't come in to check on her, she would have slept *au naturel*—her new favorite French word. She liked being a little cold. A little nude.

Her dad smoothed the hair back from her face and kissed her cheek. "Sleep tight."

"Don't let the wolf spiders bite," Racina said. She always slept well knowing he was just on the other side of the wall and that a little bit of her mother was right underneath her.

At the door, her dad paused. "Which one do you want tonight?"

"You choose," Racina said, wondering what her dad was going to do between now and when he went to bed, which was still hours away. One night, when her throat felt prickly, she'd wandered out to the kitchen for water and a cough drop. Her father had fallen asleep on the couch, which he was too big for. He was curled up around the pillow that looked like a candy cane. Even though it wasn't cold that night, Racina covered him with a warm wool blanket before she got a cough drop from the tin on the counter and went back to her room. She understood then how much love was behind him doing the same for her.

Tonight, her dad chose a song he'd been singing to her forever.

> *Go to sleep my darling, close your weary eyes.*
> *The lady moon is watching from out the starry skies.*
> *The little stars are peeping, to see if you are sleeping.*
> *Go to sleep, my darling, go to sleep, good night.*

35

⚘ Phee thought purple cowboy boots sounded like a lot more fun than the boots they made when she was Racina's age. Like Racina's dad, she wanted to go to town and get them for her right away. When Racina explained about wanting to earn them, Phee offered her ten dollars to help her organize her books, which was what the boots cost. When Racina tried to bargain her down like she did with her dad, Phee said there were two kinds of people in the world: the kind who over-estimated how much they were worth and the kind who under-estimated how much they were worth. She said it was much better to be the first kind.

"Why?" Racina said. Her dad had just dropped her off at Phee's cabin and had gone on to chop wood with Uncle Hux. Racina was going to spend the morning here and the after-noon at Dr. Beller's office in Green River so Dr. Beller could run some tests.

"The second kind of people aren't usually very happy," Phee said. "They think they don't deserve to be. They're a glum group, frankly."

"Okay," Racina said.

"Smart girl," Phee said. She handed Racina a crisp ten-dollar bill, which her cat, Liddy, tried to bat away with her paw. "Stop that. You're a mean old thing, aren't you?"

"Why does she only like me when I'm sick?" Racina said, putting the money in her pocket. The only times Liddy ever let Racina pet her without hissing or clamping down on her fingers was when she wasn't feeling right. Then and only then would she lick Racina's face. But the moment she was well again, Liddy would stop all that sweetness and turn sour.

"It's a strange habit of hers, isn't it?" Phee said, looking toward the bright yellow windowsill in the kitchen where Liddy had escaped. "The only time she doesn't mind me is when I'm opening a tin of sardines for her."

Before they got to the books, Phee poured a glass of juice for Racina and showed her a picture of a jacket she and Uncle Hux were thinking of getting her for next winter. According to the catalog, the jacket was made of goose down and weighed only thirteen ounces. It was waterproof, too. Uncle Hux was the one who picked out the color. Red onion. He thought it would look pretty with Racina's dark hair.

"I love it," Racina said.

"Then it's yours," Phee said. "Your current coat is so heavy it makes you hunch. This one's supposed to be warmer, too."

"Thank you so much," Racina said. She was hopeful that this jacket—because the description said it had been tested to thirty-seven degrees below zero and wind chills even greater than that—would convince her father to let her go out and build a snowman or make an igloo next winter.

Racina put her juice glass in the sink, and the two of them started alphabetizing Phee's books, which smelled a little rotten and a little sweet at the same time, like old leaves or wet newspaper. Phee said she'd been meaning to do this for a while but her hands were too undependable. Some days she couldn't even hold a pencil. She had special metal braces for both hands, but she didn't like to wear them because she said they made her feel like a robot. She said her hair was the only thing about her she didn't mind being silver.

"I wouldn't mind silver hair either," Racina said. "I think it's neat."

"You may be the only one in the world who thinks so," Phee said. "Getting old doesn't win most of us any beauty contests."

"Aunt Leah puts green clay all over her face to keep it young," Racina said. Last time Aunt Leah did it, she let Racina put some on, too.

"I'm afraid no amount of clay will fix me," Phee said. "I'm dealing with deep and mighty ravines. Mountains. Deserts."

Phee got out a stepladder for Racina to stand on, since she couldn't reach the top row of books on her tiptoes. "What's up there anyway?" she said.

"It looks like some books about gardening. There's one about airplanes, too."

"Can you bring those down yourself?"

"I think so," Racina said, but Phee put her hands on Racina's ankles anyway.

When Racina got all the gardening books down, she asked if she could look at the one about airplanes, and Phee said yes, of course.

"Have you ever been in one?" Racina said.

"Once," Phee said. "A little crop duster."

"What was it like?"

"Scary at first, but then I didn't want to come down," Phee said.

Racina looked at all the different airplanes in the book.

Some were small and sleek, and some were so large and bulky looking Racina wondered how they ever got off the ground. She wondered what it would feel like to fly through all that blue.

"Are people with immune disorders allowed to go on planes?" Racina said.

"I don't see why not," Phee said. "Where would you go?"

Racina went back up the ladder. "The Arctic Circle."

Ever since she'd read about it in Uncle Hux's book, she wanted to go there even though the author said there were only three things that far north—snow, ice, and regret. She wanted to see the sun at midnight.

"Where else would you fly?" Phee said.

"Wherever my mother lives," Racina said.

Racina had dreamed about meeting her mother ever since she found out she had one. Sometimes when she and her dad were in Yellow Falls, she'd pretend the women who walked past them were her mother. Once, Racina blew one of them a kiss, and the woman gave her a lollipop that looked like a rainbow, and because her dad didn't want to offend the woman, Racina got to eat it right there on the street.

Phee helped Racina down from the ladder even though Racina was standing steadily on the middle step and didn't ask to come down.

"I probably shouldn't tell you this, but I'm tired of not telling you," she said holding Racina's hands, even though it clearly hurt her and to do it she had to concentrate very hard. Anymore, her hands nearly always shook. "Your mother lives in Wisconsin, honey. I still talk to her. So does your Uncle Hux."

Ever since Racina had learned about verb tenses, she thought maybe that was true, because both Uncle Hux and Phee mostly talked about her in the present tense.

"Is she still sick?" Racina said.

"No, she's much better now."

Then why doesn't she come home? Racina thought, even though she knew the real story of her mother was much more complicated than the one her dad had told her. She knew the words "she had a very hard life that made her sick" were supposed to explain everything that had happened while her mother was in Evergreen without explaining it at all. They were like Racina's great big coat; they were supposed to keep her safe.

"She lives on a dairy farm with an old friend of hers," Phee said.

Before they finished organizing her books and Racina's dad picked her up, Phee said one last thing about her mother. "Don't be afraid to tell him you want to see her. He's stronger than you think. He'll be all right."

On the way to Dr. Beller's office, Racina was quiet. Usually she liked the drive to Green River, especially when everything was starting to bloom again like it was now, and the fields and grass and trees were such a pretty shade of green. Today, all Racina wanted to do was be at home with the folder under her bed. She wanted to write down *Wisconsin, dairy farm,* and *old friend.* She wanted to write down *she would want to see me.*

Her dad was quiet, too, but the fishing rods he was going to drop off at the Hunting Emporium on the way back were tapping against the window in the back of the truck like fingers. Racina didn't like to fish that much, but she loved to watch her dad make the rods. Each one involved splitting sheaths of wood, sanding, and lacquering them over and over again, which her dad said took a kind of patience he wasn't born with. He said he broke a lot of rods when he was first learning. He said he started making them because when Racina had learned how to stand at the edge of the river without almost falling in—when she was about three—he wanted to get her a pink rod and a pink tackle box, but nobody made them in the Northwoods. Even though it was too small for her now, the pink rod was hanging on the wall above her bed. She used the tackle box to hold her art supplies.

"How much did Phee give you?" her dad said.

"Ten dollars," Racina said, showing him the bill.

"How come you took it from her and not me?" Even though the cab was getting warm from the sun and he was still sweating from chopping wood with Uncle Hux, Racina knew he wouldn't roll down the window because of the draft it would cause. He kept eyeing the sleeves of her shirt, which she'd rolled up when she was sorting books for Phee.

"I don't want to be the kind of person who underestimates my worth," Racina said.

Her dad looked at her, but he didn't say anything.

"She let me look at a book about airplanes," Racina said. "I hope I get to go up in one someday. The big ones go hundreds of miles per hour."

"I like you being on the ground," her dad said.

"Dad?" Racina started, but she already knew she couldn't ask him to see her mother. She thought of her fishing rod. Her tackle box. She rolled down her sleeves.

"Yeah?" her dad said. A wood chip was stuck to his cheek.

Racina moved across the front seat until she was close enough to lean against him. "How was chopping wood with Uncle Hux?"

"I chopped him into the ground," he said, but it didn't seem like what he'd really wanted to say either.

When they arrived at Dr. Beller's office, the nurse took Racina back for a blood test. Usually her dad went with her, but today Dr. Beller wanted to talk to him privately. The nurse who usually drew her blood was sick, and her replacement couldn't find Racina's vein until the sixth try. She kept apologizing, and Racina kept telling her it was all right. She didn't look tough, but she was. She was from Evergreen.

When her dad saw her arm, he wasn't as nice.

"I could do better than that," he said when they were both back in the waiting room. "I *have* done better than that."

"She was really nice, Dad. My veins are tiny."

"Goddamn it," he said, raising his voice. "Why do people keep wanting to hurt you?"

"It only looks like it hurts," Racina said.

"What's going on out here? Do I have to call the police to get a little order in my waiting room?" Dr. Beller said from the doorway next to the reception window. She was wearing bright yellow shoes today that crisscrossed at her toes, a dress that looked like geometry, and a little purple flower twirled up in blond hair.

Dr. Beller winked at them, but before Racina could wink back her dad did.

"Should we all go back to the exam room?" Dr. Beller said.

"I like your shoes," Racina said when they got there. Racina took hers off and hopped up onto the exam table. "Your flower, too."

Dr. Beller took it out of her hair and with a bobby pin secured it to Racina's. "I have a whole backyard full of them right now. It's like a purple carpet."

Dr. Beller talked about how well Racina was doing and how great it was that she'd gone two whole months without so much as a sniffle. She checked Racina's heart and listened to her lungs. At the end of the exam, Racina's dad left the room so Dr. Beller could examine her chest and stomach.

"Does this hurt?" Dr. Beller said, pushing lightly around her belly button.

"No," Racina said.

"How about this?"

"Still no," Racina said.

"This is all very good," Dr. Beller said. "I'm so happy you're feeling well. I'm hoping the blood test you took today will tell us a little more about what's happening in your body when you're not sick and maybe that will help us keep you that way."

Dr. Beller leaned over Racina to take one last listen to her heart. She wore perfume that smelled like lemons. When she was finished examining Racina, she opened a cabinet and pulled out a small basket of toys. "Are you too old for one of these?"

"Should I be?" Racina said.

"You should see my collection," Dr. Beller said. "I've got the house and the barn and the tractor even. I'm only missing the old goat now."

Racina picked out a little plastic cow to add to her barnyard set at home. The cow was the color of cream with brown spots all over it. It looked proud of itself somehow.

Racina followed Dr. Beller out to the waiting room. She was lagging behind a little, looking at the cow. She didn't put everything together until she and her dad were back in the truck and on their way out of Green River. Her dad had started going a new way.

"Do you like Dr. Beller?" she said.

"Sarah?" her dad said. "Yes. She's a great doctor."

"I mean do you like her how Aunt Leah and Uncle Hux like each other?"

"I'm not going to buy her a tiny teacup if that's what you mean."

Racina looked down at her cow. "I wouldn't mind if you liked her like that."

Her dad didn't say anything for a long time. They drove past the last business and up a winding road with forest on either side of it. There were only a few houses, a few telephone poles, a few places to pull off from the road if you got turned around. Racina didn't know if he did it on purpose, but ever since he'd started going this way her dad would slow down right before they passed the orphanage her mother grew up in. Today when he did that, Racina saw a bunch of kids chasing one another around the grass, laughing and panting in a way that made Racina jealous. Uncle Hux said it used to be a very uninviting place when it was called Hopewell.

"I do like Dr. Beller," her dad finally said. "I like her a lot."

Racina liked Dr. Beller a lot, too. She was funny and smart and nice. Unlike all of the other doctors Racina had known, Dr. Beller was the only one who didn't have cold hands. She was the only one who said there was nothing more wonderful than the sound of a heart.

"The woods and lemons smell good together," Racina said.

"You think so?" her dad said. "What if she doesn't like me back?"

"She said all she's missing now is an old goat," Racina said, leaning against her dad's arm while he drove. She could already picture Dr. Beller at the cabin with them. She could see the three of them—the two of them, since she'd be stuck with the dirt tea—making coffee in the mornings and taking it out onto the porch like Racina and her dad did when it was nice outside. She could see them walking along the river. Through the forest. Eating blueberries as they went along. She could see her and her dad showing Dr. Beller all the reasons they loved Evergreen so much. She could see the three of them listening to the radio before bed. She wondered if Dr. Beller would want to tuck her in, and if she did what story she would tell. What song she would sing. What song she and her dad might sing together.

"Dad?" Racina said, picturing them at her door and feeling funny about it for minute. "Why do you drive this way now?"

They were past the orphanage, on their way out to the alfalfa and potato fields. The windows were closed, but Racina could smell the wet earth, the plants peeking up through it.

"I guess it's my way of finally saying goodbye to your mother," her dad said.

"Do you still love her?" Racina said.

Her dad put his hand on her knee. It was rough in places and smooth in others. "She gave me you, didn't she?"

Racina looked at the plastic cow in her lap and the hand on her knee. She didn't know what a dairy farm looked like or Wisconsin or even an old friend. She only knew that she wanted to know those things the way she knew the woods and the bog and the river.

"I want to see her, Dad. Phee told me she lives in Wisconsin."

Her dad took his hand away from her knee as if her knee had stung him. "She shouldn't have told you that. It isn't her business."

"Is it true?" Racina said.

"It doesn't matter," her dad said in the same sharp voice he'd used when someone from the government came out to Evergreen last year and said they were thinking about finally building that dam again. "You're not going."

"Because when I was a baby she hurt me?" Racina said.

Her dad hit the steering wheel with his hand. A wood chip went flying.

"I'm going to kill Phee."

"She wasn't the one who told me," Racina said.

"Then I'll shoot Uncle Hux."

"It's in my medical file," Racina said. "How my cheek was in the snow."

Racina didn't know why, but something about what she'd said made her dad pull the truck over to the side of the road. Something made him look like he did that night when he was sleeping and she'd covered him with a big wool blanket even though it wasn't cold.

"You don't forgive her, do you?" Racina said.

Her dad looked toward the last of the woods, which were green from all the rain. The fields up ahead were green, too. "No," he said.

Racina touched her cheek. "But I do."

Her dad looked at the woods a long time before he put his hand back on her knee, before he turned to the road in front of them, before he let out the breath he'd been holding for years, it seemed like, and said, "I guess that means I have to let you go."

36

⚘ Three and a half weeks later, Racina was standing on the airstrip in Yellow Falls. She and Uncle Hux were getting ready to go up in a bright red plane with a bush pilot her dad knew. Uncle Hux told her not to worry when she saw that there were only three seats including the pilot's; his badger, which he was bringing back to the museum personally this time, didn't count as a passenger. They were going to be gone four nights, which seemed like a really long time now that the pilot was telling them he was ready to go whenever they were. Except for when she was in the hospital, Racina had always gone to sleep in Evergreen.

Even though she'd already said goodbye to him, Racina walked back to her dad, who was standing with Dr. Beller, Phee, and Aunt Leah. The day was warm for this early in June. Dust from the surrounding fields was blowing across the runway. The women were fanning themselves with their hands and holding their dresses down at the same time.

"I'm melting," Aunt Leah said. "How much water are we made of, Dr. Beller?"

"More than sixty percent," Dr. Beller said. "Call me Sarah."

"What is it, honey?" Racina's dad said, bending over her.

Racina looked down at her purple cowboy boots, which her dad surprised her with that morning. She didn't exactly earn them, but they were special anyway just like he promised they would be. "What if it won't stay up in the air?" she said to him now.

But it wasn't the plane she was afraid of or even meeting her mother for the first time, which she was going to do with Uncle Hux in a few short hours.

She was afraid to leave him.

Her dad picked her up and hugged her close.

The first time they said goodbye he put his hands behind his head like he couldn't breathe. The first time, he told her all the things she was supposed to be careful about. The first time, he said she was the greatest goddamn girl who ever lived.

This time, her dad finished hugging her and set her on her feet again.

"Will you do something for me?" he said.

Racina looked up at her dad. She decided she wouldn't put up a fight if he'd changed his mind about her going. She'd stay here forever if that was what he wanted.

"Do you know what would make me happy?" he said. His eyes looked big and soft and open. "If you promise me you'll have lots of fun on your trip."

Racina knew how hard it must have been for her dad to agree to send her up in a plane without him, to give her what she really wanted. *"Dad,"* she said, but this time she wasn't scolding him for threatening to burn down barns. She was telling him she loved him.

"Go get on that plane already," he said. "They're waiting for you."

After Uncle Hux and the pilot finished strapping the badger's crate down to the floor of the plane with bungee cords, they helped Racina into one of the seats in the back and adjusted the straps so they were snug but not too snug. The pilot gave her and Uncle Hux headsets to wear so they could talk to each other while they were in the air. He said he was going to take them over Evergreen before they went south. He was a big believer in seeing the place you called home the way the clouds did. The birds. The sun.

"You ever been up in a plane, Hux?" the pilot said.

"No, sir," Uncle Hux said.

"That probably means you've never been anywhere but the Northwoods. Don't worry. I'll be gentle with the two of you."

"We'd appreciate that," Uncle Hux said.

When the pilot started the plane, the engine coughed and the propeller began to spin and Racina lurched forward. Even though she was strapped in securely, Uncle Hux put his hand across her shoulders like he did when they were driving sometimes and a deer darted across the road in front of them. The pilot told them not to worry.

"I'm just going to turn us around and we're off," he said. "We'll be in the air about two hours, give or take some. We can decide how scenic we want to be."

"You have any last advice for us," Uncle Hux said. He looked a little nervous. A little paler than normal. He was gripping the side of his seat.

"Every time you think you need to hold on, let go," the pilot said.

He turned the plane around so that it was facing the sun. When they started down the runway, everything began to rattle inside the plane. The windows sounded like chattering teeth. The engine was roaring. The propellers spun faster and faster until Racina couldn't see them individually anymore.

They were getting so close to the end of the runway, Racina thought they were going to go straight into the potato field beyond it and the forest beyond that. She said a prayer a nurse had taught her during one of her hospital stays. Racina didn't know if angels really lived in the clouds and looked over those who needed it, but she liked the idea of it. All that goodness floating over her and the people she loved every day.

Right before the end of the runway, the wheels finally lifted off the ground, and they headed straight up into the blue. At that moment, Uncle Hux let go of the seat.

When they were up high enough, the pilot leveled the plane out, and it stopped working so hard and making so much noise. Racina pressed her face against the window, which was cold now even though when they were on the ground it was warm. Uncle Hux pressed his face against the window next to him, too.

"I'm going to follow the river up to Evergreen," the pilot said.

From the sky, the river looked like a sheet of sparkling blue ice that someone had twisted up in places and straightened out in others. Racina couldn't see the gray stones along the banks she'd sat on for as long as she could remember. She couldn't see the river grass either or the little red butterflies and lacy moths that clung to it in the spring. But there was something wonderful about the view, too. Everything Racina had ever loved was beneath her at that moment. Phee's cabin, Uncle Hux's, her own. The river, the meadow, the forest. The pictures of her mother in the corn. What Racina had always thought was so small was really so big. Beyond the river, the forest stretched out as far as she could see in every direction.

"Everyone who wants to turn this land into parking lots and driveways should have to see it like this first," Uncle Hux said, which made Racina wonder if he was thinking the same thing about Evergreen. "If this place isn't worth protecting I don't know what is."

"At least hard winters are in its favor," the pilot said. "Not a lot of plumbing either. Not a lot of anything most people like."

Uncle Hux put his hand on the window the way he did sometimes at home on the window where he put Racina's sketches up. Racina wondered if the glass was his crystal ball the way the cross she'd found was hers.

Uncle Hux had told her the story of her grandparents building a life out here at a time when there wasn't any. He'd talked about a flood that almost swept Evergreen down the river. He'd talked about a man that came and stole something that didn't belong to him. He'd even talked about the bear trap that got Grandma Lulu and the drink that got Grandpa Reddy, the Irish poison that got both Grandpa Emil and Grandma Eveline.

But he'd also talked about the deep and pure love they all had for one another. He'd talked about a bird named Tuna. Egg pies. First fish.

The power of an old coonskin coat.

"It's *everything* I like," Uncle Hux said, letting go of the glass.

After that, the pilot steered the plane away from the river. He said they were southbound now. In a little while, the towering tamaracks and black spruces and white pines would give way to rolling green farmland with sheep and cows and horses and would stay like that all the way to Wisconsin. He said the cornfields were something to see in July and August. June was still early yet, but it would give them the right idea anyway. He said maybe that was where those cans of miniature corn came from.

Racina liked the idea of a field full of baby vegetables.

Even though she knew they cried a lot, she liked the idea of a field full of babies, too. Most of the people she'd seen in Yellow Falls and Green River did what they could to quiet their babies down. They rocked them. They bounced them. They gave them their fingers to suck on. They gave them bottles. One mother, though, cried right along with her baby in the middle of Main Street last year.

The mother was sitting on a bench in front of the general store that day with her baby in her arms, and even though Racina and her dad were in a hurry to get back to Evergreen, her dad offered to hold the baby while the mother did her shopping. He sat down right next to her and put his hand on her wrist. Before the mother could say anything he asked her what her favorite place in the world was, and though she looked surprised by the question at first she eventually said something about a lake down south she used to swim in as a girl. She said the water was so cold it took her breath away every time she jumped into it, but she kept jumping in anyway. She said she missed that.

"I used to picture being deep in the woods," Racina's dad said.

That day, he and Racina didn't end up watching the baby while his mother shopped, but the mother did let him hold the baby, a little blue-eyed boy named William. She let Racina hold him, too. Racina remembered being surprised by how heavy he was. She remembered being afraid her arms were going to suddenly stop working and he'd fall to the ground. She remembered thinking he was the prettiest baby she'd seen but wanting to give him back. She remembered wondering if her mother had felt that way with her.

Phee said her mother had tried to be less afraid by memorizing that little book about pregnancy. She said Uncle Hux used to sit on his porch with her mother while she read about what was happening inside of her. She said she'd rub her stomach. She'd tell Uncle Hux about Racina's fingernails. Her toes.

Racina had memorized that book, too. She knew about the fine hair most babies were born with. The gooey coating. She wondered if her mother had covered her eyes when she got to those parts like Racina did. What Racina loved most about that book was that her mother had held it in her hands. Some of the pages were more worn than others. Some had little question marks drawn on them, like she was going to ask someone to explain something to her. The page about a baby's first kick had a little pencil heart drawn on it.

Racina looked out the window of the plane again. Below her were rolling hills, fields with enormous silver sprinklers stretched across them, and trees that grew outward instead of straight up the way they did in Evergreen.

"We're not far now," the pilot said.

The plane started to fly lower and lower until the fields didn't look like squares stitched together into a quilt a hundred shades of green anymore. The windows and the air inside the plane got warm again. Humid. Everything started to rattle again, too.

"Are you okay?" Uncle Hux said to her. He was gripping his seat.

Racina put her hand on his. "Are you?"

"I keep forgetting to let go," he said.

The plane got so low Racina started to see the individual branches of trees. She could count the rows of plants in the fields. The pilot told her to look out her window and when she did she saw the big rectangular sign with her name on it: WELCOME TO RACINE.

Before she left Evergreen, her dad told her she was named

after a small farming town in Wisconsin and that her mother was the one who chose it. He said a kind woman lived on a dairy farm there. Sister Lydie. Just Lydie now. He said she was the first person who ever brought her mother a glass of milk or sang her a song. If it weren't for Phee's spoiled old cat, he said Racina probably would have been named after her directly.

The pilot flew the plane so close to the sign Racina could almost touch the rainbow that arched over her name. The red, the blue, the purple.

Uncle Hux unbuckled himself, got out his camera, and started taking pictures.

"Smile," he said, even though Racina was already smiling. She wanted to speak French and do the math that made her dad crazy. She wanted to multiply things! Racina thought she would be scared to fly in a plane and meet her mother for the first time, but she wasn't. Years ago, on their way back from a doctor's appointment, Uncle Hux took her to the fountain in Green River, and now her penny wish was finally coming true.

"I think I got one of you and your sign," Uncle Hux said.

They were on the ground a few minutes later, and Uncle Hux and the pilot were helping Racina out of the plane the way they'd helped her into it. The air was even warmer than it was in Evergreen. The wind was stronger, too. Racina's hair blew across her face, and when she finally found a yellow hair band to tie it back with, the wind shifted directions and lifted her hair and she saw the woman walking toward her.

Racina knew the woman was her mother not because her mother was famous for having thick black hair, which was pulled back into two glossy braids that swung in time with her hips now. She knew the woman was her mother not because she was wearing a pair of denim overalls and a white T-shirt the same as she did the day Uncle Hux took pictures of her in the corn. She knew the woman was her mother not because she had big gray eyes when everyone else in the world seemed to have eyes that were brown or green or blue. She knew the woman was her mother because she'd spent her whole life dreaming about her.

It turned out her mother had, too. *Dear Racina,* her mother had written back after she got Racina's letter. *My darling. My daughter. My dreams belong to you.*

Uncle Hux and the pilot were struggling to get the badger out of the plane when Racina lifted her legs and started running. Even if her dad were here, Racina knew this time he wouldn't tell her to slow down. This time he wouldn't tell her to stop altogether.

This time, he'd tell her to go.

With each new step, Racina heard the click-clack of her purple cowboy boots on the ground, the story they were already starting to tell. She heard the sound of the wind. She smelled the rich black earth. Before they left Evergreen, the pilot told Racina and Uncle Hux to let go the moment the plane lifted off the ground, but when Racina's feet lifted off the ground now, when she was in her mother's arms for the first time, she held on with everything she had. Her mother held on to her that way, too.

Right then, with her ear pressed against her mother's heart, Racina wanted to tell her textbook friends Watson and Crick that they were wrong. DNA wasn't the secret of life.

Love was.

Acknowledgments

Without my husband's unfailing belief that my stories are worth telling no matter how difficult they are or how long they take to tell (or how poor that may make us), *Evergreen* never would have been written. Each day that I came out of the room where I write, each time I was lost in the story, and each time I found my way out again, he managed to give me exactly what I needed: faith it would all work out. My six-year-old daughter did that, too. After watching me work for months, sometimes happily, sometimes unhappily, she came to me with a pile of paper her father had stapled together for her. She said, "I want to be a writer like you." I'm thankful for my little family. I'm thankful for my big family, too: my mom, my dad, my step-mom, and my four brothers. My friends, new and old. The Fiction Writer's Co-op. All the people I've met who love books and work so hard to support them.

Among those people is Michelle Brower, my fearless agent and friend, who doesn't give up when she hears bad news. She digs in. I couldn't ask for a better book partner. I admire her enthusiasm, grace, and remarkable instincts so much. Those instincts led her to my wonderful editor at Knopf. Without Jennifer Jackson, whole pieces of this book would have been missing. She understood the heart of *Evergreen* from the very beginning. Working with her was like coming home after a long and tiring trip. There was supper on the stove. Warmth in the fireplace. All I had to do was leave my shoes at the door.

A NOTE ABOUT THE AUTHOR

Rebecca Rasmussen is the author of the novel *The Bird Sisters*. Her stories have appeared in or won prizes from *TriQuarterly*, *Narrative Magazine*, *Glimmer Train*, the *Mid-American Review*, and other publications. She was born and raised in the green and rolling Midwest. Currently, she lives in Los Angeles with her husband and daughter and teaches English part-time at UCLA.

A NOTE ON THE TYPE

This book was set in Celeste, a typeface created in 1994 by the designer Chris Burke. He describes it as a modern, humanistic face having less contrast between thick and thin strokes than other modern types such as Bodoni, Didot, and Walbaum. Tempered by some old-style traits and with a contemporary, slightly modular letterspacing, Celeste is highly readable and especially adapted for current digital printing processes which render an increasingly exacting letterform.

Typeset by Scribe,
Philadelphia, Pennsylvania

Printed and bound by R.R. Donnelley,
Harrisonburg, Virginia

Designed by Soonyoung Kwon